PRAISE FOR MAR

~ The Wyndham

GOODBYE AGAIN

"Stewart returns to Wyndham Beach, Mass., for a lighthearted tale of love and reinvention refreshingly centered on an older heroine . . . The strength of the female friendships especially shines through, bolstering the love story. Readers will be eager for more."

—*Publishers Weekly*

"A wonderful story that will touch your heart. The book focuses on the friendship of three lifelong friends as they support each other through grief, new relationships, second chances, and hope."

—*Harlequin Junkie* (top pick, 5 stars)

"One of my comfort programs is *Virgin River*—it's a TV program I can unwind with. The Wyndham series by Mariah Stewart has become my bookish equivalent. I love that the ladies—Liddy, Maggie, and Emma—are in their fifties and navigating life and relationships as older women, as mothers, partners, and working women. This is a book filled with mostly nice people; with friendships, and family; with a glass of wine at sunset and a blooming, wonderful bookstore, and I really enjoyed my time at Wyndham Beach."

—@salboreads

"Mariah Stewart writes about women with real-world problems and does it well. A highly recommended series featuring mature heroines."

—*Bayside Book Reviews*

"An authentic portrayal of someone's messy life and there is a lot to relate to here. There's a couple of romances, lots of friendship, and some drama, too. Overall, a really enjoyable read, especially if you like character-driven stories in an idyllic setting."

—*Novelgossip*

"I love this series because it's a romance with generational characters. It is refreshing to read a romance that involves various ages and still covers real-life struggles and decisions, and is still topped with an HEA."

—@stumblingintobooks

"Mariah Stewart has been one of my favorite authors for such a long time. *Goodbye Again* has all the things I love so much. There are a lot of big themes in this book—there's substance along with the lighter love story. I love losing myself in the world Stewart builds, and if you haven't been there yet, I'd greatly recommend it."

—@shoshanahinla

AN INVINCIBLE SUMMER

"*Oh* my. This book was simply *gorgeous*! Each of the characters we're introduced to leaves a mark on your heart. The love that was both lost and found is enough to turn the biggest skeptic on to the idea of everything happening for a reason, and in its own time. All in all, it was a wonderful cast of characters with varied lives that are intriguing, heartbreaking, and uplifting in equal parts."

—*Satisfaction for Insatiable Readers*

"This is my first by this author, and it certainly won't be the last. Her writing is extremely engaging, and the author really brings to life the dynamics of longtime friendships and relationships and all the ups and downs that come with them. I couldn't help but fall in love with this book."

—*Where the Reader Grows*

"A multigenerational storyline, an idyllic setting, and a new series from one of my tried-and-true authors? Yes please! As much as I loved the setting and the premise of this one, the characterization is where it really shines. Maggie and her two lifelong friends were all such lovely, authentic women."

—*Novelgossip*

"This story hooked me from the beginning and kept me dangling all the way through: cheering, crying, and just absorbing the decisions as Maggie finds her path to true happiness. A wonderful story I just fell for!"

—*A Midlife Wife*

"What makes this book so readable are the relationships and how the past ties into the future. Isn't that the way it is for all of us? *An Invincible Summer* is a fast-paced, easy-to-read story delving into the relationships we have in life and how they both break and sustain us."

—*Books, Cooks, Looks*

"I really loved these characters and this story. The characters just felt real and flawed in the best of ways. I found myself caring about each of the characters, which has me really excited that this book is just the beginning to a series. I will definitely be continuing on, as I want to see what happens with some of these other characters. I just want more, if I'm being honest! Read this book if you are a fan of women's fiction, contemporary fiction, or are looking for a great summer read."

—Booked on a Feeling

"This book was raw and real. Stewart crafted beautifully imperfect characters that allow us to see ourselves in their struggles. I spent the majority of the novel on the edge of my chair, cheering for Maggie and her daughters. This book also gives off what I'd consider Virgin River vibes, so if you like that series, grab this one and give it a try."

—@stumblingintobooks

"What a down-to-earth, heart-filling, and sentimental read. Full of friendships, forgetting, and moving forward. The relationships and characters are realistic, charming, and the plot is a bit elusive to keep you on your toes. A very enjoyable read about love, loss, and second chances, and it is a page-turner."

—@momfluencer

"This novel by @mariah_stewart_books is what a women's fiction novel is all about. There's a bit of romance, friendship, and complicated relationships. I really enjoyed how this book highlighted the messiness that life can be, but [it was] done in a lighthearted way. And the overall theme of learning lessons from the past and the courage to move forward onto new phases of one's life was endearingly told."

—@tamsterdam_reads

"There is so much I loved about this read. The setting of Wyndham Beach is gorgeous. I could smell the sea air, feel the warmth of the sun as the women took their coffee and sat watching the horizon. I could feel Maggie's pull to return to her roots. I loved the female relationships in the book. Maggie is a strong but supportive mother who brings her children through crises but holds out for her own choices, and the independence of her own life. The gatherings with her friends are glorious—tattoos, rock concerts, and the warmth of conversations between women who really know and understand each other. This was such a celebration of life and especially of women of *all* ages."

—@salboreads

~ The Hudson Sisters Series ~

THE LAST CHANCE MATINEE

"Prepare to fall in love with this amazing, endearing family of women."
—Robyn Carr, *New York Times* bestselling author

"The combination of a quirky small-town setting, a family mystery, a gentle romance, and three estranged sisters is catnip for women's fiction fans."

—*Booklist*

"If you like the Lucky Harbor series by Jill Shalvis, you will enjoy this one. Stewart's writing reminds me of Susan Wiggs, Luanne Rice, Susan Mallery, and Robyn Carr."

—*My Novelesque Life*

THE SUGARHOUSE BLUES

"A solid writer with so much talent, Mariah Stewart crafts wonderful stories that take us away to small-town America and build strong families we wish we were a part of."

—*A Midlife Wife*

"Reading this book was like returning to a favorite small town and meeting up with friends you had been missing."

—*Pacific Northwest Bookworm*

"A heartwarming read full of surprising secrets, humor, and lessons about what it means to be a family."

—*That Book Lady Blog*

THE GOODBYE CAFÉ

"Stewart makes a charming return to tiny Hidden Falls, Pennsylvania, in this breezy contemporary, which is loaded with appealing down-home characters and tantalizing hints of mystery that will hook readers immediately. Stewart expertly combines the inevitable angst of a trio of sisters, a family secret, and a search for an heirloom necklace; it's an irresistible mix that will delight readers. Masterful characterizations and well-timed plot are sure to pull in fans of romantic small-town stories."

—*Publishers Weekly*

"Stewart [has] the amazing ability to weave a women's fiction story loaded with heart, grit, and enough secrets [that] you highly anticipate the next book coming up. I have read several books from her different series, and every one of them has been a delightful, satisfying read. Beautiful and heartwarming."

—*A Midlife Wife*

"Highly recommend this series for WF fans and even romance fans. There's plenty of that sweet, small-town romance to make you swoon a little."

—*Novelgossip*

"These characters will charm your socks off! Thematic and highly entertaining."

—*Booktalk with Eileen*

~ The Chesapeake Diaries Series ~

THAT CHESAPEAKE SUMMER

"Deftly uses the tools of the genre to explore issues of identity, truth, and small-town kinship. Stewart offers a strong statement on the power of love and trust, a fitting theme for this bighearted small-town romance."

—*Publishers Weekly*

DUNE DRIVE

"Rich with local history, familiar characters (practical, fierce, and often clairvoyant centenarian Ruby is a standout), and the slow-paced, down-home flavor of the bay, Stewart's latest is certain to please fans and add new ones."

—*Library Journal*

ON SUNSET BEACH

"Mariah Stewart's rich characterization, charming setting, and a romance you'll never forget will have you packing your bags for St. Dennis."

—Robyn Carr, *New York Times* bestselling author

COMING HOME

"One of the best women's contemporary authors of our time, Mariah Stewart serves the reader a beautiful romance with a delicious side dish of the suspense that has made her so deservingly popular. *Coming Home* is beautifully crafted with interesting, intelligent characters and pitch-perfect pacing. Ms. Stewart is, as always, at the top of her game with this sensuous, exhilarating, page-turning tale."

—Betty Cox, *Reader to Reader Reviews*

AT THE RIVER'S EDGE

"Everything you love about small-town romance in one book . . . *At the River's Edge* is a beautiful, heartwarming story. Don't miss this one."

—Barbara Freethy

"If you love romance stories set in a small seaside village, much like Debbie Macomber's Cedar Creek series, you will definitely want to grab this book. I easily give this one a five out of five stars."

—*Reviews from the Heart*

All That
We Are

The Mercy Street Series (Suspense)

Mercy Street
Cry Mercy
Acts of Mercy

The FBI Series (Romantic Suspense)

Brown-Eyed Girl
Voices Carry
Until Dark
Dead Wrong
Dead Certain
Dead Even
Dead End
Cold Truth
Hard Truth
Dark Truth
Final Truth
Last Look
Last Words
Last Breath
Forgotten

The Enright Series (Contemporary Romance)

Devlin's Light
Wonderful You
Moon Dance

Stand-Alone Titles (Women's Fiction / Contemporary Romance)

The President's Daughter

Priceless

Carolina Mist

A Different Light

Moments in Time

Novellas

"Finn's Legacy" (in *The Brandywine Brides*)

"If Only in My Dreams" (in *Upon a Midnight Clear*)

"Swept Away" (in *Under the Boardwalk*)

"'Til Death Do Us Part" (in *Wait Until Dark*)

Short Stories

"Justice Served" (in *Thriller 2: Stories You Just Can't Put Down*)

"Without Mercy" (in *Thriller 3: Love Is Murder*)

All That
We Are

MARIAH
STEWART

 Montlake

Text copyright © 2022 by Marti Robb

Published by Montlake, Seattle

www.apub.com

Amazon, the Amazon logo, and Montlake are trademarks of Amazon.com, Inc., or its affiliates.

ISBN-13: 9781542039635 (paperback)
ISBN-13: 9781542037303 (digital)

Cover design by Caroline Teagle Johnson
Cover image: © Brandon Pack / EyeEm / Getty Images

Printed in the United States of America

Welcome to the family, Gethin Peter William Jones
June 16, 2020

Chapter One

Emma Dean sat in her late husband's chair at the desk in his home office and tapped her pen on the side of the mug holding her now-cold coffee. Outside, a late nor'easter was bearing down on Wyndham Beach on the lower coast of Massachusetts, the wind whipping the bare trees in the backyard. Sleet pinging the windows sounded like buckshot against the glass, but Emma ignored it all until the lights flickered overhead. She glanced up, annoyed at the possibility of losing power. A loud crack from the backyard was followed by a thud that shook the house. She swung her chair around to look out the window just as the branch of a large tree fell, and the lights flickered once, twice, three times before the room and the hallway beyond were plunged into darkness.

"Oh, for crying out loud." Hands on her hips, she stood behind the desk in the dark, all five feet two inches of her, and silently counted to thirty. That was how long it was supposed to take for the backup generator to kick on once it sensed the electricity had shut off. She'd barely gotten to that magic number when she heard the roar of the gas-fueled equipment just seconds before the lights returned.

"Thank you, Lord." The last thing she wanted was to spend a cold, dark night alone in this two-hundred-year-old house, where the floorboards squeaked, and the radiators knocked, and the wind against the windows could sound like a child's cry.

She tucked an errant strand of short dark hair behind her ear and turned her attention back to the file that lay open on the desk, the one she'd found in the file drawer in the credenza directly behind the desk. The one where Harry had kept what he called his "tax deductions." In the ten years since her husband passed, Emma had never gone through his files, had never even thought much about them. But since she'd established the Wyndham Beach Art Center several years ago, the records she needed to keep had begun piling up. She found her tiny office at the center too small to hold more than one file cabinet, and that had already overflowed to a wire basket sitting atop the cabinet, items in alphabetical order, a most unsatisfactory arrangement. Harry had kept a well-equipped office in their home, and God knew he wasn't going to be using it again, so Emma figured, why not move his old stuff out and her new stuff in? She'd been meaning to clear out some space for weeks but hadn't had the opportunity. A stormy night in March seemed like a good time.

She rolled up her sleeves and began to purge the file drawers. She was pretty sure that tax documents had to be saved for only seven years, so those old files were well past their expiration date. She'd worked her way through three drawers, scanning the contents of each file to ensure they held nothing of import before tossing them into a box next to the desk. Once the box was filled, she'd shred the contents and resume purging. That was the plan.

But then she reached the fourth drawer, the one marked RECEIPTS in Harry's awkward uppercase print. There were files for almost every purchase he'd ever made—cars, appliances, furniture, clothing. Reading through them was like watching a quick movie reel of their life together. There was the receipt for the car Harry'd bought Emma the year their son and only child, Christopher, was born. A silver baby's cup Harry'd ordered to mark the birth of his sister Prudence's first child. A new chimney liner. The first guitar they'd bought Chris. Her eyes lingered over this one as she recalled how Harry had later "rued the day" he'd "opened that can of worms."

Emma dropped that receipt on the desk: Chris might get a kick out of it.

There was a file containing personal purchases Harry had made for himself. A three-piece charcoal suit and a lightweight summer sports coat. Three white dress shirts and the bill for monogramming the cuffs. A receipt from a jeweler in Boston for an eight-inch gold bracelet, and a . . .

"Wait, what?"

She held up the receipt and scrutinized the fine print: "One eight-inch fancy link bracelet—14K gold." The price was staggering.

Confused, she reread the receipt several times. Was she losing her mind? Had he bought her such a thing and she'd forgotten? Sure, we all lose a little as we age, and forgetting some things now and then is normal. But could she have forgotten so expensive and wonderful a gift? No, she was sure she'd have remembered that. She'd have worn it every day. She'd probably be wearing it right then.

No. Harry had never given her a gold bracelet. And since he had never worn any jewelry other than his wedding ring and cuff links, she knew it wasn't for him.

And then she noticed the print at the bottom of the receipt: "Add gold disk charm, front engrave: CJD 2-14-2012. Back engrave: My heart."

Emma felt as if she'd been punched in the stomach.

She could think of only one CJD: Carla Joan Dempsey, Harry's assistant at the bank for the last fifteen years of his life. Pretty Carla, tall and statuesque, with pale-blonde hair that fell just below her shoulders. Harry'd called her "his right hand."

As Emma stared at the receipt and the fog of confusion began to lift, she had to remind herself to breathe, but the truth was undeniable:

Harry had bought a very expensive gold bracelet for Carla, a gift that went way beyond the little tokens one might purchase for an employee.

February 14, 2012. Valentine's Day.

The inscription on the back sealed the deal: Harry'd had an affair with Carla, a woman close to his own age—one eight years older than Emma. There could be no other explanation, though she tried to think of one.

Emma's entire being filled with anger. To find this now, years later, when she couldn't even confront him and yell and scream the way she wanted, added insult to her red-hot injury.

What had he seen in Carla—what had he found in her—that Emma lacked? Why would he turn to another woman when she, Emma, had spent her entire married life doing her very best to be a perfect wife in every way? She and Harry had never even disagreed on much, and rarely argued. Neither of them had ever raised their voice in anger against the other.

Except about Chris.

Their beautiful headstrong boy, who from birth had insisted on doing things his way. Walked when he decided it was time, talked when he felt like it. Not particularly picky about what he ate but made his preferences known by tossing what he didn't like over the side of the high chair and happily eating what pleased him. Excelled in academics and athletics, to his father's pride, since bragging rights were important when you had one son and you were the president of the local bank, and a really big deal in Rotary and at the country club. From the day he was born, Chris's path had been carefully laid out by his father. Chris would go to Harvard, as Harry and his father and his father had done. And then Chris would go to work with his father at the First National Bank of Wyndham Beach, and someday, when Harry retired, Chris would follow him into that big corner office overlooking the harbor, and his name would replace Harry's on the letterhead as president.

Oh, the arguments they'd had when Chris announced he was not going to apply to Harvard, and he was not going to work in the bank his great-great-grandfather had founded, and no, he was not going to follow Harry's footsteps into the office of the bank president.

"I'm going to make music, Dad." Chris had met Harry's rantings calmly. "I'm going to put together the greatest American rock band that ever was."

"Don't be ridiculous. Dean men are bank presidents and lawyers. Not rock-and-roll singers. We have a reputation to uphold in this town, and by God, Christopher, you're going to walk the same path my father and grandfather and I walked."

"No, Dad. I'm not." Chris tried to explain patiently and calmly. "I'm not you. I can't be you. I respect you and appreciate your wanting me to have a good future. But I know myself. Making music is all I've ever wanted to do. So thanks, but no thanks. There's no bank job in my future." Chris had smiled wryly. "And no Harvard, either. I'm going to UMass."

Harry'd been infuriated that his son had defied him. His anger had spilled over onto Emma for not taking his side. Instead, she'd tried to play the role of peacemaker. When it became apparent there'd be no peace, she'd quietly supported Chris's desire to follow his own path, a decision that had become a bone of contention between her and her husband.

The argument had continued for years in one form or another. After college, Chris left Wyndham Beach with his bandmates on their first for-real tour. He never did return for any length of time while his father was still alive.

And then days after their last big blowout, Harry'd suffered a massive heart attack and died before Emma reached the hospital.

When Emma had rushed in, she'd found Carla already there.

"They wanted someone from the bank to be here until you arrived," Carla had explained hastily, her eyes red from weeping, her hands shaking, as she stepped away from the nurses' station and disappeared. Had Emma thought that odd at the time? If so, the shock of Harry's death had overshadowed everything else.

The realization that Harry had had an affair was almost inconceivable. Harry had walked the straight and narrow all his life—or at least he'd professed to. Never missed church on Sunday (well, her father was the pastor—it would have been awkward to have to explain why they weren't there). Donated generously to all the local charities. Never drank too much at parties. Always did the right thing. Always said the right thing. But here, in this file, was proof that her holier-than-thou husband, Mr. President of the Bank, the man who'd tried to shame his son into becoming a man just like him—had been having an affair.

And she had never suspected a thing.

How stupid had she been? How blind? How clueless? And how was she supposed to feel about Harry now?

When the phone rang, she automatically reached for it. If she'd thought before she reacted, she would have ignored the call. There was no one she wanted to speak with. Until she saw the name of the caller on the screen. She lifted the phone to her ear.

"Mom, you sound distracted. Everything okay?" Always sensitive, Chris needn't know he'd caught her just as her heart was breaking. "Are you all right?"

She cleared her throat and forced a cheery tone. "Oh, I'm fine, sweetie."

"Your voice sounds weird."

"I'm in your dad's old office, just cleaning out some of his files, and I guess I'm stirring up a cloud of dust. I'm making some room for the applications for the artists-in-residence program at the center this summer. We've had way more applicants than we expected."

"Any good prospects?" Chris asked, his genuine interest apparent. He knew how involved she was in the center, and he was happy to be its most generous financial donor. Anything to make his mother happy.

"Oh, way too many good prospects. It's a shame I've had to narrow them down." Emma was grateful to divert her attention away from the pain that was washing through her and showed no sign of abating.

"Why do you have to narrow them down? Why not invite all the ones who show promise?"

"Because I only have accommodations for six people." She flipped the file open and closed, open and closed, and focused on the conversation. Forget Harry. Forget the damned bracelet. Forget Carla . . .

"And you have how many candidates?"

"Oh, dozens, but I've pulled out the fifteen best. Unfortunately, less than half of them will be able to participate."

"Maybe try putting them in order of your preference."

"I can't choose—they're all exceptional. And some of their stories are so intriguing."

"Do you need an additional donation? Because I can . . ."

"No, no, sweetie. You've been more than generous. I just have to make a decision. But enough about me. What's doing on your end? And where are you?"

"I'm at Natalie's. We were hoping to get up there this weekend to surprise you, but the storm has put an end to any chance of that," he said. "The Philly airport is closed until at least tomorrow afternoon, and the flights are going to be limited. So we'll have to save our surprise for another time. I'm sorry, Mom."

"It would have been wonderful to see you." Truly wonderful. A lump formed in her throat. She hadn't realized until that very second how much she needed her son right then. "I haven't seen you since Christmas."

"I know. And that was the best Christmas ever. We loved every minute of it."

He, Nat, and Daisy, Nat's then four-year-old daughter, had been the epitome of the perfect family, enjoying all the wonderful holiday activities there in town. The Christmas house tour. The lighting of the tree down near the harbor. Breakfast with Santa for Daisy, the annual open-house parties at their neighbors' homes. Sharing holiday traditions, blending Natalie's family's Christmas Eve formal dinner with Chris's family's attendance at church on Christmas morning, followed by a casual brunch.

"I loved it, too." Every day had been perfect. Even had she known then what she knew now, not even the yet-to-be-discovered news could have taken the shine from those magical days. "Maybe things will clear up by the morning, and you could still make it."

She glanced out the window and watched the snow as it continued to swirl across the backyard. "Oh, that was just so much wishful thinking. Maybe in another week or so the three of you could come up for a weekend."

"I'm leaving for California on Tuesday," Chris told her. "We're working on some new material for next year's album."

"No tour this year?" she asked.

"Next year," he told her. "After the new album is out."

"Good," she said, and he laughed. He knew how his mother felt about his touring.

For years, she'd worried every time her rock-god son, the face of DEAN, one of the hottest bands on the planet, performed anywhere in the world. She was pretty sure it was irrational, but she couldn't help herself. Chris was all she had.

For years, she'd been afraid he would marry one of the models or actresses he'd dated since DEAN had become an international success. Emma wanted him to marry someone who'd be happy to settle down in his hometown, where she could spoil her future grandchildren every day. She was over the moon when he revealed that the woman who'd stolen his heart was his childhood friend. A girl Emma had known all her life. Natalie Flynn would have been Emma's first choice for a daughter-in-law, and joy of joys, Natalie came with a bonus grandchild, four-year-old Daisy. And bonus number two? Natalie was the daughter of one of Emma's dearest friends, Maggie.

And now Chris and Natalie had found each other, and their mothers were certain a wedding was inevitable, and neither could wait for the planning to begin.

They talked for a few more minutes before Natalie took the phone to chat. Then Daisy insisted on telling Emma about her adventures at pre-K.

"We didn't have school today because it snowed, but yesterday, snack was so exciting," Daisy told her breathlessly. "We had cheesy goldfish crackers and almond milk."

"That does sound delicious." For just a moment, Emma's spirit lightened. Few things could banish a heavy heart like a five-year-old who wanted to share their world with you.

"Mm-hmm, it was. And me and my friend Cecily wore the same socks. They are blue with little happy sunshines on them."

"You'll have to remember to bring them when you come to visit. I love happy sunshines."

"We were going to come to surprise you and Nana, but there's lots of snow, and Chris has to go away after the weekend. I like when he's here. He's so fun and makes me and Mommy laugh, and he makes us pancakes for breakfast. With blueberries in them. They're yummy."

Before Emma could respond, Daisy added, "Yesterday Mommy and I looked at lots of pictures in pretty magazines. We saw lots of beautiful fancy white dresses with big, long skirts. Like princess dresses. And there were . . ."

"All right, town crier." Natalie's voice replaced Daisy's.

"Fancy white dresses with big, long skirts?" Emma could picture Natalie and her daughter poring over the latest wedding magazines, oohing and aahing over the glossy photos.

"Oh God, don't tell my mother," Natalie pleaded, her voice lowering. "She'll have the wedding planned and a caterer booked, and she'll be looking for florists."

"My lips are sealed, but you know you can always count on Daisy to spill the beans." If Natalie was looking at wedding dresses, was a formal engagement imminent? Emma knew Maggie was anticipating it—and that she did have the caterer and the florist picked out. Emma understood completely. She wanted this wedding to happen every bit as much as Maggie did.

After the call ended, Emma held the phone in one hand for a few long moments, the fingers of the other hand tracing the letters at the top of the file on her desk: RECEIPTS. As devastated as she was, she hadn't been able to bring herself to tell Chris. He had enough baggage where his father was concerned, and she didn't want to add to it. Besides, wasn't that what a mom did, protect her kids from the unpleasant, the hurtful things in their world, as best she could?

And did she even have the right to tell her son something she knew could taint the memory of his father? Was that fair when Harry wasn't here to defend himself? Not that what he'd done was defensible, but still. Chris and Harry had had a contentious relationship. Chris had admitted once that the fact they'd never reconciled their differences before Harry died still played heavily on his conscience. Would this newly discovered secret only add to Chris's already confused feelings about his father?

Emma groaned. Why was it so hard sometimes to know the right thing to do?

~

By the second day after the storm, the sidewalks had been shoveled, the roads had been plowed, the sun had come out, and the wind had subsided. Typical for March in Wyndham Beach. Late on Friday morning, a still-downhearted Emma walked into town to meet her two best friends at Ground Me, the local coffee shop. Maggie had arrived first and was waiting at the table when Emma got there.

"Nice scarf." Maggie greeted her with a big cheery smile. "New?"

"I picked it up at that boutique next to the cheese shop." Emma unwound the scarf and slipped out of her jacket. She passed the scarf to Maggie, who'd held out her hand for a closer look.

"Alpaca?" Maggie asked.

Emma nodded and retrieved her wallet from her bag. Ground Me had no waitstaff, so one had to go to the counter to order.

"This shade of green is beautiful on you."

"Thanks, Mags." Emma hung her jacket on the back of her chair.

"The cranberry-orange scones are fabulous," Maggie said. "If they're all out, you can have half of mine."

"Thanks." Emma made her way to the counter to place her coffee order. She could no more eat right now than she could fly to Mars. The thought of actually telling her best friends what Harry'd done—saying the words out loud—made her sick to her stomach. But holding it inside was killing her.

She hoped Liddy would get there soon, because she didn't want to have to tell the story twice. She forced a smile at the young woman behind the counter, gave her order, and realized the smile was still plastered on her face while she stood at the table where the creamers and sugars were located. It was as if she thought she was personally responsible for everyone else having a pleasant day. She dropped the smile when she returned to the table. If she couldn't be herself with her friends—share the pain of her late husband's betrayal with two of the people who loved her best—who could she be herself with?

Emma had just sat back down at the table when Liddy Bryant blew in like a fierce wind.

"What have I missed?" Liddy unbuttoned her puffy winter coat and tossed it onto the unoccupied chair at their table.

"Nothing. Em just got here," Maggie told her.

"Coffee, please," Liddy muttered as she made her way to the counter.

Even with the anxiety over sharing her news, Emma had to smile at the contrast between her two friends. Maggie was petite—though not so much as Emma—blonde, active, energetic. Assured. She'd lived for years on Philadelphia's Main Line as the wife of a Center City lawyer, and she dressed like it: conservative clothes, designer labels, and real jewelry. Liddy—Lydia at birth—was taller, bigger boned, with salt-and-pepper hair that until recently had flowed down her back like a silver river. She'd broken down a few months ago and had it cut to fall to her shoulders. Where once she'd dressed mostly in T-shirts and long skirts, waves of colored beads wrapped around her neck, she'd adopted a more contemporary look when she purchased the town's only book-store. She now wore pants as often as she wore jeans, and sweaters had taken the place of her once-ubiquitous plain white tees. The three of them had gone through the local schools and had graduated together, class of 1980.

Liddy returned to the table and sat, then took a sip of her coffee. "Good but not quite as good as the kid used to make last summer. What's-his-name who left for college. He was a pro."

"You say that every time we come here," Maggie reminded her.

"Well, it's the truth." Liddy took another sip. "Boy, that was some storm." She glanced at Maggie. "Your daughter came in to work this morning loaded for bear. Apparently the storm delayed the delivery of the tile for her new bathroom."

"Gracie never did handle frustration well," Maggie said matter-of-factly. "She wants to move into that little house of hers now now now."

"I suspect her impatience could have something to do with wanting to have a place where she and Linc can be totally alone," Liddy said, referring to Grace's boyfriend, Lincoln Shelby, who by coincidence was the son of Liddy's own guy, Tuck Shelby.

Emma sat in silence as the conversation swirled around her.

"Well, it's not like they never have any time together. She stays out on Shelby Island with him often enough," Maggie pointed out.

"Where he has the responsibility for his deadbeat sister's three young children," Liddy reminded her. "But she does spend a lot of time at her house while he's there working on the renovations, so it isn't as if they don't have time to talk. Or whatever."

"I think it might be the lack of 'whatever' that might be a problem for them."

"Harry was having an affair," Emma said softly.

"Well, yes, that could be a prob . . ." Maggie stopped midsentence and turned to Emma. "Em, what did you say?"

"Harry was having an affair." Emma was well aware of the glances exchanged between Maggie and Liddy.

"What are you talking about?" Liddy leaned closer to ask.

"Harry was having an affair with Carla Dempsey." Emma whipped the receipt for the bracelet from her bag and handed it to Liddy. "Think a man spends that kind of money on a woman he's only having 'coffee' with in the office early every morning? Which he was doing, because they had 'things to go over'"—she made quotation marks with her fingers—"and that was the only quiet time of the day."

"Oh my, that was a pricey little piece of business." Liddy stared at the receipt and passed it to Maggie, who studied it.

"Oh. Well. I guess the only explanation is . . ." Maggie paused and appeared to be looking for words.

"They were having an affair." Emma completed Maggie's sentence as she retrieved the receipt, folded it, and dropped it back into her purse.

"Oh, honey." Maggie reached a hand for Emma's and gave it a squeeze.

"What are you going to do?" Liddy asked.

"What can I do? Harry's been gone for ten years. Even if I were inclined to confront her, what would I say? 'Hey, slow learner that I am, I just realized that you were sleeping with my husband. Was it good for you? And was it good for him?'"

"Emma." Maggie choked back a laugh.

"I want to slap him. But I can't because he's dead, and wherever he is, he probably isn't thinking about either of us. And I can't slap her because everyone would know that . . ." Emma's face suddenly paled. "Oh my God, do you think everyone in the bank knew? I bet they did. I bet even that smart-mouthed teller that sits up front . . . you know who I mean." She looked at Liddy to supply the name.

"Yeah," Liddy whispered. "Jeannie Brightcliffe. She's dating my ex-husband. But I'm pretty sure she wasn't there while Harry was alive."

"Look, Em. Maybe it's not what you think. Maybe the bracelet was actually from the bank as a way to mark an anniversary, not from Harry personally." Maggie continued, keeping her voice down. "You know, like ten years employed there or twenty, or . . ."

"No employer is that generous, and besides, it was dated. It was a Valentine's Day present from Harry to Carla, and it had nothing to do with her job. And it had that little 'My heart' thing on the back." Emma took a quick drink from her rapidly cooling coffee. "Do you know what he used to give me every year on Valentine's Day? One of those big dumb red-satin hearts filled with two layers of tasteless chocolates from Phillips' Drug Store. They were awful. Chris and his friends used to take it to the tree house out back, and they'd eat their way through it until they were sick."

"It could have been her birthday," Liddy suggested.

"Her birthday is not February fourteenth. It was in September. How do I know, you might ask? It coincided with the back-to-school meetings every year, and Harry never made it to one because he always took Carla out for her birthday dinner." Emma fought back tears. "One year he took her to Andre's on the Cape."

Her back to the rest of the tables, she quietly broke down. "How could I have been so blind? How could I have not seen what was going on right under my nose?"

"There was never any sign? You never felt something was off, or was suspicious of their relationship?" Liddy asked.

Emma shook her head. "No. Not once. I never suspected a thing. Carla never acted weird around me. Whenever I came into the bank, she always asked about Chris. And Harry—oh, you know Harry. He was always so . . . proper."

"Never could trust a man like that," Liddy muttered.

"I've never felt so betrayed. So . . . so stupid."

"If he never gave any sign that something was going on, how were you to know?" Liddy asked. "For heaven's sake, Em, don't turn this against yourself."

"I probably should have figured it out when he took her to Andre's." Emma sniffed. "It's a very ritzy, very intimate restaurant. At least, that's what I heard. He never took me there." She looked across the table at Maggie. "I know Brett took you a few months ago. Was it all that? Ritzy and intimate?"

"It's lovely, yes," Maggie said softly, her eyes on Emma's face. Emma knew that Maggie was understating her impression for her sake.

"Are you going to confront her?" Liddy asked. "Carla?"

"I'd like to do more than confront her, but no. I can't think of anything I could say to her that wouldn't make me look like a fool because it had taken so long for me to catch on. Maybe someday an opportunity will arise when I can let her know that I know. Right now, I don't want to do anything that will make me feel even more stupid than I already do."

"What about Chris?" Maggie asked. "Will you tell him?"

Emma shrugged. "I don't know. The mature woman in me likes to think I won't. On the other hand, the angry, vindictive part of me wouldn't mind burning down the last shred of Chris's memory of his father. But the truth is, I think it would add to Chris's negative feelings about Harry, and I don't know if that might not harm Chris somehow in the end."

"Harry earned every one of those negative feelings," Liddy reminded her.

"He did. But he isn't here to talk things out with Chris." She shook her head. "I just don't know what useful purpose it would serve at this point."

"How did you find that?" Liddy asked, pointing to Em's bag and the receipt that had been stashed inside.

Emma related the tale.

"So you just more or less stumbled across it?" Maggie moved her coffee so she could rest her forearms on the table.

Emma nodded. "In a file of paid receipts. Where it's been since 2012."

"Wow. I can't believe Harry Dean . . ." Liddy shook her head.

"Neither could I, but let's face it. There's no other explanation." All of a sudden, Emma felt weary. Worn out from crying and speculating on how the affair might have begun. "Now I question everything about my marriage. I look back on every business trip Harry ever took, and I wonder if he was really someplace with her. I think about the times when he had meetings in Boston and called home to say he was spending the night in the city because he'd taken some people out to dinner and it ran late, and he'd had a few glasses of wine, so he didn't want to drive home. Was Carla at those meetings? Was she the reason he couldn't drive home after dinner?" She sighed a sigh full of defeat. "Were those meetings even real, or were they just an excuse to spend a night away in a fancy hotel with his lover?"

"Oh, Em." Maggie's eyes were filled with tears. "I'm so sorry. I can't imagine how you must hurt. It'll be four years since my husband died, and I don't know what I'd do if I discovered that Art had kept a secret like this. It has to be so painful."

"I don't have words to describe what I feel." Emma shook her head. "Over the past few days I've felt numb when I thought about him; then I'd get this pain . . ."

"What a bastard," Liddy whispered.

"I know, right?" Emma searched her bag for a tissue. "I've been feeling all sorts of emotions I've never felt before. Like the woman scorned. One minute I feel like a fool, and the next minute I feel murderous."

"What can we do for you?" Maggie asked, her eyes brimming with concern.

"Be my best friends and let me whine and cry until it's all cried out of me. Till all this poison has drained out of me," Emma told them. "I think maybe once it all drains away, it'll be gone for good, and it won't be able to make me sick again. Just be my friends until I can breathe without it hurting."

"You got it, Em," Maggie told her.

Liddy turned her wrist in Emma's direction and pulled up the sleeve of her sweater to show off her tattoo. The same tattoo Emma and Maggie had in the same place on their forearms. Three waves—waves of the same sea—representing the endless friendship they shared. "Whatever you need, we're here for you."

And they were. Over the next weeks, the three women shared dinners, lunches, card games, margarita nights, shopping trips to Providence, whatever it took to help Emma find her smiles again. They'd even had a paper-shredding party one long weekend at Emma's, where they destroyed all Harry's old files. They had their food brought in from the best restaurant in town and sipped wine and laughed until their faces hurt over Facebook memes, funny T-shirts, movies, anything to bring some lightness back into Emma's life. Liddy and Maggie let Emma hold on to them until she felt she could stand on her own again.

Chapter Two

Weeks after winter's last storm, the only trace of remaining snow could be found in the heavily shaded areas around town. Every day seemed just a little warmer, the sun a little brighter, Emma's mood just a little lighter, though her heart was still weighed down with knowledge she wished she didn't have. She'd asked herself a dozen times if she'd rather not have discovered Harry's secret, and so far, every time she'd answered unequivocally yes. She'd rather not know. Wished she didn't know. There were moments when knowing seemed to hang over her head like a cartoon balloon, the words within changing from *How could I have not known?* to *Harry, how could you?*

But she had a life to live, and responsibilities, so she packed up and headed out to take care of the business that hadn't taken care of itself while she was licking her wounds. She pushed the Harry-and-Carla affair as deeply into the back of her mind as she could shove it, then drove to the art center and parked in her reserved spot. The center's only full-time employee, Emma had one part-time person working with her. Marion Fields worked afternoons at the art center, and mornings at Liddy's bookshop. Emma would have loved to have Marion full time, but she knew Liddy depended on her as well. During the upcoming summer months, there could be a need for two people daily at the center, and as she unlocked the door, Emma made a mental note to put out feelers for a third person. There would be new children's classes as well as those for adults, so an extra set of hands would be welcome. At the end of June Emma would be setting up a new exhibit of all local artists' work for the July Fourth weekend. The highlight would be the previously unseen work of Liddy's late daughter, Jessica, whose paintings they'd displayed over the winter, and which had brought so much positive attention to the center. And then there was the artists-in-residence program that was to begin on the first of June. Yes, an extra pair of hands would be nice.

Emma had thought it a fine idea to establish a summer artists' colony of sorts in Wyndham Beach. It was a beautiful, peaceful town with an eclectic vibe, and the six little cottages that ran behind the dune next to the center would be perfect to offer to artists to stay and have uninterrupted time to work on their craft. When the owner of those little cabins mentioned she'd be putting them up for sale, or possibly knocking them down to build a mega–beach house, Emma's mention of her disapproval to Chris had been all it had taken for him to step in and quietly purchase the property.

"What is this?" Emma had held up the thick envelope he'd handed her the morning after Thanksgiving. He'd come down for breakfast earlier than Natalie or Daisy, for which she had been grateful. She loved Nat like a daughter, but she dearly appreciated a little time alone with Chris. Those times were few and far between, and she cherished them.

"Open it up and take a look." He sat back in his chair and grinned, so she knew it was going to be something good.

And it was—once she understood what she was looking at.

"This is a deed to . . ." She read for a moment, shuffled through the sheaf of papers, then looked at her son. "You didn't."

He laughed. "Obviously I did."

"Chris . . ." Speechless, she hugged him.

He leaned over and shook the envelope. "Keys to each of the cabins."

"Oh, Chris, this is just too much." Emma hugged him again.

"It's never too much for you, Mom. I know how upset you were at the possibility of those little buildings being taken down and some monster house being built right there next to the center to spoil the view and that beach-town feel you love so much." He patted her arm. "Now sit and tell me what you think you might want to do with them."

"I don't know. I mean, I always thought it would be nice to be able to offer living space to artists who are in need of some time to work, for a limited time, of course. I remember when Jessie Bryant came back to live in Liddy's carriage house. She said she needed time to focus on her painting, and having to work to support herself took that time from her. To save on rent, she'd tried roommates, but that hadn't worked out well." Emma poured coffee for both of them and took the mugs to the table, then sat across from Chris. "Jessie was so creative—her work was so vibrant, just like her." Emma's smile held the sadness she always felt when she thought about Liddy's only child, who'd taken her life five years earlier. "Remember how lively and clever Jessie was?"

"Of course. Growing up, Jess was the sister I never had. She was so talented. Maybe the most creative person I ever met. It gutted me when she died, Mom." He ran a hand through his dark-blond hair, and his eyes clouded over. "I felt like I'd failed her as a friend, like if I'd been better at keeping in touch with her, she'd have talked to me instead of taking her life."

"Don't do that to yourself. There were any number of people she could have talked to, but she chose not to. We all love and miss her, but there was nothing any one of us could have done if she didn't want to share what was on her mind."

"That guy who abused her—the basketball coach—he's in prison?"

"Where he'll be for the rest of his life, after what he did to all those young girls."

Chris nodded, and they sat quietly for a few moments.

"What kind of shape do you think those little cottages are in?" he asked to break the silence.

"I have no idea," she replied. "I've poked around outside of them several times out of curiosity, but I've never been in any of them. I expect they're dirty and could use a good cleaning."

"Let's run over later and check them out." Still smiling at her, he added, "You'll need up-to-date accommodations if you're going to attract the kind of talent you want."

Early in the afternoon, Natalie had taken Daisy to Maggie's to give Chris and Emma time to take their first look at the tiny buildings that were now the property of the Wyndham Beach Art Center. They'd parked on Bay Street and walked the path over the dune together as Emma searched through the handful of keys that had been in the envelope.

"I guess it's too much to ask that the keys be marked," she murmured.

"We can mark them as we figure out which goes to which door. Let's start here at what we're going to refer to as cabin number one." He nodded toward the cabin closest to the center.

The fourth key she tried worked, and on the round cardboard disk attached to it, Emma wrote #1. She stepped inside, followed by Chris. It was dark, so he pulled back the curtains covering the large window that looked out toward the bay.

"Nice view," he said. "Nice to get some light in here."

Emma looked around the room. "I guess this is the sort of living room, bedroom, kitchen area." She smiled. "Talk about your open concept."

She pushed open a door, behind which she found a pedestal sink, a toilet, and a small shower. "Bathroom. Small but serviceable." She opened a second door. "Oh, I guess this would be the bedroom." She glanced over her shoulder at Chris. "Not quite as open concept as I'd initially thought, and bigger than it looks from the outside."

He peeked into the room where she stood. "You could easily fit a full-size bed in here. And one dresser if it's not too large. One chair." He pushed aside a grimy curtain and looked out. "View of the dune. Not bad."

Emma walked back into the front room. "So this could be a living room and workroom space. There's a little alcove there in the kitchen where a small table could fit. No room for more than two chairs, though. But if what you're looking to do is focus on your art, this would serve nicely. Not a lot of room to take care of, just enough to live and work in. Yes, this could suit very well."

They locked the cabin and went on to the next. By the time they'd gone through all six, which all had the same layout, Emma knew exactly how she wanted to renovate them.

"So you call someone to come in and clean them out," Chris said as they walked back over the dune. "Then call Tuck Shelby to see what has to be done to bring them up to code."

"He can arrange for the cleaning and do the construction work." And then, thinking aloud, she added, "And we'll need heat and air-conditioning."

"Not to mention a plumber and an electrician, but Tuck or Linc can take care of all that for you." He paused. "Probably not Linc. He has his hands full trying to get Grace's little house finished so she can move in. They had delay after delay with materials being back-ordered and the appliances she wanted being temporarily unavailable, and Linc said Grace is getting a little crazy at this point."

"So nice that things appear to be working out between him and Gracie. I always thought Linc was a nice boy when you were growing up, and of course, we've known and loved Grace since she was a little girl." Emma put her arm through his. "It's nice of you to invite Linc to come back into the band with you."

"It was long overdue, Mom. He was the first person I wrote songs with back in high school, and though some of them were admittedly pretty pathetic, some weren't too bad. We cleaned those up, and they're pretty darned good. It had been Linc's choice not to stay in the band when DEAN started out, after his mom died. Tuck was having a hard time of it, and his sister was just getting wilder and wilder. And then there was his dad's business. Linc felt he couldn't leave his father to deal with it all alone, said he felt like he'd be abandoning him. Being the kind of guy he is, he stayed with his family, but I know it was a bittersweet decision. Working with him now, when he can get time away, is the right thing for us to do. He sacrificed a lot back then. Honestly, the band is better with him. So much better. Even our older works, the songs we recorded after he left the band, are better with him playing on them. He puts a new spin on everything, and it works even when you don't expect it will. So win-win for everyone." He opened the driver's-side door for her. "And we're going to record a few of those songs we wrote together back then, so he'll be getting some pretty deep royalties as cowriter."

"That's wonderful, Chris. So he'll be able to follow his dream after all."

"To some extent. He still wants to work with his dad." Chris slammed the door and walked around to the passenger side. "He said Tuck's still got contracts to fulfill," he said as he got in, "and he can't leave him in the lurch. Tuck's trying to retire, and all along he planned on turning Shelby and Son over to Linc, who feels obligated to see it through, at least for a while. Plus Linc likes the business, and he still has all three of his sister's kids on the island."

Emma grimaced. "Oh, that Brenda. If I were her mother, I'd . . ." She paused, then sighed. "Of course, her mother's been gone for years, which might be the root of her problem." She started the engine. "Still, to dump your children on your brother and your father with no explanation, and then disappear like that . . ." She shook her head in disgust.

"Yeah, it's tough on everyone," Chris agreed. "Especially her kids."

Over the next months, steady progress had been made on the cabins. Tuck had gone through each of them, clipboard in hand, to outline what each cabin needed. He'd gotten the permits and put together a work crew that spent the winter fixing what needed to be fixed, adding new kitchens and bathrooms in the process. The exteriors would have to wait till spring, Tuck had told Liddy, but spring had been just around the corner. Envisioning a kind of rainbow on the beach, she'd picked out a different exterior color with contrasting trim for each little structure, and she couldn't wait to see the effect once the painting was completed.

Now all she needed were six artists to move into those little cabins come June.

She'd decided she'd offer a three-month residency to the six chosen artists. There were few strings attached to the offer, but the requirements were fair, she thought. Participation in an exhibition of any work created while part of the program would be mandatory at the end of their stay. Once the exhibit closed, the artists would be free to take their work and leave. She had an agreement drawn up that basically made the resident responsible for any damage they caused to their cabin or to the center over the course of their stay. Participants could be asked to leave if they were involved in criminal activity or behaved in such a manner that brought an unfavorable light to the program or the art center.

"I really don't want to have to spell this out," Emma had protested to the lawyer Chris had insisted she confer with. "I'm assuming these will all be adults with fully functioning impulse control and a mature sense of decorum."

"Let's not assume too much," the lawyer had told Emma. "Better to have wording in your agreement so that everyone knows exactly what you expect. And talk to your insurance agent and see what coverage you need."

"I already added the buildings to the policy that covers the center."

"That's fine, but if one of them is somehow injured on the property, you might want to up your liability limits for bodily injury."

"I'm pretty sure I did that as well, but I'll check."

"And for heaven's sake, we need to run background checks."

"Why?"

"Because we don't want a wanted felon hiding out on the beach for three months."

Emma hoped requiring the signed agreement wouldn't be off-putting to the artists, hoped they wouldn't feel they were being treated like children going off to camp for the first time. But Chris had invested a lot of money into the venture on her behalf, and she didn't want him to regret his decision. Not that he would. It made her feel guilty that he'd put so much money into the center over the years, but he'd shrugged it off, saying, "Mom, if I told you how much money I make between touring and albums and merchandise and royalties for the songs I've written, you would pass out, and it might be tough to revive you. So when I say this project of yours is a drop in the bucket, trust me. I can afford it." Then he'd grinned. "Besides, since the center is a nonprofit, I can write it all off."

Now, as April began, all Emma had to do was narrow the field of artists to six, offer the placements, get the cabins ready, and sit back and let it happen.

Choosing the final six was the hardest part. Raised by her minister father and a kindhearted mother to honor the Golden Rule, Emma hated to disappoint anyone. Ever. For any reason. Often described as the "nicest, kindest person you'll ever meet," hurting someone's feelings hurt Emma almost as much. She didn't think of herself as a pushover, but growing up, she'd observed how both parents treated others, and she'd always done the same. So denying the chance to work unencumbered on one's art to someone who'd expressed such a desperate need for the opportunity filled Emma with dread. She hated to say no, but she was going to have to, to nine talented finalists, and it weighed heavily on her mind as she fumbled in her bag for the key to the center's front door.

The remnants of last night's rain ran off the roof, dripping in large teardrops that slid down the back of her jacket as she stood on the top step and unlocked the door. The phone was ringing as she hastened to her office and turned on the overhead light. She plunked the heavy file on the desk but didn't get to the phone in time. She figured if it was important, whoever it was would call back. She adjusted the thermostat to bring up the temperature and took off her coat. She sat in her chair and eyed the file, which held fifteen letters from hopeful applicants who'd made the first cut, along with accompanying photos of their work. She'd go through them again until she could cull the herd, so to speak, and narrow it down to six. After two hours, she was no further along in her task. She picked up her iPhone and sent a text to Liddy and Maggie: Need help. Bring coffee.

Thirty minutes later, her friends arrived together. Maggie handed Emma the container of coffee and took the sole visitor's chair. After noticing the pile of envelopes on the desk, she said, "Em, please tell us you're not still working on the artist thing."

Emma nodded. "I hate to admit it—I really do hate having to tell you that I can't make a decision. I just can't seem to do it. They're all so good."

"So you called us over to tell us that?" Liddy raised an eyebrow.

"I want your opinion. Just walk through these with me, okay?" She stood and motioned for Liddy to take her chair behind the desk. "Maybe you'll see something I missed."

Emma stood at the end of the desk. "Here's candidate number one . . ." She passed around the photos. "Glorious use of color and form . . ."

She walked through all fifteen of the final applicants and displayed the photos of their work. When she was finished, she asked, "So? Anyone stand out to you?"

"Well, Em, you were the art history major, so you know much more about these things than either of us," Maggie told her, "but whether you are aware of it or not, you've already picked the ones you feel most strongly about."

Confused, Emma frowned. "I did?"

Maggie nodded and stood. She met Liddy's eyes from across the desk. "Liddy, see if you agree. Em, you spoke the most eloquently about this one." Maggie moved one of the packets to the side. "And this one." The second packet joined the first. "And this, this, this, this, and this."

Emma looked over the candidates Maggie had pulled from the center of the desk, then shook her head. "Yes. Yes, you're right. These are the best." She glanced up at Maggie. "Thank you."

Maggie shrugged. "All I did was read your body language and listen to your voice and watch the expression on your face as you spoke."

"I agree with Maggie on all points. You knew who you wanted; you just weren't ready to pull the trigger and let the others go." Liddy stood. "Except there are seven there, Mags, not six. Emma can only take six."

"Oh." Maggie counted again. "You're right. Okay, so someone has to go."

"Noooooo." Emma groaned. She didn't want to go through this again.

"Well, I will say you sounded equally enthusiastic about these five." Maggie pulled out the applicants. "For what that's worth."

"Which leaves these two." Emma picked up the two packets left from the pile. "I think they're pretty equal as far as talent is concerned, but their stories are so different." She picked up one. "This guy is nineteen. His work is brilliant. He doesn't have money for art school, so he's working in a convenience store at night, hoping to put together a strong body of work so he might get a scholarship to go to school." She set it back down and picked up the packet next to it. "This one . . . she's a sixty-seven-year-old single woman who's never had any art training. She's spent most of her life as caretaker to her disabled brother and then her mother. Her brother died last year, so now it's just her and her mother, who is in the early stages of dementia. She's eked out what time she could over the years to paint, and while she has a little more time now, she's having trouble concentrating because her mother needs so much of her attention. She's applied to the program hoping to have a few months of peace where she can focus only on her painting. Her work is lovely, what there is of it." Emma held up the photos of the woman's work. "She said in her letter that her sister has agreed to stay with their mom for the three months, if she's selected. It will be the first time in her life she's had time to paint without distractions."

"And that's the whole point of this, right? You wanted to give artists a time and a place to work without distractions or other obligations?"

Emma nodded.

"Then I'd go with her," Liddy said bluntly. "The young boy, he has his entire life ahead of him, and the chance of art school in his future. But at sixty-seven, she might not have too many more opportunities, so you should definitely go with her."

"Are their backstories supposed to count?" Maggie pointed out. "And I'm pretty sure that choosing someone only because of their age is ageism."

"You've got to look at the big picture here." Liddy took the photos of the woman's work from Emma's hand. "Look at the skill this woman has. She's had no training, but look at the angles here, and the color, oh my. So strong and so good. Now, I didn't go to art school, but I did learn a thing or two from my daughter, who you both know was a kick-ass artist. This woman"—she waved the photos—"has a natural gift, but she's never been able to pursue it. If you are looking for talented people who deserve a chance to find their inner Renoir or Georgia O'Keeffe, I say this is the one you want."

"Brava." Maggie applauded lightly.

"And spot on, Lydia. You're a hundred, a thousand percent right. She's the right person." Emma breathed a sigh of relief. "Oh God, I can't thank you both enough. You have no idea how difficult this has been for me."

"I'm just happy your decision has been made and you can write up your acceptance letters." Maggie lifted her purse from the back of her chair. "And now I am going back to planting perennials in my garden."

"Well, there are a few rejection letters to write as well." Emma sat on the edge of her desk. "Maybe I should not send those just yet. What if some of the ones we just chose decline the invitation?"

"You could hold off on those, maybe give the acceptances something like ten days to respond. If you don't hear from them, their spot goes to the next one on the list," Liddy suggested. "And hey, you never know. That nineteen-year-old kid might get that last spot after all."

~

The nineteen-year-old never had a chance. All Emma's chosen six had accepted with gratitude and happily signed the agreements. Now all she had to do was get the cabins ready for them to move into. She'd made a list of everything she'd need to buy: furniture and small refrigerators and stoves. Six scaled-down sofas and chairs, six beds, six small dressers. Six mattresses, sheets, and towels. Not to mention new toilets and sinks. Area rugs for the living rooms and bedrooms.

"I expect they'll take most of their meals in town, but not all of them will be able to afford to eat three meals a day at a restaurant, even though I am providing a stipend, so small stoves are the way to go." Then Emma had a sudden vision of someone getting so lost in their work that they might forget they'd put water on to boil for tea. "Oh, and smoke alarms. I remember Liddy mentioning that sometimes when Jessie was working, she'd get lost in it. She wouldn't want to talk to anyone or see anyone, so she blocked out everything. She said noise took her head out of her work, so she taught herself to ignore it."

"Understandable. Sometimes when you're trying to focus, just about anything can serve as a distraction," Maggie said. "What about laundry facilities?"

"There's a Laundromat on Fourth Street. They'll have to take their things there."

Once all the repairs had been made and the cabins brought up to code, Emma was eager to move in her purchases. Tuck offered his construction crew of burly young men for the job, and Emma accepted. On a Tuesday morning, the delivery trucks lined up on Bay Street. After

Tuck's guys installed the mini fridges and stoves into the kitchens and laid the rugs in the living and bedroom areas, they unloaded the truck full of sofas and chairs. Next the bed frames were assembled, and the mattresses were carried in. The cabins were starting to appear habitable.

On a Friday morning, Emma called together her people—her personal crew. Once Maggie, Liddy, and Grace were seated in her kitchen, she plied them with coffee and homemade blueberry coffee cake before making her appeal.

"The cabins are rehabbed, painted, and the furniture has been delivered. Now they need a touch of decor, and I'm asking you each to do one. Just one. Maybe some photos on the wall or houseplants on the table, something to make the place feel a little more like home. Nothing over the top, no deer heads or farmhouse implements on the walls, just a little something to warm up the interiors a bit," she told them. "Keep your receipts, and the center will reimburse you."

"Okay. What do you have in mind?" Grace asked.

"Just some little touches. Whatever you like." Emma smiled. "Though you don't have a choice of furniture. The sofas and chairs can't be changed, and they're all alike anyway, so you're going to have to work around those."

"So, if I wanted, say, a beachy theme, I could pile shells into a clear vase, or something like that," Grace ventured.

"Right. Use your imagination. Not too much, though. We don't want any of the cabins to look cluttered," Emma told her.

"Just inviting and comfortable," Maggie said, "so they don't appear institutional."

Emma nodded. "Exactly."

"We each get one cabin to work on?" Liddy helped herself to a second slice of coffee cake.

"Yup. Just one. Think of it as putting the finishing touches on a big dollhouse."

"But there are six cabins, and four of us," Maggie pointed out.

"I'm taking two," Emma said, "and maybe one of you could take an extra as well."

"I'll do two," Maggie volunteered. "I have all sorts of stuff in my attic from my last house. I'm happy to find a use for it."

"Count on Mom to bring that Main Line vibe right onto the beach," Grace teased.

Maggie laughed good-naturedly. "Hey, I brought so much stuff from Philly when I moved, and now I don't remember why I held on to any of it. There are boxes of all manner of things just sitting in the attic. So what if one of the cabins ends up looking like the Philadelphia Country Club?"

"No country landscapes on the walls, Mom. The ambience here is coastal New England."

"I think we should make it a competition," Liddy suggested. "Whoever does the best job gets taken out to dinner by the rest of us."

"Competition could add an extra little element to the project." Grace nodded, then asked, "Who could we get to judge?"

"We could always ask the chief of police," Maggie said innocently.

"And stack the odds in your favor, Mom? Not happening." Grace laughed. "Like Brett would even think of handing anyone else the blue ribbon."

"Yeah, well, if Maggie gets to nominate the guy she's sleeping with, so do I. I'm tossing Tuck's name into the hat."

Emma laughed. "I'm not sleeping with anyone, but I'll come up with someone who can be impartial."

"Anyone but Chris," Grace said. "Do not make him choose between his mother and his future mother-in-law." She paused. "Not officially future MIL, but we all know that's gonna happen."

"This will be fun," Liddy said. "I loved my dollhouse when I was little. I spent hours fixing it up. I even wallpapered every room. It might be in the attic. I'd kept it for Jess, but she really wasn't into it. Hmm. I'll have to look. I bet Tuck's granddaughter JoJo would like it."

"I remember that dollhouse," Maggie said. "You never let us play with it. So, Em, when do we get to see our blank canvases?"

"We can go right now. I'll drive."

They grabbed their jackets from the coat-tree in the front hall and chatted as they piled into Emma's car. She parked behind the center, and they walked single file along the path leading over the dune. When they came to the row of cabins, they stopped and stared.

"This isn't quite what I expected, Em," Maggie said.

"I didn't want the exteriors to all look alike." Emma folded her arms across her chest and tried to read their faces.

"Well, you certainly scored big there." Liddy laughed. "I don't know what to say."

"Then don't say anything. Don't make me feel as if I have to defend my choices."

"No need to be defensive." Maggie put her arm around Emma and gave her a squeeze. "I think it's just the thing. I hadn't expected to see every cabin painted a different color, but then again, I hadn't thought of the exteriors at all. I like all the color on the beach. It's unexpected but somehow seems just right."

"Oh, I love that they're all different. It's perfect for a group of artists." Grace added, "I especially like the second one. It looks like it was painted by the Mad Hatter."

"Then you may have that one as your project."

"I love it. Thanks, Em." Grace walked around the purple cabin, its trim the palest imaginable yellow in some places, startlingly red in others, the door a highly varnished natural wood.

"I'll take the dark-blue one, and the sage green." Maggie held out her hand for the keys. "Numbers four and six."

"I like the pink one."

"That's cabin number three, Liddy." Emma handed out the keys. "Gracie, here's yours. Catch." She tossed the key for number two to Grace.

Emma took the keys for the cabins no one else selected, and went inside Nantucket-red cabin number one and tucked the key to dark-gray number five in her pocket.

"This is so sweet," she heard Grace call from the cabin next door. "I can totally make this cozy. And I'm calling dibs on the beach theme."

"No fair, Gracie," Liddy called out from the doorway of cabin three. "You've just had months practicing on reinventing that little house of yours. I think you should have a handicap."

Grace's laugh carried over the dune, and Emma smiled, grateful for her friends, their enthusiasm for her project, and their willingness to pitch in. Her grandmother had an expression: many hands make light work. When those hands belonged to your best friends, the work was light indeed.

Over the next three weeks, it took all Emma's willpower not to watch out the center's front windows as her friends arrived carrying boxes and bags into their cabins. She'd tried to use a light touch when decorating her own, adding a lamp here and a tray of smooth stones to the coffee table in one, a stack of books and some scented candles to the other. Each of her cabins got snuggly throws and toss pillows that blended with their exteriors. Every day she'd hear a car door slam, and she'd peek through the door to watch Maggie hoist a box from her trunk and carry it to one of her cabins. Or there would be Liddy or Grace toting a bag and grinning as she no doubt pictured how her choices would transform the plain little interior into something unique and comfortable. Emma was thinking about an appropriate person to judge when her cell phone rang.

The screen read Owen Harrison—the first man—the only man—in recent history who'd made Emma's heart rate tick up. At her age, she thought it embarrassing to think of herself as having a crush on anyone, but if she did, it would be Owen. They'd shared several dates in the past, but he was a busy guy, so they'd never had a chance to develop the kind of relationship Emma thought she might want with him, the relationship she hoped her future held. He wasn't the most handsome man Emma had ever met—he was of average height and build, had thinning brown hair, and wore tortoiseshell glasses. He'd been casually dressed most of the times she'd seen him, khakis mostly, with a sweater or a button-down shirt, but when he'd taken her to elegant restaurants, he'd done his suits proud.

"Oh," she exclaimed softly as her heart took a tiny tumble before she answered the call.

"Emma? Owen Harrison here." The voice was as she remembered, deep and precise with just a touch of a British accent.

She cleared her throat. "Owen, good to hear from you. How are you?"

"I'm well, as I hope you are." Before she could respond, he said, "I'm going to be in Wyndham Beach Sunday through Monday morning, and I was hoping we could get together for dinner."

"I'd love that."

"Does Sunday night work for you?"

"It does."

"Any place in particular you'd like to go? I know there are a number of new places in the area. Of course, there's always the Cape. What's your preference?"

"You decide. I'll be happy wherever we go."

"I'll pick someplace special. It's been months since I've been back, and I've been thinking about you."

She could have added, *And I've been thinking about you, too,* but she merely smiled. It took a moment for her to realize he couldn't see her. This wasn't FaceTime.

"I'll make reservations, and I'll text you and let you know the details."

"I'll wait to hear from you." She paused. "Owen, where are you?"

"I'm in London. I've had some meetings to attend, but I'll be going to Italy in the morning."

"You have a business there as well?"

"Yes. Well, it's more of a hobby at this point. I bought some property in Tuscany, and the villa that came with it has suffered years of neglect. It needs a total overhaul."

"Oh." Emma thought of all the novels she'd read recently where someone inherited or purchased a run-down villa in Tuscany, renovated it, and voilà! Suddenly they're the owner of a thriving vineyard whose wine goes on to win international acclaim. *What a cliché,* was her first thought, but her better angel prevailed, and instead she said, "That sounds wonderful. I imagine it's a lot of work, though."

"It is. It's not as easy to find contractors there as it is in the States. The local workers are excellent, but it's difficult finding someone who isn't already busy on another project."

"Well, I hope you'll bring some pictures."

"I will, yes. The orchard needs attention, but I've been assured that, in time, the trees will do just fine."

"Trees?" Emma was confused. "I thought grapes grew on vines."

"They do. But my house came with an olive orchard."

"Olives," she mused.

"Olives. Now bring me up to date on the goings-on at your art center."

She did. One of the things she liked about Owen was the fact that he always wanted to know about her, her projects, her life. For a man who appeared to own half the known world, in the year or so she'd known him, he'd never seemed to be overly impressed by himself or his worth, but, rather, was more interested in her.

"And your son is well?" Owen asked.

"He's fine, thank you for asking."

"Will he be coming to London anytime soon?"

"Probably not till next year."

"You'll have to let me know," he said. "My nieces have all his music. My stock has risen immeasurably in the eyes of my nieces since I told them Chris Dean's mother was a friend of mine."

"If you want that stock to rise even more, we could probably arrange for tickets for them."

"Oh my. I see favorite-uncle status in my future for sure. Thank you, Emma."

"Email their names to me when the time comes, and I'll ask Chris to have the tickets put aside for them."

"That would be wonderful," he said. "In the meantime, I'll see you next weekend."

They said their goodbyes, but Emma continued to hold her phone even after the call disconnected. She and Owen had met at the first showing of Jessie Bryant's paintings the winter before last and had gotten together a few times since then. There was something about him that appealed to her, and it had nothing to do with the fact that he was not just a member of the Harrison clan, but the one in charge of the current generation of Harrisons.

Everyone in Wyndham Beach knew about the Harrison family. For generations, they'd been the wealthiest family in town. Their home was a mansion on acres of land that stretched from the highway all the way to the beach on the northeastern side of town, though it wasn't known if anyone actually lived there other than a housekeeper and a groundskeeper. They'd made their money first in whaling, some of which they turned into shipping, some into real estate, some into manufacturing, much of which was later channeled into careful investments. Emma wasn't sure what they were invested in these days. Emma didn't really care. She didn't need his money, and at the moment she wasn't looking for a long-term relationship, thank you very much. She'd had one of those, and look how that had ended up. That solid, steady marriage she thought she'd had turned out to have been nothing but a pile of sand.

But Owen was fun and made her feel special and important. It was at her urging that he reinstated the decades-long tradition of bringing out of storage a carousel that had been commissioned by his great-great-grandfather, Jasper, and making it available to the town children to ride on the Fourth of July. Their conversations were always interesting, and his humor never failed to make her laugh. So when she'd told him she'd love to see him again, she meant every word, but she wasn't sure she was interested in anything other than friendship. Yes, she admitted to herself that he made her feel things she hadn't felt in a long time, but thanks to Harry and his little secret, her self-esteem had taken such a beating. Could she imagine trusting a romantic relationship again? She wasn't sure, but if she did, Owen would be her first choice. Then again, someone who had homes in cities all over the world could have an "Emma" in every one of them.

Since the day she'd discovered Harry's infidelity, Emma hadn't felt the same about herself. She'd devoted years—decades—of her life to a man who had cheated on her. His regard for her obviously hadn't been nearly as high as her regard for him, but she'd never caught on. As long as he continued to be the same man at home she'd always known, she'd had no reason to doubt him when he said he had a business dinner or trip. When he'd said he had to work late, she'd not questioned him. In retrospect, she marveled at his acting ability. Now she wondered how well she'd really known Harry, and how she could have been so blindly naive.

And how it was possible that a man who'd been dead for ten years could still break her heart.

Chapter Three

Emma wanted her date with Owen to be special, and she wanted to look her best. She felt a slow rise of anxiety inside and smacked it back down. She wanted to enjoy their time together and not think about the situation with Harry or anything else that might weigh heavily on her mind. She wanted to focus on Owen and enjoy his company. Her doubts about relationships aside, she always smiled when she thought of him.

She changed her clothes three times before deciding what to wear. What she thought of as her go-to dress—black knit, long sleeves, high neck—had been returned to the closet after she remembered the last two times she'd worn it had been to funerals.

She frowned. "Rest in peace" was not quite the look she was going for.

Number two was a red-and-black-checked sheath that made her look like she was off to chop wood in the great Northwest.

"What was I thinking when I bought this?" she'd muttered. "All I need is an axe to sling over my shoulder and I'm good to go."

As soon as she took it off, she folded it and placed it on a chair with a mental reminder to drop it off at the thrift shop on her way to the center in the morning.

Back to the closet.

She finally decided to celebrate the new season with something a little lighter. The spring-green dress was just the thing. It was sleeveless, but there was that lovely multicolor cardigan Natalie had given her for Christmas. Chastising herself for spending so much time dithering over what she would wear for a simple dinner date, she fastened her opera-length pearls around her neck and popped a pearl earring into each lobe. She had pearls in several lengths and was rarely seen without them. The earrings had been an engagement gift from Harry's mother, and the necklaces had belonged to Harry's mother and grandmother. At the time she'd been presented with them, she'd been flattered and felt she'd been accepted as a member of the Dean clan. Pearls had become her go-to, her signature. Now she stared in the mirror at her reflection, the loop of pearls seeming to glow, and not in a good way. It was as if Harry himself was mocking her for still wearing his mother's necklace even knowing how he'd deceived her. She slowly unhooked the long strand, carefully placed it back into its box along with the earrings, and closed the dresser drawer she kept them in. Perhaps one of Harry's nieces would want them. Emma wouldn't wear them again.

She'd dried her hair after her shower, so her modified pixie cut lay perfectly around her heart-shaped face. Bess, her hairdresser, had tried on several occasions to tempt her into a different look, but Emma, who'd worn her dark hair in the same style since her school days, had always declined. With the current popularity of short cuts, her salon had renamed the pixie as the Emma, much to her amusement.

"I don't know that you want to do that," she'd told Bess. "I'll bet there are a lot of women in town who might not want their hair styled like a woman who's pushing sixty."

"They might if they thought they'd look as good as you," Bess had replied.

Emma had laughed. "Way to earn a big tip."

She finished her makeup—just mascara, a swipe of color on her cheeks, and a touch of dark pink on her lips—and was ready when the doorbell rang promptly at seven. She turned off the bedroom light and made her way down the wide staircase to the first floor and answered the door with a smile, her heart in a bit of a flutter.

"You're right on time," she greeted Owen.

"My time with you is always limited, so I hate to waste a minute of it." He stepped inside and leaned close to place a soft kiss on her cheek, then handed her a large bouquet of pink tulips.

"Oh, they're lovely. And this shade is one of my very favorite colors. Thank you, Owen. This was very thoughtful of you. Come with me while I find a vase worthy of them." She beckoned him to follow as she headed toward the back of the house. "I love that these old houses have butlers' pantries," she said as she opened a cupboard door. "Ah, this will do nicely."

She brought out a crystal vase, took it to the sink to fill it with water, then slid the flowers into it. "Perfect. I'll tend to them a bit better later, but for now I'll just give them a good drink, and we can be on our way." She caught him looking at his watch. "Are we going to be late?"

"I think we have enough time." He leaned against the doorjamb. "You look beautiful, Emma. I should have said that first."

"There's no wrong time to tell a woman you like the way she looks." She fought back a blush. The way he looked at her gave her butterflies. "Let me just find my bag, and we can go."

Minutes later they were walking to his car, which he'd parked under the porte cochere of the large house.

"You haven't mentioned where we're going," she said as she slipped into the passenger's seat.

"Right." Owen nodded, closed the door, and walked around to the driver's side and got in.

"So are you going to keep me in suspense?"

"A friend of mine opened a restaurant in Marshfield last year, and I've never been. I thought tonight might be a good time."

"I know Marshfield," she told him. "It's a lovely town."

"And what do you know about it?" He smiled as he backed down the driveway.

One of the things Emma most liked about Owen was his attentiveness to everything she said. He listened to her, heard her, and expressed an interest—and often a curiosity—in her life and her thoughts.

She'd bet her last dollar that Owen was not a man who'd buy his wife a big satin heart filled with cheap chocolates for Valentine's Day while presenting his lover with a pricey gold bracelet. For that matter, she doubted Owen would cheat on his wife if he had one. Then again, she'd never suspected Harry would have, either. One thing she was sure of was that Harry had never hung on her every word the way Owen did. Maybe that should have told her something about her husband. It was certainly telling her something about Owen.

"I know that John Thomas was born there, and that his wife, Hannah, was the first woman lighthouse keeper in the country."

He glanced across the front seat to her, one eyebrow raised.

"Oh yes," she assured him. "The Gurnet Point lighthouse in Plymouth where they moved after they were married. The lighthouse had been built on their land, so John Thomas, who was a doctor, became the lightkeeper. But when he left to join the Continental Army, the lighthouse was left in Hannah's hands. He eventually made general, but he died while he was away. Smallpox, I seem to recall, but she continued to run the lighthouse."

"What happened to the lighthouse?"

"Oh, it's still standing, but it's automated now."

"I wonder how Hannah feels about that," he mused.

"Well, there have been rumors that she's never left, so I suppose one could ask her. I think the lighthouse is only open once a year to visitors, though." She turned slightly in her seat. "Obviously, if you'd gone to school in Wyndham Beach, you'd know these things. We went there on a field trip in fourth grade."

"I did go to school in Wyndham Beach, at Alden Academy, but only for a few years."

"A lot of boys from town went there. My late husband, for example."

"It wasn't my idea, and would not have been my choice." He cleared his throat. "My father insisted."

Emma sensed a story there but wasn't sure she should ask. She was still debating with herself when he solved the dilemma for her.

"Do you know anything about my dad? I mean, like from rumors in town, maybe?" he asked.

Emma shook her head. "I don't think so. Should I have?"

"Probably not. I just thought maybe . . . you know, stories might have gone around."

"Did he ever live in Wyndham Beach?"

Owen stared straight ahead at the road. "He was born there in the family house, though he only lived there till he was five. My grandparents sent all their kids off to boarding school at a very young age, so my father did, too. It was supposed to 'build character.'"

"Oh. I can't imagine . . ." Not one to pass judgment, Emma didn't finish her thought. But she knew there was no way she'd ever have sent Chris away to school as a small child. It had been difficult enough to see him off to college.

"That was the thinking back then."

"So did you go to Alden from kindergarten?"

"Yes, I started boarding there when I was five." He flicked on the turn signal and made a right onto Route 6. "I stayed there until second grade; then I went to school in England. That left my father and mother to go and do as they pleased." He cast a quick glance at her but returned his gaze to the road. "Which, in my father's case, was to leave my mother and hunt for wife number three."

"Your father was married three times?" How had that tidbit escaped the local gossip mill?

"Four, actually. He was working on divorcing that one when he died. Fell overboard from one of his boats and drowned. My mother remarried and died about four years after my father."

Emma regarded his grim expression. "I'm so sorry, Owen."

"Thank you, but the truth is, I never knew either of them very well. I hate admitting that, and I hate talking about it, but I thought you should know right up front that I'm from a totally dysfunctional family." He tried to force a smile. "Mine was certainly not a made-for-TV childhood."

She placed a sympathetic hand on his arm. "But you have siblings, right?"

"I have several half siblings and a couple of stepsiblings. My oldest half brother—well, let's just say he followed in Dad's footsteps. I haven't had anything to do with him in years. My youngest half brother, Ethan, is all right, though. He's the only one of the lot I'm close to. He's helped me build back the family businesses after our father did just about everything he could to bankrupt us. Ethan's happily married now for almost twenty-five years and has wonderful kids. His daughters are the ones who are delirious over the fact that I actually know Chris Dean's mother."

She laughed, grateful for the conversation to take a lighter tone. "My sole claim to fame. And you—did you ever marry?"

"Too busy trying to put Humpty Dumpty back together again." He smiled. "That's how Ethan and I thought of the family's holdings. Like one big broken thing that we had to reassemble, piece by piece. It took me almost thirty years to rebuild; then I spent the past few years making sure everything was solid. By the time I realized I'd successfully done my part for future Harrisons and I could slow down and relax a bit, I found myself alone and wondering why I bothered. I had no children of my own to leave my share to. No one to spend my time with when I retired."

She couldn't think of anything to say other than "I'm sorry."

"Well, I don't feel so alone now." He reached for her hand, and her fingers instinctively curled around his. "I'm sorry I didn't spend more time in Wyndham Beach all those years. There was nothing to bring me back here. Until now. Look what I've been missing. I'm glad you harassed me into coming back. I might never have met you."

"I'm glad you didn't hold that harassment against me." Emma laughed, recalling how fiercely she'd tracked him everywhere he went for months to get a commitment from him to bring out the old carousel for the Fourth of July.

"At first I thought it was cheeky of you, keeping after me the way you did. Then I became intrigued, and I had to meet this bossy Emma Dean who'd been writing and calling me. When you finally wore me down, I had to come to Wyndham Beach and meet the woman who'd chased me halfway around the world. Could possibly be the best decision I ever made."

"You just showed up at the art center. That was the first big exhibit we did," she said, remembering.

"I wish I'd come back years ago. We might have met sooner." He paused. "But, of course, you were married then, so . . ." His voice trailed off, and he disengaged his hand as he made a left turn.

Emma stared out the side window, a tangle of what-ifs racing through her mind. What if she had met Owen sooner? And what if Harry had asked for a divorce—a laughable thought since no Dean had ever been divorced—so he could marry Carla? Emma would have been a free woman. What if she and Owen had . . .

"Emma?" Owen touched her arm. "I said, we're here."

"Oh. Sorry. My mind just wandered for a moment." She felt her face go red.

Owen turned off the car and got out, and by the time she unhooked her seat belt, he'd opened her door and was offering his hand. He helped her from the car, then looped her arm through his as they walked to the entry of the restaurant.

"Beautiful view." He nodded toward the bay that spread out behind the building that sat upon the rocks above the water.

"Oh, it is," she readily agreed.

Along the far side of the restaurant, pines stood in a straight line and spread along a very narrow stretch of land that stuck out into the bay like a long thin finger. The remaining light was golden and soft and cast hazy shadows, and overhead the first stars were just beginning to blink in the early evening sky. It was a lovely night, a romantic night, Emma thought as they entered through the large double doors, and a slight bit of current raced up her spine. When was the last time she'd thought of anything in her life as romantic?

Her mind went straight to those damned red-satin hearts again. Romance hadn't been high on Harry's list of things to do. At least not where she was concerned.

"Is something wrong?" Owen asked after they'd been seated at a table with a gorgeous view of the bay. "You've gone so quiet."

"Oh, no. I was just taking in the decor. It's lovely." She waved away his concern as their waiter brought their menus. They both listened attentively as he recited the specials; then she discussed the different dishes with Owen to divert conversation away from her.

She managed to keep things light for the rest of the evening. They talked about books they'd both read, and she told him about a show she'd been watching. They lingered over coffee and dessert, then listened to eighties music all the way home, Emma surprising herself by how many lyrics she recalled, Owen chagrined by the fact that he remembered so few. He walked her to her door when they returned to Wyndham Beach, declined an offer to come in for a drink ("Early meeting in Boston in the morning") but kissed her soundly in the doorway—not once or twice, but three times, the first time he'd given her more than a peck on the cheek—and promised to call when he knew he'd be back in town.

"When I get the villa company ready, you could visit." He kept his arms around her to keep her close. "You could be my first guest."

"I'd love that." She took a breath, then let the feeling of shared closeness flow through her as her arms wound around his neck.

"How's your Italian?"

"Ciao. Arrivederci. Grazie. Scusi. Prego. That's about it. You know, the usual phrases you pick up from old movies."

"Enough to get by in a pinch, I suppose, but I hear there are some really good foreign language programs available."

"I'll look into it. Thanks for the tip."

Owen waited until she locked up the house before driving away. She stood in the front window and watched until his taillights disappeared at the end of the street. She turned off the hall light and wondered if he'd been as reluctant to leave as she was to see him go.

Emma sat in the darkened living room, thinking about how different things could have been had she discovered years ago what she now knew about Harry and their marriage. If he'd been honest with her back then, who knew where she might be today? It wasn't a given that she and Owen would have ended up together, but maybe she'd have found someone else who valued her opinion, who enjoyed talking with her and spending time with her. Someone else who might not have been unfaithful, but who might have cherished her for the woman she was and for what she had to bring to a relationship.

"Damn it, Harry, you rat," she murmured as she started up the stairs to go to bed. "Why didn't you just tell me?"

Thinking how they both might have lived happier lives—more honest lives—if only Harry had fessed up years ago, Emma fought a flush of bitterness. She got ready for bed but sat on a chair in the corner of her bedroom, thinking how she hated the thought of getting back into that bed she'd shared with Harry.

"I don't have to keep your damned bed, Harry. I don't have to sleep in that bed ever again," she said aloud. "I can buy a bed of my own."

It was late, but she went downstairs and sat at Harry's old desk with her laptop open in front of her. She pulled up the websites for every furniture store she could find and checked out the beds. She thought maybe a queen size would be nice this time around. The bed she'd shared with Harry had been a double, which had been pretty much the standard for married couples for so many years. While she was at it, she might as well replace the rest of the furniture from that room. New dressers, new rug, even a new light fixture—things she chose, things that were all hers. Of course, since practically all the furniture in the house were antiques belonging to the Dean family trust, she couldn't sell anything, but nowhere in that odious document that she'd signed when she and Harry had married did it address moving furniture from one room to the attic. And that was exactly what she was going to do.

She found something she liked at a store in Boston, so she emailed the site to herself and vowed to check it out in person over the coming weekend. Maybe she'd see if Maggie and Liddy would want to accompany her. They could shop and have dinner, maybe see a movie, spend the night in a hotel known for its fabulous room service breakfasts.

And she'd learn to speak Italian, so she searched for foreign language programs and marked several for further investigation. She'd see what Liddy had available at her bookstore, Wyndham Beach Reads. She pulled up a map of the Tuscan region and wondered where Owen's property was located. She looked at photos of the area and pictured herself there. Feeling a little better having taken control of not one but two areas of her life, she turned off the computer and the overhead light and crept back up the steps. She walked past the room in which she'd slept for the past forty years and went directly to one of the guest rooms, where she tucked herself into an unfamiliar bed. When sleep came, she dreamed she was walking through the misty rows of an orchard, her hand reaching overhead, her fingers trailing the slender green leaves of the olive trees, chatting happily with Owen in perfect Italian.

"Mrs. Dean." He rose from his seat when he saw her approach. "How nice to see you. You're looking well on this fine morning."

"Mr. Sanchez, it's good to see you as well." She extended her hand. He held out his own. "How's that boy of yours?"

Emma smiled. She suspected that Mr. Sanchez and older employees of the bank would always think of Chris as the young boy who used to bring in his savings book to deposit a portion of that week's allowance.

"He's all grown up now, Mr. Sanchez," she reminded him.

"What a nice little boy he was, back in the day."

"He was, thank you. Now he's a nice big boy."

"I heard he was something special, playing that guitar."

"Oh yes, he is." She knew from experience that Mr. Sanchez would chat mindlessly for the rest of the afternoon, if given the chance. So she took the key for the safe-deposit box from her bag and held it up for him to see. "I need to get into our box. Would you mind opening the gate for me?"

"Oh, certainly." He rose slowly and unlocked the old-fashioned metal gate that stood guard over the vault. "What's the number of that box again?"

Emma told him, and he found the box and set it on a table for her. "Just let me know when you're finished, and I'll set it back up there for you."

"Thanks, Mr. Sanchez." Emma waited till he'd left the vault before she sat and unlocked the box.

It had been so long since she'd had occasion to check the contents that she'd forgotten much of what had been stored there. She sorted through some bond certificates, the deed to the house in which she lived as well as a few other properties Harry had purchased in town for rentals, a copy of his will. The wills of Deans going back generations. A leather box containing the most valuable pieces of his mother's and grandmother's jewelry, another holding some miscellaneous papers she didn't bother to read. Harry's birth certificate along with Chris's and her own. The passports were on the bottom. She checked hers and found it was long overdue for renewal, even more than she'd realized. A quick look at Harry's, however, revealed that he'd renewed his three years before he died. Curious, Emma flipped through the pages.

Harry had taken a trip to Bermuda in February 2006? She had no recollection of that. Three days in Belize in 2005? Another three days in Mexico in 2007? She sat immobile, her brain processing the information. Harry had never expressed an interest in any of those places to her, and he never would have traveled to any of those places alone. He never took the time for anything other than a work trip, but there'd been plenty of those. Could he have been in Bermuda when he'd said he was going to Dallas?

He could have if someone else had wanted to spend a few days on a beach, far away from the New England winter.

Emma sighed deeply. The hits just kept on coming.

She slipped her passport into her bag and locked the box. Forcing a smile as she passed Mr. Sanchez, she managed to get out the words, "It's all yours. Thank you."

"You have a good day now, Mrs. Dean," he said.

Too late for that, she thought as she made her way to the lobby, anger bubbling inside her and threatening to spill over, which she simply wouldn't permit. Emma Dean was not one to make a scene.

She smiled pleasantly to the old-timers who remembered her as Harry's wife but made it a point not to maintain eye contact with anyone lest they wanted to chat. She was in no mood for small talk. At the bank's double front glass doors, she reached to open one just as an arm shot out from the outside and pulled it open. Emma stepped aside to permit the person who opened the door to enter, then noticed the arm was attached to Carla Dempsey's body—and at the end of that arm dangled a bracelet, its shiny fat gold links wrapping around each other.

So that was what a really expensive solid gold bracelet looked like.

"Oh. Emma." Carla's voice held surprise but no warmth. "It's been a while."

"Yes, it has." She deliberately directed her attention to Carla's arm, which was still extended and holding open the door. She let her gaze fall on the bracelet. "Oh, what a lovely bracelet. Is it new?"

Carla took a step back as if to encourage Emma to pass through the door and leave.

"I've had it for years." She pulled the sleeve of her jacket down to cover the bracelet.

"Really? It looks brand new." Emma reached out and tugged the bracelet back down, then flipped over the gold disk attached to it. She read the inscription aloud. "CJD—2-14-2012." She met Carla's eyes and said innocently. "Ah, a Valentine's Day gift from 2012? How touching that you still wear it after all this time. The person who gave it to you must have meant a great deal to you."

She stared at Carla for a very long moment.

"He did," Carla said defiantly.

"I totally understand." Emma released the other woman's arm. "Such a coincidence, though. Harry bought me a very similar one from a jeweler in Boston. I believe it was the same year, too."

Carla looked as if she'd been struck. Then, speechless, she walked past Emma into the bank, while a smiling Emma crossed the street and headed for Wyndham Beach Reads. She was still smiling when she went inside and waved to Liddy, who was behind the counter, wrapping up a sale. Emma found her way to the foreign language books.

"What was that look for?" Liddy asked when she joined Emma.

"Which look was that?" Emma glanced at the titles on the shelf, seeking something that could have her speaking Italian like a native, just in case.

"That look. The one on your face right now."

"Oh. I just told a huge lie," Emma admitted. "But right now, I'm at that point between feeling good about myself—you know, that I asserted myself—and being embarrassed that I actually told such a bold lie."

"You told a lie? Deliberately lied about something?" Liddy's eyebrows rose almost to her hairline. "Emma, you are the most painfully honest person I've ever met. Who did you lie to?"

"Carla. And it was a whopper." Emma related the brief conversation she'd had with Carla.

"You told her Harry bought you a gold bracelet for the same Valentine's Day?" Liddy burst out laughing. "What did she say?"

"She didn't say anything. She just turned white and went into the bank. She looked so upset, I almost felt sorry for having lied. I still can't decide if I do or not. I just wanted her to know that I knew about their affair."

"You could have simply said, 'I know you were having an affair with my husband.'"

"I could never admit that out loud to her, Liddy. I don't know why, but I couldn't. It's strange, because I admitted it to you and to Maggie, but I can't to her."

"I know it's hard for you to be confrontational. It's just not your way." Liddy gave Emma a little hug. "I think you got your point across."

"Yeah, but I hate being mean."

"Carla deserves to be called out. You let her know that you know about the affair."

"That's all I really wanted. I don't want an apology—which she'd never give me anyway—and I don't want excuses. I just hated that she and Harry thought I'd never find out. I want her to wonder how much I know and how long I've known." Emma folded her arms over her chest. "Of course, it took me ten years to figure it out." She rolled her eyes. "They don't call me Speedy for nothing, you know."

"Okay, so now it's her turn to wonder. Don't give her another thought, Em. You can't change what was." Liddy had turned over the book in Emma's hand to read the title. "Now, why are you holding that copy of *Learn Italian in Ten Days!?*"

"The short answer is Owen bought a run-down villa in Tuscany that has an olive grove. He's going to restore the entire place, the orchard and the villa. He's invited me to visit once the renovations to the house are completed, so I thought I'd start to learn some conversational Italian. I'm sure I have more than ten days, though."

"A run-down villa in Tuscany, huh? You know that's almost a cliché these days."

"That's just what I thought, too. But clichés are clichés for a reason. Do you know anyone who wouldn't buy an old villa anywhere in Italy, if they could afford it?"

"Good point. So, if you're going to go to Italy, you're right. You will want to speak the language." Liddy gestured for Emma to follow her to the end of the aisle, where she picked up a box and handed it over. "This is one of the better programs on the market. It has CDs you can listen to, and you can read along in the books. You can find it online for less money, but I'll give you the family discount."

"I'll take it." Emma gave Liddy a little shove in the middle of the back, urging her in the direction of the cash register. "Let's do this before I have second thoughts."

Liddy stopped in the middle of the aisle. "Why would you have second thoughts?"

Emma shrugged. "I don't know. Maybe unconsciously I do wonder if . . ."

"No. Don't say one more word. You're not going to let Harry do that to you." Liddy took Emma by the arm. "Listen, I get that finding out all these years later that you were betrayed is heavy. But you're not going to let that color every new relationship from here on. Owen hasn't given you any reason to doubt his sincerity, has he?"

"No. He has not, but I don't really know what he does when he's not in Wyndham Beach."

"So google him and find out."

"You mean look him up online? I wouldn't do that." Emma was aghast.

"Then that makes you probably the last person on Earth with access to a computer who wouldn't."

"That's like spying on someone. It would make me feel creepy."

"Then don't look for trouble, my friend. But the man wants you to visit him in Italy, you say, *Yes please*, you learn to speak a little Italian, you read up on olives, and you book that flight. I'll drive you to the airport. You'll return with several bottles of Chianti that you, Maggie, and I can enjoy while you tell us all about your romantic time in Tuscany." The two old friends shared a long moment of unspoken, longtime understanding and love.

Emma nodded and handed Liddy the box of books and CDs. "Ring me up."

Chapter Four

It had taken several discussions and a bit of negotiating, but finally the four would-be interior decorators agreed that Kathleen McDonough from the Garden Patch, the local nursery, should judge the little cabins on the dune and decide the winner. After solemnly swearing not to give away which cabin was whose, they all met on the beach at high noon on Tuesday, as agreed upon.

"Let's get this show on the road, ladies. I don't have all day. Memorial Day is coming, and you know what that means," Kathleen said when she arrived.

"No, what's that mean?" Grace asked.

"It means the summer growing season is right around the corner, and I have a lot of plants to sell. I have a tractor trailer of annuals arriving this afternoon, so let's get going."

"You do like a bit of nostalgia, don't you, Kathleen?" Liddy put an arm over the nurserywoman's shoulder. "Echoes from your childhood, that sort of thing?"

"Hands off the judge, Lydia," Maggie scolded. "Kathleen, ignore Ms. Bryant's efforts to sway your opinion. We've all agreed that the judge should not know who decorated which cabin."

Kathleen, a tall, slender woman with salt-and-pepper hair cut blunt to her chin and held off her face with an old-school headband, put her hands over her ears. "Not to worry. I didn't hear a word."

"Yes, well, some of us are better than others at blocking out noise," Grace said dryly.

"Excuse me. Do you still work for me?" Liddy pretended indignation.

"Yes. And you're damned glad of it," Grace reminded her.

"Actually, I am," Liddy conceded.

"All right, ladies." Emma sought to silence the small group. "There will be no efforts to influence the judge. We will all stand back over here and keep our mouths closed. Kathleen, you just go on inside the cabins and look around. Take notes if you want. See which one you think is the best decorated."

Kathleen strode on long legs to the first cabin in the row. She paused at the front door, then stepped inside. Moments later, she emerged, smiling, then went on to the second cabin. The four women watched as Kathleen went in and out of each, smiling each time she emerged.

"Tough to get a read on her," Liddy whispered. "She seems to like them all."

"Of course she does," Emma said. "They're all great."

"How would you know if you hadn't peeked in on the others, Em?" Maggie asked.

"I didn't have to peek," Emma replied archly. "I'm assuming you all put your singular touches on your decor."

"Shh." Grace elbowed her mother and nodded as Kathleen closed the door to Maggie's sage green cabin number six. "Looks like Kathleen is finished."

"Well, what do you think?" Liddy asked as the group of four moved forward.

"I think they're all special." Kathleen stood with her hands on her hips. "Seriously, they're all so well done. Emma, when your artists' residency is over, I think you should consider renting them out."

"Yeah, yeah, fine. But which one did you like best?" Liddy asked impatiently.

"What does the winner get?" Kathleen asked.

"We all take her out to dinner," Maggie said.

"And it has to be to someplace nice," Grace added. "As in, not Ray's for pizza and a milkshake."

"And what does the judge get?" Kathleen folded her arms across her chest and looked from one of her friends to the next. "I mean, without my input, there's no winner."

"Fine," Liddy said. "We'll take you out with us. Now which one did you like best?"

"As I said, they're all really well done, and I'd be happy to stay in any of them, but I'm going with cabin number two. Grace's."

"Yes!" Grace pumped her fist into the air.

"Why?" Liddy frowned. "What does hers have that mine didn't?"

"This is a beach town. These places are on the beach, and she went with a beachy theme. It just seemed to fit." Kathleen nodded in the direction of the purple cabin with the yellow-and-red trim.

"Well . . . that didn't take much imagination," Liddy protested. "What about my dollhouse?"

"Oh, the third one? The pink house?" Kathleen laughed. "It's very cute inside, Liddy. I'll give you that. But I don't know how an adult might feel living with those shadow boxes set here and there with the miniature family and their little furniture and their tiny dog. Some might find that just a little, well, creepy." She leaned close to Emma and whispered, "You might want to take them down before the artist has to move in. I wasn't kidding when I said it was a little creepy."

"I suppose I might have gotten a little carried away," Liddy admitted. "I'll take them down and bring over some books." Then she pointed at the second cabin. "But how did you know that was Grace's?"

"Elementary, my dear friend. It wasn't tough to figure out who did what. I remember the dollhouse you had when we were kids, so when I saw those little people? No-brainer." She looked at Maggie. "My grandparents lived with an uncle and his family in Haverford, Pennsylvania, probably not far from where you lived in Bryn Mawr. I know Main Line Philly when I see it. That black watch plaid wallpaper in the one bathroom reminded me of my cousin Mindy's school uniform, and those foxhunting prints in the other bath? My uncle had those in his study.

"Grace's had the youngest vibe, the lightest colors, which we'd expect because she is the youngest, so her place had a lighter, brighter touch. There were two left over, so they had to be Emma's." Kathleen shrugged.

"Well, now that we can see what each of us did, I think we need to take the tour," Maggie said.

"Whose dumb idea was it to make this a competition anyway?" Liddy pretended to grumble.

"I'm pretty sure it was yours, Lids." Maggie gave her a friendly pat on the back.

They all traipsed into Grace's cabin and, after looking around, agreed that she'd nailed it. There was a thick fishermen's knit throw on the sofa, over which she'd mounted crab nets. There were bowls of shells and a metal bucket holding a variety of fishing poles. A lobster trap topped with a slab of raw-edged pine served as a coffee table, and a clock in the shape of a lobster hung on the wall, its tail moving from side to side as it ticked off the seconds. In the bedroom, a large whale made of wood was affixed to the wall behind the bed, which had toss pillows that reflected the beach theme—shells, crabs, a school of shiny fish. She'd done the walls in the colors of the inside of the shells: creamy white, palest pink, sand.

"Okay, so you did a good job, Gracie." Liddy glanced around approvingly. "Where'd you get that piece of wood for the coffee table?"

"Linc found it for me."

"Wait . . . was that against the rules? Getting help from an outside source?" Liddy asked.

"I don't believe there were any rules." Grace smiled smugly.

"So where are we taking you for dinner?" Maggie asked her daughter.

"I'll have to think about it." Grace grinned. "I'll come up with someplace really good."

"Well, then. Place, date, and time to be announced. Lock up, everyone. Then I'll take the keys." Emma turned to Kathleen. "Thanks for taking the time to come over here and humor us. We'll let you know when we have a date for dinner."

"Any day except Saturdays," Kathleen said. "I'm usually beat by the time I get home after lugging plants around all day."

"I'll call you," Emma promised.

As Kathleen turned to walk away, Grace said, "If you're going back to your nursery, could I catch a ride? I've been meaning to stop by to talk to you about some plantings I'm going to need at my new house."

"Sure." Kathleen waved Grace along as she walked to her pickup truck.

"I guess Grace is going to be moving into that little house of hers soon." Maggie watched her daughter cross the parking lot. "I'm going to miss her, but it sure is time. Much as I love her, she needs her own place."

"Tuck told me her kitchen appliances finally arrived," Liddy said, "so as soon as they're installed and the HVAC guys are done, she'll be able to move in. Seems like the longest renovation in history, doesn't it?"

"Yes, it does." Maggie laughed. "Especially to Gracie. I know she and Linc are looking forward to having a place where they can be alone. Unless I'm staying at Brett's apartment—which between us I hate to do because it's so small, or unless we're away for a weekend, well, let's just say three's always a crowd. Whether it's me, Brett, and Grace, or me, Grace, and Linc, it can get awkward. By the time you're in your midthirties, as she and Linc are, you need a place of your own."

"Agreed. And God knows there's no privacy on Shelby Island, especially with Brenda's three kids there and Tuck's father and his live-in nurse. If three's a crowd, I don't know what you'd call seven. Nine, if you add in Grace and me," Liddy said.

They reached the parking lot, and Liddy continued walking toward her car. "I need to get back to the bookshop so Marion can go to lunch. I'll talk to you guys later."

"See you, Liddy. Maggie." Emma started up the steps to go into the building.

"Wait, Em." Maggie walked toward her. "You're awfully quiet today. Are you all right? Everything okay?"

Emma shrugged. "It's been an odd week. I'll get over it."

"Get over what? What's wrong? You know I'm here if you need me."

For all she hated talking about it, Emma couldn't resist the offer of her friend's shoulder. She knew from their shared past that Maggie was not only a great listener, but a compassionate one as well.

"Come on in." She unlocked the door and Maggie followed her into her office.

"I ran into Carla yesterday at the bank." Emma wasted no time, jumping right into the heart of the situation. "She was wearing the bracelet."

"The gold bracelet Harry gave her?"

"The very one. I admired it; then I lied and said Harry'd bought me a similar one the same year as hers." She threw her bag onto her chair, then leaned back against her desk.

"You didn't!" Maggie laughed. "And . . . ?"

"I did, and, well, we both know that's not true." Emma could feel her face flush with shame at the admission.

"That's it? That's what's bothering you?"

"Well, yeah. At first, I thought, 'Yay, me! I slapped back at her and Harry.' Like I'd had the last word. I'm not going to lie, Maggie. I saw red when I saw that bracelet on her arm. But then I realized that she's still wearing it, all these years later. You know what that must mean."

"What must it mean?" Maggie sat on the visitor's chair and crossed her legs.

"That she really loved him. That she still does. That it was more than merely an affair. They were in love." Emma's eyes were filling with tears. "He was the love of her life, and she was his."

"Honey, you don't know that. Maybe she just likes wearing a beautiful and expensive gold bracelet." Maggie played the skeptic. "I know I would."

"I suppose there's that." Emma covered her face with her hands for a moment. "It's all so complicated. It makes me angry to think he played a role with me for so long, like I was a prop in his respectable life. In my heart, I feel that if he'd met Carla first, he'd have married her. But he met me first, and married me, and we had a son. Then she came into the picture, and I think he must have fallen in love with her, but he couldn't marry her because of me."

"If he loved her that much, Em, he could have asked you for a divorce."

"He never would have done that. A Dean divorce? Uh-uh. It never would have happened. No one in his family ever got divorced. So all those years he was married to me and loved someone else. Which means all those years he didn't love me."

"You don't know that. Stop trying to fill in the blanks. You have no idea what Harry was thinking or feeling, and since he died, you will never know."

"No, I do know. In my heart, I do. I lived with that man for almost forty years. He wouldn't have left me, but he continued his relationship with her. He could have given her up, but he never did. I told you she was at the hospital after he had his heart attack. She was with him before I was. She left when I arrived, but I'll never forget the look on her face. I don't know why I didn't figure it out right then and there. Why it took the receipt for a piece of jewelry for the truth to finally dawn on me.

"And knowing just makes me so angry. He could have told me. If he hadn't been so concerned with what other people thought or what they'd say, maybe we both could have been happier."

"Oh, Em, I don't know what to say." Maggie sat on the desk next to Emma and put an arm around her. "But go ahead and vent if you need to."

"I'm angry with him on so many levels. Suppose he'd been honest with me. Suppose we went our separate ways. Maybe I could have met someone else who really loved me, and he could have spent the rest of his life with someone he did love." A tear ran down her cheek. "And as much as I hate her, I hate what I did even more. I made her think he'd given me the same gift he'd given her. I meant to make her feel that she was not so special after all." She brushed away the tear with her fingertips. "I made her feel the way I felt when I realized he'd betrayed me. I could see it in her face. Of course that's what I'd wanted, but when I saw how hurt she looked . . . Maggie, I'm ashamed of myself for stooping so low."

Maggie was momentarily speechless.

"Emma . . . geez. Who cares how she feels? You certainly shouldn't. She's the one who had the affair with your husband. Not the other way around."

"I think she loved him very much, and still does."

"Maybe so, but that's not the point, Em. She's not the injured party here. You don't owe her anything."

"I'm the daughter of a minister. I was brought up to believe that causing pain to someone else is always wrong. Even if that person has wronged you." She picked at the nail polish on her left thumb with her right. "I'm angry with Harry and I'm angry with Carla. But I'm angry with myself, too. I took something from her, and I did it deliberately, and with a lie."

"Oh my God, are you even a real person?" Maggie stared at her; then she sighed. "Okay, so you made up something to . . ."

"To make myself feel better by hurting her."

"Em, you're thinking too much about this. I think it's part of being human to want to strike back when someone hurts us. Carla hurt you. You wanted to hurt her. It's understandable."

"No. *Harry* hurt me. I wanted to hurt him, but I can't get to him. So I hurt her instead. It wasn't right. No matter how you look at it, or how you try to rationalize it, it was wrong. I'm disappointed in myself. My mother always said, if you know better, you need to do better." Emma shook her head. "I know better."

"I'm sorry, Em. I don't know what else to say except that I'm sorry about all of this."

The phone on Emma's desk began to ring. "I should probably get that."

"All right, but you call me if you need to talk some more." Maggie stood and grabbed her bag from the floor where she'd dropped it. "Even if you do something that disappoints you, you never disappoint me. I'll always be on your side."

"I know you will. Thank you, Mags." Emma gave her a quick hug, then turned away and answered the phone. "Wyndham Beach Art Center. Emma speaking . . ."

~

The following morning, Emma sat in her kitchen, feeling tired, grumpy, and no happier with herself than she'd been the day before. She'd barely slept, and the only good thing she could think of was that today was one of the two weekdays the art center was closed. She wouldn't have to see or talk to anyone for any reason if she didn't feel like it—and today she didn't feel like it. Of course that would change once summer arrived, but for now, she'd happily take the two days off.

She knew her friends loved her, and they tried to understand her, but neither Maggie nor Liddy had grown up in such a highly religious home, where right and wrong had been clearly defined. She'd heard her father preach selflessness and kindness and compassion for one's enemies from the pulpit every Sunday. In her parents' eyes, there were no gray areas. She couldn't remember the last time she'd deliberately gone against her own deeply ingrained beliefs. Taunting Carla had felt good before the little whispers of doubt began to curl around her conscience, and she couldn't shake off the tangled feelings of guilt and anger and shame for the way she'd behaved, all of which had had her staring at the guest room ceiling all night. At four, she'd gone downstairs and eaten a quart of strawberry ice cream standing up, looking out at the night sky and wondering why she hadn't been able to control her emotions any better than Harry had been able to control his apparent passion for Carla.

She spent most of the day sitting in her kitchen shopping for furniture on her laptop, her earlier plans to have a grand weekend in Boston with her two best friends for company scraped in the wake of her current funk. She'd find a bed and a dresser she liked, and she'd have it delivered. No fuss, no muss. When her phone rang, she let it go to voice mail. She still didn't want to talk to anyone, and she had a raging headache. She responded to Maggie's late-afternoon voice mail with a text: I'm fine. Just having a busy day. Talk to you later. Thanks, Mags. xxox

The Italian language program was still in its bag from Wyndham Beach Reads, so she took out the book and was flipping through it when the doorbell rang. Her first reaction was to let it ring, but the sound was so shrill it seemed to echo inside her already aching head. Conscious of the fact that she looked exactly the way she felt and hoping it wasn't anyone she knew, she crossed the foyer toward the front door. She smoothed down the ancient threadbare sweatshirt she'd pulled on that morning over a pair of faded jeans and looked askance at her feet, which were still in her bedroom slippers.

"It would serve me right if it were Owen," she grumbled as she made her way to the front of the house.

When she reached the door, she peered through the glass in the upper panes, but no one was there. She opened the door and looked down. A small, thin girl with auburn pigtails who appeared to be seven or so stood on the porch to the left of the door. She held a piece of paper with Emma's address written on it.

She must be selling something, Emma thought when she saw the box at the girl's feet. Candy bars for the local school? It was too early for Christmas cards, wasn't it? And hadn't the season for Girl Scout cookies passed?

"Yes?" Emma tried to sound kinder—certainly less cranky—than she was feeling. She'd been wallowing all day and hated to have to share her wallow time with anyone. She'd buy whatever the child was selling and get back to her online shopping and her now-cold coffee.

"Are you Miz Emma Dean?" The girl's voice was soft with a decidedly Southern accent. She gazed up at Emma tentatively, her blue eyes uncertain behind her bright-orange glasses.

She spoke so softly Emma had to lean forward to hear her. "Yes, I'm Emma Dean."

"Oh, good." The child exhaled a very deep breath. She stuffed the paper into her backpack.

Emma leaned against the doorjamb with her hands in the pockets of her jeans and waited for the sales pitch.

But instead of a rehearsed speech about whatever it was she was trying to sell, the girl picked up the box at her feet. "Granny said I'm going to stay with you now. She said there was no point in sending me back to her or Angel this time 'cause she was tired of all the back-and-forth."

Emma frowned. What was this child talking about?

"I'm sorry, what? What angel?" A confused Emma couldn't even finish the sentence.

"Angel Lobell? She's Mama's best friend? I stayed with her after Mama left, but then she sent me to my granny's, but *she* said it was too much for her, so she sent me back to Angel, but then *she* sent me back to Granny again when she had to go out of town. Then Granny said it was 'bout time you took your turn."

"I'm sorry, I'm not following you." Emma put a hand to her face. Her head began to spin. "My turn for what?"

"To take care of me."

"I don't understand." Emma wondered for a moment if she'd fallen asleep at the kitchen table, and this was a dream and everything the child had just said was so much jabberwocky.

"Because you're my grandma. My *other* grandma."

For a very long moment, Emma's world stood perfectly still. Jabberwocky, indeed.

"I'm sure there's some mistake. I don't have any grandchildren."

"Well, ma'am, you have me."

Emma took a deep breath. "Let's start with, well, who are you? What's your name?"

"Winter Sky Pine." The child's face turned red, as if it hurt to say the name aloud. "But could you call me Winnie?"

"Your name is Winter Sky?" Emma's eyebrows scrunched toward each other.

The girl nodded with evident reluctance and said hopefully, "Winnie?"

She put the box down and set her backpack on top and rummaged through it for a moment. She took out an envelope and handed it to Emma. "Granny said to give you this."

Emma took the envelope but didn't open it. "Look, Winnie, I don't know who your mother is, or your grandmother, but . . ."

"ArlettaJo Pine is my granny. It's in the letter." She pointed to the envelope she'd just given Emma. Behind her glasses, Winnie blinked as if to hold back tears. "Ma'am, do you think I could use your bathroom? Granny told me to be careful around the bathrooms in the bus stops since I was alone."

Emma stepped back, almost without thinking. "You came here by bus? By yourself?"

"Yes, ma'am." Winnie followed her into the foyer and looked around, eyes wide. "Is this a mansion or something?"

"Where did you get on the bus?" Emma asked, ignoring the awe-struck look on Winnie's face.

"Atlanta, ma'am."

"You came all the way up here from Georgia on a bus?" Emma tried to calculate how long a trip that must have been, but could not. "How long did it take?"

Winnie shrugged. "A long time."

"When did you leave Atlanta? Do you know?"

"Yes, ma'am. It was pretty early in the morning."

"So you've been on a bus since this morning . . . ?"

"No, ma'am. Yesterday morning."

"Where did you sleep?" a horrified Emma asked.

"Oh, I slept on the bus. It was okay. The driver was a real nice lady. She let me sit behind her and sleep on the seat. Then when we got to New York and I had to get off her bus and get onto another one, she found it for me and talked to the driver, so he let me sit behind him, too. Then we got to Rhode Island, and I had to take another bus, but Larry—that was the driver's name, Larry—he found that bus for me and he told the new driver—his name's Wayne—to make sure I got here. And he did. I showed him the paper with your address on it, and he knew where to go 'cause he used the navigation on his phone. He let me out right up there on the highway and told me to walk straight down that street to the tennis courts and turn right and go to Pitcher Street and to this house. And I did."

"You walked here from the highway?"

"Yes, ma'am."

"That's well over a mile."

"Yes, ma'am."

Emma tried to process the fact that the child had been traveling for more than twenty-four hours—alone—on a series of buses—from Georgia to Massachusetts. Was that even legal?

Winnie dropped the box and the backpack on the ancient Persian rug that covered half the floor in the foyer. "Ma'am, the bathroom . . . ?"

"Oh. Of course. Right down here, off the kitchen." Emma closed the door behind her, then led the way down the hall and through the kitchen. She opened the powder room door and turned on the light. "You go on, Winnie. I'll be in the kitchen when you're finished."

Emma was standing in the middle of the kitchen when she opened the envelope and slid out two pieces of paper. The first was a letter. Emma skimmed it quickly. "What the hell . . . ?"

Dear Emma Dean—I saw you in *People* magazine last year when some photographer put your picture in there and said you were Chris Dean's mother and you were living on a beach in Massachusetts. I've been raising this girl on and off for the past couple of years, but I'm done. If you don't want her, just send her over to children's services there up north and they can put her in foster care. If my daughter comes back and wants her, she can let you know, but I'm over it. If she'da let me know sooner that the girl's father was <u>that</u> Chris Dean—that's what she told Angel, so I'm taking her at her word—I'da sent her to you a long time ago.

ArlettaJo Pine

Emma read it again, and then again.

Neither the third nor the fourth read-through made any sense to Emma. No, ArlettaJo Pine did not know what she was talking about. Her daughter may have gotten pregnant by someone named Chris

Dean, but it was not *Emma's* Chris Dean. He'd have told her. He'd have had that child with him.

Who was this ArlettaJo Pine, anyway? Who was her daughter? Was this some sort of extortion scheme? A joke?

Angry fingers opened the second sheet of paper, and then Emma had to sit. The birth certificate had the state seal of Georgia on it, and the names of the parents of the child born on March 3, 2015, to Patricia Summer Rose Pine and Christopher Dean.

Emma glanced out the window. There had to be hundreds, maybe thousands, of men named Christopher Dean in this country. What made this woman so sure *her* Christopher was the father?

It was too preposterous to imagine for one minute that it could be true.

She glanced back at the birth certificate. Winter Sky Pine. Seriously? Who named their child Winter Sky?

Apparently someone whose two middle names were Summer and Rose. Someone who'd point to a rock star as the child's father. But if she'd been so sure Chris was the father of her child, why hadn't she notified them sooner? She could have cashed in years ago.

None of this made sense.

Emma held her head in her hands, thinking back over all those years Chris spent touring . . . she'd read about groupies. Why, wasn't she in his California home when some strange woman managed to slip past security and scaled the back fence, stripped naked, and jumped into his pool? What if he wasn't always as careful as he should have been? As smart as he should have been?

In which case Winnie could well be his. Had he known about the child but not told his mother? Had he been keeping this secret for eight years?

Emma saw red.

She grabbed her phone from the table and punched the icon for Chris's number. When he answered after the third ring, she all but growled into the phone: "Come home. NOW!"

"Mom? What's wrong? Are you sick?" a concerned Chris asked. "Are you okay?"

"No, I'm not sick, and no, I'm not okay. I need you here *now*."

"Can this wait? I'm on my way to Natalie's and I planned to . . ."

"No. It cannot wait, and I don't care what your plans are." It was all she could do not to shout. "You get up here now. Tonight."

"I can't possibly . . ."

"Yes. You can. You have your own damned plane. Get on it." She disconnected the call just as the bathroom door opened and Winnie tiptoed out, holding up her hands.

"I washed my hands with your soap. Those little roses were so pretty but there wasn't any other soap in there. Was that all right? That I used your rose soap?"

Emma took a deep breath to calm herself. "Sure. That's what it's there for."

Her phone began to ring. One glance told her that her son was calling her back. She ignored him. She'd said what she had to say. He needed to get up here and fast. She didn't know what to do with this child who claimed to be his daughter. It was his mess to straighten out, not hers.

If she *was* his daughter—but of course she wasn't—he had a lot of explaining to do. And even if she wasn't, he was going to have to help Emma figure out what to do. Send her back to Georgia with a note around her neck that said *Return to sender*? Thanks but no thanks?

No one is that cruel.

"Granny told me to make sure I was real polite and did everything right or you'd send me to some home for kids that no one wants," Winnie announced as if it was a given that Emma would toss her out if she didn't wash hands after she went to the bathroom.

Emma stared at the child standing in her kitchen. That any child would say what Winnie had just said—and so matter-of-factly—was heartbreaking. Who told a child something like that?

"Winnie, what have you had to eat since yesterday morning?" Emma asked. Whatever the circumstances, however she'd come to Emma, for now, Winnie was here, and she needed to be cared for. Emma could feed her and give her shelter for the night, and then tomorrow they'd try to get to the bottom of this. Maybe when Chris got there, they could get some answers.

"Well, yesterday Granny made me waffles for breakfast—the frozen kind?—and I had some strawberries, so I wasn't hungry for a while." She sat on the floor and dug into her backpack. "I brought some of the berries with me, see?" Winnie held up a plastic sandwich bag that held three sorry-looking berries, mashed and swimming in their juice. "They were real good, only they don't look so good now. And I had some granola bars—they were kind of dry; that's why I ate the berries with them. And I had a bottle of water, so I drank some of that. The driver from Atlanta—Miss Lois—bought me a burger and a few more bottles of water at one of the stops."

Hot anger built inside Emma. Whoever sent this child alone on a bus with nothing but a bunch of berries and some snacks should be put in jail. Thinking about all the things that could have happened to Winnie between Atlanta and Wyndham Beach made Emma's knees weak. Whatever she thought about this child's parentage, she was someone's offspring, and that someone had shown little regard for Winnie's safety.

"Did you have any money with you? In case you needed to buy something to eat, or if you lost your ticket?"

Winnie brightened. "Oh, yes, ma'am. It's in my backpack. Granny said I was to give you whatever I didn't spend." She started toward the foyer, where she'd left her belongings. "I didn't spend much. We can count it."

"No, no. You don't need to do that." Emma didn't even want to know how much cash had been put into that child's hands. "Winnie, are you hungry?"

"Yes, ma'am."

"You sit right down here at the kitchen table and I'll see what we have." Emma opened the refrigerator door and scanned the contents. She turned back to look at the little girl sitting still as a stone, a little girl who looked so lost but looked nothing like Emma's son, nor anyone else in her family. Despite her effort to "do everything right," she was probably terrified and intimidated. The awestruck look when she first came into the house told Emma that the girl was likely accustomed to more modest surroundings. "Do you like grilled-cheese sandwiches?"

"Oh, yes, ma'am. That's one of my favorite things." Winnie nodded vigorously, and the too-large glasses slid down her nose. She pushed them back up with her left index finger.

"I think I'll join you, and we can talk a little more, okay?"

"Yes, ma'am."

Emma proceeded to prepare two sandwiches, and as the butter melted in the frying pan, she watched Winnie out of the corner of her eye. The girl's jeans hit her above the ankles. She wore dirty white sneakers, and her T-shirt had pale red stains on the front, probably from the strawberries she'd been eating on the bus. Her braids appeared to have been done hastily and without much care, the tails secured with unmatched rubber bands. Someone—either this Angel person or Granny ArlettaJo Pine—had been all too eager to send Winnie on her way. Emma still had to sort all that out.

She took the fruit bowl from the counter and carried it to the table. Setting it before Winnie, she asked, "Do you like grapes? Bananas? Apples? Why don't you help yourself while I make our sandwiches?"

"Thank you, ma'am." Winnie reached for some grapes. "I love red grapes. They're my favorite. Angel didn't like fruit, so we never had them. She said if she was going to buy red grapes, they'd be in a bottle. My friend, April, sometimes had grapes in her lunch sack at school, and sometimes she shared them with me, but Granny never bought them.

She said they were too dear. She said April's daddy and mommy were both teachers, though, so they could afford them."

Emma wondered if Winnie had told April her father was a rock star.

"Why aren't you in school, Winnie?"

"I was. But school got over for the summer on Friday."

Today was Wednesday. Apparently Granny couldn't wait to get Winnie on that bus. The anger inside Emma continued to grow. There were so many questions . . .

"What grade were you in this year?"

"Third." Winnie sat up a little taller. "I did real good on my reports. All As." She paused before admitting, "Well, not quite all. I got a C in physical education." She dropped her eyes and lowered her voice as if confessing a sin. "I wasn't very good at softball."

Before Emma could tell her she hadn't been very good at softball, either, Winnie whispered, "Do we have to tell my daddy that? That I wasn't good at softball?"

Emma froze at the stove, grateful her back was toward Winnie. Obviously, she assumed that Chris was her father.

"We don't have to tell anyone anything you don't want them to know." Emma flipped over the sandwiches to let them brown for another minute.

She grabbed two plates from a cupboard, plated the sandwiches, and carried them to the table.

"Here you go, Winnie."

"Thank you, ma'am."

She sat across from Winnie and watched the girl eat. She could tell she was really hungry, but she was trying to eat slowly. Something else "Granny" must have told her to do lest she be sent to a place for kids no one wanted. Emma closed her eyes and said a silent prayer that she did not unload on Granny the way she wanted to when she called her. And Emma was going to be giving that woman a call. Angel, too, if she had to, to get to the bottom of this nonsense.

"Winnie, where's your mother?"

Winnie shrugged her thin shoulders. "Angel said she went to the desert to see a band show."

She went to a desert? What did that even mean? Was that code for something Emma was too old or too uncool to understand?

"Do you know which desert she went to?"

Winnie shook her head.

"How long ago did she leave?"

Winnie shrugged. "A long while back now."

"She didn't say when she'd come home?"

Another shrug.

"Wasn't she living with you and your grandmother?" Emma tried to phrase her questions in such a manner that she didn't appear to be criticizing Patricia Summer Rose, but it wasn't easy.

"Oh, no, ma'am. She lived sometimes with Angel. That's why I was there, too. But then sometimes she had to go see a band, so she'd go away for a while." Winnie took a bite of her sandwich. "This is the best grilled cheese I ever ate."

"Thank you. Winnie, did your mother go away often?"

Winnie nodded slowly. "All the time. Most of the time she was gone. Once in a while, Angel would go with her—that's when I had to stay with Granny."

"Do you know the name of the bands your mom liked?"

"I never heard her say. I saw the cover of a record one time, though."

"Was the name of the band on the cover?"

Winnie shrugged. "I don't remember."

"Did your mother ever stay at your granny's with you?"

"Oh, no, ma'am." Winnie put her sandwich down and bit her bottom lip. "Granny said Mama had made her bed, and she was just going to have to lie in it somewhere else. She let me stay with her when Angel was working at night or if she was away with my mama, but mostly she didn't let Mama in her house."

"So you always split your time between Angel's place and your grandmother's? You didn't live anywhere else?"

"No, ma'am. Just those two. I don't remember ever being someplace else." She appeared to think for a moment, then said, "Angel worked most times, so she didn't usually go away with Mama. She had an apartment and a car, and she said someone had to work to pay for them."

"Your mother doesn't work?"

"Sometimes. When she was at Angel's, she worked at the diner sometimes, and sometimes she worked at a bar."

Emma was beginning to get a picture of a young woman who worked long enough to get her where she wanted to go and support her for the time she was there. Then she'd go back to Georgia and stay with her friend just long enough to earn enough to take herself back on the road again. Did she pay Angel to take care of her daughter? Emma couldn't bring herself to ask Winnie.

"What about when you were a baby? Who took care of you then?"

"I don't know, ma'am. I was just a baby."

"Of course you were. That was silly of me to ask." Emma took a few bites of her sandwich and chewed absentmindedly. "Winnie, do you know how old your mama is?"

Winnie shook her head. "Just that she's a grown-up."

Debatable, Emma thought.

"Would you like another sandwich?" Emma noticed how quickly Winnie had dispatched the one that had minutes before been on her plate.

"No, thank you."

"Oh my goodness. I didn't give you anything to drink. Would you like a glass of milk?" Emma paused, trying to remember if in fact she had milk. "Well, it's almond milk."

"How do you milk an almond?" Winnie asked.

75

At first Emma thought it was going to be a joke and started to respond, "I don't know. How do you milk an almond?" But she realized Winnie was serious.

"I mean, I heard about it, and I saw some kids had it at lunch, but it doesn't make much sense to me. When I was little, I watched my grampa milk his cow, but almonds are nuts, right?" Winnie yawned.

"When was the last time you slept, Winnie?"

"When I was on the bus." She yawned again.

"Let's go into the other room, where you can take a nap on the sofa. Would you like that?"

"Yes, ma'am."

Emma led the way into the family room and pointed to the sofa. "Why don't you take off your sneakers and get comfortable. I'll get a pillow and blanket for you."

"Okay."

She watched the little girl untie her sneakers with awkward fingers that told of her fatigue as clearly as her yawns. Emma went upstairs to one of the unused bedrooms and took the pillow and a crocheted blanket from the bed. She carried them downstairs, and as she entered the family room, she said, "This lovely soft blanket was made by my mother when . . ."

Winnie was curled up on the sofa on her side, her head on one of the decorative toss pillows, her glasses sliding half-off her face, her mouth open in a tiny O. Emma stared at her for a while, her emotions running wild. She felt no connection to the child, but her heart ached for her all the same. She couldn't imagine being so small and being set adrift the way Winnie had been. Tossed out into the world with a couple of bus tickets and some snacks and a little bit of cash.

What was wrong with people?

She was pretty sure Winnie wasn't Chris's daughter—for one thing, no one on either side of the family was a redhead—but she didn't have the heart to tell her that. When Chris got there, they'd clear it up.

He'd know if he'd slept with someone named Patricia Summer Rose Pine, wouldn't he? Had she contacted him in the past to tell him about Winnie? Had she asked for support? If not, why not, if she was so sure Chris was the father? Had Chris been paying child support he'd never told Emma about? After all, he was an adult, and no law said adult children had to tell their parents everything. Then again, as she'd previously thought, surely her son wasn't the only Christopher Dean in the world.

But was he *this* girl's Christopher Dean? Someone must have had a reason to believe Chris was the father, or they wouldn't have gone to the trouble and the expense to pay for Winnie's bus tickets. Had that been ArlettaJo Pine, or had her sole contribution to Winnie's trek north simply been a breakfast of frozen waffles, a bag of strawberries, some granola bars, and a bottle of water?

Emma sat in the wingback chair next to the fireplace and watched Winnie sleep, one question tripping over the next. Was she Chris's daughter, and if so, did he know about her?

And if he did, why hadn't he told Emma?

Chapter Five

Emma half slept in the chair by the fireplace for most of the night, afraid Winnie might wake up and panic, not knowing where she was. But the child never opened her eyes and barely moved the entire night. Emma had just tiptoed into the kitchen for a glass of water when she saw headlights in the driveway and heard a car's engine shut down near the garage. A moment later, she heard her son's footsteps on the path that led from the driveway to the back porch. She went to the door and opened it to find Chris with a key in his hand and a worried expression on his face.

"Mom, are you all right?" He stepped inside and wrapped his arms around her. "I got here as soon as I could."

"Shh." She held a finger to her lips. "I knew you could do it if you wanted to."

"What, was this some kind of a test?" He leaned back. "Why are you whispering? And why are you up at four forty in the morning?"

"She fell asleep on the sofa in the family room, and I don't want to wake her." Emma wearily closed the back door and locked it. "I'd just gotten up to get a glass of water when I saw . . ."

"Mom, start over." No doubt about it, Harry had passed on his impatient nature to his son. "Who is sleeping in the family room?"

"Winnie. Your daughter." Emma folded her arms across her chest and watched his face for a sign that he knew about the girl.

"Win . . . what? What are you talking about? I don't have a daughter." He looked as confused as she had felt when Winnie first arrived. "Mom, are you sure you're all right?"

Emma opened the envelope she'd left on the kitchen table and handed Chris both pieces of paper.

"What is this?"

"Just read." She lowered herself to a chair and studied her son's expression, which went from annoyed to incredulous to a sort of horror.

When he was finished reading, he waved the papers he held. "I don't understand any of this."

"Neither do I. But imagine my surprise when the doorbell rang yesterday and there was this little girl announcing that she was my granddaughter, and she'd come to stay with me because her *other* grandmother had decided it was my turn to take care of her. Actually, I think she was starting with me because she didn't know where you were to send Winnie to you."

"Mom, I don't know anyone named . . ." He looked down at the birth certificate. "Patricia Summer Rose Pine. I swear I've never heard of her."

"Well, she's heard of you. She not only officially named you right there on her child's birth certificate but apparently told her best friend and her mother that you were the father. God only knows how many other people she told."

"There must be other men named Christopher Dean," he said.

"I'm sure there are. That was my first thought, too. But none of the others have a mother whose picture and hometown were mentioned in an article in *People* magazine a few years ago."

Chris's eyes were glued to the paper in his hand. "I don't know who this woman is," he repeated. "This girl was born in March of 2015, so she just turned eight . . ."

"She looks younger than eight. I thought she was seven at the most. She's small. Looks a little undernourished. Which could be close to the truth since she said she hardly ever had fruit to eat because this friend of her mother's whom she stayed with didn't like it, and her grandmother said it was too expensive." Emma shook her head. "Honestly, what this kid has been through. Bounced around between two homes. Her mother comes and goes in and out of her life. She's put on a bus by herself in Atlanta. There are so many blanks in that story, Chris. But first I want to know if she is in fact yours."

"I can't imagine anyone waiting eight years to tell someone they have a child, especially if they figure that someone has deep pockets, so she probably isn't mine. But there's only one way to find out for sure." Chris stuck the letter and the birth certificate back into the envelope and tossed it onto the table. "We'll do a DNA test."

"That goes without saying. But, Chris, where were you in the summer of 2014?"

"Offhand, I don't know." He sat in one of the chairs and appeared to think. "Melissa would know, I guess."

"Your agent?"

"Agent, manager. Back then she was a one-woman band for us. No pun intended." He tried to smile but failed.

"She's still with you?"

"Right. I'm sure she could send us a copy of the itinerary for the entire year."

"Ask her for it. Right now."

Chris looked at his watch. "Mom, it's not even five a.m., and she's in LA. Which means it's barely two o'clock in the morning where she is."

"Send her a text now, and she'll see it when she wakes up. I'm serious, Chris. We need to get to the bottom of this as soon as possible. For the sake of this little girl, if not for your reputation."

"Please. My reputation won't take a hit from something like this, even if it's true. In the music world, this is not a deal-breaker. But don't worry. The DNA test will prove one way or the other."

"DNA tests take time. If this woman has walked away from her daughter, we need to track her down, and we need to find out your involvement with her. This little girl has gone through a lot. I don't know what to do with her." Emma leaned back against the chair. "Whether you are her father or not, we can't just put her on a bus or a train and send her back to Georgia. I couldn't live with myself if we just tossed her back to someone who doesn't want her. Her grandmother suggested we turn her over to child services if we weren't going to keep her. Can you imagine being that coldhearted?"

"No. You're right," he agreed, though he sounded reluctant. "We need to get all the information we can while we wait for the results of the DNA test, which we should take care of today. So we'll start with 2014." Chris took out his phone and began to type. When he finished, he put the phone in the pocket of his jeans.

"I think we need to talk to this friend of Winnie's mother and her grandmother as well. Winnie probably has their phone numbers. The friend would probably be the best source of information, though. Winnie said her grandmother more or less kicked out her own daughter—not sure when or why—and that Winnie only stayed there when the friend—Angel—was working at night or was away."

"Then we talk to the friend first. She's more likely to have the best information, since it sounds like this Patricia and the grandmother weren't particularly close. Women confide more in their friends than their mothers, right?"

"You're right. The friend is the place to start. But do you think you should be the one making the calls? Shouldn't you hire someone, an investigator, in case this is a scam?" Emma tapped her fingers on the table. "Actually, since Winnie was sent here to me, and since the letter was addressed to me, I should be the one making the calls."

"Mom, I hate for you to have to deal with these people when we don't know what they're after. The more distance you keep . . ."

"What distance, Chris?" Emma laughed ruefully. "Winnie is here. In my house. There's no distance. I'm going to take the lead on this and get as much information as I can, then you can give whatever I find to Melissa, and she can take it from there. In the meantime, Winnie is here, and we have to do what's right for her." She rested her elbow and put her chin in her hand. "I'm just not sure what that is."

"I'm sorry, Mom. I'm really sorry."

"I know."

"Crap, what am I going to tell Natalie?" He ran a hand through his short but slightly shaggy blond hair. "Man, this is the last thing I expected when you told me to come home right away."

"And it's the last thing I expected when I answered the door yesterday, but here we are, Chris. There's a real little girl sleeping in the room next door. She believes you are her father. You're going to have to tread easily with her. One way or another, we have to get to the truth, for her sake." No need to let him know that, up until the minute her doorbell rang, she'd been immersed in a different sort of mess. Harry and his mistress and Emma's guilty conscience would all have to take a back seat for a while. The affair lost its immediacy in comparison.

What a week. Didn't they say things came in threes? Emma was afraid to wonder what might come next.

They sat in silence for a few moments; then Emma asked gently, "Chris, were you ever contacted by anyone who claimed she'd gotten pregnant by you?"

Chris snorted. "Are you kidding? Only about once every other week."

"That many?" Emma frowned. "What do you do? How do you respond?"

"I don't. Melissa has someone who handles that sort of thing. For the record, Mom, not one of those has ever panned out. I'd never even met ninety-nine-point-nine percent of those women. As far as I know, there are no kiddos running around with my DNA."

"As far as you know." She turned that around in her mind for a moment. "But you don't know one hundred percent."

"If I fathered a child, of course I would take responsibility for it. But I have always been very responsible when it comes to the women I've dated. I don't sleep around. I haven't even looked at another woman since Nat and I got together. I wouldn't do that to her. She's my future, Mom. I'm going to marry her."

"I'm glad to hear you say that. But from what Winnie's told me, her mother sounds like a professional groupie to me, follows bands all over the country."

"There's no shortage of those on the tour trail, Mom."

"So you could have met her and . . ." Emma couldn't bring herself to say the words *and had sex with her*.

"Mom, that's not quite my thing."

"But eight or nine years ago . . . ?"

He sat quietly for a while, then shrugged. "Maybe I wasn't quite as discriminating back then."

"So you might have crossed paths with this woman."

"Anyone ever tell you you'd have made a great lawyer? Or CIA agent? Private investigator?"

"No." Emma wasn't in the mood for banter.

Chris sat with his hands in his lap and seemed to be deliberately avoiding her eyes. "I don't know, Mom. I met a lot of women back then."

"Your father always was afraid you'd fall into that sex, drugs, and rock-and-roll thing. You know, the lifestyle you read about."

He looked like he wanted to speak, but he remained quiet.

There was a shuffling sound at the doorway. Emma and Chris both turned at the same time.

"Winnie! Did you just wake up?" Emma rose immediately and went to the little girl, who swayed slightly in the doorway.

Winnie nodded sleepily.

"Are you all right?"

She nodded again. "I can't remember where the bathroom is."

"It's right over here. Come on." Emma took her by the hand and led her to the powder room, where she turned on the light. Winnie blinked several times.

"I'll be right out here, okay?" Emma told her. She closed the door and walked back into the kitchen.

"That's her?" Chris asked. "That's Winnie?"

"Yes. Winter Sky Pine."

"She's tiny." He was still staring at the powder room door. "Does she have red hair?"

"She does."

He glanced across the room at Emma. "Don't bother asking me if I ever dated anyone with red hair. I have. Many times. But that doesn't mean she's . . ."

The powder room door opened, and Chris fell silent. Winnie came into the room and was almost past the table when she noticed him. She stopped and stared at him, squinting without her glasses, which she must have left in the family room.

"Winnie," Emma said softly. "This is . . ."

"My daddy." Winnie's voice was so low, breathy, and infused with awe, Emma barely heard the words.

Emma watched Chris's face and tried to read his expression. His head was cocked to one side. After a moment he said, "Hello, Winnie. I heard you've come on a long trip."

"Yes, sir." Winnie still had not moved. She simply stared at him with big eyes and a blank expression, as if she didn't know what to think of this strange man she'd come so far to find.

The moment was excruciatingly long and awkward for everyone.

"Winnie, you know, it's still nighttime." Emma took the girl's hand. "Why don't we go upstairs and get ready for bed. Did you bring pajamas with you?"

Winnie nodded.

"Are they in your backpack?"

"Yes, ma'am."

"Well, then, let's get them and we'll go upstairs, and you can put them on. We have a bed you can sleep in, and I'll tuck you in so you can sleep for the rest of the night. Then in the morning we can all have breakfast together. The three of us." Emma held out her hand. "What do you say?"

"Yes, ma'am." Winnie was still staring at Chris.

Chris was staring back. "I'll see you in the morning, Winnie."

"Yes, sir." Winnie took the hand Emma held out to her, her eyes on Chris until they reached the doorway. Before she turned away, she said, "Night, Daddy."

"Good night, Winnie. Sleep well."

Emma glanced back over her shoulder at her son and nodded to him to acknowledge that small kindness on Winnie's behalf. He wouldn't tell Winnie he was pretty sure he wasn't her father, especially at five in the morning, after she'd gone through so much to get there. Emma knew her boy's heart, knew he wasn't about to needlessly burst the bubble of a tired, worn-out child who surely must be hoping she'd finally found a parent who maybe—just maybe—would want her.

~

Emma had already been up for over an hour and was on her second cup of coffee when Chris came into the kitchen.

"Our little visitor isn't awake yet?" he asked as he poured himself a mugful of coffee.

"I haven't heard her, but that doesn't mean she isn't lying awake in that bed, wondering what comes next." Emma glanced up at the ceiling as if she could see right through the plaster into the guest room, where she'd left Winnie the night before. "I suppose I should check."

"Mom, I'm sorry this problem landed on your doorstep."

"Let's not refer to her as a 'problem.' The situation is certainly problematic, but that poor little girl is not the problem."

"She is when she arrives at your door unannounced and expecting to be welcomed with open arms."

"Honey, I don't think she expected that at all. I think she was terrified she'd be turned away. Actually, I think that's what she was expecting. That I'd refuse to take her in." Emma couldn't help but worry how the situation was playing out inside Winnie's head. "She isn't like Daisy, who has a loving family and has always known where she belongs. And Daisy has you, a loving father figure.

"This is a little girl who was bounced around between her mother and her mother's friend and her grandmother, which makes me suspect that no one really wanted her or knew what to do with her. Winnie is not the problem. The adults she's been saddled with all her life are the problem."

Chris stared into his coffee as if reflecting on his mother's words. Finally, he said, "But the fact remains that there are questions—who is this child and where does she belong? Where's her mother? Does she know her daughter's here? I agree with what you said last night—we will not send her off to spend the next ten years as a foster child. I feel reasonably certain she isn't mine, but she's someone's. Maybe we can discover whose."

"We have a game plan, Chris. Let's stick to it," Emma reminded him. "First up—you'll arrange for the DNA testing. And I'll make those phone calls today to this Angel woman and Granny ArlettaJo."

"How are you going to do that with Winnie around? She shouldn't hear the questions you're going to have to ask."

"Good point." Emma sipped her coffee and found it had cooled. "I'll take her to Liddy's bookshop and let her pick out some books. While she's doing that, I'll slip into Liddy's office, or I'll go outside and make the calls."

"If I don't hear from Melissa by nine a.m. her time, I'll call her. Just in case somehow she didn't get my text. Any thoughts on how to get Winnie's DNA without alarming her?"

"She must have a hairbrush or comb, and a toothbrush. We'll use what we can."

Chris stared out the window to the backyard. "I should call Natalie this morning. Fill her in. She's probably already called Maggie or Grace to see if they know what's going on."

"I'm sure she has. And she's probably wondering when you're coming back."

Chris laughed and held up his phone. "I already got a text from her at six."

"What did you tell her?"

"I told her I'd call later. She's teaching most of the day anyway." He slid the phone back into his pocket.

There was the sound of a soft shuffling in the doorway, and Emma and Chris both turned. Winnie stood there in too-small pajamas and bare feet, her pigtails pulled out of the elastics that had held them together, her hair suffering from a severe case of bedhead.

"Well, good morning, Winnie." Emma waved the girl into the room with as much of a smile and cheer as she could muster. "I'll bet you're hungry and ready for breakfast. What would you like to eat?"

Winnie shrugged. She noticed Chris seated at the table, and her eyes lingered on him.

"Winnie, I make great pancakes," he told her. "Would you like me to make some for you?"

She blushed slightly, then nodded. "Yes, please."

"Mom, do you have blueberries?" he asked.

"I believe I do." Emma turned her attention back to Winnie. "Do you like blueberries in your pancakes?"

"I guess I might. I never had them," Winnie said.

"Oh, well, then. Blueberry pancakes it is." He got up and started to arrange the ingredients. "Daisy likes them, too. I make them for her on Sunday mornings."

"Who's Daisy?" Winnie still stood in the doorway.

"Daisy is the daughter of my girlfriend, Natalie. Daisy is five now. She lives in Pennsylvania. Do you know where that is?" He got a mixing bowl from one of the upper shelves. "Mom, ever think of storing this on a shelf a short person like you can actually reach?"

"I reach it very easily right where it is. Of course, I have to use a stepladder, but still. I can get it when I need it." Emma went to the refrigerator. "Winnie, do you like orange juice?"

"I don't know." Winnie stepped into the room, never taking her eyes off Chris.

"I'll pour a little into a glass and you can decide." Emma put the carton of juice on the counter along with a container of blueberries. "Here you go, Chris."

"Thanks, Mom." Chris grabbed the berries and dumped them into a colander and ran them under water.

Winnie watched them silently.

Emma poured some juice into a small glass and placed it on the table. "Come sit, Winnie, and see if you like this juice."

Obediently, Winnie walked straight to the table and sat in the chair Emma had pulled out for her. She tasted the juice tentatively. While she didn't comment, her expression said it all.

"It's okay, Winnie," Emma assured. "You don't have to like it."

"It's not too bad," Winnie said, but her expression told Emma otherwise.

"How 'bout a glass of almond milk? Would you like that better?" Emma took the glass that Winnie still held in her hands.

"Yes, ma'am. Thank you."

"You are very welcome." Emma left the juice on the counter while she poured the milk and handed it to Winnie. "Chris, how are you doing with the pancakes?"

"Just heating up this old griddle of yours. And I do mean old. I remember this from when I was a kid."

"It was my mom's. She used to make pancakes for us when your uncle Dan and I were children." If Emma closed her eyes, she could smell the pancakes cooking, hear the sizzle of the bacon or the sausage her father loved, and the sound of the morning coffee percolating in the tin pot her mother used until the end of her life. Emma wasn't sure, but she thought maybe her brother had taken that pot after her mother died and her father moved to an over-fifty-five community.

"I don't remember either of my grandmothers being much of a cook," Chris was saying.

"Your dad's mother had cooks all her life. I don't know if she even knew how to boil water. But my mom was a great cook." Emma got plates from the cabinet and flatware from a drawer.

She noticed Winnie carefully following the conversation, looking up at Emma as if her words were vital.

Emma searched in the refrigerator for the bottle of maple syrup she kept there. She poured some into a small pan and proceeded to heat it on the stove.

"Winnie, do you like your syrup warmed?" she asked as she returned the large container to the fridge.

"I never had it like that." She paused as if thinking it over. "I might like it, though."

"Good." Emma nodded. "It's good to be open to new things. To try new things. You certainly do not have to like everything you try, but you should try. You might find some new favorites."

"Or you might find it tastes like orange juice," Chris teased and put a plate of just-off-the-griddle pancakes on the table.

Winnie blushed.

"How about we start you with two?" Emma asked. "If you finish those, you can have another, okay?"

"Yes, ma'am. Thank you."

"Would you like me to put some butter and syrup on your pancakes?"

"Yes, please."

Emma proceeded to fix Winnie's pancakes and cut them up for her. She tossed a few blueberries onto the plate.

"Thank you, ma'am." Winnie looked down at the plate before her but didn't raise her fork.

"You don't need to wait for us, Winnie. I know ordinarily you should wait until everyone is seated and has their food, but you don't want yours to get cold while Chris is making more. So go ahead and start eating. I'll just fix a few for myself and . . ." She glanced at Winnie. "What's wrong?"

Winnie pointed to the blueberries. "Inkberries. Granny says they're poison."

"Oh, no, honey. These are definitely blueberries. See, it says right here on the label." Emma got up to retrieve the container and bring it back to the table. Did Winnie really think they'd poison her? Emma ate a few to show Winnie they were fine.

Winnie picked one up between her right thumb and index finger and examined it. She looked Emma straight in the eye before popping it into her mouth, then sat as if waiting for something to happen. When nothing did, she ate another, and a third.

"Want a few more?" Emma asked.

"Yes, please, ma'am."

Emma loaded a spoonful onto Winnie's plate, thinking that, as much as she appreciated the girl's politeness, sooner or later, all those "ma'ams" were going to have to go. Or at the very least cut back some.

Chris came to the table with two plates of pancakes. He handed one to his mother and put the other in front of the place where he'd left his mug of coffee. Then he took out his phone and read, "Inkberry is a common name for pokeberry. And Winnie's right. It's toxic. Every part of the plant from the root to the leaves, stems, and berries is poisonous." He glanced up from his phone and said, "Definitely not something you want to eat."

"No, sir. That's what I told Granny." Winnie pushed a piece of pancake into the puddle of syrup before nibbling at it.

"I'm surprised she didn't know," Emma said.

"Oh, she knew." Winnie took a sip of milk, then went back to the pancake on her plate.

"She wouldn't really have given inkberries to you," Emma assured her.

Winnie nodded. "Uh-huh, she would. She said she gave some to Grampa, but he was too onery to die."

Emma put down her fork. "I'm sure she was kidding, Winnie."

"Uh-uh, she wasn't," Winnie insisted. "She said God made it to feed to little kids who were bad, but it worked on husbands just as good." She paused. "But it didn't because Grampa didn't die from eating inkberries. He died when a tree fell on his pickup."

Chris and Emma stared at each other, their eyes wide. Had Winnie's grandmother seriously threatened to poison her own husband and her granddaughter? What kind of person was this ArlettaJo Pine?

Emma's nod to her son was almost imperceptible, but he nodded back as covertly. There was no way this girl was going back to her grandmother. Whether she'd meant the threat or not, ArlettaJo didn't sound like a woman you'd want around a child. Emma was beginning to think maybe her daughter leaving home had been a matter of self-preservation.

"Winnie, I'm going to give your friend Angel a call today," Emma told her. "Do you have her phone number?"

Her mouth full of berries, Winnie nodded.

"You know your grandmother's phone number as well?"

Winnie swallowed. "Yes, ma'am."

Emma got up and opened one of the cabinet drawers and removed a small pad of paper and a pen. She handed them to Winnie.

"Could you write the numbers down for me?"

Winnie nodded and began to write. When she was finished, she passed the pad and pen back to Emma, who looked down at the carefully formed numbers. "Winnie, your numbers are so neatly written. Is your handwriting as lovely?"

"Oh, yes, ma'am." Winnie's smile went ear to ear. "I won the penmanship prize this year."

"Congratulations. It's important to have nice, legible handwriting," Emma said.

"That's what Miz Haldeman said. She's my teacher." Winnie corrected herself: "She was my teacher for third grade." Her expression grew pensive. "I guess I won't see her again since I won't be going to school there anymore." She looked up at Emma. "Will I be going to school here next time?"

"Well, we'll see. There's lots of time between now and when school starts up again at the end of the summer." Emma tried to sound as neutral as possible. What would this little girl understand about DNA tests?

"Winnie, have you finished eating?" Chris picked up on his mother's attempt to answer Winnie's question without answering the question, and changed the subject.

"Yes, sir."

He reached out for her plate, and she handed it to him, and she smiled. Emma was pretty sure Chris saw what she saw in that smile—hope and trust and the need to be accepted here and loved. When he smiled back at Winnie, Emma's heart smiled, too.

"So, Winnie, why don't you get dressed, and we'll go to the bookstore together. Maybe you'll find a book or two you'd like to have." Emma stood and touched the back of Winnie's head, where her hair was matted from having been in braids for who knew how long. She couldn't wait to brush it out.

"I don't think Granny gave me enough money for books," Winnie said softly.

"That's all right. We'll consider them a present from me to you, to welcome you. Would that be all right?" Emma asked.

"Thank you, yes." Winnie got up from the table and started to walk away before turning back, pushing her chair in, and finishing the last bit of milk in her glass.

"You go on and get dressed, then," Emma called after her as Winnie left the room. "Bring your hairbrush down with you, and I'll fix your pigtails, if you like."

"Yes, ma'am." Winnie disappeared through the doorway.

Seconds later her footsteps could be heard pounding up the steps.

"She's got a heavy foot for such a little kid," Chris remarked. "And clever you asking for her hairbrush. Nice way to get her DNA without her suspecting something might be up."

"I wasn't thinking about DNA, Chris. The girl's hair is a mess. I wonder when it was last washed." Emma couldn't keep echoes of disgust and annoyance from her voice. "I'm taking her to Target today. We'll get her a new hairbrush and toothbrush—the one she brought with her is worn down practically to the ends—some mild shampoo. Oh, and some clothes. The pants she had on when she got here were too short, and the shirt was stained. Her nightgown is at her knees, and she has no shoes other than the sneakers she wore, and her toes are right to the tip. I asked her why she didn't pack other clothes, and she said her granny packed for her. Like she almost expects us to send the kid back to her. Maybe with a fat check?"

"After reading that letter, I doubt she wants Winnie back. But a fat check? Yeah, I bet she'd take that." Chris looked as annoyed as his mother. "Just get her what she needs, and I'll reimburse you."

"No need. We're in this together. You just focus on getting your DNA testing done so we can find out if she is in fact yours. If she is, we know what we have to do."

Chris nodded. "While you're out, I'll call Melissa and let her know what's going on. Send her a copy of the letter and the birth certificate so she can send them to my lawyer. But first I need to call Natalie. She needs to know."

"I'll leave Winnie's hairbrush and her toothbrush on the sink in the bathroom upstairs," Emma told him as she opened the door that led to the back stairwell.

"Mom," Chris said. "We know what to do if it turns out she's mine. But what do we do if she isn't?"

Emma thought for a moment, then shook her head. "I don't know."

Chapter Six

Natalie had heard the text notification ping softly on her phone while she was right in the middle of the course review for a class of freshman English students one week before their exam. The text would have to wait, even if it killed her to ignore it. The second the last of her students left the room, she scrolled through messages until she found one from Chris. Her fingers began to twitch. Something big had to have happened for Emma to demand that Chris drop everything and head to Wyndham Beach immediately.

Natalie couldn't recall Emma ever having demanded anything of anyone. Whatever was going on, it had to be a bombshell. Speculation had kept her tossing and turning all night, and her uneasy feeling only intensified when the call she'd made to Chris first thing that morning had gone unanswered.

She opened the text and began to read:

> We need to talk. ASAP. No one's sick or hurt but this is important.
> Call me as soon as you can.

She leaned back against the blackboard and stared at the screen. He'd given no hint as to what was going on.

Taking a deep breath, she speed-dialed Chris's number.

"What's happened up there?" She'd wanted to remain calm, but her good intentions went right out the window after she heard his voice.

"It's kind of hard to explain. I hate to do this over the phone. I apologize in advance for not telling you face-to-face."

The hesitancy in his voice filled her with dread. Was he going to break up with her? And over the phone? After they'd been talking about getting engaged and setting a date and having a family together?

"This is just so awkward," he muttered.

Oh God, he is breaking up with me. The room began to close in on her, and she lowered herself into the nearest chair.

"Just say it. Put it out there." She tried unsuccessfully to keep the quiver from her voice and the tears forming in her eyes from falling. "Whatever it is, just say it, Chris."

"Okay. Here goes." He took a deep breath, and her heart sank further. "Yesterday, a little girl showed up at my mom's house and said she was my daughter."

"Wait . . . what? Say that again?" She couldn't have heard what she thought she'd heard.

"I said, a little girl . . ."

"What little girl? You have a daughter?" Natalie's heartbeat had risen so rapidly she was afraid for a moment she might pass out. "What do you mean she just showed up at your mom's? Who is she? Where did she come from?" She was trying to keep herself from panicking, but it was too late. That button had already been pushed.

"Nat, calm down. Well, as much as you can. I know this is a shock—I mean, I'm still in shock, and my mother . . . well, you can imagine."

"Who is this kid? Are we talking about a *baby*? Like, someone left a baby on Emma's porch? How did she get there? Who's her mother? And where is she? Do you know her?" Natalie snorted. "Well, of course you would know her, right? If this kid is yours, you must know . . ."

She could feel herself edging toward hysteria, but she couldn't stop the roaring freight train of doubt that was tunneling through her head.

"Nat, slow down." Chris exhaled a long breath. "She's not a baby. She's eight years old. I know the name of the girl's mother—it's Patricia Pine. I got the impression she's a groupie. But I don't know who she is. I have no recollection of ever having met someone with that name."

"How do you know her name?"

"It's on the birth certificate. The grandmother was kind enough to send that along." The sarcasm was unmistakable.

"Is your name on there as the father?"

"Yup."

It was worse than Natalie thought. Why name him as the father if he isn't? And why wait eight years to tell him?

"Why now? Why wouldn't she have contacted you before or right after the baby was born if she's so sure you're the father?"

"I have no idea, Nat. There are a lot of things that aren't adding up."

"So what happens now?"

"We're going to do a DNA test right away. Mom got her hairbrush and toothbrush, and I'm overnighting them to Melissa. She'll take care of the testing."

"What are you going to do if this kid is yours?"

"Well, Nat," he said calmly, "right now, I'm more worried about what we'll do if she isn't mine."

"What is that supposed to mean? You seriously think this kid is yours?" She squeezed her eyes shut, and tears plopped onto her lap.

"Actually, I'm pretty sure she isn't. And would you do me a favor and stop referring to her as 'this kid'? Her name is Winnie, Nat, and she's just a child, one who's been shipped up here on a bus from Atlanta by her grandmother with a note that said . . . well, basically, it said that no one wants her down there, so they were sending her to us, and if we didn't want her, we could put her into foster care."

"I don't understand any of this." Natalie put a hand to her head. She'd tried to follow along with him, but nothing he said make sense.

His laugh was brittle and brief. "Yeah, well, neither do we."

"So I guess our wedding-planning weekend is off."

"Just for now. I'm supposed to be in California on Monday, as you know, but I'm taking a few days at the end of the week to come back for the reception at the art center. I hate to leave my mom to deal with this by herself, so I can at least give her a few days before I go back to California again to finish up."

Natalie heard voices in the background, heard Chris say, "Okay, you guys have fun shopping. I'll see you when you get back."

She heard the voice of a child, a voice touched heavily by the South, and she heard Emma's laugh. A moment later, Chris returned to their call.

"Mom's taking Winnie shopping. I guess for some clothes—Mom said the few things she brought with her are all too small. And they're going to the bookshop."

Natalie fell silent as she tried to process what was happening.

"Nat?" Chris was asking. "You there?"

"Sorry. I'm just having a hard time wondering what this will mean for us."

"I don't understand. What *what* will mean?"

"If you have a child with another woman . . ."

"I don't think she's my child."

"But if she is . . ."

"Then we'll deal with that together. Same way we deal with everything else. This won't change us. Trust me."

"I trust you. I do. But . . ."

"Nope. Nothing after that, except maybe that you love me, and you know how much I love you. That's between you and me, Nat. The rest of it, this thing with Winnie, we'll get it straightened out one way or another. Either way, I hope you're going to be there for me and whatever happens."

"Of course I will be. And of course I love you, and I do know you love me. It's just that . . . this is . . . it's . . . it's . . ." Natalie didn't even have a name for what was happening.

"Yeah, babe. It is. For everyone. We'll work it through. But we have to do it in a way that no one gets hurt, understand? Least of all Winnie. Whatever I think of her mother and her grandmother—and it's not much, believe me—Winnie's the innocent party here, and she needs to be protected."

"You're right. Of course you're right." And he was right. She took a deep, calming breath and, with the back of her hand, wiped the tears from her face. "Chris, do you think this might be an attempt to extort money from you?"

"It's possible. Hell, anything's possible since we don't have any real facts other than that she's here and we're not going to toss her out on her ear. She knows no one wants her, Nat."

"But if you're not her father . . ."

"Then we'll do our best to find out who is."

And she knew that, Chris being Chris, he would move heaven and earth to do what was right for this girl, whether that was owning up to the fact that he'd fathered her or using his resources to find out who had. Natalie knew Chris would always do the right thing. It was one of the many things she loved about him.

She stayed seated for a minute or two after they ended the call, and she tried to put it all into perspective. Finally she stood and muttered, "What a mess!" Then she gathered her things and walked through the back exit door to the parking lot. Once in her car, she did the first thing she always did in times of crisis. She called her sister.

Grace picked up on the second ring with a cheery, "Hey, girl! How're things in the Keystone State today?"

Before she could respond, Grace went on: "I hope you're calling me to tell me you're going to be visiting soon. I need you to help plan my surprise housewarming party."

"Gracie, I just got off the phone with Chris. You're never going to believe what happened."

"He popped the question for real?" Grace squealed. "I mean, I know you've been talking about it, but he finally did it!"

"No, no, Grace, listen . . ." Natalie related everything Chris had told her about Emma's surprise visitor.

"Wait, Chris had a baby with a groupie? Are you effing serious, Nat?"

"No, he thinks the child—Winnie—probably isn't his, but she showed up at Emma's house with a birth certificate naming him as the father and a letter from the grandmother saying, basically, 'Here you go.' He's going to go through the whole DNA thing, but in the meantime it looks like she's going to stay at Emma's. Oh, I bet they're at the bookshop right now. Emma was going to take her—Winnie—to get a book."

"So I'm guessing you want me to run right down there and check it all out."

"If you wouldn't mind. I mean, you are working there today, aren't you?"

"Not till this afternoon, but I can go in early. But, Nat, this is just so hard to believe. Chris having a baby with a groupie? It's so out of character."

"That's what I thought, too, but she's eight years old, and I guess back then—when she would have been conceived—maybe Chris was still sowing some wild oats. Maybe she *is* his wild oat. I don't have any illusions about how things were when they first started out and the band was growing in popularity. Becoming DEAN. I guess the whole experience could have gone to his head for a while, so maybe . . ." Nat sighed. "Maybe she could be his."

"Wow. That's very possibly the last thing I expected to hear today. But how are you feeling about all this?"

"I want to be supportive. I want to be open minded. Honest to God, I do. But Gracie . . ." Natalie sniffed. "I wanted his first child to be with me. I never thought for a minute it would be any other way. It feels like that's been stolen from me. And not by someone he was involved with or in love with, but a one-night stand? I'm not gonna lie, Grace. It hurts, even though I know it probably shouldn't."

"Nat, how would you feel if Chris felt that way about Daisy? If he felt he'd lost something because he'd wanted your first child to be with him?"

"Chris has always known about Daisy. She wasn't brought out of the blue after we'd been together for a while."

"That's immaterial. The question remains."

Natalie thought for a moment.

"I guess it would hurt me—and her—that he couldn't accept her as his. That he didn't think of Daisy as his real child."

"And yet he has, most graciously. Can you give him the same if you're called to?"

Natalie laughed in spite of herself. "You know, sometimes you're like a bucket of cold water tossed in my face."

"I believe it's part of my role in your life. Just accept whatever he decides, okay?"

"Well, I don't have a say in whatever he decides to do."

"I don't know that that's true. If she's his child, he'll be raising her. Which means you'll be raising her. You'll be her stepmother. How did you leave it with him?"

"That I'd be supportive of his efforts to figure out who the father is and blah blah blah."

Grace laughed. "Nat the brat. Tell us how you really feel."

"I'm trying to do the right thing, but I feel rattled. I don't know what to think."

"Understandable. It's been a shock, I'm sure. You'll come around, and you'll graciously accept Winnie if and when the time comes, because while you are a brat at times, you are, at heart, a good and kind person. And you love Chris, and he loves you," Grace gently reminded her. "And think about how this little girl must feel. You know, when you stop to think about it, you have a child who was rejected by a parent, too."

"Yes, but Daisy doesn't understand that her father rejected her. He's just never been in her life." Natalie shook her head even though her sister couldn't see her. "There's a world of difference there. Jon and I were in a relationship and were starting to think about marriage until . . ."

"Until the day he found out you were pregnant. Imagine how Daisy's going to feel once she understands that he walked out on you when you told him you were going to keep the baby, and that baby was her. That's rejection, kid. It sounds like Winnie's already been rejected by her mother and her grandmother. And she is old enough to understand she isn't wanted anywhere."

"Except maybe by her father and Emma. If Chris is her father. Yeah, I get it."

"Look, let me change and get up to the bookshop. I'll call you back."

Natalie rolled all the windows down in the car and took a few deep breaths. Yes, she would be totally supportive of Chris. But she couldn't help herself from hoping that the DNA test would prove this child wasn't Chris's and they'd find out who was, and it would be Winnie's real father's obligation to fit her into his life. Everything would go back to being normal, and she and Chris would finalize the plans for the wedding they'd been talking about for months. And someday she would have his baby, and it would be his first child. She closed her eyes and envisioned him in the delivery room, beaming as he held their squirming, squalling newborn in his hands just moments after she gave birth. He'd fall in love with their baby, and he'd fall in love with her all over again. That was the way their story was meant to be. That was the way it would be.

She just had to trust that everything was going to be all right, that soon enough, Winnie would be with her real father, and she and Daisy would have Chris all to themselves again.

~

When Grace was on a mission, she rarely disappointed. Natalie had no sooner arrived home and poured herself a glass of wine—yes, in the middle of the day, something she never did, but today had turned out to be a doozy, as her grandmother would have said, when the phone rang.

Natalie cut right to the chase. "So was she there? What's Emma saying? What's she look like? Does she look like Chris?"

"Yes. Not much. Dunno. And no."

"Stop being a smart-ass, Grace. This is serious."

"Emma and Winnie are still here. So's Mom."

"Ha! I knew it!"

"Well, yeah. You have a crisis, you call in the cavalry. Emma's not said much beyond good morning, but she's been in the office with Mom and Liddy, and I got stuck on the cash register as soon as I walked in. Liddy lit up like fireworks on the Fourth of July. 'Great. Here's Gracie. She can take the register.' And off the three of them went and closed the office door. So I'm stuck working an extra two hours." Grace paused. "You're welcome."

"But the little girl . . . where is she?"

"Right at this moment, she's sitting in one of the wingback chairs—actually, it's the one I use for the Saturday-morning story hour—and she's reading a book. She has a stack of about four or five books in her lap—I guess Emma's trying to keep her busy so she can talk to Mom and Liddy."

"What does she look like?"

103

"I don't know, Nat. She looks like a little girl. Maybe a bit small for her age if in fact she's eight. Red hair up in a ponytail and tied with a blue ribbon."

Natalie heard some shuffling sounds before hearing her sister say, "Oh, I can take that for you right here. How are we paying this morning? Cash or . . . yes, of course. Cash is always fine . . ."

Grace had apparently put her phone down on the counter while she rang up a sale.

"Okay, I'm back. Where was I? Oh, right. What does the kid look like? Pale skin. Freckles. She wears glasses that are way too big for her face. She's almost cute in a geeky kind of way. If eight-year-olds can be considered geeky."

"What do you mean by 'almost cute'?"

"Oh, you're going to make me say it, aren't you?" Grace sounded annoyed. "I hate to call any kid homely, so I won't. She just . . . she needs to grow into her looks, like Mom used to say about that boy who lived across the street from us in Bryn Mawr." She laughed. "And he certainly did, if you remember. He was such a hunk back when we . . ."

"Stick to the subject. So if she's not really cute, then she's probably not Chris's." She knew Chris's children would all be beautiful, adorable, right from the womb. How could they be otherwise?

"Natalie, I have to say this right up front. You're my sister—my only sister—and I love you unconditionally. But right now, you sound, well, mean. You don't sound like the sweet, kind, loving, openhearted girl I grew up with."

"Well, that girl didn't have an almost fiancé who out of the blue had a child shipped to him, a child he was being accused of having fathered by some woman he can't even remember."

"Well, get a grip. I honestly hate to be the one to tell you this, but this is not about you. It's about Chris, and it's about this little girl." When Natalie tried to interrupt, Grace talked over her. "Does this affect you? Yes, of course it does. But you are not the star here, Nat. You're part of the supporting cast, and you have to take that role seriously. If it turns out that Chris is her father, she's going to be part of his life from here on out. Which means she will be part of your life. You know Chris. You know if she's his, he will be a devoted dad. He'll make her part of his world. And if you want to stay in that world . . ."

Natalie let her sister's words sink in.

"You're right. I know you are. I just hate that this is happening—for everyone involved—and I hate that you're all there together, and I'm here alone."

"So you'll finish grading papers, and you'll administer those exams, enter all the grades into the system, and you'll pack for a visit. We'll all be here waiting for you." Grace paused. "Including Winnie."

"Okay. Yes. Good plan. I have two exams next Thursday, then another on the following Tuesday, but as soon as my grades are in, we'll be on our way." Natalie could feel tears creeping up on her, and she wanted off the call before they began to fall.

She knew Grace was right: she always seemed to know the right thing to do, where sometimes Nat was a little slower to catch on and see the big picture. She hated that she felt so isolated from what was going on in Wyndham Beach and wished she could be in the thick of things the way everyone else was.

And there was one other little thought nagging at the back of her mind. If Chris was determined to be the father, Winnie could become her stepdaughter. What if she and Winnie didn't get along? What if she was called upon to raise a child who didn't like her?

How had life suddenly become so complicated?

Chapter Seven

"So the worst thing that could happen is that you have a granddaughter. You know you've been wanting one." As usual, Maggie tried to put a positive spin on the situation Emma had just laid out for her and Liddy.

"I'm not sure this is what Emma had in mind, Mags." Liddy sat at her desk, her arms folded in front of her on the stained blotter she'd inherited from the bookshop's previous owner. She'd kept it only because it had the phone numbers of most of the town's businesses and many of its occupants written on it.

"No, it isn't. But if she's ours, she's ours." Emma caught Liddy's eye. She knew that look. "What, Liddy? You know you have something to say, so spit it out."

Liddy hesitated. "Emma, you have the kindest heart of anyone I know. Suppose you go through the testing—which you know takes some time, you're not going to have the results overnight, right? So what happens when the tests come back, and Chris is not Winnie's father? She's all settled in with you and she believes she's part of your family, and you've bonded with her, then bam! Turns out she's not Chris's child. Maybe you get lucky somehow and figure out who her father is—"

"How in the world would she do that? How would they know who to test? And if they had that information, they'd be testing him now," Maggie pointed out.

"I don't know, Mags. This is all hypothetical. So you find out who the father is, or the mother shows up and she's changed her mind." Liddy's voice softened. "You get where I'm going here, Emma? You're going to have your heart broken."

Emma nodded slowly. "I understand where you're coming from, and I appreciate that you're concerned about me. But what's the alternative— right now—to keeping her until we find the truth? She has no place to go. Oh, sure, I could send her back to her grandmother, but God knows that's the last thing I want to do. The woman doesn't want her, and she doesn't deserve her. We can't send her out to California with Chris when he leaves on Sunday. Like he knows what to do with a child. Besides, he's going out there to work for the next however many weeks it takes for him to be happy with what they record, so who's going to be taking care of her?" She looked from Liddy to Maggie. "So you tell me what you think you'd do if you were in my shoes."

The room was silent for a moment.

"I'd do the same thing you're doing. Of course I would," Maggie said.

Liddy nodded. "I guess I would, too."

"Look, I know there's no telling how this is going to play out. But this is all so much harder on Winnie than it is on me. I'm an adult. I've handled plenty in my time." She forced a smile. "I'm still working through Harry's infidelity. I'm still upset and angry over that. But Winnie's just a child. None of this is her fault. Whatever the outcome, it's going to change her life forever. So while she's here, I'm going to do what I can for her."

"And we'll do whatever we can to help you," Liddy said.

"Whatever you need," Maggie assured her.

"Thank you. What I need right now is some time alone to call"— Emma took a sheet of paper from her handbag—"Angel Lobell, who's our best bet for figuring out where the girl's mother is, and ArlettaJo Pine. She's the grandmother, the one who sent the girl to me. Liddy,

I'm going to ask you to give me some privacy here while I make these calls. It would help if you'd keep an eye on Winnie. If she asks where I am, tell her I had a few phone calls to make but I'll be back out there as soon as I've finished. Maybe help her to find a book or two if she's read through the ones we already gave her." Emma turned to Maggie. "Maggie, would you be a dear and run across the street to Ground Me and get me a large coffee?"

"Of course." Maggie rose and leaned over to whisper in Emma's ear. "Give 'em hell."

Liddy was already at the door. "Take no prisoners."

"Thank you both."

Emma watched them leave the office and heard the click of the door as it closed behind them. She stared at the names and the phone numbers Winnie had given her, then took a deep breath. This wasn't going to be easy, especially for someone whose default reaction was generally nonconfrontational.

～

The call to Angel went unanswered, so she tapped ArlettaJo's number into her cell phone, then sat back and listened to it ring.

"Yes?" The voice that picked up the call was deep and raspy, as if years of cigarettes had had their way with her vocal cords.

"Is this ArlettaJo Pine?" Emma asked.

"Depends who's asking."

"This is Emma Dean."

"Well, well." A cough followed a chuckle. "So I guess you're calling to let me know the girl got there okay."

"She did." Emma thought of all the things she really wanted to say. Like, *How could you have put that child on a bus and sent her off like that? Did it occur to you that she might not have been safe? That any one of a long list of terrible things could happen to a little girl alone at a bus stop?*

But Emma needed answers, and she needed them from the woman on the other end of the call. So Emma swallowed hard and said, "We're in need of some information we're hoping you can provide."

"Like what?"

"Like, where is your daughter, and does she know you've sent her child away?"

Another raspy laugh, another cough. "I have no idea where that girl is, and I doubt she'll give a rat's ass about her kid. She's spent more time away from her than she's spent with her. She's got this wild hair, gotta be on the move all the time. I swear I don't know where she gets that from. I told her the first time she took off the way she does, 'Don't come running back to me when you find yourself knocked up, 'cause I raised my kids, and I'm not raising yours.'" ArlettaJo sniffed, and for a moment Emma thought she might be more emotional about her daughter than she'd let on. Then Emma heard her blow her nose and mutter, "Damn allergies."

ArlettaJo continued: "Anyway, I can't afford to be raising a kid. I don't have the money or the time. Besides, I've carried this burden for the past eight years for the girl's mama, and I figure it's time for her daddy and his kin to do their share. Don't be thinking you'll be sending her back to me, because I don't want her."

"I think you've made that perfectly clear." The woman's referral to Winnie as a burden made Emma's blood pressure soar. She had to fight to keep a civil tongue. "So you're telling me you don't know where your daughter is."

"That's what I'm telling you."

"How long has she been gone?"

"Well, let's see . . . the last time I saw her was around Thanksgiving. She brought the girl here for dinner. I didn't invite her, and I didn't want either of them, but my late husband's sister and her family were here, and I didn't want to make a scene. So I invited Tish in and fed her and her kid. Afterward, Tish said she was running out for cigarettes. Haven't seen or heard from her since."

"And no idea where she was headed?"

"She was headed back to her friend's place, and they left for a long weekend. Least, that's what I was told when I finally tracked down her friend."

"You mean Angel Lobell?"

"Uh-huh. I called over to the Bluebell Diner, where Angel works. One of the waitresses there told me she was off until Tuesday the next week. So on Tuesday I took the girl over there and told Angel to take her home with her so Tish could take care of her own. Angel said Tish hadn't come back with her, and she wasn't sure where she'd gone. But I told her, since she was responsible for having taken Tish wherever it was they went, she could take the girl until Tish decided to come home."

"So you haven't seen or heard from your daughter in . . ." Emma counted forward starting with December. "Six months?"

"That'd be about right."

"Have you called the authorities?"

The woman on the other end of the line snorted. "What authorities? Where? I have no idea where that girl is. She could be in Alaska, for all I know."

Emma was speechless.

"She'll turn up like a bad penny one of these days," ArlettaJo added.

"Hasn't it occurred to you that something may have happened to her?" Emma couldn't imagine a world in which she wouldn't be frantically looking for her son if she hadn't heard from him after a week and couldn't get in touch with him.

"If something has, it's long overdue." A long coughing spell followed. When she stopped, she said, "If you're thinking about sending the kid back, it's gonna cost you."

"We're not sending her back."

"Good. Then I guess we don't have anything else to say." ArlettaJo coughed.

"Just one thing." Emma tried to think quickly before the woman hung up. "You have other children?"

"Two sons and another girl. They're all settled. Married, kids. Jobs. None of this nonsense like she does. None of them wild like her."

"Could I get their names, phone numbers, their . . ."

"Don't be bothering them about her." ArlettaJo's temper flashed. "They all know what Tish is and not a one of them wants anything to do with her."

"I just thought maybe, if she was in trouble, she might reach out to a sister, or a brother, and maybe if I . . ."

"If she's in trouble, she got there on her own, so you'll not be bothering my kids on account of her. I got nothing more to say. You have a nice day now." And with that, ArlettaJo Pine ended the call.

Emma stared at the phone. Well, that was productive.

She took a deep breath and again entered the number for Angel Lobell.

Emma counted four rings before the call was answered by a sleepy voice that whispered, "What?"

"Is this Angel Lobell?"

"Who's this?"

"My name is Emma Dean. Winnie Pine gave me your name and this number."

"You have the kid?" Angel seemed to come awake. "Is she all right?"

"She's fine."

"Oh, good." Angel cleared her throat. "I didn't think Miz Pine was really going to put that kid on a bus like she always threatened to do, but I guess she did."

"You didn't try to stop her?"

"Lady, you know how many times that woman said she was going to do something about that girl?" She snorted. "How many times she said she was calling children's services? Or leaving her at the orphans' home? Please. Sending her to her daddy was the only decent thing Miz Pine ever thought to do." Angel paused. "But I never thought she'd really do it." Another pause. "Are you really Chris Dean's mother?"

"Yes, but the real question is, Is my son really Winnie's father?"

Angel laughed. "Tish always said he was, but who knows?"

"Do you know if she ever actually met my son?"

"I'm pretty sure she did. The band was down to Atlanta for a weekend, and there was a big storm, so they were stuck in the city for a while. Not sure how long."

"Were you there?"

This time the pause was more awkward. "Well, yes. I mean, I wasn't with her for all of those four or five days. I went to Atlanta with her, but I came back by myself. I had to work, but she'd lost her job." A harsh laugh followed. "And for Bobby Hendricks to fire her, you know she'd pushed him too far. I mean, she'd take off whenever she felt like it and always managed somehow to keep her job. Then again, we all knew what she was doing to keep Bobby under her thumb, so—"

Emma interrupted her. She didn't really want to know what Tish did with Bobby to keep her job. "So she had been working. What did she do?"

"She worked as a dancer at the Tip Top."

Maggie pushed open the door and set a large coffee on the desk in front of Emma, who mouthed, *Thank you*, earning her a thumbs-up as Maggie closed the door behind her.

"She was a dancer? Really?"

"Probably not the kind of dancer you're thinking, if you don't mind me saying, Miz Dean."

"Oh. Okay." Emma figured by *dancer*, Angel meant *stripper*, or something akin to that. "So back to that weekend. Where did you—or she—meet my son?"

"In the bar of the hotel the band was staying in. We'd heard DEAN was in Atlanta, so we drove down there to the city, and we were in another bar down the street. Some girl came in and said she'd just seen them in this other hotel, so we thought, *What the hell? Let's go check it out.*"

"And you're sure the band was DEAN? It couldn't have been someone else?" Emma pried the lid off the coffee with one hand, careful not to knock it over, and took a sip of the hot, perfect goodness.

"Oh, no, ma'am." Angel laughed. "Don't mind me saying it, but your son is hot. I mean, yes, we recognized him right away, first thing when we went into the bar."

"What happened after you got there? Did you talk to him?"

"Tish may have. I don't know if she did. But I did not. I started talking to this guy—he said he was the drummer with DEAN—and he was buying me drinks and then more drinks and then one thing led to another, and I lost track of Tish."

"Do you remember the name of the drummer?"

"It was Buddy."

Buddy Lang. Emma nodded to herself and took another sip of coffee. The only drummer DEAN ever had was Buddy Lang.

"Angel, did you see Chris with Tish that weekend?"

"Not really. I don't remember. I was pretty much out of it." She added under her breath, "I'm lucky I remember what I was doing."

"Now, this last time Tish left . . ."

"Last Thanksgiving weekend."

"Right. Do you have any idea where she went?"

Emma heard the click of a lighter, and the deep inhale of smoke followed by a long exhale, after which Angel said, "Las Vegas."

"Are you sure?"

"Positive. We drove out there together at the butt crack of dawn the day after Thanksgiving. I mean, it was early. Took us a couple of days, but we made it."

"Did you tell Tish's mother where she went?"

"I did, but she didn't care. Tish's kid was waiting on my front porch when I got home. I called ArlettaJo, and she said Winnie could wait with me till her mama came back, since I was the one who'd taken her mama away." Inhale. Exhale. "It wasn't the first time. I swear that child spent more time with me than with her own kin. Didn't bother me none. She's quiet and she's a good kid. I felt sorry for her, you know? Tish didn't care about her, and no one in her family wanted her, and for the most part I didn't mind having her. I worked during the day, and she was in school, so she wasn't alone at night. We worked it out. Tish never stayed away too long, so she'd come back, work for Bobby Hendricks for a few weeks, then she'd take off again. That girl's a real rolling stone, Miz Dean. It's just her nature to keep moving." Angel's voice dropped low. "It's like she can't help herself."

Emma rubbed her hand over her face. "Angel, do you know where she is now?"

"No. I haven't heard from her since . . . oh, maybe late January?"

"And that didn't alarm you?" Emma sighed. What was wrong with these people?

"It did, and it didn't. I mean, Tish might have met up with some-one she really liked and just took off with him, stayed stoned, and forgot about everything else." Emma could almost see the woman shrugging. "Wouldn't have been the first time, you know? Though she never did stay away this long. Maybe a month was the most before she came back."

"Hasn't it occurred to you that something really bad could have happened to her?"

"We talked about that one time, about the chances she took, taking off the way she did, not telling anyone where she was going or who she was going with. She always laughed and said she'd been born under a lucky star, and she'd still be partying when she was ninety.

"But, yeah, I wondered if maybe . . . I don't know, something might have happened to her. ArlettaJo didn't seem worried, though, so I thought maybe she'd heard from Tish and was just not telling me, just to be mean. She's like that, Tish's mom. She's a mean old snake. That's pretty much why I let Winnie stay here so long. I figured any place was better'n staying with ArlettaJo."

"No idea where Tish could have gone?"

"When we were in Vegas, there was some talk about a big concert out in the desert. It seemed everyone we met was going, so I'm guessing Tish hitched a ride with someone."

"Do you remember where in the desert, or any of the bands that were mentioned?"

"I don't, I'm sorry. If I knew, I'd tell you. I just didn't pay that much attention. I had a job to get back to, and I couldn't afford to lose it, so I wasn't interested in hanging around."

"Angel, is there anything else you can tell me? Anything at all?"

"I can't think of a thing."

And the $50 million question: "Angel, do you think Tish was serious about Chris being Winnie's father?"

"I can't answer that. Sometimes she just said things to get a reaction out of you, you know?"

"If she really believed Chris was the father, any idea why she never contacted him to tell him he had a daughter?"

"I wondered that myself. I mean, if I believed some rock god was the father of my kid, you want to believe I'd be all over that. Child support? Hell, yes. So . . . I don't know. I don't know what she was thinking. Could well be he's not. Then again . . ."

"Will you call me if you think of anything that might help us track her down?"

"Sure."

"Oh—last thing. Do you have a photo of Tish you could send me?"

"I have a bunch on my phone. I can send you a few right now."

"That would be great, Angel. Thank you."

Emma was just about to hang up when Angel said, "Miz Dean, tell Winnie I said hi, would you? She's a good kid. She doesn't deserve this crap of a life she's had. I only took her back to ArlettaJo's because I was going out of town for a few days. I didn't know she was going to make good on her threat to send the kid away."

"I'll give her the message, Angel. But I promise you, the crap in her life is all behind her."

Emma's phone had gone silent, but she kept it in her hand next to her cheek, trying to process both conversations. From ArlettaJo, she'd gained nothing of value except maybe the conviction that she would never send Winnie back to that hateful woman. Angel had been helpful to the extent that Emma knew where Tish had gone after she left Angel in Vegas. She also now knew that Chris had possibly met Tish in Atlanta. But beyond that, what did she really know?

The phone buzzed to indicate the receipt of a text, then buzzed several more times before Emma opened up her messages and had her first look at Tish Pine. The woman was of medium height and curvy in short shorts and a tank top, then in tight pants and a jacket, standing next to a motorcycle, and finally in a very short, very low-cut dress and tall heels. In each picture, she exuded sex appeal and confidence. There was no denying that she was a very pretty young woman with her long red hair, flashing eyes, and an abundance of cleavage. Emma's first thought was that Tish didn't look like someone Chris would be attracted to—then she laughed. What young man wouldn't have given Tish Pine at the very least a second look? And how could she really know who her son had been attracted to nine years ago, or what type of woman he spent time with on the road?

She saved the photos to her phone, then sent them to Chris. **Does this woman look familiar? Chances are you could have met her in a bar in Atlanta.**

Less than a minute later, her phone rang.

"No, she doesn't look familiar. I'm assuming that's Winnie's mother. Where'd you get the pictures?"

"Yes, that's Tish, and I got those from her friend Angel. The one who took care of Winnie whenever Tish disappeared." Emma sighed and drank her coffee, wishing she'd asked Maggie to bring her a scone as well.

"I can't say I never met her, Mom. She looks like a lot of girls I've met over the years. And why specifically Atlanta?"

"Angel said she and Tish were there one weekend and heard you and the band were in a bar down the street from where they were staying, so they went looking for you guys and found you in the bar. She doesn't know if you actually met Tish, because she, Angel . . ." Emma paused. "I guess the term is *hooked up* with Buddy. That she met him, and he kept buying her drinks, and she doesn't remember much more than that."

"Maybe I should ask the rest of the guys for their DNA," Chris said.

"You think they'd volunteer to do that? The consequences . . ."

"They would. They're stand-up guys. I'll see them on Monday, but meanwhile I'm going to send them these pics and ask if anyone remembers her from . . ." He fell silent. "Mom, that was a long time ago. I'm guessing a whole lot of pretty redheads have come and gone through their lives since then. The odds aren't good that anyone would remember anyone in particular. We played Atlanta several times."

"Angel did say that you'd been held over in the city due to a big storm that kept you there for a few days."

Chris fell silent for a moment. "I do remember being stuck for a few days in Atlanta once due to bad weather. That could have been right about that time, eight, nine years ago. Yeah, I remember that, but I don't remember this woman, Mom."

"Ask your guys. Oh, and Angel also said that she and Tish were in Las Vegas last year right after Thanksgiving, and that Tish didn't come home with her because she was going to some big concert in the desert where there were rumored to be a lot of bands."

"Desert Rose, yeah, I heard about it."

"So . . ." Emma urged her son to elaborate.

"So it was a bunch of bands—no one famous, just a lot of wannabe famous. Lots of groupies, lots of drugs. It's an annual thing, first week in December every year out there. Two years ago, two guys died, not sure if they'd OD'd or if they were murdered. And a couple of years ago, there were rumors about a few women's bodies being found half-buried when the sand shifted and everyone had left but the cleanup crew. But every year there are rumors of people having gone missing. Whether or not any of that's true, I don't know. Could just be hype, you know? Amp up the drama? If Winnie's mom had gone last year, and no one's heard from her since, chances are something could have happened to her."

The way he'd said *something* sent a chill up Emma's spine.

"That's what I'm afraid of, though when I mentioned the possibility to her mother, she didn't seem at all disturbed by it, or by the fact that she hadn't heard from her daughter in six months."

"That doesn't sound good, Mom."

"No, it doesn't." Emma picked up a pen and made a tiny drawing of a flower on one end of the desk blotter, her go-to doodle when she was feeling pensive.

"All right, I'm going to send Buddy the photos you send me and see if he remembers her from that weekend. I guess while I'm at it, I'll call all the guys. You never know how things might have played out. We'll get everyone's DNA and have Melissa send it all in to the lab. I'm also going to call the LVPD and ask about any incidents at the Desert Rose concert last year."

"Do you think you should be the one making the inquiries about that?"

"Oh. Well . . ." Emma could almost hear him thinking.

"Probably not. Melissa can do that as well. Not that I'm hoping for the worst, but you never know. Maybe they found her but can't identify her."

"I suppose it's not beyond possibility that she could be . . . well, we just don't know. As her friend suggested, she could have met someone there and took off with him and gone somewhere else entirely."

"We'll start in Vegas, and we'll hire a PI to investigate for us. We may have to do that anyway to find Winnie's father. How's she doing? Winnie?"

"She seems to be doing fine." Emma stood and opened the door partway. "Right now she's sitting in Grace's storytelling chair with a stack of books in her lap, and she looks happy. She's okay for now, but I think the sooner we have answers, the better it will be for her. She can't stay in limbo forever." Emma sighed. "Of course she doesn't realize she's in limbo. She thinks you are her dad and I'm her grandmother, so all is good as far as she's concerned."

"Then let me get started on this end. I'll see you back at the house, Mom."

"All right." She was just about to press "End Call."

"And Mom? Thanks. For everything. But especially for being my mom."

"It's been my pleasure since day one, Christopher." Emma disconnected the call and leaned back against the desk. It seemed that life had been strange recently, and it just kept getting stranger.

She drank the last of the coffee before pitching the empty cup into the trash next to Liddy's desk, then went out into the bookstore to see what her maybe-granddaughter was up to.

Winnie looked up and smiled a huge and happy smile when she saw Emma coming toward her, and Emma's heart twisted just a little. The girl hadn't inherited any of her supposed parents' beauty, but her smile could light the room. Emma suspected that in Winnie there was a real swan hiding beneath the plain, awkward eight-year-old. Which didn't really matter. This was no daydream grandchild. This girl was real flesh and blood. Maybe not Emma's flesh and blood, but there was something earnest and winsome about her. Winsome Winnie, indeed.

"Do you think you found enough books?" Emma pointed to the stack on Winnie's lap.

"Oh, I know I can only have one." Winnie sat up a little straighter in the chair. "I'm just reading a bit of each of them to see which one I have to finish." She pushed her glasses up on her nose. "It's so hard to choose."

Emma made a mental note to call the eye doctor to make an appointment for Winnie to get new glasses. Ones that actually fit her would be nice.

"Did you ever read a book that just trapped you inside, and you knew you just weren't ever gonna sleep again till you knew what happened?"

"Why, yes. I believe I have, so I totally understand. Let's see what you have there." Emma knelt next to the chair and looked over the selections Winnie had made.

"That one there—*Amelia Bedelia*—I read that last year, but I sure loved it. I thought I wouldn't mind reading it again," Winnie said. "But I could probably get that one from the library, so maybe put that one back."

"Oh, no." Emma shook her head. "A book you've read and loved deserves a place on your bookshelf."

"I don't have a bookshelf," Winnie pointed out.

"We'll take care of that this afternoon. There are several in the attic, and you're welcome to choose one." Emma picked up the next book on the stack. "We'll put it in your room so your books are always handy."

"Like when you wake up in the middle of the night and you're alone and maybe a little bit scared." The tone of Winnie's voice told Emma the child knew what she was talking about.

"Yes," Emma said softly. "Exactly like that."

"Do you ever wake up and be alone and scared of . . . something?"

Reminded of the findings in Harry's files, *Not until lately* was on the tip of Emma's tongue. "Of course," she said. "Everyone feels alone sometimes."

"And that's why there's books."

"One of the many reasons," Emma agreed. It may well be that Winnie turns out to be someone other than Chris's daughter, but that she so obviously loved books and loved to read was a common thread between them and brought a smile to Emma's lips and to her heart.

They went through the books Winnie had amassed, Emma finally telling Winnie, "Since you have no books at my house, I think we should buy all of these so you can start your little home library."

Winnie looked dumbstruck. "All of . . ."

"Yes. Let me go find Liddy and see if she's ready to ring us up. Can you wait here for me?"

Winnie nodded, still apparently trying to comprehend that a windfall of books would be coming home with her.

Emma met up with Liddy and Maggie at the cash register. She waited until the customer ahead of her finished her transaction and walked away from the counter.

"So what did you find out?" Liddy whispered.

"I found out that come hell or high water, that child is never going back to that witch of a grandmother in Georgia."

Maggie rolled her eyes. "Em, we knew that before you called her, since she'd already struck out by putting that little girl on a bus by herself. What else?"

Emma recited the conversations she'd had with Angel and ArlettaJo.

"Chris is following up with the guys in the band to see if any of them recognize her." She took out her phone and pulled up the pictures Angel had sent her.

"Oh, she's pretty," Liddy exclaimed.

"She is," Maggie agreed.

"But apparently totally devoid of any maternal instincts or responsibility or heart or decency or . . ."

"Okay, Em. We get it." Maggie patted her gently on the back.

"Some animals are better at parenting than she's been." Emma shook her head. "And her mother is no better." She paused. "Which I guess explains why Tish is the way she is. But still. Anyone would know abandoning your little one and taking off on your own is no way to raise a child."

"We both agree," Maggie assured her, "but Tish is in the rear mirror right now, and it's Winnie who matters."

"Right. And if Chris can find out where her mother is . . ." Liddy frowned. "What happens if Chris finds her?"

"I have no idea. Frankly, I think I'd almost rather he skipped that part and just tried to focus on who her father is. Hopefully he's someone with more sense than Tish."

Emma felt a stab of guilt mixed with something that felt a little like fear. Even if they were able to identify the man, would he readily step up for Winnie? Chris seemed to think any one of his bandmates would, but Emma secretly thought that was optimistic. Several of the guys were married and most likely would not be happy to be presented with a physical reminder of their early days on the rock-and-roll highway. The single guys could be even less likely to welcome such news.

And then there was Winnie. How was she going to feel if Chris actually found her real father, and she had to be sent off once again?

There were no good answers to any of this, Emma realized as she walked back to the children's department to get Winnie and her books.

"Oh, she's right there," Emma heard Winnie say as she rounded the tall bookcase that set off the children's section.

"Who's right there?" Marion, who'd come in early for her afternoon shift, turned and was staring at Emma.

"My grandma. She's right there." Winnie, who sounded a bit exasperated, pointed directly at Emma.

"That's Mrs. Dean, honey," Marion said.

"Yes, I know. She's my grandma."

"But . . ." Marion's confusion was apparent.

Winnie got off the chair, the stack of books sliding as she did so. Several books slid to the floor. "Oh no."

Emma moved past Marion to help Winnie pick up the books. "It's okay, Winnie. Not to worry. The books are fine. Was there anything else you wanted?"

"No, ma'am."

"You take those in your hand right up to the counter there and hand them to Miz Bryant. You tell her I'll be right behind you."

"Yes, ma'am." Winnie sent an unspoken *I told you so* glance in Marion's direction before disappearing around the corner.

Marion turned to Emma, who held up her hand as if to ward off any questions or discussion of the obvious. "It's a long story . . ."

Chapter Eight

A large take-out pizza—half cheese only, half pepperoni and roasted vegetables—occupied much of the center of the kitchen table. Winnie was seated on one side and Chris on the other, and for a moment Emma debated which side to join before taking the chair next to Winnie, lest the child look across the table and see Emma and Chris sitting together as if aligned against her.

"We had a fun outing to Target after we went to the bookshop today, didn't we, Winnie?" Emma said just a little too brightly. If she'd sounded forced, Chris hadn't seemed to notice.

Having just taken a bite of cheese pizza, Winnie nodded. She chewed, swallowed, and then said, "Yes, ma'am."

"We bought books," Emma told Chris. "Lots and lots of books. Some for me, some for Winnie. Liddy made a killing."

"What, and nothing for me?" Chris tried his best to engage in conversation with a teasing comeback, but it was clear his mind was elsewhere. Emma suspected it might be on the phone call he'd taken from Natalie right before they'd sat down to eat.

"Is there something you've been wanting to read?" Emma asked.

"There was a book out last year I meant to pick up. I can't remember the title offhand, but Liddy would know it. It's by Jon Meacham and Tim McGraw." He leaned closer to the pizza box and selected a slice from the pepperoni-and-roasted-veggie half.

Emma raised a questioning eyebrow. "Jon Meacham the historian and Tim McGraw the country singer?" When Chris nodded, Emma said, "That seems like an odd pairing."

"Not really. It's about how the music of our country reflected the times, the politics. One of the roadies was reading it last year and said it was great. I've been meaning to order it, but I keep forgetting."

"You have roadies?" Emma frowned, then tilted her head ever so slightly in Winnie's direction. "Maybe you should speak with them."

"Possibly. I already called the guys in the band, but no go. No recollection." He took a second slice of pizza and put it on his plate. "It's all in Melissa's hands now, Mom. But I will suggest she expand her list of contacts. I'll see her while I'm in LA, and we'll get it straightened out."

Emma nodded to show she understood everything that had not been said. "So tomorrow Winnie and I are going to the art center. I have a few things to take care of before my artists arrive on the first of the month."

"I'd forgotten about that." Chris sat back in his chair and stared across the table at his mother. "You're going to have your hands full. Are you sure you want to . . . take on everything at the same time?"

"Pfft. You forget who you're dealing with." Emma made light of his concerns, though all afternoon she'd been having second thoughts about the artist-in-residence program. Why had she been so quick to act on that impulse, so insistent that it happen that summer? It had seemed like a good idea at the time, but now she felt overwhelmed, unprepared where the program was concerned. For a moment, her life seemed like one big tangle of loose ends, and totally out of control, something she'd never been in her life, which had always been so managed. Planned and executed on schedule.

"If you're sure, Mom."

Emma made a dismissive gesture with her right hand, as if brushing his worries away in one swoop.

Winnie was staring at the pizza Chris was eating, piled high and loaded as it was with all manner of green and red things.

Observing her interest, Emma asked, "Winnie, would you like to try a slice that has veggies on it?"

Winnie leaned forward to get a better look. After a moment, she shook her head. "No, thank you, ma'am."

"Then how 'bout another slice of just cheese?" Emma offered.

"Yes, please."

As Emma added a slice to Winnie's plate, she said, "Winnie, maybe you could help me put together some booklets for the artists who'll be coming to the art center in June."

"What artists?"

Emma explained the setup for Winnie while Chris excused himself to take a phone call. When he returned, she glanced at him and asked, "Everything okay?"

Avoiding her eyes, Chris nodded but did not elaborate other than to say, "Nat."

Emma frowned. After all the years she'd waited for Chris to find the love of his life, to have his one true love turn out to be Maggie's daughter—well, that was a dream come true for so many reasons. "Is she okay?"

"She will be. She's going to have to be."

"That doesn't sound good, son." *What must Natalie be thinking?* Emma wondered. Being told that the man you're in love with—the man everyone knew you were going to marry—might possibly have fathered a child with another woman, however long ago that may have been, has to sting, to put it mildly.

Chris shrugged. "Nat's a loving person. She has a huge heart. She's just been caught off guard, that's all. She'll be fine."

Winnie silently followed the conversation, her eyes moving from Emma to Chris and back again.

"Well, give her and Daisy my love when you speak with her again."

"You can tell her yourself." Chris took the last slice of pizza on the loaded side and took a bite. "She'll be here as soon as she finishes up with exams and grades and all that end-of-the-school-year stuff."

"She's coming here? But you'll be in California."

"I don't think she's coming to see me, Mom," he said pointedly.

"Oh. Well." Emma understood perfectly. Natalie was coming to check out Winnie. "We can talk about that, if you'd care to."

He frowned. "What's there to talk about?"

Emma opened her mouth, then closed it again. Was he really so dense that he couldn't see the potential for trouble brewing?

She sighed. Yes. Yes, he was.

Later, Emma sat on the side of Winnie's bed, listening as Winnie read from the pages of *Matilda*, which she'd proclaimed one of her very favorite stories. Emma wondered if Winnie identified with the beleaguered but oh-so-clever title character. From time to time, Winnie paused in her reading to show Emma an illustration before continuing on with the story.

"You read very well, Winnie," Emma told her when they'd reached a point where they both agreed they would stop for the night. She hadn't kept current on the latest thinking on when to expect children to do what at what level, but it seemed Winnie, who read smoothly and without hesitation, was doing remarkably well for an eight-year-old.

Winnie nodded vigorously and slid down under the blanket and covered herself up to her chin. "I do. All my teachers said so. It's the thing I do best."

"Your teachers must be very good to have taught you so well." Emma took the book and closed it, and set it on the table next to Winnie's bed.

"Oh, they didn't teach me how to read." Winnie yawned.

"Who did?" Emma stood and reached toward the table to turn off the lamp. First guess? Anyone other than Granny Pine.

"I did, ma'am."

Emma's hand hung in midair for a moment. "You taught yourself how to read?"

"Yes, ma'am."

"How did you know how to do that?" Emma didn't think she'd ever known anyone who'd taught themselves how to read.

"I don't remember. I was only three."

Emma processed the information. Winnie had impressed her as resourceful and smart, but she wondered if she hadn't totally underestimated the girl.

"You must be very smart."

"They said so at my school. They let me move into the next class up last year."

"You mean you skipped a grade?"

"Yes, ma'am. At the end of first grade they moved me to third."

"Well, then, you must be very smart indeed."

"They said I have a picture memory," Winnie said proudly.

Emma had to think about that one. "You mean, a photographic memory?"

Winnie nodded.

"Did you like skipping a grade?"

"I liked the learning part, but I missed my friend April. She didn't skip second with me. We still got to walk home from school together sometimes, though. She lived closer to town than me, so we only walked half the way together."

"How far did you have to walk by yourself?"

"A ways. It took a while. Angel and Granny both lived pretty far out of town." Winnie yawned again, wider this time, and her eyes began to close. "Is my daddy going to come in to say good night?"

Emma hesitated. She didn't want to give Winnie false hope. What if she stayed awake, waiting for Chris to appear?

"He had a meeting tonight, so I don't think he'll be home for a long while yet. But you'll probably see him in the morning."

She waited for a *yes, ma'am*, but Winnie was already asleep.

Emma stood over the bed and gazed down at the sleeping child. Winnie's red hair was spread over the pillow on one side and fell across her face on the other. After she'd helped Winnie wash her hair the night before, Emma had offered to braid it for her, but Winnie had declined.

"I really don't much like braids," she'd confided. "My granny made me wear them so she wouldn't have to brush my hair or fix it up before I went to school. She'd just put in the plaits and leave 'em till they started looking scrappy; then she'd take them out. After I washed my hair, she braided it up again. She didn't like to fuss much." Winnie had taken one braid in her hand, given it a hard look, and said softly, "I sorta hate it."

"How would you like to wear your hair, Winnie?" Emma had asked.

"I always wanted a ponytail," Winnie had replied wistfully, "but she always said it was too much trouble cause it would have to be fixed new every day."

Emma had bit back the words she had for ArlettaJo and her indifference, and silently brushed Winnie's hair back from her face and secured it in a ponytail. She'd paused once and asked, "High or low?"

"Oh, high, please, ma'am." Winnie's grin had been wide and unexpected. "My friend April, she always had the highest ponytail in the whole entire school."

"Higher than this one?" Emma had held Winnie's hair in her hand at the crown of her head.

"Oh, no, ma'am. That's . . . that's really high." Winnie's eyes had been shining with approval.

Emma had secured it with one of the rubber bands from the braids she'd unwoven. Watching Winnie preen uncertainly in front of the mirror had brought a smile to Emma's face. Emma had made a mental note to pick up some pretty hair ties tomorrow.

"Thank you." She'd beamed as she admired her reflection.

Something about a new hairstyle perked everyone's spirits, Emma told herself, but she sensed Winnie's pleasure went deeper than that.

Maybe it was because someone had asked her what she wanted, and in doing so had given her a tiny bit of control over something in her life. Maybe for a child who'd been tossed back and forth between two houses, neither of which were really a home, forced to wear a hairstyle she hated and outgrown clothes because no one cared about her appearance, something as simple as letting her choose, to decide for herself how she wanted to look, was a gift. Impulsively, Winnie had turned from the mirror and hugged Emma, and Emma knew she was in deep, deep trouble, the results of the DNA tests be damned.

~

Emma arrived at the art center in midmorning, having taken the time to go through the box of new clothes she'd ordered online for Winnie for overnight delivery. She'd never seen anyone so totally gobsmacked as Winnie had been when she was told that everything in that box was for her. Winnie had stood staring, her jaw dropped, as if she'd not understood what she'd heard.

"Let's go through these things, and you can pick out what you'd like to wear today." Emma had begun to take the items out of the light plastic bags they'd been shipped in.

Winnie had continued to stare.

"What do you think, maybe jean shorts and one of these shirts?" Emma had continued to sort things as she removed them: pants, shirts, tops, underwear, sleepwear, a dress or two. "Do you like yellow, or do you prefer this light blue? Or this one . . ."

"Ma'am . . ." Winnie shook her head slowly. "I . . ."

Emma sat on the sofa next to the piles. "Is something wrong? Do you not like what I ordered? I'd be happy to take you to one of the malls to find something you like better, or we can look online, but I thought I'd order a few things to be delivered right away so you'd have something new to wear." She softened her voice, lest she sound critical. "The clothes you were wearing when you arrived looked a little . . . small on you. So I thought we'd try the next size up. Was that okay?"

Winnie nodded. Her gaze went from one pile to the next. "Those things . . . they're for me?"

"Yes. They're for you."

Winnie touched the piles, one by one.

"Do you see anything you'd like to wear today?" Emma asked.

Winnie pointed to the jeans in Emma's hands. "Those. And that shirt . . ."

"You don't have to choose these because I'm holding them. You can pick any of the others."

"No, ma'am. Thank you, but I like those."

"So you like pink?"

"I do. I like pink. My friend April has a pink bedroom. It's the prettiest bedroom I ever saw."

Emma handed Winnie the clothes, adding a set of underwear on top. "You go on up to your room and change, and when you're ready, we'll go to the art center."

"Yes, ma'am." Winnie took her new things and ran up the steps.

If it came time to do over the guest room for Winnie, Emma knew what color the walls would be. She'd seen a pale-pink shade in a magazine not too long ago that would be perfect. Oh, and maybe a bedspread with a creamy background and pink flowers. Where had she seen one of those recently?

Emma sighed. She knew she was jumping the gun. Who knew how long Winnie would be living with her? For all Emma knew, the child would be gone in two weeks if they were able to determine who fathered her or if Chris was successful in locating her mother. It was up in the air which of those possibilities was the less likely, though Emma was pretty sure Tish Pine wouldn't be found alive unless she wanted to be.

She brushed aside all such thoughts when she heard Winnie bounding down the steps, then pause.

"Winnie?" Emma went into the foyer and found the girl standing on the bottom step, staring at her reflection in the mirror on the opposite wall.

"Don't you look pretty?" Emma exclaimed. "You know, a lot of redheads can't wear that shade of pink, but it's lovely on you."

"I don't look the same," Winnie said flatly.

Emma walked to the bottom of the stairs, reached up, and pulled the sides of Winnie's ponytail just enough to tighten it a little.

"Do you not like the way you look?" Emma asked.

"I like it." Winnie's head bobbed up and down. "I like it a lot, but I don't look like me."

"Oh, I think you look exactly like you," Emma assured her. "Exactly like you're supposed to look."

Winnie continued to scrutinize her image for a few moments, then grinned from ear to ear.

"Okay," she said brightly. "Are we still going to your art center?"

"We are. If you're ready."

Winnie's ponytail waved as she nodded. "I'm ready."

Winnie shared her thoughts on whatever popped into her head from the time Emma pulled out of her driveway.

What a little chatterbox, Emma mused. But then maybe Winnie hadn't had much of an audience these past few years. Whatever the reason for her steady stream of words, Emma enjoyed seeing her hometown through the eyes of a child.

"There are a lot of big houses here. How many people do you think live in that place right there?" Winnie'd pointed to Liddy Bryant's home.

"That's Miz Liddy's house. You met her at the bookshop."

Winnie nodded. "But how many people live there?"

"Right now, it's just Liddy and Dylan. He's a boy she took in last year when he didn't have anyplace else to go." Emma caught herself before she told the rest of the story. The now-eighteen-year-old high school senior's situation wasn't exactly like Winnie's, but he had been homeless after his parents had been arrested and imprisoned for armed robbery. He'd come this close to being put into foster care because he was still seventeen. But he was an excellent student and a gifted athlete with state ranking in baseball, pursued by many colleges offering scholarships, and several professional baseball teams had their eye on him. He'd chosen the University of Massachusetts so he could come back to Wyndham Beach on weekends and continue to help out Liddy in the bookshop and do odd jobs around her house for her. He was totally devoted to Liddy for giving him a home when he'd needed one and for not prosecuting him for all the nights he'd sneaked into the bookshop to sleep in an unused third-floor room before she'd discovered him. Emma knew that Liddy'd done what she herself acknowledged was the best deed of her life, and she loved having Dylan around.

"It's win-win-win," she'd told Emma and Maggie one night. "He gets a home, and I get company at home those nights I'm not out with Tuck, a helping hand around the house, and he'll work part time whenever I need extra help in the shop. Last fall, Dylan did all the yard work at the house and at the shop, cleaned up the garden beds, raked the leaves. And I've gotten a promise for tickets to all the baseball games I will ever want to attend, once he goes pro. And everyone knows that's his path. I'm proud of him that he's chosen to get an education first. Some of those pro scouts were pretty tenacious."

Dylan was going to be just fine, and Liddy was a big part of the reason. She'd hosted a graduation party for him at the bookshop two weeks ago, and he'd presented her with a UMass sweatshirt he'd bought when he'd visited the school to accept their scholarship offer.

Winnie pointed to a house barely visible at the end of a long drive they were passing. "That right there, down that long driveway? That's a for-real mansion. I saw one like that in a movie at Angel's one time. Does a king live there?"

"That's the Harrison house, and no, a king doesn't live there."

"But who lives there?" Winnie turned back to Emma after they'd passed the house.

"Well, no one, really. Not full time, anyway. Sometimes the owner comes back and stays for a day now and then. Most of the time it's just a housekeeper and a groundskeeper who also serves as the maintenance man."

"Where does the owner live?"

"Most of the time he's in London. That's in England."

"He must be very rich." Winnie's glasses had slid down her nose, and she pushed them up. "How rich is he?"

"I have no idea." That Owen was wealthy was no secret. How wealthy, exactly? Emma mentally shrugged. Wealthy enough to have homes in London and Wyndham Beach and who knows where else. Wealthy enough to buy a villa in Tuscany.

Thinking of Owen reminded her of the Italian language course she'd bought for herself. Her enthusiasm for learning to speak Italian and visit Owen at his villa had faded from the foreground along with the artists she'd be greeting soon, and the Harry-and-Carla affair. Everything else had been pushed aside in the wake of the arrival of this one little girl.

Not that that was a bad thing. But she didn't want to lose sight altogether of her future getaway to Italy with the first man who'd made her heart beat faster since Harry had died.

Every time she thought about Harry, she had to restrain herself from launching into a most unladylike string of profanities.

But with Winnie's presence and the looming opening of the artists' retreat, at least when Emma found herself wide awake and still staring at the ceiling at 3:00 a.m., it wasn't her broken heart keeping her awake.

Emma pulled into the lot behind the art center and parked in her usual reserved spot. "Winnie, can you carry that tote bag and the folder I left on the seat back there?"

"Yes, ma'am." Winnie unhooked her seat belt and grabbed the requested items. She was out of the car before Emma was.

"Let me get the bag from the back, and we can . . ." Emma paused.

A boat out in the bay kicked its engine up full throttle and sped off, leaving its wake churning the bay right off the jetty outside the art center. Winnie's head jerked up, and she stopped in her tracks, gazing out past the row of little houses.

"Oh!" She gasped.

"What is it?" Emma looked past Winnie to the water beyond the dunes.

Speechless, Winnie pointed to the bay, where gentle whitecaps rolled quietly onto the pebbled beach.

"I never saw the ocean before." Winnie was still staring.

"Oh, that's not the ocean. That's the bay. Buzzards Bay. It's salt water like the ocean but much, much smaller, and it's set apart from the ocean. See the way the land curves out that way and wraps around the water? It separates the bay from the ocean. The ocean's on the other side of that curve."

Winnie couldn't take her eyes off the expanse of water.

"Would you like to walk down to the water and take a closer look?" When Winnie nodded, Emma put the box on the top step. "Put the bag and the folders right over here on the steps by the door. We'll take a little walk before we start work, and we'll get the rest of our things from the car when we come back; okay with you?"

Winnie nodded and did as she was told, then reached for Emma's hand. Silently, she walked with Emma over the dune and past the cabins to the beach.

"It's so big." Winnie was still wide eyed and in awe. "Are you sure that's not the ocean?"

"Positive," Emma assured her. "The ocean is much, much bigger. But we can take a drive to the Cape one day and you can see for yourself."

"What's the cape?"

"Cape Cod. It's a long stretch of land that goes right out into the ocean."

"That sounds scary."

"No more scary than standing right here and looking at the water from here," Emma assured her, but Winnie looked unconvinced. "I guess living near Atlanta, you never got to see the ocean."

"I saw a lake once. It had lots of little boats on it. I got to go in one. My friend April's granddaddy had one, and he took us for a ride around the lake." She turned her face up to Liddy. "It was a big lake, but it wasn't nothing like that." She pointed to the bay.

"Did you like the boat ride?"

"Uh-huh. April's granddaddy made it go real fast. That was fun, 'cept he made a lady fall in the water. She was on these skis going behind a boat." Winnie shook her head. "Watching her fall wasn't fun."

"Probably not much fun for the lady who was waterskiing, either."

"I guess not, but he thought it was funny. That wasn't very nice of him. Me and April felt bad for the lady. Her boat came back around, and someone pulled her outa the water, and the man driving it yelled at April's granddaddy." Winnie pointed off to the left. "What's that over there?"

"That's Shelby Island. A family lives there." Emma smiled. So much more child friendly than, "The man Miz Liddy sleeps with lives there with the children whose father's in jail because he's a drug dealer and whose mother dumped them with their uncle and grandfather before she took off for God knows where."

"Are there dinosaurs there?" Winnie looked worried.

"Why would you think there might be dinosaurs there?"

"Granny let me watch this movie on the TV with her once. There were dinosaurs on this island, and they got loose out of their pens and chased people and ate them." Winnie's focus was still on Shelby Island, as if not convinced.

"Winnie, that wasn't real. It was made up for the movie."

"The dinosaurs looked real. Granny said they were."

"She was just kidding with you, honey."

"Granny never kidded with me."

Granny Pine went down several more notches in Emma's estimation, which left her pretty near rock bottom, since Emma hadn't thought much of her to begin with.

"I promise there are no dinosaurs there. Just a big old house and a barn and some gardens and trees and a lovely beach and some very nice people who I'm sure you will meet before too long."

Winnie nodded wordlessly. After a few moments, she glanced down at her feet, where a wave had ventured closer. She took a few steps back, then leaned over to pick up something the receding water had uncovered. Holding it up to Emma, she said excitedly, "This looks like a big green diamond."

"It's sea glass," Emma told her. "Somewhere a piece of glass fell into the water, and over a long time, it got turned over and over by the waves, and it was polished and the rough edges smoothed over until it landed on this beach."

Winnie examined it carefully. "Do I have to put it back?"

Emma held out her hand, and Winnie dropped her prize into the palm.

"No, you found it. It's yours. I used to love finding sea glass when I was a girl, but I guess it's been a long time since I looked." Emma turned it over and over in her palm, remembering a time when finding such a treasure was the highlight of her day. Those days when she'd find more than a few pieces, or a piece of an usual color, she'd run home to excitedly show her mother; then she'd put it in a box she kept under her bed. She wondered what had happened to that box in the years since. Perhaps it had gone into the attic at the manse, where the Lewis family had lived for years until her father retired and her brother, Dan, had taken over as pastor at the church in the center of Wyndham Beach.

She supposed it could still be there, if it hadn't been tossed out after her mother passed away.

She handed the glass back to Winnie.

"Maybe someday I'll find more." Winnie slipped it into the pocket of her jeans.

"If you look carefully, you will. Mornings after a storm are a particularly good time to look. The tide scatters things onto the beach every day, but the tide can take them all back as well."

Emma glanced at her watch. The morning was slipping away, and she had work to do to prepare for the artists' arrivals as well as the summer classes. But she hated rushing Winnie, who was experiencing something new and seemed to be enjoying it. Suspecting there'd been few such moments in the child's life, moments of discovery when she'd had the total attention of the adult with whom she'd found herself, Emma was reluctant to turn back from the beach and head inside.

"Winnie, we can come back another time, but right now, I do have to get to work. We can have a picnic on the beach sometime if you like."

Emma held out her hand and Winnie took it, and together they walked back toward the building, Winnie pausing to take a good long look at the little cabins that lined the beach.

"Who lives there?" she asked. "In those funny little places?"

"Those are for the artists who will be arriving soon."

"Why are they painted all those colors?"

"Just to make them unique and fun."

"I thought they were outhouses. But I never saw an outhouse painted up like that."

Emma tried to keep a straight face as she explained her idea for a mini artist colony as they walked to the art center. Winnie gathered her things from Emma's car, and Emma grabbed a box from the trunk. After they arrived at the back door, Emma unlocked it and they went inside. She set the box on the top of her desk and brought in what they'd left on the steps, then wondered what to do with Winnie while she put together the packets of information to be handed out to the artists when they arrived.

"I could help you work," Winnie offered. "I'm a good helper. Miz Edwards—she was my teacher in first grade—always let me help because I'm very good at doing things. I follow directions real good."

"I bet you do. Well, I could use your help." Emma opened the box in which she'd packed the printed pages for the handouts. The whole booklet would contain local phone numbers, lists of restaurants, shops, and local attractions along with information about the town. The pages would need to be collated and stapled before Emma'd add the cover piece she'd had made from an illustration Liddy's late daughter, Jessica, had drawn years ago.

Emma made stacks of the pages, put them in order, and showed Winnie how to assemble them, page by page, then place the individual stacks on a worktable out in the main section of the art center. Watching her brought a smile to Emma's face. Winnie was totally focused on her task, checking the numbered pages to make certain none were out of order before she set them on the table, and was careful to keep the stacks neat.

What a treasure this child is, Emma thought while she watched. *What a sweet, sweet treasure.*

For the first time since Winnie'd arrived in Wyndham Beach, Emma found herself hoping that the DNA tests would confirm the child was Chris's. Yes, it would create problems for her son, but for Emma, Winnie was turning out to be the granddaughter she'd wished for. And the longer it took them to sort through the test results, the harder it was going to be to let Winnie go.

Emma watched Winnie work for a few minutes, then turned her attention to other matters. She listened to all the voice mails that had been left over the few previous days, making notes on whom to call back and in what order, occasionally glancing at Winnie, who was humming softly to herself. She'd just picked up the phone to begin her return calls when the door opened and Marion strolled in.

"I didn't realize I'd scheduled you to work today." Emma opened the top side desk drawer and pulled out the calendar she'd made up at the beginning of the month.

"Oh, you didn't." Marion cast a quick glance at Winnie. "I just saw your car and thought I'd drop in and see if there was anything I could help you with."

Emma pointed to a chair, and Marion sat. "I have things pretty much under control. The only real news is that Kelly Markus, one of the artists, left a voice mail letting us know she's pulled out of the program. Regretfully, she said, but one of her kids was in an accident and needed to be cared for around the clock for a while, so we're down to five."

"You don't want to call one of the others who'd applied and offer them the opportunity?"

"No. Too late. Everyone else will be arriving a week from tomorrow. Besides, it's one less person to deal with, and I'm all for that, at this point." Emma leaned back in her chair and for the moment thought that all the artists could decline to show up and she'd be grateful for it. She was feeling more and more that there was less and less of her to go around.

"That's not like you, Emma." Marion leaned forward. "What's really going on?"

Of course Emma knew Marion's visit had more to do with Winnie and less to do with the artists.

"You're asking about Winnie."

"Well, not that it's really any of my business, but let's be real, Emma. If I suddenly showed up with a young child who called me *Grandma*, you'd be damned curious."

Emma laughed. She *would* want to know what the story was. Keeping her voice low so Winnie couldn't overhear, she gave Marion the abbreviated version. When she was finished, Marion frowned.

"No way that kid is Chris's," Marion said emphatically.

"How can you say that when none of us know, and we won't know until the test results come back, which won't be for weeks?"

"Any redheads in your family, Em?"

Emma shook her head. "Not that I know of."

"Harry's?"

"I never heard of one. His sisters are both dark; his mother was blonde."

"And that girl looks nothing like you, or Chris, or Harry. Or any of his sisters, now that I think about it. I went to school with Prudence, you know. I've known all the Deans, all my life."

"I know. But family resemblances can be fickle. Traits can skip generations, and lots of time there's a resemblance to someone way back on the family tree."

"Have any idea what her mother looks like?"

"I've seen pictures. She's beautiful."

"She's beautiful, and Chris is extremely good looking. No offense, but that child is neither."

Emma bristled. "What are you trying to say, Marion?"

"Don't get your back up, Emma. I'm just saying that I don't see a smidgen of Dean in that girl, or any of your Harper relatives, either. So maybe not go all in on the grandmother thing until you know for sure."

"I appreciate your concern." Emma nodded slowly. "And I understand. But she's here, and I can't not take care of her the way a child needs to be cared for. I don't think anyone ever has, so as long as she is under my roof, she's ours, and we're treating her the way we'd treat our own."

"Chris too?"

"Chris is having mixed feelings. I think he's more afraid to accept her as his own until he has proof. If she's his, he'll be all in. I'm sure of that. But until then, he's trying as best he can. He's hired an investigator to look for her mother, so . . ." A noise from the doorway drew Emma's attention. "Winnie, did you need something?"

"No, ma'am. I just wanted to let you know I was all done so you can put the covers on those little books." Winnie stood with one foot behind the other, her body at an angle to the door, as if ready to run if she had to.

"Thank you. Can you say hello to Miz Marion?"

"Hello, Miz Marion. I remember you from the bookshop."

"And I remember you, Winnie. How nice that you're able to help your . . . to help out here today."

"Yes, ma'am."

"Here, Winnie. Take the covers out and just place them on the booklets, and I'll get the big stapler. I'll be out in just a minute."

Winnie came into the office and picked up the covers. She smiled at Marion as she left the room.

"She does have a sweet smile," Marion said.

"She does indeed."

"It's pretty clear there's a connection between the two of you, but just keep in mind that she might not be staying with you. You know, in case it turns out that Chris isn't her father." Marion looked over her shoulder to the big room where Winnie had gone. "I just don't want to see your heart broken."

Emma smiled wryly. Too late. That ship had sailed, with Harry at the wheel.

"I appreciate that, Marion. Thank you."

"Well, I guess if there's nothing you want me to do here, I'll go on down to the bookshop. See what trouble I can get into there."

Marion gave Emma a thumbs-up before leaving the office. Emma heard her say something to Winnie, then heard the front door open, then close.

Emma went to the small supply closet and searched for the large stapler, then checked to make sure it was loaded. She went out to the main room, where Winnie waited with her completed task, and wondered how long the girl had been standing in the doorway, and how much, if anything, she'd overheard of the conversation with Marion.

~

Despite Emma's best intentions and her efforts to remain calm and organized, the day the artists arrived the following week bordered on chaotic. Two of the artists arrived at the same time, well before two; then the others began trickling in, and after being greeted were shown to their cabins. Just before the welcoming reception Emma had planned, when she finally had them all together at the same time to go over the booklets she'd prepared, she discovered three of them—more than half—had left to stroll through the town even though she'd told them when they signed in they'd have Sunday to explore.

"Why did I think this was a good idea?" she'd grumbled to Chris, who'd arrived from California the night before to attend the reception as he'd promised. Now it was in full swing with art lovers along with the merely curious locals crowding the exhibition space. He'd had Winnie in tow, but she'd disappeared with Maggie, who'd offered a walk on the beach, which was quickly becoming Winnie's favorite place.

"Are you referring to the party or the whole concept of 'artists' retreat'?" He made quotation marks with his hands before swiping two glasses of champagne from the tray of a passing waiter. He handed one to his mother.

"The whole . . ." She waved her hand to include the entire room. "This whole thing."

"You thought it was a good idea because it is. You're giving something precious to a few people who couldn't pull this off on their own. A few months to devote to their art, some time to themselves away from whatever in their lives prevents them from doing their thing, being at peace with themselves, maybe." He kissed his mother's cheek. "The way you used to do for me when Dad would go on a tear about me ruining my life because I'd rather make music than sit behind a desk and someday have my portrait hanging on the wall in the bank next to his and Granddad's and all the other Dean former presidents of the First National Bank of Wyndham Beach. You were my champion back then, and you're their champion now, in a way." His gaze went beyond her to the child who was just coming into the room with Maggie, then stopped to look at a painting of a sunset. "The way you're Winnie's champion."

Emma sighed. "Someone needs to be."

"I know you think that should be me. I don't know what to say to her, Mom. I don't know how or if I fit into her life. I picked her up at the bookshop after Grace's Saturday-morning story hour was finished and drove her home for lunch, like you asked me to do. If I hadn't bought her a copy of the book Grace read to the kids this morning, I wouldn't have known what to say to her. She spent the trip between there and here telling me about the story, and once she got started, she just kept going, so I didn't have to say too much. Sorry, Mom, but I'm not used to being around kids, except for Daisy."

"Winnie believes you are her father. She wants you to be."

"So if I feed into that and it turns out that I'm not, that someone else is, then what? And if we can't locate whoever wins the DNA paternity lottery? What will that mean for her?"

"I wish I knew."

"Well, you're acting as if you do. It's clear she's already accepted that you are her grandmother." He took a sip of champagne. "Mom, I'm not criticizing you or what you're doing with Winnie. It's obvious she's starved for true affection and kindness, and I don't know anyone more affectionate and kinder than you. I just can't make that leap to making believe we're going to be a happy family when I don't know. For her sake more than anyone else's."

"Especially since you already have a happy family of your own. You have Natalie, and Daisy already looks to you as her father figure."

"They are my happy little family. Should I try to fit Winnie into that family when I don't know if she'll be staying? Would that be worse for her? At the same time, I can't totally reject her, either. She's had plenty of that."

"She has. And that's why I'm trying to be what she needs right now."

"Mom, you've always been the best at making everyone you care about feel loved and wanted. Dad was the luckiest guy in the world to have had you. I hope he appreciated just how lucky he was."

That would be a big no, but he was lucky, all right. Lucky I never caught on to his affair while he was alive. Oh, what a delicious scandal that would have been.

"Mom? You all right?" Chris leaned forward and touched her arm.

"Oh. Sorry. I was just thinking about your father." She forced a smile.

"Do you still miss him?"

Before she'd found the receipt for the gold bracelet that Harry'd bought for the woman he'd loved, Emma's response most likely would have been a quick and certain, "Of course I do."

Now, she went for honesty. "No. Not anymore."

"Good. I'm glad. No disrespect to Dad, but he's been gone a long time."

Emma was surprised by Chris's reaction, but before she could say more, Maggie appeared with Winnie.

"We had a nice stroll on the beach," Maggie told them. "It was a little chilly, so we headed back."

"Did you find any more sea glass, Winnie?" Emma asked.

Winnie shook her head no. "But we found some shells." She dug one out of the pocket of her jeans and held it up, then handed it to Chris.

"Ah, a quahog shell." He turned it around in his hand, then gave it back to her. "And a very nice one, too."

"What's a quahog?" Winnie held the shell in both hands.

"It's what folks around here call clams." He stood with his arms folded across his chest and looked down into her inquisitive face. "They have hard shells, like the one you have there."

"Oh." Winnie looked up at Chris as if searching for something. The silence between them seemed to expand inch by quiet inch.

Finally, Chris said, "Winnie, why don't you and I take a stroll around the gallery, and we can look at the paintings together?"

Her eyes lit up and she nodded. "Okay."

Chris squeezed Emma's arm with one hand and put the other on Winnie's shoulder. "I guess you have art in school, right?"

"Uh-huh. I like to paint."

"Well, then, Chris, be sure to show Winnie the children's corner over there on the left."

"Maybe we should do that first. What do you say, Winnie? Shall we start there?"

Winnie's response was another beaming smile, another happy, enthusiastic nod of her head.

Emma watched as Winnie put the shell back into her pocket and tentatively slipped a hand onto Chris's arm. When he patted her hand, Emma sighed. While he may not be ready to fully embrace the role of father, he was making an effort to let her know she was welcome here, that she had a place there with them.

It was the first step he'd taken in Winnie's direction, but Emma knew in her heart it wouldn't be the last.

~

The reception at the art center had been crowded, but it had gone well. When the guests had all left, Emma successfully herded the artists into the conference room for the more personal meet and greet she'd planned to have earlier before they'd all taken off in different directions. She'd looked around the room and memorized names and faces. She'd been both amused and surprised, mentally matching the in-the-flesh artists with her recollections of their photographed works as submitted with their applications.

There was tall, willowy Eva Sadler, elegant in her midforties but looking so much younger. Soft spoken with sparkling brown eyes the same color as her hair, dressed as if she'd just spent the day buying out Talbots, Eva had been one of the surprises. The photos of her work had displayed several large canvases, smeared with slashes of black and white and enlivened with one or two streaks of one primary color per canvas. They were bold and interesting, but Emma would never have matched Eva with such vibrant contemporary work.

Pasquale Morrone, one of two men in the group, dark hair and dark eyes, his manner patrician and genteel. His landscapes were lovely and lush, beautifully detailed. *No surprise,* Emma thought.

Stella Martin, thirty-three years old, who reminded Emma of a tiny blonde, blue-eyed wood-sprite, a Tinker Bell of a young woman. Hers had been one of the few photography portfolios submitted, and Emma had fallen in love with her perfectly balanced, lovely compositions. She'd hoped for a chance to tell her so, but Stella had kept to herself and had been the first to leave when the event concluded.

Preston Hall, sixty-five, a tall, bald, aging preppy, who arrived wearing faded Nantucket-red chinos and a white button-down shirt with the sleeves rolled to his elbows, painted still lifes in oils with all the finesse of a Renaissance master. He was congenial and interacted with the others, but there'd been a sadness about him.

And then there was sixty-seven-year-old Irene Peterson, who, upon arrival, had signed in as Luna Moon, explaining to Emma that Luna was the name of her artistic persona, that part of her that had been suppressed all the years she'd spent caring first for her disabled brother and then for her mother. Her watercolors were almost ethereal, her subjects varied. In particular, Emma remembered a photo of Irene . . . er, Luna's, painting of connected hands, an age-spotted hand with swollen, gnarled, and twisted fingers linked with the chubby pink fingers of a toddler. It had been the one painting that had most captured her imagination.

It was, Emma mused, quite the collection of personalities. All talented, all eager to get to work, all grateful to have an opportunity to devote an entire summer to their art. After fielding their questions and going over the "house rules," such as they were, Emma dismissed the group. She watched as they filed out to get settled into their respective cottages and wondered how this venture was going to play out. Having more than enough chaos in her own life—all unforeseen, none of her own making—she was hoping her artists had left all their personal drama at home. But watching Stella Martin, the only one of the five not to engage with the others, Emma had the feeling the young woman carried more than enough baggage to go around. What was causing Emma's silent alarm to go off? There was something there, in her eyes, in her face, that gave her a twinge of concern, but she couldn't put her finger on what that might be.

Emma went into her office and pulled out the files she'd set up for each of her artists. She sat at her desk with Stella's file and read over the woman's application, noting that while Stella had initially noted her status as *married*, she'd crossed it out and entered *separated*. Emma sat for a while with the file still open, her right index finger tapping the application. She went through the packet of papers that had been returned with Stella's acceptance of Emma's offer, then through the file of background checks her attorney had insisted on and had compiled for each artist. In all the confusion of Winnie's arrival and the rush to get the accommodations livable, Emma had neglected to notice the reports. In Stella's, she found the criminal report relative to Stella's filing of assault charges against her husband, George Martin, and a protection-from-abuse order signed by a West Virginia judge. Accompanying the report were photos of bruises to the young woman's face, arms, and, worst of all, throat. The husband had been arrested but had received a light sentence and a long period of parole. She glanced at the dates. If Martin had begun his sentence on time, he could be out of prison now, but there was no way of knowing if there'd been any delays or appeals.

Emma closed the file, trying to decide how she was going to deal with this distressing information. The only thing she knew for certain at that moment was she'd have to speak with Stella, but first, she'd speak with Brett, Wyndham Beach's chief of police, first chance she had.

Chapter Nine

With Daisy off on a playdate with a friend from school, Natalie spent the Saturday of Emma's reception reading and grading the papers her students had turned in during the week. All but one of the exams had been administered, and if she could grade everything and submit the final grades to the college by Wednesday night, twenty-four hours later she could be in Wyndham Beach. True, Chris would be on the opposite coast by then, but his would-be love child would be at Emma's, and Winnie was the one she most wanted to see. Natalie prided herself on her ability to read people, and she actually considered herself to be a better judge of character than anyone she'd ever known. God knew, for all his worldliness, Chris was still a little naive when it came to assessing the motives of others. Natalie had to see for herself this eight-year-old girl who claimed to be his daughter, see if she could figure out what the endgame was for Winnie.

"What, you think the kid has ulterior motives?" Grace, who'd called on her lunch break from the bookshop, asked after Natalie told her she'd be there before the end of the week. "Like she's part of some plot to steal your soon-to-be fiancé? Part of some widespread conspiracy to deprive you of your happy-ever-after? She's eight freaking years old, Nat!"

"I'm just saying no one really knows who she is or where she really came from. This story about her coming to Wyndham Beach by herself after changing buses here and there assisted only by kindly bus drivers . . . it just sounds a little crazy to me."

"Let me remind you: she has a birth certificate naming Chris as her father." Grace's voice was level, low, and slow, the way she spoke when she was explaining something simple to someone who wasn't paying attention. Natalie imagined that was the way Grace had sounded when she was in court and addressing a particularly annoying and uncooperative witness. "And yes, Mom said she heard from Emma that Chris's manager checked. The birth certificate is legit. I honestly don't understand why you feel so threatened, Nat. It just isn't like you. Why are you feeling so insecure?"

Natalie took a deep breath. "Okay, here's the truth. I started thinking, what if they find her mother and Chris meets with her and realizes she's his long-lost one true love—his soul mate—and he wants her back in his life?" She swallowed back tears she would not permit to fall.

"Do you know how far-fetched that is? For one thing, if she'd been his one true love, he'd never have lost her. And I'm pretty sure you're his soul mate."

"But what if they decide to try to work things out between them for the sake of their child?" Her voice was barely a whisper as she spoke aloud the fear she realized had been gnawing at her heart since the moment Chris had told her about Winnie's arrival.

"I think if Patricia Pine had been inclined to do anything for Winnie's sake, she wouldn't keep disappearing from the child's life and dumping her on whomever was willing to take care of her until she felt like showing up again. If she sincerely cared about Winnie, she'd have let Chris know they shared a child—if in fact they do—and she'd have demanded he step up a long time ago. And Winnie would have been more than an occasional thought to her."

"But what if . . ."

"No more what-ifs. You're making yourself crazy, you know that, right? Do you want to know what I think?"

"You're going to tell me anyway."

"That's right, I am. Because I am your big sister, and I love you in a way that no one else does. We've always had each other's backs, and if I thought for one second there was something shady going on, I'd be the first to speak up. But I really think this situation is exactly as it appears. I think this woman had this child fathered by someone—ha ha, well, obviously—but didn't know who. So maybe she picks a famous singer on a lark because, hey, that would be cool, right? And besides, who's to say she's wrong? Maybe it's just a big joke to her. Maybe it was wishful thinking. Maybe it was another man named Christopher Dean. We're not going to know until the DNA tests come back, and that won't be for another few weeks."

"But, in the meantime, everyone is assuming she is Chris's daughter."

"No. In the meantime, everyone is just trying to do their best for this scared little girl." Grace took a deep breath. "You know I do story hour at the bookshop every Saturday, right? This morning Emma dropped Winnie off on her way to the art center because her artists-in-residence were due to arrive, and Emma had to be there to greet them. Winnie sat on the floor while I was reading, off all by herself, and it was pretty clear she felt not only out of place but out of her element. She looked scared to death. The other kids coming in mostly knew each other, and they sat in little groups, chatting and laughing, but no one spoke to her, and she didn't try to initiate conversation with anyone. When Chris came to pick her up to take her to the art center reception, the kid's relief was palpable. She's trying really hard, but I think, deep inside, she knows she might not belong here. Emma's trying really hard, too. I don't think she believes for one minute that Chris is Winnie's father, and neither does Chris." Grace paused. "They're just trying to be kind, to give Winnie a secure place until they can figure out who she belongs to and where she's going to wind up.

"Nat. You need to get on board." Grace had said her piece, had put it out there, and Natalie could tell her sister was waiting for a response.

"I'm trying."

"No, you're not. You're trying to protect your place in Chris's life."

"Not just. And don't say it like it's a bad thing. I love Chris. We're going to get married. I'd die if anything happened to break us up." Natalie swallowed hard. "I never thought anything could, but this, this child . . . her mother out there somewhere—I don't know what to think anymore."

"Please. I know you're feeling insecure. And while I don't understand why, I'm telling you, you don't have to be. All I know for certain is that if you can't find it in your heart to put Winnie first right now, chances are it will harm your relationship with Chris in ways we can't even imagine. You need to be the person we all believe you to be. The woman we know you are. Like I said, you need to step up."

"I will. Of course I will." Natalie took a deep breath. "I'll see you in a few days."

"Great. You can help me move into my little house."

She paused. "I thought Linc would be doing that."

"We brought in some furniture, and we spent the last few nights there. We'll stay there tonight, too, but tomorrow he'll be heading back to California with Chris. I need help with the rest of the furniture and the details. Decor. I still don't have any curtains or drapes, and I'm not sure I want them, but we can talk about that. You and Daisy are welcome to stay with me if you don't mind sleeping on the pullout sofa. And we'll have to borrow some sheets and blankets from Mom until I can buy some. Unless you want to bring sleeping bags." Grace paused. "Maybe I should invest in a few of those to keep for occasional overnight guests."

"We'd love to stay with you. Mom said we could stay with her, but now that you're in your own place, I think she and Brett should be allowed some time alone, just the two of them."

"Agreed. They're long overdue. How long are you planning on staying in Wyndham Beach?"

Natalie hesitated. "I haven't decided yet. I guess it depends on how things go."

"Make the effort, Nat, and you won't be sorry. Things will work out just fine."

"Or as Mom always says, they'll work out the way they're supposed to."

Natalie sat and stared out the window after she ended the call. But what way was that?

Every day, her mental image of this woman, Patricia—Tish—Pine, began to look more and more like a supermodel, and who could compete with that? She hated that she felt so insecure. But most of all, she hated that she'd had a chance to be that loving, supportive woman Chris believed her to be, and she'd let her insecurities get in her way.

Natalie had never felt beautiful, not in the way she thought of her sister as beautiful. Where Grace was petite and curvy with dark hair and blue eyes, Nat was tall and lanky, green eyed and blonde. Grace was the "it" girl of her class, the girl who got all the cards on Valentine's Day, the girl all the boys wanted to go out with in high school, the girl everyone invited to their parties, the one everyone wanted to call their best friend. Natalie was the quiet one, the one who didn't make friends as easily but who cherished the friends she had. Two years behind her sister, Natalie had always been invited to the same parties, but she'd suspected it might have been Grace's doing, as in, "My sister's invited or I don't come." Grace was like that—fiercely loyal and protective of Natalie, who always felt she faded in her sister's shadow. Growing up, there'd been times she felt she'd disappeared completely.

Grace's very presence commanded respect. Before her skunk of a husband had pulled the rug out from under her and drained away everything she'd once believed about herself, Grace had had an authoritative manner that had served her well as a lawyer. She could intimidate with a glance. While her ex, Zach, had robbed her of so much, moving to Wyndham Beach and finding new challenges had done wonders to bring back Grace's mojo. Of course, that meant Grace had come roaring back as the older sister who thought nothing of putting the younger in her place, no filter.

Well, someone had to do it.

Natalie pulled her laptop closer. She'd read the remaining papers, and on Tuesday night she'd grade the last of the exams, enter all the data into the school's files on Wednesday, and put aside all thoughts of Chris and Winnie and Winnie's mother. She'd focus on her job—her students deserved her complete attention—and when she finished and submitted the last grade, she'd pack what she and Daisy would need for an undetermined length of time in Wyndham Beach.

But before a half hour had gone by, Natalie's thoughts had drifted back to Chris.

Had there ever been a time in her life when she hadn't been in love with him?

Natalie was four or five when she first became aware of Christopher Dean. He was four years older, but he'd never treated her like a nuisance whenever she was around, like some of the other older kids did, including Grace and her friends. Back then, Natalie had been painfully shy, and her shyness had been exacerbated by the fact she was merely a summer visitor to Wyndham Beach, not a resident. Maggie wanted her daughters to spend most, if not all, of their summers in her hometown in the house where she'd grown up, getting to know their grandmother. Natalie had loved the house and had adored her grandmother and would have been happy to spend all day every day in the backyard, gardening with Gran, or on the front porch with a book in her hands, but inevitably her mother would insist she join the other kids in the neighborhood on the beach or at the playground. Back then, the highlight of Natalie's days had been when Grace and Jessica Bryant would pile into Chris's Radio Flyer wagon, and he would pull them around the block. If Nat was around, he'd tell Grace to move over and make room for her little sister.

When Natalie was nine and she'd fallen off the jungle gym at the playground, thirteen-year-old Chris had carried her home, iced her knee, and stayed with her until her mother returned from wherever it was she'd been. Luckily, nothing had been broken, but a secret place in her heart had opened up and let him move in. Then, three years later, when she'd seen Chris kissing Emily Jones behind the lifeguard stand on the Cottage Street beach, that poor young heart had been ripped in two. By the time she'd turned fifteen, she'd become resigned to the fact that not only was she totally, impossibly in love with him, but that Chris was way out of her league—and always would be.

But then sometime over the summer she turned sixteen, something had changed. That summer—that special summer—Chris and Natalie always seemed to be in the same place at the same time. They spent hours on the beach in the mornings, sometimes as part of a group, sometimes just the two of them, just talking about . . . everything. Sometimes later in the evening, when the sun was just about to set, he'd show up, and they'd go for a walk.

"We're just friends," Natalie insisted to whomever commented on the fact that she and Chris seemed to be spending a lot of time together. "Our moms are best friends, and Chris and I have always been friends. It doesn't mean anything," she'd protested, though deep in her heart she wished that it had. He'd never even tried to kiss her, much to her disappointment.

The following summer, Nat was in Wyndham Beach for less than a week. About to embark on a study-abroad program—to Florence to study art—she'd spent her last night in town on the Cottage Street beach, where she could see the harbor and all the way out to Shelby Island. She'd been sitting alone on the big rock overlooking the water, thinking about all the adventures to come once she was beyond the watchful eyes of her parents and her older sister, when someone had called her name. She'd turned to see Chris at the end of the jetty, slipping out of his flip-flops, then walking toward her, picking his way over the rocks to join her at the end.

"How'd you know I was here?" she'd asked as he'd lowered himself to sit beside her.

"I stopped by your grandmother's, and Grace said she thought you might have gone to the beach." He leaned back on his elbows and stretched his legs out in front of him, his toes just skimming the water. "So you leave tomorrow. Italy. Excited?"

"Of course. It's the first time I've ever gone away for three months without my family. I'm going to take advantage of every minute."

He'd frowned. "What's that supposed to mean?"

She'd flipped her hair back over her shoulder and made a comment about sampling the tall, dark, and handsome talent she'd meet in Florence.

Chris hadn't seemed to like the implication that she could meet someone who'd sweep her off her feet. "Don't," he'd said. "You might not come back."

And then he'd said something about wanting to be able to think about her there, in Wyndham Beach, which had thoroughly confused her. He'd dated several other girls over the summer but had always kept her at arm's length even while spending a lot of time with her, so why should it matter where she was or whom she was with? Especially since he'd be God knew where, doing God knew what with God knew whom. He was only there that summer because he and his bandmates were rehearsing for their first big gig—one of the opening acts for a semi-famous group. She'd known in her heart that he was heading toward fame and glory, and when they saw a shooting star overhead, she'd told him to make a wish.

When he'd asked her what she'd wished for, she'd told him she'd wished that his wish for his band to make it big would come true.

"Aw, Nat, that's sweet," he'd said. "But you don't have to waste your wish on me. Wish something for yourself."

"That is for me," she'd insisted. "I wish for you to be happy, and that's what will make you happy. So that's my wish. It wasn't wasted if it comes true."

He'd looked into her eyes for what had seemed like a lifetime.

"I will never forget you, Nat. And I will always remember this." He'd kissed her then, the first knock-your-socks-off kiss of her life.

"I'll remember, I swear it," he'd said, his voice a whisper. "No matter where I go, whenever I see a shooting star, I'll think of you."

It would be years before she'd had an inkling of just how much that night had meant to him, and how much he'd remembered. A year ago, after not having seen him in a very long time, she'd been surprised when he'd sent front-row tickets to his concert in Philadelphia for her and Grace. Midway through the performance, he'd stopped to address the audience.

"You all know I like to stop about halfway through the show for a little story time. So settle down, boys and girls. This is a story I've never told before and may never tell again. But tonight is special, so here goes."

He'd paused for a moment—and then he'd talked about that night before she'd left for Italy, and the shooting stars. And then he'd sung the song he'd written about it, and Natalie knew it was about her, and about how much her belief in him had meant to him, and she knew in her heart that what had begun that night so long ago had been only a promise of someday, of something more to come. After that night in Philly, they'd fallen into their relationship easily, naturally, and they both recognized it for what it was: a one-of-a-kind forever love. For all her insecurities, Natalie had never doubted Chris's love for her or the fact that they were fated to be together always, to eventually settle down here in Wyndham Beach and raise their family. She'd never questioned that sure path—until now. Now that path to their happy-ever-after seemed strangely out of focus.

And she couldn't help but wonder why, when everything in her life was going so perfectly, fate had to toss a grenade into it.

~

"Nana! I'm here!" Daisy shot through Maggie's front door, a girl on a mission, her mother following along behind loaded down with luggage, which she promptly let drop in the foyer.

"Who's there?" Maggie called from the kitchen. "Is that my sweet pea?"

"It is! It's me, Daisy! I'm here!"

"So you are." Maggie met Daisy and Natalie midway between the kitchen and the front hall. She blew a kiss to her daughter and scooped up Daisy in both arms.

"We had to drive a long way today," Daisy told her. "I thought we were driving to the moon."

"Well, that would be a much longer drive, I'm pretty sure." Maggie set Daisy on the ground and turned to hug her daughter. "Hello, sweetie. I'm so glad you're here."

"Hi, Mom." Natalie returned the hug. "I'm happy to be here."

"Come into the kitchen. We were just talking about . . ." Maggie led the way.

Natalie stopped in the doorway. Brett, her future stepfather, and Emma were seated on stools at the big granite island in the middle of the kitchen. It had never occurred to her that her mom would have company when she arrived. Brett was usually at the police station in the afternoon, and she'd expected Emma to be at the art center since she'd only welcomed her artists for the retreat over the previous weekend.

She took a quick glance around the room. Where was Winnie?

"Emma, I didn't know you were here." Natalie hugged her with genuine fondness. "So good to see you."

"I was hoping you'd arrive before I left." Emma returned the hug. "Chris said you should get to Wyndham Beach by late afternoon."

"We'd have been here an hour earlier if we hadn't hit traffic this side of New York." Natalie turned to Brett, who was wearing his Wyndham Beach police uniform, and hugged him, too. "How are you, Brett? Are you off for the day now?"

"Ah, no. I stopped over to talk to Emma about . . ." His gaze went quickly from Emma to Maggie and back to Emma.

"I'm interrupting something." Natalie had followed his gaze. "I'm sorry. We can go outside and . . ."

"No need," Emma told her. "I was just filling Brett in about a possible situation at the art center."

"Is everything all right? Are you all right?" Natalie's brows drew closer together. "Is it Winnie?"

"Oh, no, no. Winnie's fine. She and I are getting along wonderfully. It almost seems she's always been here." Emma's demeanor changed in the time it took Natalie to drop her handbag on the nearest chair. Or the time it took for Natalie's stomach to drop just a little as she caught the glow in Emma's smile and the light in her eyes. "She's fit in just fine. No problems with Winnie."

"Well, thank God for that," Natalie heard herself say.

"You're going to love her, Nat," Emma assured her.

"I'm sure." Natalie focused uneasily on a spot on Emma's forehead just the teeniest north of Emma's eyes, hoping she didn't look as guilty as she felt. What if she couldn't love this child? What if, when it really mattered, she wasn't—couldn't be—the person everyone believed her to be? "Has there been any word yet about the DNA results?"

"Oh, much too soon for that, I'm told," Emma said. "But it's okay. Winnie needs a bit of time to settle down from all that's happened to her."

"Someone's in your yard, Nana. A girl." Daisy's voice held a mixture of concern and curiosity as she looked through the screened door. "Who is in your yard?"

"Oh, that's Winnie. She's . . . staying with me for a time," Emma responded.

Natalie made her way to the back window for her first glimpse of this child whose presence threatened to send her world out of control. Winnie was seated on one of the swings Maggie had installed for Daisy's visits, but she wasn't swinging. She was staring at something in a nearby lilac bush. Nat wasn't surprised by the fact that Winnie's hair was red—really red—because she'd expected that, but she was startled by the fact that the child was sitting so still for such an extended period of time without seeming to move a muscle.

"I want to see her." Without waiting for a response, Daisy bolted through the back door. Winnie's head turned in her direction; then she held a finger to her lips. Natalie could almost hear her whisper, "Shhh."

Natalie watched as Winnie hopped off the swing, then stood as if waiting for Daisy. When the younger child reached the swings, Winnie again placed a finger on her lips and knelt down. She pointed to a spot in the lilac, and Daisy craned her neck to see whatever it was Winnie found so mesmerizing.

Behind her, Nat could hear bits and pieces of the conversation as it resumed.

". . . not sure if I have any legal obligations." Emma's voice.

Then Brett's: "Em, unless she tells you he's threatening her, or she feels she's in physical danger from him, I don't know what we can do."

"Do you think she's in danger?" Maggie's voice, heavy with concern. "Are you afraid he's going to come after her?"

"I don't know what to think. On the one hand, I tell myself to mind my own business. On the other . . ." Emma sighed. "Don't I have a responsibility to her and the others at the retreat to make sure no one comes to harm?"

"Well, you do, and you would," Brett said pointedly, "but right now, there's no reason to think something will happen while she's in Wyndham Beach. Unless she knows of a threat. In which case, she needs to tell you. What I can do is request the complete file from the police in West Virginia as a precaution, and I'll find out where Martin is now. If he's still in jail, there's no problem. If he's already out on parole, well, then we need to know that. We also need to know if he knows where she is, and if he's contacted her in any way." He paused to take a sip from the mug of coffee Maggie'd placed before him, then smiled at her, a smile overflowing with not merely thanks but the deepest love.

Natalie knew that look. It was the same way Chris looked at her.

"Give me a minute . . ." He excused himself from the kitchen and took out his phone as he walked toward the front hall. Seconds later he was speaking to someone in a low voice.

Natalie caught the look that passed between Emma and Maggie. Torn between watching the two children in the backyard and the conversation behind her, Nat had missed bits of both.

Turning to her mother, she asked, "Is something going on in town that I need to know about?"

"Emma found out that one of her artists was the victim of domestic abuse," Maggie told her.

"What tipped you off?" Natalie asked.

"Her behavior was . . . I don't know. I just had a feeling something was off." She looked up from her coffee. "My attorney insisted I have everyone sign a release so we could do background checks on all the artists. The firm followed up on everyone. Included in her background was information regarding the arrest of her husband for assaulting her, complete with photos. He was arrested and sentenced to jail time, but I don't know if he's still there."

"Em, you didn't read the reports when they came in?" Maggie asked.

Emma shook her head. "For one thing, I thought it was unnecessary. Just some legal thing. The reports all came together from the law firm right around the time I found the receipt for the bracelet—" She paused, glancing at Natalie, with whom she did not wish to share Harry's affair. "Then Winnie showed up, and I forgot all about the file with the reports. It just wasn't on my radar at that point."

"So you haven't discussed this with her?" Natalie leaned against the cool stone top of the island.

Emma shook her head. "I thought I should speak to Brett first. I don't know the best way to handle this."

"Oh, that's terrible." Natalie thought of a roommate of hers from college, who'd been stalked and eventually beaten by an ex-boyfriend. "Mom, remember Amy and what she went through?"

"I do. It's the first thing I thought of," Maggie said. "She filed charges and he was arrested and eventually went to prison, didn't he?"

Natalie heard Brett's footsteps as he paced back and forth in the front hall, his voice indistinct.

"He did. Amy had no qualms about prosecuting him," Natalie said, "but unfortunately everyone isn't able to do that for one reason or another. Sometimes the victims just want to put it behind them. Sometimes they're too afraid of their abusers to pursue a legal case."

"Fear is a very potent motivator. One we need to respect," Brett said when he returned to the kitchen. His expression said volumes. "Good call, Emma. I checked with the police down there. George Martin was released from prison three days ago."

"I wonder if Stella knows," Emma thought aloud.

"More importantly, I wonder if he knows where Stella is," Brett said. "He's served his time, but he's on parole so should be checking in with his parole officer, and he shouldn't leave the state. So far, there hasn't been a crime committed, so until we can confirm he's still in West Virginia, there's not much we can do other than be observant, maybe keep an eye out for this guy in case he shows up in town."

"If he shows up, you can arrest him, right? Because of the court order?" Emma asked.

"There's a ninety-day order that was signed in West Virginia, so it does have legal teeth here in Massachusetts for as long as the order is good, that is, ninety days from the day it was issued in West Virginia. The order was signed eight weeks ago, so it's still good for another month."

"I wonder if he knows where she is," Maggie thought aloud. "I doubt she told him where she was going when she left town."

"What happens when the ninety days expire?" Emma asked.

"She can apply to have the time extended. But she'd have to do that in West Virginia. Any time before the ninety days expires, she can request an extension." He paused. "She may be able to do that remotely, though."

"What if the ninety days are expiring and she wants to stay here or go somewhere else to live?"

"Then she has to file for a new order in the state where she's going to be living," Brett explained. "Of course, then he'd know where she is, if he doesn't already."

"And if she feels threatened here, she does what?" Emma asked.

"She needs to bring the order to the police station, and we'll keep a copy on record. That way, if he shows up, we can pick him up for violating the order. Of course"—Brett nodded—"she'd have to take us into her confidence for that to happen." He thought for a moment.

"If you have the background checks on the other artists, you should check them out as well. You never know what might show up—a repeat DUI offender, scofflaw . . ."

"Serial killer. Axe murderer," Maggie chimed in.

Emma frowned at them both and tossed in, "Superhero. Teacher of the year. Doctors without Borders alum . . ."

"Okay, we get it." Brett laughed softly. "And you're right. You're just as likely to find someone who stands out in a positive way. But you should know, for everyone's sake, if anyone has a disturbing background. But in the meantime, we can keep an eye out for him." Brett's phone pinged, and he swiped the screen several times, then held up the screen for Emma to see. "The police chief I spoke with down there is on the ball. This is her husband. If you see him around the art center, or in town, call the station right away. I'll make sure everyone on the force is aware."

Maggie leaned in to take a look, and Natalie drifted over from the windows.

"He's innocent enough looking, isn't he?" Emma observed. "Blond, blue eyes, big smile, friendly expression."

"A wolf in sheep's clothing," Brett said as he headed for the hallway. "Maggie, okay if I run a few copies off on your printer?"

"Of course."

Minutes later, he was back with several sheets of paper. He handed one to Emma.

"Take a good look; then I'll head back to the station and make sure everyone on the force sees it."

"I've seen what I need to see." Emma passed the photo to Maggie.

"Me too." Maggie nodded, and Natalie leaned over her shoulder.

"Yup. Got it." Natalie studied the image. "That's what a cherub would look like all grown up. His is a face you'd remember." Natalie turned her focus back to the yard, where both girls were staring at a shrub. She wondered what they were talking about.

"I should go out and introduce myself." Natalie watched as Winnie led Daisy close but not too close to the lilac.

Both girls covered their mouths and seemed to be giggling.

"Something is tickling their funny bones." Maggie stepped up behind her daughter.

"Looks like they're getting along well enough," Emma observed. "I'm so happy you're here, Natalie. Winnie hasn't had anyone near her age to talk to or to play with."

"She's eight, and Daisy was just five. I wonder how much she and Winnie have in common. Winnie's in what, second grade?"

"Third. They skipped her a year." Emma's voice held a touch of pride in the girl.

"They're doing all right out there," Maggie noted. "Which is a good thing, since they could end up as . . . well, I guess stepsisters, at some time."

Leave it to Maggie to address the elephant in the room head-on.

Natalie studied her mother's face, wondering if she knew something Natalie hadn't been clued in to yet.

"There's a fifty-fifty chance," Maggie added. "And I did say *could*, because right now, we don't know."

"Has something come up that I should know about?" Natalie raised an eyebrow. "Do you all know something I don't know?"

"Oh, no, dear," Emma assured her. "We're still waiting for the DNA results so we have a clearer picture of how to proceed. If we knew something definitive, we'd let you know."

"Okay, well, good." Natalie poured herself a glass of water from the refrigerator door, took a few sips, then left it on the counter. "I think I'll go out and make Winnie's acquaintance now."

"No time like the present," Maggie said as Natalie opened the back door and stepped down onto the deck.

Late afternoon on a sunny day in Wyndham Beach brought soft shadows from the shade of Maggie's oak trees, a hint of salt from the bay, and a whiff of the good rich earth that Maggie had recently turned over in preparation for her spring planting. On the deck, flats of hardy annuals—pansies and dusty miller, zinnias and cosmos—sat next to pots of this year's perennials: phlox, echinacea, butterfly bush, and hollyhocks. Maggie was predictable in her choices. Every year she replanted whatever had been growing in her mother's garden beds once upon a time.

"What's so interesting, girls?" Natalie called out as she descended the deck steps.

"Shhh! You're going to scare her away!" Daisy had turned to her in near panic.

"Scare who away?" Natalie lowered her voice and slowed her steps as she approached the spot where Daisy and Winnie still stood motionless.

"The mama bird," Daisy whispered. "She has a nest, and she's sitting on her eggs."

Natalie placed her hands on her daughter's shoulders and tried to see past the leaves that guarded the inner branches of the lilac.

"I don't see her," Natalie said softly.

"You need to make yourself smaller," Winnie told her without turning around.

Natalie crouched lower until she reached about the same height as Winnie, who pointed toward the bush.

"I think I see . . . oh, yes, there she is." Natalie spotted the tiny bird seated on her nest of twigs. The poor thing stared back at the three sets of eyes that watched her. Natalie wondered if the bird was having the same sort of fight-or-flight reaction she herself might have if some huge unknown species moved proportionately and dangerously close enough to stare at her and her child. "Maybe we should take a few steps back and give her a little breathing room. She looks a little frightened."

The girls quietly backpedaled until they were back at the swing set.

"Mama, do you think she feels better now?" Daisy asked.

"I'm sure she does. You know, it's never good to get too close to wildlife if you can avoid it. You'd hate for her to feel scared so she has to abandon her nest and go somewhere else to start over, right? If her eggs hatch here, you'll be able to watch the baby birds grow all summer. From a polite distance, of course."

Daisy nodded enthusiastically. "I would like to see baby birds. We could leave birdseed on the deck, and they could eat there, and we could watch them."

"I think birds need to learn how to feed themselves in the summer when there are lots of seeds and worms and bugs to eat. We save the birdseed for the winter, when there's not so much food for them. We don't want them to not learn how to feed themselves."

Daisy giggled and turned to Winnie, who'd been watching Natalie as if trying to figure how she fit into this new life of hers. "Worms and bugs! Yuck!"

At her outburst, the bird took off.

"Oh no! She's gone!" Daisy wrapped herself around her mother's waist. "Now there won't be babies!"

"She'll be back," Winnie told her. "We were just here for a few minutes. She's watching from somewhere. We just have to go away for a while so she sees it's safe, and she'll come back."

Natalie took the moment to introduce herself, pausing as an urge to extend her hand washed over her. While she normally wouldn't think of shaking hands with most eight-year-olds, something about Winnie seemed so . . . well, old. As if somehow a thirty-year-old was living inside that small-for-an-eight-year-old body. "Winnie, my name is Natalie. I'm Daisy's mother."

"It's nice to meet you, ma'am." Winnie stuck her hands in the pockets of her denim shorts.

"Nice to meet you, too, Winnie." Natalie tried to put some genuine warmth in her smile even as she studied the little girl. Everyone was right about one thing: she looked nothing like Chris. Winnie was scrawny, pale, and her eyes had a wary, worn-out look. Natalie was curious, a bit wary herself, and at the same time saddened that a child of so young an age should have that air of defeat about her.

"Winnie came all the way on a bus to stay with Nana Em," Daisy related to Natalie as if she'd memorized what Winnie had told her. "She's staying in her house, and they went to the bookstore where Aunt Grace works."

"I met Grace," Winnie said. "She's your aunt?"

"'Cause she's my mommy's sister, right, Mommy?"

"That's right. Grace and I are sisters. Maggie—Mrs. Flynn, who lives here—is our mother," Natalie said. "We should probably go in now, if we want Mama Bird to come back to her nest."

She began to walk toward the house, Daisy following, and a moment later, Winnie did as well.

"What kind of bird was that?" Daisy asked.

Winnie shrugged. "Maybe some kind of sparrow. Or maybe a wren or a finch."

"If you remember what it looked like, maybe we can look it up," Natalie suggested as she walked into the house.

"What bird?" Maggie asked.

While Daisy filled her grandmother in regarding the backyard excitement, Natalie checked her messages. She'd sent a text to Chris before they left home, and another when they were halfway to Massachusetts and had stopped for another of Daisy's potty breaks, which were really a cover for a trip to the rest stop's snack bar. He hadn't responded to either text, but she sent a third. **Arrived safe and sound. Call when you're free?**

She signed off with her usual, mulu (miss u love u), and sent it on its way.

"Did you hear from Chris?" her mother asked, apparently having observed Natalie's attention to her phone.

"Just texting to let him know we made it." She dropped her phone into her bag even as she noticed Winnie's watchful eye. "So. We're going down to the bookshop to meet Grace for dinner."

"Oh?" Maggie's eyebrows raised. "I thought you'd be having dinner with us."

"I figured you and Brett would enjoy a dinner alone." Natalie looked around the room. "Where is Brett, anyway?"

"He went back to the station to pass around the photos of . . ." Maggie glanced at the two young girls, who were leaning on the island counter.

"Got it." Natalie nodded. "Anyway, with Grace finally out of your hair, I thought you'd appreciate a little privacy."

"That's very thoughtful, sweetie, but we do see each other every day, and I haven't seen you and Daisy in several months," Maggie pointed out.

"We're not leaving Wyndham Beach anytime soon, Mom. And I think Gracie wants to show off her new house. How 'bout we have dinner tomorrow night?"

"One of Brett's officers is getting married tomorrow night. The officer—Emma, you know her, Audrey Toller—has no family, and she's asked Brett to give her away, which of course he's honored to do."

"Nice of him." Natalie smiled. She was grateful that he and her mother had found each other again after so many years apart. High school and college sweethearts, they'd gone their separate ways and lived very different lives before eventually ending up in the same place at the same time, and discovering their love was as strong as it ever had been. Nat and Grace had both agreed that Maggie was due for something wonderful in her life, after having given up the child she'd secretly had with Brett at eighteen, and having lost her husband—the girls' father, Art Flynn—to cancer almost five years ago. To see her mother so happy, to see the sparkle in her eyes and the joy she exuded, was sigh worthy. Romance was alive and well in Maggie Flynn's life, and her daughters couldn't be happier. Being reunited with her son, Joe, who'd searched for and found her through Natalie's participation in a genealogy site, had been a joy Maggie never thought she'd experience.

"Well, I have no plans, so why don't you and Daisy have dinner with Winnie and me tomorrow night?" Emma asked.

"We'd love to, Em, thank you. And Mom, maybe we can all get together on Saturday night."

"Sounds like a plan. We should invite Liddy. And Tuck. Maybe we should do seafood . . . fish and something else." Maggie went to her kitchen desk and began to make a list.

"Mom, is there life without lists?" Natalie teased, knowing her mother rarely did anything without having mapped it out first on paper.

"No, there is not. Or shouldn't be." Maggie looked up. "Or do we want to go out? I could make reservations . . ."

"You decide. Just tell us where and when, and we'll be there." Natalie watched her daughter open what she referred to as Nana's cookie drawer and take out a bag of Oreos. "Nana, can me and Winnie have a cookie?"

"Of course." Maggie didn't bother to look up from her list-making.

Winnie's eyes gravitated to the photo of George Martin that Brett had left on the counter. Emma slowly moved it from view, but not before Winnie'd taken a good long look.

"One cookie, and you may eat it on our way to the bookshop. Aunt Grace is going to wonder what happened to us. And Mom, do you have any old sheets we could take to Grace's?"

"I do. And since I suspect your sister doesn't have extra blankets, I'll give you some of those, too. It's still cool here at night."

While her mother disappeared in search of sheets and blankets, Natalie helped herself to a cookie, and Daisy passed the bag to Winnie, who looked to Emma for permission. Emma smiled and winked.

"Thank you, ma'am," Winnie said softly, and dipped her hand into the bag. She wandered toward the windows, stilled for a moment, then whispered loudly, "Daisy! She's on the deck!"

Daisy ran to the window. "Is that our mama bird?"

Natalie leaned over Emma's shoulder. "Is she always so polite?"

Emma nodded. "Her grandmother told her if she wasn't, I'd send her to a foster home."

"What?" Natalie was horrified. "What kind of . . . ?"

"Exactly." Emma turned, and her eyes met Natalie's. "I'm sure you understand why it's important to us that Winnie feels secure and accepted. She hasn't had any stability in her life, and she's been told she'll be sent away if she says or does the wrong thing. Since there's a very good chance she will leave us sometime in the not-so-distant future, assuming Chris finds her real father and perhaps her mother, we don't want her to believe that it's her fault that she's going somewhere else to live. We want her to know she's worthy of a family, worthy of being loved, and that pretty much everything she'd been taught about her life—that no one wants her, that no one cares about her—has been a lie."

Natalie's jaw dropped while that ugly fact of Winnie's young life sank in.

Emma stood and hugged her. "We're so grateful, Chris and I are, that you're here to help smooth things over for her. By showing up for Winnie, you've shown up for my son and for me, and I'll always be grateful."

Natalie shrank into the embrace, grateful that Emma couldn't read her mind, or her heart, which right at that moment felt roughly the size of the Grinch's before his epiphany.

Chapter Ten

"Wow, this looks nothing like it did the last time I was here." Natalie gazed around Grace's front room, which served as a combination living room, with its white sectional and plaid wing chairs, and dining area defined by a large farmhouse table. She was genuinely amazed by what her sister had accomplished in the old building that had once served as the offices for Liddy's ex-husband's insurance agency. There were green potted plants on the wide windowsills and bright-pink peonies in an old-fashioned crock in the center of the coffee table. A stone fireplace with a thick mantel of dark wood took up much of the left side of the room.

"I know, right?" Grace beamed her obvious pride and pleasure at the opportunity to show off her finished home. "It seemed like it took forever, but now it's done, and I am so in love with my little house."

"I love that you named it the Little House. I saw the plaque by the front door."

"It's how everyone refers to it, so I figured we should make it official."

"Mommy, can I go look at the pond?" Daisy leaned on the wide windowsill and stared out the window.

Natalie hesitated. "Maybe wait until Aunt Grace is finished giving us the tour of her house."

"Uh-uh. I want to go now."

"I think she sees the ducks," Grace said.

Daisy's face was smooshed against the glass. "I think there must be ducks on that pond."

"Okay, but don't go too close to the edge," Natalie said.

"Not to worry," Grace told her as Daisy opened the back door and sped across the patio toward the small pond. "Right now the water is about three inches deep at the edges and not much more than four feet at the center. We haven't had much rain."

"A kid can drown in less water than that." Natalie stood in the doorway and watched Daisy approach the pond on tiptoe.

"She'd have to actually get into the water to drown, and right now it's grossly sludgy and muddy. I know my niece. She's not about to get her fancy sneakers muddy."

"You have a point. She can be a bit of a priss when it comes to her clothes."

"We'll keep an eye on her. We have windows all around the back here." Grace's hand made a sweep toward the back wall, which was almost entirely made of glass.

"Your view is spectacular, the woods, the pond, that field." The natural setting was picture perfect.

"The back of Liddy's house, her carriage house . . ." Grace mused before her expression turned sober. "The carriage house where Jessie decided to die."

Natalie placed a hand on her sister's back for a second, then rubbed between her shoulder blades to offer a bit of comfort. Liddy's daughter, Jessica, had been Grace's best summertime friend from the time they were toddlers until they were in their teens. It had been Grace who'd discovered the reason Jessie took her life.

"I will be forever grateful to Liddy for letting me buy this parcel of land and this little house from her," Grace said. "I can't even tell you how much this place means to me. It's anchored me, Nat. I'm happier here than I have ever been anywhere at any time in my life."

"Is it because of Linc or the house?"

"Linc is the icing on the cake that is my new life." Grace smiled. "But it's more than falling in love with an amazing man who's fallen in love with me. I feel like myself here, like I belong here."

"Do you miss practicing law?"

"Not really. I thought I would. I expected to mourn the passing of that life. The challenge, the drama of the courtroom, the putting together the puzzle pieces of a winning case. But I don't miss it. I barely think about that time in my life, except when I'm cursing out my jackass cheating ex-husband. That all seems so far in the past, even though it was just a few years ago. Right now I'm happy building websites. I know that's hard to believe. I never considered myself even a little bit techy. But I like being creative and giving our local businesses a fabulous platform—and if you've seen my work, you know those websites are in fact fabulous."

"I haven't really had cause to look up any of the shops in town," Natalie confessed, "but I will."

Grace laughed good naturedly. "Start with one of the *Me*s. Dazzle Me. Ground Me. Or the Stroll." The locals' name for the small group of shops behind the center of town. "Oh, and Dress Me Up? That one will knock your socks off."

"I'm making a mental note." Natalie stepped to the wall of windows and looked toward the pond. Daisy had parted the stand of cattails that grew along the water's edge and was peering through the opening she'd made. "I guess she found the ducks."

"Yeah, there's a pair of mallards nesting out there. I've been watching them myself."

Assured that her daughter was safely occupied, Natalie was ready to resume the tour. She gestured toward the wide expanse of windows. "Won't all this glass make the house cold in the winter?"

"Nope. It's tempered, double pane, yada yada. All the things to keep out the cold. Linc's idea. He was high on the technology, so I said,

Sure, order some of those. The only problem is that I could spend all day just staring outside."

Natalie headed into the kitchen, which once had served as the small, dark break room for the Bryant Agency. "And look at you with your granite countertops and all those stainless-steel appliances. Upper cabinets white, lowers that luscious shade of mossy green. Green leafy plants, a copper bowl filled with oranges, African violets blooming in that atrium window overlooking the sink. And OMG, this island! Someone's been watching a whole lot of HGTV."

Grace laughed. "Someone still does. And those countertops are quartz, by the way, not granite."

"Pardon my faux pas. Apparently I've fallen behind on the latest in trendy decor. Thank God there's not going to be a test." She turned to her sister and gave her a hug. "You've done an amazing job, Gracie. It's perfect. No one could have envisioned this would turn out the way it has."

"Linc did the amazing job," Grace corrected her. "He knew what I wanted before I did, and he worked like a demon to get it done for me." She ran a hand over the wood top of the island.

"Oak?"

"Walnut. Last summer, a tree half toppled in those woods out there. Linc went out to take a look to see if something could be salvaged. He saw it was walnut, so we had the rest of the tree taken down and some large sections planed so we could use it here. The island top is actually two solid slabs of wood. Isn't it gorgeous?"

"Beyond gorgeous." Natalie's fingers traced the grain. "That is one multitalented guy you've got. Construction god by day, hit songwriter by night."

"He's one in a gazillion, that's for sure."

"So is he going to think about giving up the construction business to be part of DEAN from now on?"

Grace shook her head. "No. Chris has given him that option, but Linc's content with how things are. He likes working with his hands, likes working in his hometown, being with his family. He said he starts to feel restless if he's away from home for too long. Plus, he wants his dad to be able to retire, which Tuck isn't about to do if Linc isn't around. Linc's afraid Tuck will work himself into an early grave."

"You'd think that having lost his chance to be a rock star when he was in his teens, he'd be happy for the second chance. Most guys would jump in with both feet."

"Oh, he's grateful that Chris is giving him the opportunity to work with him in the studio, and to join the band onstage whenever he wants, but that's not Linc's heart. He's a small-town guy. He likes the slow small-town life. He's said he's not built for the road." She leaned back against the island. "He admitted it bothered him for a time, having given up that chance back then, but his family needed him here. That selflessness is one of the things that first attracted me to him. He leads with his heart, and his heart has no boundaries. That he could give up so much for people he loved, and not be bitter about it—well, like I said, he's one in a billion."

"Actually I think you said *gazillion*," Natalie teased. "But seriously, he must have resented it at some point."

"Oh, sure, when DEAN first broke big and everyone was talking about the band and how they were so good and so cool—that he'd been part of the original group and had quit before they made it? Yeah, that got under his skin. But he said that he knew he could never look himself in the eye if he'd left his father to deal with everything on his own."

"And then his sister rewarded him by dumping her kids on him." Natalie rolled her eyes. "Like the guy can't catch a break."

"He doesn't really see it that way. The money he's making with DEAN has been mind-blowing, and a good deal of it is going into trusts for the kids' educations. He's furious with Brenda for leaving them, but he really does love them, and they love him. Even Bliss, who can be a royal pain in the butt, has come around. She adores him."

"You thinking about marrying him? Having a family together?"

"We're talking about all that. We're both in our midthirties, so yeah, we need to plan ahead," Grace confided. "I think Mom and Brett should be first down the aisle."

"Hey, what about Chris and me?" Natalie poked Grace with her elbow. "Don't be butting in front of us."

"Are you ready to do that?"

"We are. It's just a matter of timing for us, but yeah, Mom deserves to go first. And then there's this thing with Winnie."

"What did you think of her?"

"She isn't what I expected at all." Natalie frowned. "I feel so sorry for her. I didn't expect to, but I can't help myself. She seems so tightly wound, you know? Like she's waiting for the other shoe to drop."

"Ahhh, my sister, master of the obvious."

"Well, yeah, I guess she would be. But . . . I don't know, she seems like such an old soul in that skinny little body. She watches every move everyone makes, like she's trying to figure out where everyone fits."

Grace jumped as they heard the back door slam.

"Tired of watching the ducks?" Natalie asked when Daisy came flying into the room.

"I saw these little fishes with long fat tails," Daisy said excitedly.

"Tadpoles," Grace told her. "They'll turn into frogs soon."

"You have frogs?" Daisy asked.

"I do."

"How do tadpoles turn into frogs? Is it magic?"

"It's nature. Which in a sense is magical," Natalie told her.

"Maybe we could go back to Nana's and maybe Nana Em will still be there and I can play with Winnie. I'm bored."

"Maybe tomorrow."

"Nana Em?" Grace raised an eyebrow.

"Emma's idea."

"What does Winnie call her?"

"She calls her *ma'am*. I don't think she knows what else to call her, and Mom said Emma doesn't want to push it, in case . . ." Natalie glanced at Daisy, who'd taken an orange from the bowl and was kneeling on a barstool rolling the fruit around the island. "In case, you know . . ."

Grace nodded. Emma didn't want Winnie to get in the habit of calling her *Nana* or *Gramma* in case she wasn't going to be staying. In case it turned out that someone else was really her grandmother.

"What does she call Chris?" Nat asked.

Grace shook her head. "I haven't heard her call him anything except *sir*."

Natalie took the orange from Daisy's hands and began to peel it. Damn that Patricia Pine.

What a mess that woman had made. How many other people's lives were going to be disrupted because of her irresponsibility, how many people were deeply hurt because Patricia Pine couldn't be bothered to raise her own daughter? And who doesn't tell the father of her child that he is the father? Who takes off and leaves everyone else to figure out where her child belongs, and to whom? Who does that?

Anger began to build up in Natalie, for Winnie, for Emma, for Chris, for herself, for everyone who'd been drawn so deeply into the woman's drama. They were hapless innocents—people who would always do the right thing—caught like gnats in a web. It wasn't until later that she realized she'd included herself in the list of Patricia's victims.

~

"I took a shower in Aunt Gracie's bathroom." Daisy, her hair still wet, plopped down next to her sleeping mother on the sofa bed where they'd slept the night before. "It was so fun. The water comes at you from everywhere."

"Is that right?" Reluctant to leave the cozy cocoon she'd made in the lofty down comforter, Natalie rose slowly and leaned upon her elbows. Sunlight poured through the windows and spread over the dining area to cast a pale glow across the polished top of the wooden table.

"Uh-huh." Daisy jumped off the bed and raced into the kitchen, where Grace was making breakfast.

"I'll put a shower like that on the list for our someday house." Natalie yawned and grabbed her phone from under her pillow to check the time. Almost 9:00 a.m. Late for her. She checked to see if Chris had texted her overnight, but there were no messages.

"You're welcome to try it out if you can hurry." Grace stood in the kitchen's arched doorway. "We're having french toast, and I'm just about ready to start."

"You two go ahead and eat." Natalie threw her legs over the side of the bed, then stood. "I can be quick."

Ten minutes later, she was back in the kitchen, dressed in shorts and a plaid cotton shirt, her wet hair wrapped in a towel. "That shower is mind-blowing. Big enough for half the neighborhood."

"Well, I'm not sure of the legal capacity, but it accommodates Linc and I quite nicely."

"I bet." The ingredients for french toast were on the counter, so Natalie turned on the frying pan that was still on the stove top and tossed in some butter. "Where did Daisy go?"

"Back out to check on the tadpoles. She called them her 'baby frogs' and wanted to make sure they're still there." Grace took a carton of half-and-half from the refrigerator and placed it on the counter. "Coffee's made. And I'm happy to make your breakfast."

"I don't mind doing it. I just need to heat up the frying pan a bit more." She poured herself a cup of coffee while the butter melted.

"Did you sleep well?" Grace settled onto one of the stools at the island.

"I slept like the dead," Natalie told her. "It's so quiet here. So different from our neighborhood, where you can hear cars going up and down the street at night, radios blaring. The occasional police siren."

"What? You live in such a nice area."

"It is a nice area, but if there's any place in the Philadelphia metro area where there's the kind of quiet you have here, I've yet to find it."

"Wyndham Beach has a very low crime rate. I can't remember the last time I heard a police siren. Oh, sure, every once in a while a couple of guys go down to Dusty's and tie one on and get a little rambunctious. Brett sends out a patrol car to settle them down or takes them home to sleep it off. And we get car accidents, mostly on the highway, people in a hurry to get to the Cape. But all in all, things are pretty low key here."

"Do you ever wonder if Brett misses being a big-time professional football player? I mean, to go from that to being chief of police in a small town like this one?" Natalie shook her head. "It's gotta be a comedown, wouldn't you think?"

"I don't know. Mom said he'd told her that if he hadn't played ball, he'd have gone directly to the police academy. That if he didn't make it in the pros, he'd want to be a cop."

"Mom never says much about the time she and Brett lived in Seattle right after they graduated from college. I don't think she was very happy there. But that wasn't long after she'd had Joe and gave him up for adoption. It had to have been very tough for her."

"And after Mom left him, there were those three marriages of his." Natalie rolled her eyes. "All to petite blonde women. Think he was stuck on a type much?"

"He was still stuck on Mom. Liddy told me that his last wife, Kayla, looked just like Mom when she was younger. I heard she moved to Boston and filed for divorce right after Mom moved back."

"And then he and Mom found each other again. So romantic."

"Except for the fact that our dad had to die for that to happen," Grace reminded her.

"Well, yeah, there is that." Natalie took a few sips of coffee. "Dad would have wanted Mom to be happy. He wouldn't have wanted her to live alone for the rest of her life."

"But do you think he would have wanted her to be happy with Brett? Her first love?"

"I don't know what you feel once you pass over. Maybe he's just happy that she's happy."

"Would you be that generous? If you died, would you want Chris to find happiness with someone else?"

"I don't know." Natalie looked out the window, and Grace laughed.

"Liar. You know you wouldn't."

"Well, I like to think that for a while he'd be distraught without me."

Grace pointed to the stove. "Nat, your french toast is about to burn up."

Natalie grabbed a spatula and flipped the pieces of well-cooked bread onto a plate. "They're still good."

Grace observed the darkened toast and laughed. "If you say so."

Natalie poured syrup onto the plate and was just about to take a bite when her phone rang. She glanced at the screen, then swiped to accept the call.

"Emma, hi."

"Good morning. How's everything at the Little House?"

"Great. We're having breakfast. What's going on there?"

"Natalie, I hate to impose, but I'm going to have to run over to the art center this morning, and I'd prefer not to take Winnie with me. If it's convenient for you . . . if you don't have other plans and wouldn't mind, could Winnie hang out with you and Daisy for a while?"

"Of course. And it's not an imposition, Emma. Daisy mentioned last night that she'd like to play with Winnie, so that'll work out just fine."

"I appreciate it, Natalie. Are you going to be at Grace's for a while? Could I drop Winnie off in about fifteen minutes?"

"Of course. We'll be here." Natalie paused. "Emma, is everything all right? Did something happen . . ."

"No, no. I just have a few things to tend to. Not to worry."

"Well, then, whenever you're ready, bring her over."

"If you're sure . . ."

"Positive. I was going to go to the beach for a while this morning. It's not warm enough to swim, but the girls can play on the sand or look for shells."

"Perfect. Winnie will love that. I'll see you soon."

Natalie disconnected the call and placed her phone on the island. "So you heard that."

Grace nodded. "Daisy will have a playmate today. That's good. It'll give you some time to get to know Winnie."

"I wish she were a little closer to Daisy's age."

"Three years isn't so much." Grace refreshed her coffee.

"I guess. And they did get along well yesterday, so we'll see."

True to her word, Emma arrived fifteen minutes later, Winnie in tow with a tote bag over her shoulder.

"She has some snacks in her bag, a couple of books, and a change of clothing in case they get wet on the beach." Emma stood on the front porch, having declined Grace's invitation to come inside. "I shouldn't be all day, but one never knows."

"Is there a problem at the art center?" Grace asked.

"No, I just feel like I should be spending more time there. You know, in case any of the artists have questions or need something. I did try to think of everything, but who knows?" Emma's response had been a beat or two late, and her laugh held an almost imperceptibly false note. She handed Natalie a key. "If you need to get back into my house for something. Or if the girls get bored at the beach and want to go back there to read or whatever."

"I doubt they'll get bored at the beach, but you never know with kids, right?" Natalie tucked the key into her pocket.

Apparently having seen Emma's car, Daisy came back into the house. "Winnie's here!" She greeted her new friend with a hug, which Winnie returned somewhat awkwardly.

Emma turned to Winnie. "Have a good time with Natalie and Daisy, Winnie. I'll see you later."

"Yes, ma'am." Winnie stood in the middle of Grace's front room, her hair pulled up into a high ponytail, bony knees and matchstick legs emerging from her shorts, her thin arms poking out from the sleeves of a light-blue T-shirt, her face unreadable.

"So, Winnie, you've had breakfast?" Natalie asked as they watched Emma get into her car and drive off.

"Yes, ma'am." Winnie's red ponytail bobbed up and down.

"Would you like to go to the beach with Daisy and me? See if you can find some shells, or pretty stones?"

Another nod. "Yes, please."

Daisy piped up, "Mommy, we don't have a bucket or a shovel to dig in the sand with."

"We'll stop at the general store. They should have their beach toys in by now." Natalie looked from Daisy to Winnie. The contrast between the well-fed, well-loved child with one who'd been, while not starved, probably not provided with the proper nutrition, and who'd been treated like an unwanted burden, couldn't have been more obvious. As a mother, Natalie felt her heart twist inside her chest.

The Winnie she'd imagined and Winnie the real-life child solemnly looking up at her had little in common. Natalie wasn't sure how to reconcile the two, but she understood exactly why Emma immediately had taken her into her heart.

~

The beach was warm if a bit windy, but the two girls found endless ways to pass the time. They stopped at the Wyndham Beach General Store, where Natalie purchased two sets of buckets with matching shovels—blue for Daisy, orange and yellow for Winnie—along with some sand molds Daisy found ("If we build a castle, it will need turrets") and some snacks, cold beverages, and a cooler bag to keep them in. Grace left them there to cross the street to the bookshop, where she'd be working much of the day with Liddy, after promising Daisy a surprise for dinner. Nat turned on Cottage Street and parked in front of her mother's. Maggie's car wasn't in the driveway, so instead of popping in for a quick good morning, Natalie and the two girls walked the half block to the beach. Natalie spread out the blanket she kept in the trunk of the car, and after everyone was slathered with sunscreen, the girls ran directly to the water's edge.

"Watch your feet, girls," she called to them, "or you're going to have wet sneakers."

Daisy pulled off her shoes and left them on the sand, and Winnie followed suit. Already barefoot, Natalie walked to the water and dipped in a few toes.

"Whoa! Cold!" She laughed, and unable to resist seeing for themselves how cold, the girls did the same, screaming with playful exaggeration and gleeful alarm while they hopped up and down and splashed themselves and each other.

When they began to chase along the shoreline, Natalie smiled and walked back to the blanket, content to let them play and get to know each other. She was avoiding acknowledging what her mother had alluded to, but yeah, they could end up stepsisters one day in the not-too-distant future. If they got along now, at least they'd have that when their lives were turned upside down.

How would Daisy adjust to Winnie being Chris's daughter when she alone had played that role in his life for almost two years? And how would Winnie feel upon realizing that Chris looked upon Daisy as his own, that he and Natalie and Daisy had established their own family unit, of which she was clearly not a part?

No more today. Natalie wanted only to rest on the blanket in the warm sun with her eyes closed and her mind blank. Occasionally she'd lift her head to see where the girls were and to ascertain they were still playing without incident, but for the most part, she was happy to be on her beach again for the first time since last summer. Her beach—the Cottage Street beach—where she'd played as a child younger than Daisy, where she'd collected shells to stow away in her suitcase to share with her father when they returned to him and Bryn Mawr at the end of the summer. The beach where she'd gossiped with her summer friend, Jessie, and dug for quahogs, and watched the big boats head out toward Buzzards Bay. The beach where Chris had kissed her for the first time. She'd never forgotten that kiss, and when they finally caught up with each other again as adults, she'd found that his kisses were every bit as wonderful as she'd remembered. Her only regret was knowing that he'd probably shared those kisses with a lot of other girls over the years.

No matter. He was hers now. They had only to pick a date, and then they'd be married and he'd be hers forever.

She was still smiling when her phone rang.

Emma. *Probably running late,* Natalie thought.

"How are the girls getting along?" Emma asked.

"Really well. I haven't heard a peep out of them. Well, except laughter. They've been cracking each other up for some time now."

"That makes me so happy." Emma paused. "Nat, I need to ask you for a favor. Please feel free to say no, and I can . . ."

"Anything for you, Emma, you know that. What do you need?"

"I just had a call from Owen. He's going to be in town for just a few hours tonight, and he's asked me to dinner. I didn't ask, but it would probably be okay if Winnie came with me, but . . ."

Natalie laughed out loud. "No, that would not be okay. I'm sure Owen is looking forward to spending some time with you." She paused. "Does he even know about Winnie?"

"I mentioned her briefly today on the phone, but I didn't go into detail."

"Winnie will be fine with Daisy and me. Not to worry."

"She hasn't been with me for too long, and I'm concerned she'll think I'm running off with a man. You know, the way her mother does," Emma said quietly.

"I doubt that's what she'll be thinking, but even if she did, she'll see that you come home."

"I need to consider how she's going to feel."

"You need to consider yourself, and your relationship with Owen. You don't see each other that often. You need to get dressed up and go out for dinner and have a great time. This is the perfect way to show Winnie that not everyone takes off when they walk out the door. That people who care come back when they say they will."

"That's an excellent point. You're right. I know we talked about having dinner together tonight. Are you sure you don't mind . . . ?"

"Not a bit. I'll take the girls out for dinner or do takeout, and we'll be fine."

"I'm not sure when I'll be home, though. I don't know what Owen has planned, though he did say for me to dress casually. Could you possibly sleep over? There are several unused guest rooms. You can have your pick."

"We could do that," Natalie said without hesitation. "Don't spend a second worrying about Winnie, Em. I've got this."

And for the rest of the day, Natalie did. When the girls began to show signs of restlessness on the beach, she took them to the bookshop, where she bought them each a book. Grace joined them for pizza at Ray's on Front Street, and from there they went back to the Little House. Daisy and Winnie spent an hour watching the ducks and counting tadpoles, then came in for snacks and some quiet time while they all read their new books. Late in the afternoon, Natalie packed up pj's and toothbrushes and clothes for the next day for Daisy and herself and drove to Emma's. For dinner, she ordered Thai, which Winnie had never had but bravely sampled. The pad thai had been a winner, but the curries—both red and green—had been too much for her.

By the time Emma was home and ready for her dinner date, Natalie was feeling pretty good about herself. Both girls had been fed, had baths, were in their pj's, and were ready to kiss Emma good night. She and Winnie had gotten along wonderfully, and she had to admit she was beginning to see the child in an entirely different light, and she couldn't wait to tell Chris about her day. He'd texted her earlier to let her know he was still in the studio but would call her cell around nine her time when they took a break.

Natalie went upstairs and had started to push open the door to the room she and Daisy would share when she heard Winnie's voice.

"I don't know where my mama is. But my daddy's going to find her and bring her back, and we're going to live together, and we're going to be a family. Mama, Daddy, and me. I heard Daddy say it. He's gonna find her, and then we're going to be together forever and ever . . ."

Chapter Eleven

Emma had barely gotten her seat belt buckled before Owen asked, "So how are your Italian lessons going?"

"They're going nowhere." She smoothed the skirt of her dark-blue linen shirtdress. Owen had said casual, but not how casual, so she'd gone with a classic. "I just haven't had time, with the artists arriving last weekend, and Winnie the week before."

"Ah, yes. Winnie. You mentioned her earlier on the phone." Owen came to a slow rolling stop at the corner, then made a right onto the highway. "You promised me a long, complicated story."

"And you shall have one." Emma proceeded to bring him up to date on the saga of Winnie and Chris.

"Did you cover everything? Leave anything out?" Owen cut to the chase. "Or is the bottom line that you really don't know much about this child?"

"I've told you everything we know to date, and yes, that's the bottom line."

"How did the grandmother know how to find you?"

"A few years ago, an article in an entertainment magazine mentioned that Chris's mother still lived in Wyndham Beach, where he grew up. She assumed correctly that I was still there."

Owen's eyes narrowed as he appeared to think through it. "How did she know which house was yours? How did Winnie know which doorbell to ring?"

"I guess maybe she went to one of those websites that look up anyone's address for a few dollars. Anyway, it doesn't much matter how ArlettaJo Pine—that's the grandmother—found where I live. Winnie had my address right, and she rang my doorbell and I let her in."

"And now you're stuck with her."

"Oh, no, Owen. Please don't look at it that way. I don't feel stuck at all. Winnie's a smart little thing, and I enjoy her company. She's had a very hard time for most of her life, but she's coming out of her shell a little more every day. I've grown very fond of her."

"Is Chris equally as fond?"

Emma shifted uneasily in her seat. "He hasn't spent as much time with her as I have."

"You mentioned DNA tests . . . ?"

"He and all his bandmates have submitted their DNA to a lab, and we're just waiting for the results to compare to Winnie's. I gave her old toothbrush and hairbrush to Chris to give to his manager, and she's coordinating the search."

"And if no one's a match?"

Emma shrugged, then stared out the passenger-side window.

"No plan B?"

"No plan B, C, or D. Not even sure about plan A, which is to find her mother. Chris hired an investigator to do that."

"Wow. What a mess." Owen shook his head.

"Mostly for Winnie."

"And for Chris. And for you, Emma. You're the one who's taking care of this girl."

"I'm enjoying it. If you detect anger in my voice, it's for Winnie and all she's been through. It's for Chris, who, if he is her father, has been deprived of her for eight years. If he isn't . . ."

"And if he isn't, and he can't find who is?"

"I don't know, Owen." Emma rubbed her temples, which were beginning to throb. "Could we talk about something else?"

"Of course. I'm so sorry. I should have noticed you were getting a little stressed. What would you like to talk about?"

"Olives."

Owen laughed softly and reached a hand across the console and looped his fingers with hers. "I'm afraid I don't know nearly as much about them as I'd like, but I'm going to learn. Someday I'm going to make the best damned olive oil to come out of Italy. It's going to take a while, though, which is too bad for me, because I'm not a patient person. My trees have been abandoned for a long time, but I've been assured that with the right kind of care, they'll flourish."

Like Winnie, Emma thought. With the right care, the sky's the limit for that child.

"I can't wait to see your olive trees. I've seen pictures, and they always look so graceful." Emma closed her eyes and tried to envision the loveliness of an entire grove of olive trees, branches swaying in a light breeze.

"I'm afraid they look a little scraggly right now, but they won't always. I meant to bring pictures for you and I forgot. Next time, for sure."

"I would love that. Thank you. I'm sure your olive adventure will be successful."

"I hope so. That's my retirement goal."

"I'm not so sure farming fits the definition of retirement."

"It will for me. No more running all over the world. That whole international routine, the travel, the constant meetings—it has grown very thin after so many years. That's been my entire life. Except for my brother Ethan and his family, all my relationships have been business acquaintances. I've never really had a place I thought of as home. I own several houses, but they're all merely convenient places for me to stay from time to time."

"You don't think of the Wyndham Beach house as your home?"

"Not really. I never thought of any place as my home. But the minute I walked into that villa in Italy, something inside of me sighed with relief. Welcome home, it said. I bought it on the spot, and I'm looking forward to spending the rest of my life there."

"I'm having trouble picturing you as a farmer."

Owen grinned. "Ah, but you have to see me as I see myself—in a big wide-brimmed hat and tan cargo pants, walking through the olive grove, picking the fruit to see if it's ripe."

When she laughed, he said, "Hey, scoff if you like, but it's my fantasy, and I'm determined to make it happen."

He pulled into the parking lot behind a small building with weathered cedar siding. There was a sign out front, but it was small, poorly lit, and too far away to read other than one word: LOBSTER.

"What is this place?" Emma leaned forward and squinted, hoping to get a better look.

"Uncle Steve's Place."

"Your uncle owns a lobster shack?"

"No, no. That's the name: Uncle Steve's Place. The home of the best lobster rolls and the best lobster potpie on the planet. And the homemade cranberry sauce? You haven't lived. There's nothing fancy about it, but the food is delicious. They've been locally sourcing since the nineteen forties, when the original Uncle Steve took over that old fisherman's shack and started selling the sandwiches and the potpies his wife made using the lobster he caught and the vegetables she grew. I don't know of another place like it." He turned off the car and got out. By the time he reached Emma's door, she was just about to step out. "And for those of us who like to finish a meal with some chocolate . . . well, you're just going to have to see for yourself . . ."

As promised, dinner had been delicious. Emma went with the pot-pie, fat chunks of sweet lobster encased in a flaky crust, swimming in an herby broth, partnered with fresh carrots, peas, potatoes, and onions, served on a faded melamine plate. The cranberries were tart and cold with just the hint of sweetness and came piled high in a ramekin.

"This is unbelievable," she said after one bite. "Which is not to say I am not lusting after that lobster roll you're eating."

"It's delicious." He grinned. "You don't know what you're missing. But we can come back again, and you can have one if you like."

"That's a deal. But why haven't I heard about this place before?"

"Small place in a small town, and they don't advertise. You have to hear about it from someone else. And now you have." He looked around the room. "A dozen tables, they don't take reservations, and when they run out, they put the CLOSED sign on the door."

"I have to come back and bring everyone I know. And next time I want the lobster roll."

Owen leaned forward and lowered his voice conspiratorially. "Are you sure you want to do that? The more people who know, the more likely they'll sell out while you're waiting in line."

"Takeout?"

"Only between eleven in the morning and two in the afternoon." Owen sat back as the waitress cleared their table of plates and bowls to make way for coffee mugs and dessert. "So what did you think of Uncle Steve's lobster potpie?"

"Hands down, one of the best things I ever ate. It makes me wish we'd just arrived so I could eat it all over again."

"You could have ordered a second."

Emma laughed. "One was more than enough. I'm not sure I'm going to be able to dive into your chocolate whatever, though."

"You can have some of mine"—Owen glanced around for their waitress—"because I'm not leaving here without my chocolate fire and ice. Chocolate ice cream with cayenne pepper."

"Is that really a thing?" She tried to put those two things together but couldn't get her head around it.

He nodded. "Specialty of the house."

"Why would anyone put pepper in their ice cream? Why would anyone even want to? Who would even think to do that?"

"Someone with a good imagination and asbestos lips. But it's a taste treat like no other," he assured her.

The waitress made an appearance, and Owen placed his order, adding, "Two spoons, please."

When the dish of ice cream was set before him, Owen handed Emma a spoon. "Ladies first. Go ahead. Try it."

It sounded like a terrible combination, but lest she look like a wimp, she dipped the spoon into the ice cream.

"Well, it's certainly different," she said after she'd tasted it. "It's very chocolaty, and it's really cold . . . but it has that heat."

"Right. Fire and ice. What do you think?"

"I think it's interesting," she said slowly, adding, "but rocky road is more my speed."

Owen laughed. "I suppose it is an acquired taste."

On the drive home, he asked, "So tell me about your artists' retreat. How's that going?"

"It's going quite well. We'd accepted six, but one had to drop out, so we only have five. All so very different, and all so talented."

"Anyone you think might be a 'name' someday?"

"Oh yes. They're all impressive in their own right. But Eva Sadler—you'll be hearing about her for sure. Remember that name. She paints the most vibrant, energetic contemporaries. Wide swashes of color." Emma paused. "Now that I think about it, her work reminds me of Jessie Bryant's."

"Your friend's daughter? The one who took her life?"

"Yes," she said, pleased that he had remembered. "Jess had that same energy, that same passion. Oh, and Luna Moon. She paints . . ."

"Luna Moon?" His amusement was obvious.

"I know. Raised my eyebrows, too, when she introduced herself. But I get it. I get her." Emma angled her face toward the driver's side. "Her next big birthday will be her seventieth. She has so much natural talent, but she's never had time to flex those artistic muscles. She's spent her entire life caring for other people. Her work takes my breath away. She said she took an unearthly name for her work because she's had to suppress the artistic side of her for so long. While she's here, she wants to be the person she'd always dreamed of being."

"I'd love to see her work since you think so highly of it."

"Come back at the end of August. We'll be having a huge gallery-type showing of the work they've produced over the summer. Most if not all the pieces will be for sale."

"Well, I hope to see you again before the end of the summer, but I will definitely come for that. Maybe I'll find a few things for the villa," he mused. "Ah, now there's a concept: bringing the works of unknown American artists to one of the great art centers of the world. When you set the dates, let me know. I will be there."

She heard a beeping sound but didn't realize what was causing it until Owen apologized.

"Sorry. That was my watch reminding me that I should be somewhere right about now."

"Oh, I'm sorry."

"No need to be. The plane won't leave without me." He smiled, then took her hand again and gave it a squeeze before turning off the highway onto Front Street. "Emma, I'd like to see you more often. It may only be for a few hours like tonight, but I want to see you as often as I can. For the rest of the year, I'll be doing a lot of traveling. I'm trying to set up things for my brother so he can walk into my shoes without missing a beat and the company will not even notice I'm gone. But after that, my time will be my own."

"So you're really serious about retiring this year."

"I'm committed to it. Life's too short, which I've realized all too late. I woke up one morning and bam! I was fifty-five years old and I felt I hadn't lived at all. I'm going to spend the next fifty-five making up for it."

Fifty-five? Owen is fifty-five? Emma had assumed he was at least her age.

"Em?" he was asking as he pulled into her driveway and turned off the ignition.

"I'm sorry, what?"

"I said, I'll be back to see you as often as I can. I like you. Very much." He leaned across the console and kissed her. "I can't remember the last time I felt like this. If maybe ever. I don't think I've ever known a woman like you."

"Well, for the record, I like you, too." She smiled in the dark. "And I don't think I've ever met another man like you."

Least of all the one I married.

"Once I get this elephant off my back—Harrison Holdings—I'd like us to spend more time together. There are things I need to tend to if I'm going to retire on schedule. But if you can hang in there with me, I'll fit in as many trips to Wyndham Beach as I can, as long as you don't mind last-minute dates . . ."

"I don't mind at all, Owen. Right now there's so much going on, between this thing with Winnie, and the art center, the artists, the summer classes . . ." She shook her head. "I'm fine taking it slow, because right now I don't have a fast-forward button. I just need to take things one step at a time."

"Then that's what we'll do. Let's set our goal for the end of the year to have our individual issues wrapped up as best as we can, so we can spend more time with each other. I'll see what I can do to speed up the renovations at the villa. Maybe we could spend the holidays there together."

She shook her head. "Not Thanksgiving or Christmas. I can't imagine not being here for the holidays."

"Of course you would want to be with Chris."

"Oh, it's the whole Christmas thing we do here."

"Well, then, how 'bout we plan on ringing in the New Year in Italy?"

"I like the sound of that. And thank you for understanding. It isn't just about Chris, though. It's Maggie and Liddy; it's Natalie and Daisy. And, of course, if she's still here . . ."

"Winnie."

Emma nodded, wishing she had a crystal ball. Would Winnie still be with them, or would she be seated around someone else's holiday table, her presents under someone else's tree? The thought saddened her, but if it meant Winnie had found her father, and perhaps even a half sibling or two, Emma would be fine with that for Winnie's sake. The child needed stability and to be part of something bigger. She needed to land where she was supposed to be. Hopefully wherever that might be, it would be a place where she was appreciated and loved.

"But maybe you could join us here, if you like. Wyndham Beach is so much fun between Thanksgiving and Christmas. So many events and activities."

"I'd love to be part of your family for the holidays. And after Christmas, we can celebrate the New Year together, just the two of us."

"That sounds very romantic."

"I've never thought of myself as a romantic guy, but I'm beginning to think maybe I've underrated romance."

Owen put an arm around her and leaned in to kiss her. She turned her face up to his and placed a hand on the side of his cheek, and waited happily for the touch of his lips on hers. The only other man she'd ever kissed had been Harry. The last time she'd kissed Owen, he'd outkissed Harry by a mile, leading her to wonder: Was Owen really that good a kisser, or had Harry been that uninspired?

Yes, and yes.

Owen walked her across the lawn and up the front steps, holding hands, and at the door, he took her fully into his arms and kissed her again.

"I'll talk to you this week." He took the door key from her hand and slid it into the keyhole. "Text me anytime. I promise I'll text back. I love hearing from you. I like knowing that you're thinking of me from time to time. I smile whenever your name pops up on my screen. It warms my heart in ways I never . . . well, it warms my heart."

"I'm glad. That makes me happy to hear. I do think about you, Owen. I like knowing I can share things with you. I understand now why the kids are so into texting." She laughed self-consciously. "Not that Chris is technically a kid . . ."

"But he's still your kid. I get it." He unlocked the door, removed the key, and handed it to her, and then he kissed her again.

"Thank you for dinner, and for such a pleasant evening."

"Believe me when I say it was my pleasure."

Emma was reluctant to let him go, so for a long moment, she held on, letting the drumming of her heart flow through her. She kissed him one more time before stepping out of his arms, and tugged on his hand toward the house.

His phone beeped again.

"Someone's getting antsy," she said.

"They can wait."

They said reluctant good nights before Owen gave her one last long kiss, then hastened toward the car, checking his watch as he did so.

She stayed in the doorway until he'd backed out of the driveway, and raised her hand to wave goodbye even though she was pretty sure he couldn't see her. After she locked up, she went into the living room and sat on the love seat and toed off her shoes. She packed a couple of throw pillows behind her and drew her legs up under her and just sat, reflecting.

She liked the fact that he knew he was due elsewhere, had people waiting for him, but hadn't rushed through his time with her. She tried to remember if Harry had ever ignored other responsibilities to spend a few easy minutes with her, but she knew he never had. Owen made her feel important.

She tried to think if she'd ever been important to anyone before. Oh, sure, when Chris was little, she was pretty much his world. She was sometimes treated like a VIP for the mere fact she was Chris's mother. But that was because of who Chris was, and, really, that had nothing to do with her other than a happy accident of birth. Owen was different. He made her feel important. Important enough to interrupt business meetings, to drive to Wyndham Beach to take her to dinner at a place he'd enjoyed and wanted to share with her. Important enough to put his own busy life on hold to spend even just three hours with her.

She'd never come first to Harry. She'd never been worth a pause of his schedule.

Chris. Liddy. Maggie. She knew she meant the world to them, just as they knew they meant the world to her. But Harry? That would be a big fat no.

Tonight had been such a good night, a night filled with the promise of something new and wonderful. She felt like a lighter, happier, younger Emma when she was with Owen. Being with him made her remember what it was like to fall in love and have the world at your feet. The undercurrent that flowed between them made her feel alive in ways she hadn't felt in . . . well, maybe forever. Had Harry lit a spark in her? If he had, it must have been long ago. But Owen lit something deep inside her and gave her a glimpse at a life she thought she'd never have. Listening to him, she could believe he felt the same way about her.

There was such mystique about Tuscany. The capital, Florence, was one of the great art centers of the world, and as an art history major in college, once upon a time Emma had dreamed of going to all the storied art museums and galleries there. Now the thought she might actually go to the Uffizi Gallery and, hand in hand with Owen, see Botticelli's *The Birth of Venus* and Caravaggio's *Medusa*, to the Galleria dell'Accademia and stand before Michelangelo's *David* and look upon that magnificent sculpture . . .

"Emma? Are you all right?" Natalie stood in the doorway, dressed in a DEAN tee and sleep shorts.

"I'm fine." Emma smiled but then realized in the dark, Natalie would not see it.

"I heard Owen's car leave a while ago, and when you didn't come upstairs, I wondered if something had happened . . ."

"No, no. We had a great night." Emma patted the cushion next to her on the sofa. "Come sit. Unless you want to go back to bed."

Natalie walked across the ancient Persian carpet, turning on a lamp as she passed the table on which it stood, and took her place on the sofa, her bare feet pulled up under her, her back against the arm so she'd be facing Emma. "Where did you go?"

"Owen knew of this place where they make the most delicious lobster rolls and lobster potpies."

"Well, a delicious lobster anything would go a long way to make any night of mine great. But I suspect it was the company at least as much as the food."

"Owen is . . ." Emma paused. "A very special man."

"I only met him a time or two, but I thought he was nice. I remember how he brought out the carousel last summer for the kids to ride. Remember how Daisy loved that black horse?"

"I do. She was so indignant when another child rode it." Emma smiled, remembering.

"I guess she'll have to wait another five years to ride it again. That was the deal, right? The Harrisons brought out their carousel for the town kids to enjoy every five years?"

"Actually, Jasper Harrison's will specified it was to be no less than every five years." Emma stared into space for a moment. "Maybe we could convince Owen to do it more frequently."

"I bet you could."

"I'll have to remember to bring it up next time we speak."

"I'm so happy you found someone who puts such a smile on your face. I can't remember ever seeing you so . . . well, you're glowing, Emma. I guess it's tough being alone all these years since Chris's father died."

Emma stared into space. Had it been so tough? Maybe not so much since she'd learned the secret the skunk had kept for all those years. But maybe back after he'd first passed away?

"Oh, Em, I'm sorry. I didn't mean to bring up something hurtful."

"No need to apologize. I was just thinking about how to respond. For a while after Harry died, I did miss him. I'd gone from my mother's house to his, so I had never lived alone. Chris's band was just starting to get real jobs, so I was by myself, and it took some getting used to. Since then, though, I've made a life for myself. So, no, it's not tough at all, being by myself. And no, I don't miss Harry." She added quietly, "I don't miss Harry at all."

"I don't think Chris does, either." Nat's voice was quiet as well.

"I don't suppose he does. You know Chris and his father had a very contentious relationship."

"I know his dad wanted Chris to be a banker."

"Can you imagine Chris in a three-piece suit, in a nine-to-five job?"

Natalie laughed. "Nope. He's right where he always said he wanted to be. And it sounds like maybe you are, too. Though I have seen Chris in a three-piece suit, and I have to say he rocked it."

"Did I tell you Owen bought a property in Italy? An olive grove in Tuscany. He invited me to spend New Year's Eve there with him. That's one of the things I was thinking about while I was sitting here. The thought of going to Florence, seeing all the world-famous art I've only seen in photos, I can barely believe I'll really get to go, to see those museums, the ones I'd read about in college."

"You never went to Italy when you were in school?"

Emma pointed to herself. "Pastor's daughter. We couldn't have afforded it, so I never even asked. You went, though, didn't you? One summer?"

"We'd gone to Europe several times as a family because my dad loved the museums. He'd spend days in the British National History Museum, another full day in the Louvre. The summer I turned seventeen was the first time I went abroad alone. I did an entire semester in Florence and lived with a family there." Natalie closed her eyes, and a smile crossed her lips. "That was the year I knew in my heart that I loved Chris and would never love anyone else the way I loved him." She opened her eyes and grinned at Emma. "And I was certain he'd never love me."

"How wise of him to prove you wrong." Emma leaned forward and squeezed Natalie's hand. "Will we be hearing about a wedding sooner than later?"

"We're working on that, but we need to confirm a few things before we make an announcement. Stay tuned."

"Then I will not pry." Emma's heart still skipped a beat. She couldn't wait to see her son settled down and married to this sweet girl, but she and Maggie both had so many questions. Would the wedding be in Wyndham Beach or Bryn Mawr, where Natalie grew up? As soon as early fall or later in the year in winter or even as late as next year? Would they be buying a house here in town, or would Natalie and Daisy move into Chris's house in Los Angeles? Best to change the subject before she began to sound like a prying almost mother-in-law. "How was Winnie this evening?"

"She was fine. I ordered in some Thai, then we walked down to Jackson's for ice cream and took the long way home through the park. Both girls had bubble baths, watched a little TV, and I read to them before lights out. Daisy wanted to sleep in the room with the blue wallpaper, so I put her in there. I hope that was okay."

"Of course. She may sleep wherever she wants." Emma glanced at her watch. "I was hoping to have heard from Chris by now. I sent him a text this afternoon. Not knowing what's going on is making me nervous."

"Oh, he called a while ago. After the kids were in bed. He didn't have a lot of news, just that his investigator is in Las Vegas and has an appointment with the police department tomorrow morning. He said he'd let us know what the investigator finds. Charlie Gannon is the guy's name, and Chris said he comes highly recommended, so we'll see."

They sat in silence for a few moments, Emma sensing Natalie had something more to say. But a minute later, Natalie stood and stretched and said, "I think I'll go back up to bed now. I'm glad you had a good time, Emma." She leaned over to kiss Emma on the cheek. "And I'm glad you're going to Florence. You're going to love it there."

"I know I will."

Natalie's drooped shoulders as she left the room was a dead give-away that there was something unspoken on her mind. Had Chris said something to upset her? Nat's eyes had lit up when she talked about him, the way they always did. So maybe not . . .

"Sweet dreams, Nat," Emma called after her.

A moment passed before Natalie's soft reply. "You too, Emma."

Chapter Twelve

Emma pressed her fingers against her temples and tried to push back on the headache that had been plaguing her for the two weeks since she'd learned about Stella's court order. She'd tried ice, warm washcloths, and more ibuprofen than is medically approved, but she couldn't banish the pain. She lowered the shade on the lone window in her office, hoping to block out the pain along with the sunlight, but so far it hadn't worked. Nothing had brought her relief since the headache had settled into both temples when she'd accepted the fact that she was going to have to talk to Stella Martin about her husband. Emma had procrastinated for as long as she could, but Brett had been right. If there was a chance George Martin could follow her to Wyndham Beach, everyone at the center had to be on the alert. At the very least, Emma had to determine whether George Martin knew that Stella was there, and if so, Stella had to give a copy of the protective order she'd obtained from West Virginia to Brett so he'd have it on record.

It was a conversation she didn't want to have, but she couldn't put it off any longer. Winnie was on the Cottage Street beach with Natalie and Daisy, and would be there for most of the day, so today was going to have to be the day. There'd be none of the usual interruptions—"Come see!" or "What is this? I found it on the beach!"—all in that sweet Southern way Winnie had.

Bless Winnie. Everything was new and exciting to her. Every shell, stone, piece of driftwood, every gull she encountered on the beach—nothing was too small or too unimportant for her curious mind to turn over a time or two. Emma suspected that prior to her arrival in Wyndham Beach, Winnie's life experiences had been limited. As best as Emma could tell, she hadn't been to very many places other than school and the diner where Angel—and sometimes her mother, Tish—worked. Life in Georgia hadn't prepared her well for life in Wyndham Beach, just as Emma's life as the mother of one adult son hadn't prepared her for instant grandmotherhood of an eight-year-old. She knew the latter could end tomorrow with little more than a phone call from Tish Pine, telling them she'd turned over a new leaf and wanted her daughter. Numbers on a lab report could change things as well, so she was in no hurry for the DNA results. Of course she wanted to know if Winnie was Chris's daughter, but not in the edgy way that Natalie needed to know. She tried not to show it, but Emma could tell Winnie's presence made Nat nervous in a way Emma didn't quite understand, especially since they seemed to get along so well. And since Natalie's place in Chris's life was unquestionably solid, what was there for her to be nervous about?

Voices drifted in through the open door as the artists converged in the exhibition area to discuss how each might like their work displayed at the August showing. Apparently it was never too soon to worry about how one's work was hung.

Emma waited a full minute before stepping out into the gallery area. She made small talk with Pasquale, who complimented her on the accommodations, and Eva, who announced she loved her cabin and could live there forever.

"It's just the perfect little place. I don't need another thing to be happy. I sense there's a story behind them, though. You'll have to tell us some time," Eva said. "Do you think it would be all right if I bought a beach chair so I could sit out there at night and watch the stars? It's so peaceful and beautiful here."

"Oh, of course," Emma replied. "I wish I'd thought to provide them. It's lovely at night as long as the breeze is blowing the right way. The mosquitoes can be quite vicious once we get into July, and not to frighten you, but later in the summer, the greenhead flies are merciless."

"Oh, I grew up in Maine," Eva laughingly told her. "I know when to stay inside, and I know what to slap on my skin to keep those little buggers away."

From the corner of her eye, Emma saw Stella Martin trailing behind everyone else, walking alone, as always.

"I believe the hardware store in town has beach chairs," Emma said.

"Thanks. I think I'll pay them a visit." Eva started toward the door.

"I think I'd like to buy one, too." Pasquale followed her. "Eva, if I could grab a ride with you . . ."

Emma waited until Stella was almost to the door before calling to her.

"Oh, Stella. Do you have a minute?" Emma tried to keep her voice light, her smile casual.

The young woman paused, then nodded. "Sure."

Emma stepped back into her office, holding the door open. When Stella stepped inside, Emma closed the door behind her.

"Have a seat." Emma pointed to the lone guest chair, then realized Winnie's sweater was draped over the back. "Oh, let me just move that. My eight-year-old granddaughter was in earlier."

"Oh, the little girl with red hair?" Stella's voice was soft, melodic. "I saw her yesterday. She was with another child and a woman."

"Yes. My future daughter-in-law and her daughter." Emma chatted casually, hoping to establish some sort of rapport. She thought perhaps the best way to do that was to offer something personal if she was going to expect something personal in return.

Stella sat, her hands folded in her lap, and appeared to be waiting.

"So. How are you enjoying your stay so far?" Emma asked.

"It's wonderful. I love my little cabin, and I love being alone. I mean, having time to myself. To experiment with different techniques. Different exposures."

"Do you work full time?"

"I'd been working for a florist, but I quit to come here. She couldn't hold my job for three months. Too many summer weddings."

"Do you have children at home?"

Another shake of her head.

For a moment, Emma wondered where to go next, how to broach the subject of her being abused.

Oh, hell. Just go for it.

Emma took a deep breath and plowed ahead. "Stella, do you remember the forms you were asked to sign when you were accepted to the retreat?"

Stella shrugged. "I remember there were a lot of them."

"An agreement to a background check was included."

Emma watched the color slowly drain from the young woman's face.

"One of the things that came back was the assault report from the police and the protection-from-abuse order you filed against your husband."

"Ex-husband," she whispered.

"Your application said you were separated." Emma nodded.

"That was true at the time I filled it out. The divorce was final ten days ago." She cleared her throat. "After that incident"—she pointed to the order—"I pressed charges, and he was arrested. He insisted I was lying, of course. There was a trial, and he blew up in court, so the judge sentenced him to ninety days in the county prison. He's still there as far as I know."

"Actually, he's not. He's out on parole."

"He is?" Stella went white. "How could they let him out?"

"I don't know the circumstances, but once I found the order in your file, I had to talk to the police here. The chief called your department in West Virginia and was told the man was free." Damn, this wasn't easy. Emma wasn't comfortable in the role of inquisitor, but she knew for Stella's sake and the sake of everyone at the retreat she had to put it out there. "Does he know where you are? That you're here?"

Stella shook her head adamantly. "Oh, no. God, no. I took every precaution possible to not let him know I'd even applied."

"So you don't think he might show up here one day looking for you?"

"I don't know how he could find me. I was very careful not to leave a trail. No credit cards. I left my car at home and traveled by train and bus. I didn't bring anything he could have planted a tracker into. I left my phone on the kitchen counter and bought a burner."

"Did he know or suspect you were leaving town?"

"I think he knew I wanted to, but I don't think he believed I would do it. That I'd be smart enough or strong enough to go." Shame crossed her face. "I'd tried it before. It didn't end well for me."

"Is that when you filed for the protection-from-abuse order?"

"Not that time." Her voice was barely audible.

"Stella, do you have a copy of your protective order with you?"

"I do." Stella fumbled with the clasp of the bag she'd been holding in her left hand. She opened it with shaking fingers and pulled out an envelope. "Do you need to see it?"

"I'd like you to take it down to the police station here in Wyndham Beach. Ask for Chief Crawford. Leave a copy of the order with him."

Stella stared at her hands, clearly embarrassed. "I'm sorry. I shouldn't have come here. I'd debated for weeks after I saw the newspaper article about the retreat. Three months on a Massachusetts beach. It was as if someone was speaking directly to me. Like, here's your chance. I thought if I could just get away. Just have my life back. To finally be free." She swallowed hard. "I shouldn't have come."

"Nonsense. Of course you should have. But now you need to take steps to protect yourself while you are here, and at the same time protect all of us at the center."

"You think he'd . . . well, of course he'd come if he was out and he knew I was here." Stella's laugh sounded more like she was being choked. "But Mrs. Dean, he's never hurt anyone but me."

"What do you suppose he'd do if he did manage to find you? How would he deal with anyone he thought had helped you?"

"But there's no way he can find me here," she insisted. "I didn't tell anyone I'd applied. I didn't tell anyone I was leaving. No one knows I'm in Wyndham Beach. I can't think of any way he could figure it out."

"Stella, I have to insist that you take that order to Chief Crawford this afternoon."

"All right." She began to gnaw on the nail of her right index finger. "Do the others have to know?"

"I think they should be aware of the situation."

"I'm sorry, Mrs. Dean. It never occurred to me that there could be a problem with me being here." Stella's fingers moved to her throat.

"If he should find you, the police can arrest him for violating the order." Her voice softened. "But they can't do that if they don't have it on file, you understand?"

Stella nodded. "All right. I'll go this afternoon."

Emma stood. "There's no time like the present. Come on. I'll drive you."

For a moment, Stella appeared torn. Then she exhaled, nodded, and said, "Okay. Thank you. Let's go."

~

Emma's head was still pounding when she arrived home from the station after dropping Stella off at the art center. Marion had come in to fill in for the afternoon. Emma had called Brett to let him know she and

Stella were on their way, so he was available to speak with them. He'd listened to Stella's story without interrupting, took notes, and opened a file into which he placed a copy of the protection-from-abuse order from West Virginia.

"You understand this order is only good for ninety days from the date it was signed," he'd said.

Stella had nodded. "They told me I could extend it, but I think I might have to go back to West Virginia to do that, and I'm not sure that's the smartest thing for me to do. Court order or no court order. He has family there."

"I hear you. Your alternative is to file a new order in whichever state you plan to stay in. If it's Massachusetts, I can give you a hand with that."

"But then he'd get a copy of the order, and he'd know where I am, right?" Stella had bitten her bottom lip.

"That's correct. But Massachusetts is a big state, and you have plenty of time to think about what you want to do between now and the end of the summer, when this one expires." He'd turned to Emma. "Thanks for giving her a hand, Em. We'll take it from here."

"What if I filed for an order in Massachusetts and he comes here?" Stella had asked.

"If he's in Wyndham Beach, he's in violation of the order, and he's probably violated the terms of his probation, and we can arrest him." Brett had stood behind his desk. "It goes without saying that if you see him, think you see him, or hear from him, your first call is to me."

"Thank you. I don't think that will happen, but it's good to know there's a plan in case . . . well, in case something crazy happens."

"If I've learned one thing after all my years as a cop," Brett had said, "it's to never rule out the crazy."

"Thanks, Brett." Emma had watched Brett shake hands with Stella before guiding the young woman from the chief's office.

"He seems really nice," Stella had said after they left the station.

"He is very nice, and a very good chief of police."

"You seemed to know each other well."

"We grew up together. Went all through school together." They'd reached Emma's car, and she had used the remote to unlock the doors. "And he's marrying one of my best friends. So, yeah, we know each other very well." Emma had opened the driver's-side door and gotten in. "Gotta love small towns, right?"

"I lived in a small town all my life, until I met George, that is. Then we moved to Charleston—that's the state capital. It's a pretty city, but it wasn't home. I never felt like I belonged there," Stella had said softly.

"What does he do for a living?" Emma had turned on the ignition and backed out of the parking spot, pausing to wave to one of the officers walking across the lot.

"He worked for the city maintenance department. Word got around fast once he was arrested, so of course he was fired. Needless to say, besides being infuriated with me for having the audacity to call the police, him losing his job made him nuts. George tried to deny everything, said I'd made it all up, but they told him he should consider anger management once he gets out of prison." Stella had laughed ruefully. "Like a few hours with a counselor is going to change him. Nothing will ever change him. It would be nice for him and any future relationships he might have, but it's not going to help me."

"I'm very sorry you've had to go through all this, Stella. You seem like a good person."

"Thanks. I used to be. Now I don't know who or what I am anymore." She had turned her head and gazed out the window. "I was hoping to find out while I'm here."

"Have you ever worked as a professional photographer?" Emma had driven through the center of town and had been tempted to drive past her house to see if Natalie and the girls had returned from the beach, but she'd headed straight for the art center. "Your work is so good, so poetic. The photos you sent in with your application had an almost dreamy quality."

"Oh, thank you." Stella had turned back to Emma quickly, her eyes brightening at the compliment. "No, I've never worked professionally. I just took it up a few years ago. I started taking pictures with my iPhone," she'd said almost apologetically. "Then I saved up to buy a secondhand digital camera, and things sort of went on from there. I was hoping to sell some of my photos one day, or find some way to make a living with it."

"There are ways to make a living with a camera besides selling your photos to a gallery."

"I know, but I don't have any education in the field, and I have no professional experience." Stella had sighed. "I guess I hadn't really thought it through very well."

Emma had parked the car and turned off the engine. "I invited you here this summer because I thought your work was extraordinary. If you want to make a living with your photography, you'll have to get creative. It may take a while, but eventually, maybe . . ."

"Thank you. It's nice to know someone believes in me."

The conversation and Stella's dilemma played over and over through Emma's mind all night. The headache she'd had when she'd gone to bed was still raging the next morning, making her snappish and ornery even after she'd had coffee. Winnie was spending the day with Natalie and Daisy again, so Emma left home a little early. She made one stop along the way.

Marion was already in the office when Emma walked in.

"Oh." Marion, seated behind Emma's desk, began to stand. "I thought you weren't coming in till later."

"Don't get up. I just stopped in for a moment." Emma looked out the window toward the little cabins. "I guess everyone's working now."

"I'm assuming. There seems to be a lot of energy among them this morning. They were all chatty and animated on their way back from breakfast a while ago."

"Good." Emma tossed her bag on the visitor's chair and dug in for her phone, which she slipped into her pocket. "I'm just going to walk down to the beach, see if anyone's about. I'd love to get a peek at what they're all working on, if it won't distract them."

Emma left through the side door, slipping her sunglasses on as she stepped into the morning sun. She walked along the dune until she reached the row of colorfully painted little cabins. It always made her smile to see them, the various color combinations giving each little shelter a different personality. There were some in town who thought she'd desecrated the tiny buildings. But others were as amused as Emma to see them standing along the dune, facing the bay, bright multicolored sentries keeping watch over the beach.

If she'd encountered anyone, she'd have stopped to talk. But no one was outside, except for the lone figure who was crouched over something on the sand. Emma walked toward her, trying to make enough noise to let the woman know she was coming, something easier to do on asphalt or concrete, where you could scuff your shoes. Sand was mostly silent. But her shadow preceded her, and the woman rose.

"Good morning," Stella greeted her.

"Good morning to you. Did I interrupt you?"

"No, I think I got the shot." Stella looked down at her camera, smiled, then held it up to show Emma what she'd been working on. "What do you think?"

It took a moment for Emma to realize what she was seeing.

"Oh, this is lovely. The way the sun is illuminating those grains of sand . . . remarkable." Emma looked closer. "Oh, and there are little prisms." She handed the camera back to Stella. "I hope you plan on exhibiting that one when we have our showing at the end of the summer. It's just beautiful."

"Thank you." Stella gazed back at the screen. "It's amazing what you can see through the lens of a camera. The lighting here at different times of the day changes everything. I was just thinking about shooting this same bit of sand several more times as the day progresses. I think it would make an interesting series."

"I'm sure it will." Emma paused, trying to decide how best to approach the subject she'd come to discuss. "Were you able to speak with the others? About the situation with your ex?"

"I did." Stella exhaled deeply. "Everyone was wonderful. They were very understanding and supportive. I'm glad I shared that with them. They all said they'd watch my back."

"I'm so happy to hear that. Now you have any number of people keeping an eye out." Emma's headache began to recede, but she had one other thing to discuss with Stella. "What will you do when you leave here?"

"I have no idea."

"Do you have enough money to set yourself up somewhere?"

"No. I only have a few hundred dollars. Of course, if I'm lucky enough to sell some photos while I'm here, it would help a lot."

"But you'll need a job. What kind of work experience do you have?"

"Not much. I worked in a bakery for a while before I worked at the florist, and I waitressed when I first got out of high school. I did work for a trucking company for a couple of years. I worked in the accounting department. But that was years ago. Why all the questions?"

"I was just thinking it would be good if you could find a job where you could use your photographic skills."

"Well, sure. That would be ideal. But you're talking about, what, newspaper work?" Stella shook her head. "I'd never qualify for a job like that. I'm pretty much self-taught."

"Are you squeamish?" Emma asked.

"What?"

"Are you squeamish? Do you freak out when you see blood?"

"No." She laughed self-consciously. "I've had to clean up my own blood more times than I care to think about. I've even given myself stitches on more than one occasion, so no, the sight of blood doesn't bother me. Why are you asking?"

"A few months ago, Chief Crawford was lamenting the fact that he didn't have a decent photographer on his staff who could take pictures at crime scenes. Oh, nothing terrible happens around here, but there are always traffic accidents in the summer and the occasional burglary, stolen cars, that sort of thing. Wyndham Beach isn't a high-crime area, and I'd be hard pressed to recall any violent crimes over the past five years. Which doesn't mean there will never be one."

"So, your point is . . . ?"

"Maybe you could offer your services to the police while you're in town this summer. Just on an on-call sort of basis. It probably wouldn't pay a whole lot—you'd have to talk that over with the chief, but it would give you experience and a reference for when you move on." Emma smiled. "A reference from Brett Crawford would be a good thing to have, especially if you're going to stay in New England. He's sort of a legend since he played in the NFL for several years. Everyone in law enforcement in this part of the country knows him."

Stella appeared momentarily stunned. Finally, she asked warily, "Why would you care? Why would he do this? You don't even know me."

"Because no one has the right to do to anyone what your ex-husband has done to you. No one. If you need help, I'm happy to do what little I can. But also because I'm the mother of a young man just a little older than you. He's been able to pursue his passion because he defied the man who tried to control him. He's happy and he's successful because he was able to pursue his dream. I see that same passion in you. You deserve a chance, just like my Chris did."

Stella was silent, as if turning Emma's words around in her head. "Chris. Chris Dean? I know who he is. You're his mother?"

"I am. His very proud mother. He could have given in to his father's demands a hundred times, but he held his ground no matter what he was threatened with. He was going to be a musician, and that was that."

"You supported him? Against your husband's wishes?"

"I did."

"How'd that sit with your husband?"

Emma shook her head and was overcome by a feeling of sadness. The arguments back then had been fierce and personal, with Harry often accusing Emma of wanting to see Harry humiliated. Every confrontation had dug a little deeper into the schism that had developed between Harry and Emma. Had that been when the seeds of his infidelity had been first sown, with a wife who defied him to the point he felt entitled to look elsewhere for the support he wasn't getting at home? Had he seen her actions as an excuse to fall in love with a woman who would idolize him the way his ego had demanded?

All these years later, did it matter?

Probably not. She would have supported Chris no matter the cost.

"You know, not all abuse is delivered with a slap or a punch." Stella appeared to study Emma's face.

"Water over the dam," Emma said curtly.

"I'm sorry. I greatly overstepped. I shouldn't have . . ."

Emma waved away the apology. "If you want help, it's here for you. Brett—Chief Crawford—could use someone to take photos for the department when the need arises. If you are interested, you should speak with him."

"Thank you, Mrs. Dean. I will definitely do that. I don't know how to thank you."

"Just be true to yourself, Stella. Find your place," Emma told her. "And stay safe."

Emma felt Stella's eyes on her as she turned her back and walked across the beach. She regretted having snapped, but the woman's comment had hit too close to home. Emma had never really thought of

Harry's loud tirades, followed by long silences and snide remarks, as a form of abuse. It had felt more like punishment, a bully's way of getting his point across, because it had always been about Chris and his betrayal of Harry, his insolence and his selfishness at denying his father the pride he'd counted on as he someday would watch his only son take his place as president of the bank his ancestors had founded. Had Emma felt abused at the time? She couldn't remember having felt anything more than hurt, embarrassed, and confused for herself, but angry on Chris's behalf. Their son was everything anyone could ever want in a child. Why hadn't that been enough for Harry? Why had his expectations been more important than the reality of their beautiful son? It had taken Emma a long time to understand that Harry's ego had taken a blow every time Chris defied him. Chris had refused to be bullied, and he and Emma had both paid the price.

It seemed to Emma that, having discovered Harry's infidelity, she was still being punished. But the pain had been losing its fangs as time had passed. Now she simply did not care.

As for Stella? Maybe Emma had recognized another soul that had been beaten down. Maybe she saw in Stella the beginning of the strength and the will to defy a bully that her own son had shown. Or maybe she was just a kind person who wanted to help a stranger.

~

"Chris called a little while ago," Natalie announced almost as soon as Emma joined them on the patio behind the Dean house.

"Oh? Good news?" Emma lowered herself onto a lounge and slipped off her sandals. "The DNA tests . . . ?"

Natalie shook her head. "Not back yet. I know we're all impatient—especially Chris—but I guess we have to accept that it takes time. Labs are so overwhelmed and . . . well, you know all that. He does think we could get those results any time now, though."

Emma watched Daisy and Winnie playing some sort of game that vaguely resembled tag across the wide backyard. Their laughter traveled all the way to the patio, and the sound made her smile. She thought, not for the first time, about having a play set built back there, with a tree house in one of those old oaks. Winnie would love that, wouldn't she?

"Chris said the investigator reported in. He's met with the police department in Las Vegas. Apparently there are concerts that last for days and raves out in the Mojave Desert every year, and inevitably, there are deaths reported. Some are drug overdoses, some are murders. The Nevada State Police have officers undercover at all of these events. But every year there are reports of missing persons. People who went out into the desert and vanished. The detective he spoke with is newly promoted and sharp as a tack. She told him the reports were always vague, and there'd been no reason to suspect that the missing persons hadn't just taken off without telling anyone. But after his initial call, she started reviewing all the reports for the past five or six years, and guess what she found?"

"Tish Pine?"

Natalie laughed. "No. Well, maybe. She found that something like ninety-five percent of the people who'd gone missing were women. And she discovered by following up with their families, those women are still missing."

"They'd just disappeared?"

"Without a trace, as they say. She also told him there have been rumors of a killing field and a secret graveyard where bodies were buried."

Emma frowned. "I think Chris said he'd heard something about bodies in the desert. I don't remember exactly what it was, though."

"Well, Gannon—the PI—drove out into the desert himself to the area where these concerts and week-long parties took place, and he said if there are bodies there, good luck finding them unless they know where to look."

"That doesn't sound very promising."

"Well, apparently this detective thinks she might have a confidential informant who could be willing to pinpoint locations where some of the bodies could be found."

"So there's already an active investigation ongoing?"

"There is now. The detective said they didn't want to even utter the words *serial killer*, but it sounds like that's what she's thinking. I guess since the city's livelihood depends so much on tourists, they don't want that getting out. Though if they find a bunch of graves, they're going to have to go public with it, give warnings for people to stay away from those events."

Emma sat back and digested this information, her mind racing ahead. If Tish had been one of those victims, would they ever really know for certain?

"Meanwhile, the PI is also going to take a few days to show Tish's picture around to the casinos and the bars and clubs to see if anyone recognizes her. She has bartending experience and has worked as an 'exotic dancer'"—Natalie made quotation marks with her fingers—"in the past, so maybe she found a job and just stayed there."

"So the bottom line is, we may never know."

"No. We might never know." Natalie blew out a long breath. "And between us, I don't know which is worse. To find remains that match Winnie's DNA or to learn that all this time Tish's been living it up in Vegas. I'm not sure which would be more damaging to Winnie."

Emma murmured thoughtfully, "How would you feel if you knew that your mother would rather go on with her life and forget about yours? And what would we tell Winnie, either way?"

"I guess that would depend on whether or not it's Chris's decision to make. If he isn't her father, he won't have to tell her anything. That would be someone else's decision," Natalie pointed out.

"What a mess. Every time I try to remind myself to be charitable to that woman, even in my thoughts, the way I was taught, something like this pops up to remind me why I would love nothing more than to give her a good shake."

"It seems her whole family has washed their hands of her. The PI spoke with her siblings—the ones who would speak to him, anyway. None of them had anything good to say for her. No one seemed particularly upset. They just don't care. The consensus seemed to be that whatever happened to Tish, she'd brought it on herself."

"I wonder if they even asked about Winnie."

Natalie shrugged. "There was no mention of Winnie in the email Chris read to me."

"So I guess no one cares about her or her future."

"I guess not." Natalie brightened just a bit. "But maybe if her father is located and he's willing to take her, things might turn out all right for her."

"Being willing to take her and wanting her are two different things. Something like this could likely turn someone's life upside down. Not everyone is going to want to do that." Emma ran a hand over her face. The headache she thought she'd outrun that morning was back. "I think I'm going to go inside and get a cool drink and some Advil."

She sat up slowly and rested her feet on the ground before she stood. Giggles from the back of the yard drew her attention. She watched the two girls for a few moments before heading into the house, unable to understand how anyone could turn their back on a child who, despite all that had happened, had somehow managed to keep her little spirit bright enough to find joy in every day.

Chapter Thirteen

"Are you sure you're ready to take on all four girls today?" Grace looked out her back door to where Winnie and Daisy had been joined by Linc's nieces, Bliss and JoJo, at the pond.

"Sure. Hey, you're talking to the woman who hosted eight five-year-olds for Daisy's birthday two months ago." Natalie poured herself a second cup of coffee and grabbed a jelly doughnut from the box she'd bought at Ground Me when she'd driven to Liddy's bookstore to pick up the two newcomers to the playgroup.

"Thanks for being such a sport. The babysitter Linc lined up to watch the girls until the end of the month apparently found a full-time gig. Brett's fifteen-year-old daughter, Alexis, arrives in a few weeks from California for the summer, and she'll take over."

"Daisy is so excited that she's coming. They got along so well last year, even with the ten-year age difference." Natalie watched Bliss, who was eight going on eighteen, snap a long-dried cattail and hold it over the pond like a fishing pole. The three other girls followed suit. "What's Linc's nephew doing for the summer?"

"Duffy has sports camps lined up. Baseball, soccer, football. Linc thinks they need to keep him moving—he's an eleven-year-old boy, which I know nothing about, but Linc does. After football, he's going to STEM camp. It's for all age levels, so the girls are going, too. In August."

"Emma said Daisy and Winnie can take classes at the art center in the second half of the summer. Maybe Linc should look into something there for the girls."

"I'll mention it to him. I bet they'd love that if there's a lag in their schedules." Grace glanced at the clock on the stove. "I gotta go. I promised Liddy I'd open up the store for her today. I'm working till two, but I have several websites to finish up, so I might not be back here until four or so. Is that too late?"

Natalie shook her head. "No. I have a full day planned, starting at the beach."

"It's not much of a beach day." Grace nodded toward the sky, where the sun played cat and mouse with big white fluffy clouds.

"They don't need sun to have fun on the beach. Maybe we'll walk from Cottage Street Beach out to the point. The kids like to sit on the dock and watch for dolphins."

"Is it early for dolphins?" Grace rummaged through her bag looking for something.

"Maybe, but they don't know that. Watching is half the fun."

"Keep telling yourself that." Grace laughed and found what she'd been searching for in her bag. She handed Natalie a key. "For the front door so you can lock up on your way out. You can drop off Bliss and JoJo to Liddy at the bookshop later. I'm pretty sure she's staying with Tuck out on the island tonight." Grace grinned and wagged her eyebrows. "Such a scandal! The divorcée and the widower, Liddy Bryant and Tuck Shelby, shacking up on Shelby Island. And at their age! They're old!"

Natalie laughed. "I think the scandal element has pretty much run its course. I think everyone's used to the two of them being together. These things have a way of blowing over. Especially since Liddy's made it pretty clear she doesn't give a rat's ass what anyone has to say about her or her life."

"I want to be like Liddy when I grow up," Natalie said.

"I hope I live long enough to see you grow up." Grace dodged the wadded-up paper towel Natalie tossed at her head. "Missed. Sad that your aim isn't any better than it was when you were eight." Grabbing her bag and laughing, she headed out the front door. "Love you."

"Love you, too." Natalie was still smiling as she watched her sister walk the length of her long driveway.

Natalie was happy for Grace. And Natalie was happy for their mother, too. Maggie was back where she belonged—Natalie sent a silent apology to her father—and she and Chris were back where they had started so many years ago. Who would have thought that Wyndham Beach would turn out to be just what everyone needed?

Natalie locked the front door and went out through the back to check on the girls, who were still "fishing."

"Catch anything yet?" she asked as she neared the pond.

Bliss turned around, a scowl on her pretty face, her disdain for Natalie's cluelessness in full view. "We're not really fishing. We're just pretending."

"I'm really fishing," Daisy said.

"No, you're not. That's not a real fishing pole." Bliss turned to Natalie. "Tell her it's not a real fishing pole."

"Lighten up, Bliss," Nat told her. "It is if she wants it to be."

Bliss rolled her eyes and muttered, "Whatever."

How, Natalie wondered, did an eight-year-old child become so cynical? Had she learned that from her mother before Brenda had taken off for God knows where and left her kids behind?

Natalie debated between driving to the beach, which would take five minutes at the most, and walking, which, with this crew, could easily take more than twenty. She opted to walk, stopping at the general store in the center of town for bottles of water and snacks for later: oranges, apples, and a box of raisins. On her way to the cashier, she tossed in a package of wet wipes for cleanup.

The morning was starting to warm, the sun finally was coming out, and Natalie figured by the time noon rolled around, it would be pretty much a perfect day. The group of five meandered to Cottage Street, and once at the beach, Nat tossed the tote she'd carried over her shoulder onto the sand.

"Guys, you can put your feet in the water, but no higher than your ankles. If you get tired and just want to sit on the beach for a while, I have a blanket. I also have beach towels if you get wet and want to dry off. Now let's see who can find the most sea glass."

As she opened the blanket and spread it on the sand, Natalie watched the girls scatter and kneel on the beach as they searched for treasure. She lay back, arms folded behind her head, and watched the sun dance off the water. She was right: it was going to be a beautiful day. She closed her eyes, mentally scrolling through the online catalog of wedding gowns she'd looked at the night before. So many delicious options! Long sleeves or none, strapless or not, halter or sweetheart neckline, lace or satin, or a combination of both. No veil—she just wasn't the type—but flowers tucked into a slightly untidy bun, maybe. Or a jeweled pin to hold back her hair on one side. She did like that look.

"I don't know where my mommy is," Natalie heard JoJo lament. "She's been gone for a long time."

"Not as long as Daddy," Bliss reminded her.

"I don't have a daddy," Daisy announced blithely, apparently unconcerned by the fact. She never had known her father, so she didn't feel his loss. And for the past year, she'd had Chris, who'd treated her like his own.

Then Winnie: "I don't know where my mommy is, either, but my daddy is looking for her, and he's going to find her, and then we're going to live together and be a family." Winnie's voice was solid and sure.

Oh crap. Natalie raised up on her elbows and tried to see the expression on Daisy's face, but then she realized that Daisy wasn't aware that

Winnie was referring to Chris. It was the second time Natalie'd heard Winnie's statement, so obviously she believed it.

"Hey, look what I found!" JoJo exclaimed, excited about whatever it was. Natalie couldn't see from the distance. "It's a snake." JoJo tossed it away.

"Dummy. It's a shoelace." Even from the distance, Natalie could see the way Bliss dismissed her sister.

"Hey, Bliss. That's not acceptable. No *dummy* talk, do you hear me? No name-calling. It's unkind," Natalie called across the beach.

Bliss ignored her and pretended not to hear.

Natalie's phone rang, and she answered without looking at the screen.

"Hey, beautiful woman."

"Hey, yourself, beautiful man. What's up?"

"Just taking a break and thinking about my number one girl. What are you doing today?"

"I'm on Cottage Street Beach with the girls. Yours, mine, and Linc's."

"Ahhh, the very spot where we shared our first kiss. Revisiting the scene of the crime, are you?"

"I am."

"How's Winnie? You two getting along?"

"Better every day." Not a lie, Natalie told herself.

"That's good."

From across the sand, Natalie heard Winnie say, "He will so find her. He will so bring her back."

Natalie groaned.

"What, babe? What's going on?"

"Oh . . . nothing."

"Natalie Flynn. I've known you since you were a wee tot. I know your voice. I know your moods. What is going on?"

"I really don't want to get into it."

"Nat."

Natalie sighed. "Okay, but remember, you asked." She took a deep breath. "It seems Winnie is under the impression that you're looking for her mother and—"

"I am looking for her. You know I am."

"You didn't let me finish. She believes you're looking for her mother so that the three of you can be a family and live happily ever after."

Silence.

"Chris? You there?"

"I'm here, but I don't know why she would think that. I haven't even told her that we're looking for Tish."

"She must have heard you talking to Melissa or your mom or me, or heard Emma say you were searching, but that's what she believes. This isn't the first time I've heard her say it, so I'm pretty sure it's what she believes."

"And it's upsetting you."

Natalie sniffed back a tear she refused to allow to fall. "Maybe a little."

Chris blew out a long stream of air. "I guess I need to talk to her. We can't let her keep thinking that. It isn't fair to her when we know she'll be disappointed when it doesn't happen. She needs to understand the truth."

"Someone needs to tell her, but it shouldn't be Emma, and it shouldn't be me."

"Definitely not my mom. It's something I need to do, but I wouldn't mind if you were with me for moral support."

"I'm always here for you; you know that."

"I do. Just one of the many reasons why I love you. I know you're always on my team. And I hope you know I'm always on yours."

"I do."

"And Nat—you know that the only reason why I'm spending so much time and resources looking for Tish Pine is because I want to get to the bottom of Winnie's parenthood. I have no interest in Tish beyond that. You're my only girl, Nat."

"I know. And you're my only guy."

"Well, then, we should have a very happy life together, you and me." She could hear that he'd turned away from the phone. "Okay, just a second." Back again. "Nat, I need to run. But I'll talk to you soon, okay? Very soon."

"Okay. Love you."

"Love you, too."

Bless him. Natalie dropped the phone into her bag. Chris always seemed to know when something was eating at her, and he always knew the right thing to say. *He'll talk to Winnie and make certain she understands the situation.* It wasn't fair to let her think there would be a fairy-tale ending with her mother and Chris. For Winnie and Chris . . . maybe. But Tish wasn't going to be in the picture, and somehow Chris was going to have to make her understand that.

∼

Two days later Natalie was in Emma's kitchen with Winnie and Daisy readying for their trip to the bookstore. Saturdays were story-hour days at Liddy's store, and it was Grace's job to read to the children who gathered at 10:00 a.m. to sit on the floor and hang on every word that fell from Grace's lips. She dressed like Mary Poppins and fell into the role naturally. It was the part of her job she loved the most, she'd told Natalie.

She'd just picked up her bag and slipped on her sunglasses when she heard a car horn beep from the driveway. She glanced out the kitchen window in time to see a blond-haired man get out and walk toward the house.

"Chris!" Natalie rushed to the front door and swung it open, then ran across the yard to jump into his arms.

Daisy went to the door. "Chris is here! Yay!" she yelled and started to follow her mother out the door, as Natalie expected her to do, but Emma held Daisy back.

"You didn't tell me you were coming home this weekend," Natalie said between kisses.

"I wanted to surprise you." He swung her around.

"Did your mom know?"

Chris set her feet back on the ground. "She did. Actually, I met up with my mom earlier this morning."

"She didn't mention it." Natalie frowned. "Why wouldn't she tell me? And it must have been much earlier. It's barely nine thirty."

"I asked her not to say anything. I met up with her when she went to Ground Me to pick up those doughnuts I expect you made short work of."

"Why all the secrecy?"

"It wouldn't have been very romantic for my mom to dash out of the house, slap this into my hand, and rush back inside. Might have been a mood breaker."

Natalie laughed. "What are you talking about? Slap what into your hand?"

"This." Chris went down on one knee.

"Oh my God, Chris."

"Natalie Lloyd Flynn, I have been in love with you for so long, I can't even remember when I first knew. Maybe the night we sat on the rocks and watched for shooting stars."

"Chris, no." She tugged at him.

"No, that wasn't when I fell in love with you?" He frowned.

"No, I mean don't kneel." Natalie's emotions got the best of her, and she burst into tears. "It means you're begging me, and you don't have to beg." She tried to pull him up, but when she realized he wasn't budging, she knelt down in front of him.

"I'd beg you to marry me if I had to. I'd do whatever it would take, Nat. You and me, we were meant to find each other again. That day when I made Gracie go to Dusty's with me to have a beer—remember? You and I hadn't seen or spoken to each other in years, but I made her call you, FaceTime with you, because you were in my head so much. I had to see your face, to see if it was all real. I took one look at you, and I knew why you were still with me. It's always been you, Natalie."

"It's always been you for me, too, Chris," she said through her tears.

"So . . . ?"

"So what?"

Chris laughed. "So will you marry me?"

"Oh my God, yes! Yes!" She put a hand on either side of his face and kissed him. "A million times yes!"

"You haven't even looked at the ring." He tapped her left ring finger.

She took her first good look at the platinum band on her hand. The large center diamond was set slightly higher than the two light-blue stones on either side. Natalie didn't know much about gemstones, but she knew Ceylon sapphires when she saw them. "Oh, it's gorgeous! Oh, Chris . . . it's just beautiful. I've never seen a ring like this."

"It was my grandmother's engagement ring. Before she died, she told me she was saving it for me so that someday I would give it to a woman I loved as much as my granddad loved her." He brushed the tears from Natalie's face, then from his own. "And that's what I'm doing."

"Aw, Chris . . ." The tears began again.

He was kissing away the tears when they were both rocked by something that felt like a small runaway sedan. "Oof!"

Daisy landed on them at the same time. "What are you guys looking for in the grass? I can help."

"Life with a five-year-old," Natalie told him. "I guess you'd better get used to it."

"I'm already used to it." He laughed. "I just wasn't expecting to be blindsided."

"Sorry, you two." Emma followed Daisy across the front lawn. "I tried to keep her in but she just bolted."

Chris stood and pulled Natalie with him.

"Natalie, I hope you know how happy this has made me." Emma, too, was misty eyed.

"Thank you, Emma." Natalie returned the hug. "Does my mom know?"

"No, I thought you'd want to tell her yourself."

"I do, thank you. But how did you keep this a secret?"

"Willpower. Lots and lots of willpower. But I had to tell Gracie. I knew we needed to have the ring sized down to fit you—Mother Dean had larger fingers than you—but I had no idea what size, so I had to ask someone."

"Which explains why the ring fits so perfectly." Natalie held out her hand to admire it. "It's the most beautiful ring I've ever seen. But I can't believe my sister knew and didn't even give me a hint."

"Linc bribed her with the promise of a trip to Paris when the album is finished," Chris told her.

"Huh. Good to know my sister can be bought with a plane ticket."

"I want to see." Daisy grabbed Nat's hand. "Ooh, it's so sparkly!" She touched a small fingertip to the diamond. "Can I wear it?"

"That would be a big fat no." Natalie turned to Chris. "We should go inside. People are driving by, and they're going to figure out what you were doing down there on one knee. Before you know it, photographers from *People* magazine will be on the front porch."

"I don't care. We'll announce it ourselves. Here, stand right here and hold up your hand." With one hand he pulled his phone from his pants pocket, and with the other he held up Natalie's left hand. Before she could move, he'd taken the picture. "This is going right onto Twitter. And Instagram."

"Oh no. No. Look at my hair . . . and my clothes! I'm not dressed for a PR shot, Chris," she protested.

"I don't want a PR shot. I want our shot. And I think you look gorgeous. There's nothing wrong with your hair—that ponytail is you." He gave it a tug. "And you're dressed just fine. Shorts, a tank top. Sandals. Just right for an early summer day in a beach town."

"But someone will see it and tell my mom."

His fingers had been tapping away on his phone for a few seconds, but he stopped.

"You're right. I'll save it till after we tell Maggie." He returned the phone to his pocket. "When do you want to tell her?"

"Let's see if we can have dinner with her and Brett tonight, and we'll tell her then." Natalie imagined the look on her mother's face when she saw the ring on Natalie's finger. She'd be ecstatic.

"Good plan," Chris agreed.

"Have you thought about a date?" Emma asked.

Natalie shook her head. "We haven't had time."

"I have," Chris told her. "I was thinking Labor Day weekend."

"Labor Day weekend? Are you serious?" Nat stopped in her tracks. "That's, like, two months away."

"The rest of June, July, August. Yeah."

"Do you know how much time it takes to plan a wedding?"

"No clue."

"It'll take months. I can't possibly put together a wedding in two months, Chris."

"Sure you can. Look at the crew you have to work with." He nodded in the direction of his mother. "You've got my mom, your mom, Liddy—that's the big three right there. And you've got Gracie."

"But why so soon? I mean, you know I want to marry you, but a big wedding takes a long time. Why can't we put it off till maybe Christmas? I mean, even that's not much time, all things considered, but we could do a gorgeous winter wedding." She was already picturing the altar at the church in town alive with red poinsettias. Or maybe all white ones. A white winter wedding could be just stunning.

"I have a lot coming up over the next year—a new album, a tour, all the promotion that comes with the territory—and I know that I want our wedding to happen before all that madness begins, because I want to have some time to focus on you. On us. I don't want to be looking over my shoulder to see who I have to talk to or where I have to be."

From the tone of his voice, Natalie could tell how much thought he'd put into timing his proposal, and how much it meant to him.

She smiled and nodded, her fantasies of a poinsettia-covered altar fading fast. "All right. I'll think about Labor Day weekend. We'll talk about the details later."

"You know, it doesn't have to be a big wedding," Chris suggested.

"Are you kidding?" Emma spoke up. "This is Wyndham Beach. Our families have been in this town for centuries. There is no way we could leave anyone off the guest list, Chris. I don't want anyone's feelings to be hurt because their neighbor was invited and they weren't." She paused. "I'm sorry. I know it's your wedding, but I'm just thinking . . ."

"No, no, Mom. You're right to point that out. You and Maggie invite whomever you want. We'll figure it all out."

When they'd gotten as far as the front porch, Chris stopped and looked around. "Where's Winnie?"

"She's upstairs," Daisy said. "I told her to come outside with me but she just ran up the steps and went in her room and closed the door."

Emma glanced at Daisy, then said, "Daisy, please go inside and . . . and see if you can find my phone for me. I'll be just a minute, and when I come in, we can make chocolate milk."

Daisy skipped up the steps and into the house. When she was safely beyond hearing, Emma said, "Winnie saw you pull up, and she looked about to run outside to see you when she saw you with your arms around Natalie, and you were kissing. Then you went down on one knee, and I guess she figured out what was going on."

Natalie turned to Chris. "I told you what she was thinking . . . that you would find her mother and . . ."

"And we'd live happily ever after, just the three of us." Chris blew out a very long breath. "I'll go up and talk to her."

Emma said softly, "She believes you are her father, you know."

"Well, that's the other reason why this weekend was a good time to come home." Chris looked from his mother to his fiancée and back to his mother. "Melissa called when I was on my way here this morning. The DNA tests are back. I'm not Winnie's father."

Everyone fell silent for a long moment. Then Natalie said, "Maybe someone in your band, or someone on your crew back then . . ."

Chris shook his head. "Melissa tracked down everyone who worked with us that year and had them test as well. She sent them to the lab along with the swabs from the guys in the band. There wasn't a match to anyone."

"So how do we tell Winnie?" Natalie thought aloud.

Emma sat on the top step, as if all the wind had been knocked out of her lungs. "How do we tell her . . . oh Lord, she's been doing so well here. She's . . . oh, dear . . ."

"Maybe we shouldn't tell her," Chris said softly.

"How can you not tell her?" Natalie asked. "Should she know?"

"We just don't tell her, that's how."

"Is that the right thing to do?" Emma's expression clearly defined her confusion.

"Look, on the one hand, Winnie should know who her parents are. She has a right to that information." Natalie sat next to Emma. "On the other hand, we don't know who her father is." She looked up at Chris, who was obviously as torn as Emma. "But we can't really tell her that. She's only eight. How could she understand something like that at her age? She's been told by her mother that you are her father, so we tell her you're not, so she either won't believe us . . ."

"Or she'll think we're just trying to get rid of her, the way her grandmother did," Emma said, still rubbing her head slowly.

Natalie nodded. "Or she'll think there's been a mistake, or that you're lying. I don't think she'll take it as truth, because that would mean that, on top of everything else, her mother was a liar. Which we know she is, but we don't have to beat Winnie over the head with that." Natalie felt an unexpected desire to protect Winnie from being hurt more than she'd already been, but she was at a loss to know how to go about doing that.

"You know, when Winnie first came here, she had to have been scared out of her wits. Look at all she'd been through. Tossed back and forth between her mother and her grandmother, then her mother's friend. Put on a long bus ride alone—at eight!—going who the hell knew where. She's dropped off here somewhere, made her way to this house, and stood on this porch and rang that doorbell without knowing what awaited her on the other side. I bet she was expecting more of the same. Another adult who didn't want her. Someone else she couldn't depend on. Someone else she might want to trust but who'd let her down and hurt her little heart all over again." Emma slapped her thigh. "We can't send her away, Chris. She's happy here. She's adjusted to being here. I've grown so fond of her. She's delightful and smart and oh, Chris, if you don't want her, she'll stay here with me. We have to keep her, one way or another."

"I didn't say I didn't want her. Of course we're going to keep her with us."

Chris sat next to Natalie, and it was apparent he was deep in thought. "I still don't really know her very well, so it's tough for me to say what I want. But I do know what I don't want: I don't want her hurt more than she's already been. Mom is right about that. But should I lie to her and tell her I am her father? And, keep in mind, we don't know where Tish is, or even if she's alive. There's a chance she may not be. Gannon reports that the Las Vegas police are running DNA tests on some remains they've found. We've had the lab we used send Winnie's DNA to their lab. So supposing we find out for sure that Tish is dead, and we have to tell Winnie, and that comes on the heels of me telling her I'm not her father, and no, kid, we don't know who is."

"So just not tell her for now? Just not address it directly?" Natalie asked. "And, you know, there's always the possibility that Tish is still alive. She might someday have a change of heart and want her daughter back."

"I would be shocked if that happened." Still, Emma looked worried at the very thought of Tish coming back into Winnie's life.

"I don't think we can plan for every possible contingency. I think we just need to decide how we're going to proceed from here, then stick with it." Chris's voice softened even more. "And you know the chances that someone—anyone—finding out about her now and being willing to step up are very slim."

"You did," Nat pointed out. "You're willing to step up, even now, even knowing you don't have to."

"Ah, but I do. I can't not."

Natalie kissed him full on the lips. "Thank you for being the kind of man who would do that." She turned to Emma and kissed her cheek. "And thank you for raising a man who steps up even when he doesn't have to."

Emma cleared her throat. "I'm a very proud mom. I've always been proud of you, Chris. Especially now."

"Stop. You're making me feel like I should be tracing a line in the dirt with the toe of my shoe and muttering 'Aw, shucks.'" He stood. "I should go speak with Winnie."

"What are you going to say?" Emma asked.

Chris shrugged. "I have no idea."

"Do you want to go it alone, or would you like me to come along?" Natalie asked.

"I'd appreciate the backup," he told her. "Just in case I can't find the words."

"You? Not find the words?" She smiled, hoping to lighten the mood. "You're a songwriter. You'll know what to say."

And he did. Chris and Natalie went up the steps after settling Daisy in the kitchen with Emma, a glass of chocolate milk, and a cookie. Chris knocked quietly on Winnie's bedroom door, and waited. When there was no reply, he said, "Winnie? May we come in?"

After what seemed like a long moment, they heard her resigned "Okay."

Chris pushed open the door and, followed by Natalie, stepped into the room. Winnie was standing dead center, as if to meet them head-on, her feet planted solidly apart, almost in a battle stance.

"I haven't been in this room in a long time," Chris said. "My great-aunt Rosie used to stay here when she came to see us. She was my grandfather's sister, and she always visited in the summer, and she always stayed in this room 'cause it had been hers when she was growing up."

"Where'd she come from?" Winnie asked, her Georgia accent more pronounced than Natalie had recently noticed.

"She lived in Iowa. Do you know where that is?"

Winnie pointed to the map of the United States on her wall. "It's right here."

"That's right, it is." He walked to the map. "This is a great map, but I don't remember seeing it before."

"Miz Liddy gave it to me. At the bookshop? She owns all the books and things, so I guess she can give stuff away if she wants."

"I'm sure she can. That was nice of her." Chris pointed to the chair in the near corner. "Is it okay if I sit?"

Winnie nodded and appeared to be bracing herself for something that she thought might be bad.

"We—Natalie and I—were hoping you would come outside with my mom and Daisy before. I had a big surprise for Natalie, and I wanted to share that with everyone. With you, too."

When Winnie did not comment, Chris continued. "I proposed to Natalie. Do you know what that means?"

Winnie nodded. "Mama and Angel always watched *The Bachelor* on TV. The last show, the man always kneels down and gives the lady a ring. I saw you . . ." She pointed to the window, meaning outside.

"But do you know what it means, to propose to someone and give them a ring?"

Natalie couldn't tell if Winnie knew and didn't want to say the words, or if she didn't know and was waiting for an explanation.

Chris didn't bother to wait. "It means I asked Natalie to marry me, and she said yes."

Winnie's bottom lip began to tremble. "I thought you were going to find my mama. I heard you say someone was going to find her."

"We do have someone looking for your mama, Winnie," Chris said as gently as possible, "but not so that I can marry her. We want to find her to make sure she's all right, because no one's heard from her in a very long time. You know that, right?"

Winnie nodded.

"What happens if you never find her?" Winnie's question was barely more than a whisper.

"Then you stay right here." Chris got off the chair and sat next to Winnie on the bed. "You stay right here, okay?"

Another nod, this one uncertain. "Will you be here?"

"Well, not for a while. Right now, you'll be staying with my mom and Natalie, because I'm working a lot and I'll be traveling some. But then I'll be back here, with you, and my mom, and Nat and Daisy. Is that okay?"

Winnie nodded with a little more enthusiasm than she'd shown since they'd entered the room. "I'd like that."

"Then that's the plan, right?"

"That's the plan," she repeated.

"Now let's go downstairs. I think I heard my mom and Daisy talking about chocolate milk and cookies . . ."

Winnie was the first out the door and the first one on the stairs.

"See, you didn't need me at all." Natalie whispered to Chris.

"I always need you." He took her hand as they began the downward climb.

Neither of them mentioned the fact that Chris had neither confirmed nor denied he was Winnie's father. The word had never been mentioned, and they were both okay with deferring that part of the conversation for another day.

~

"Mommy, we were supposed to go to the bookstore! Aunt Gracie was going to read us a story." Daisy turned to her mother accusingly and said, "You forgot!"

"I did, and I'm sorry. We can stop by the bookstore later and buy a copy of the book for you." Natalie corrected herself. "Two copies, because Winnie didn't get her book this morning, either, and we can read it later."

"It's not the same as having Aunt Gracie read it to us." Daisy looked like she was working up to a full-blown pout.

"Maybe it's a book I can read to you." Winnie sat across from Daisy at the kitchen table. "I know how to read."

"You're not a grown-up." Daisy blew bubbles in the last of her chocolate milk with her straw.

"You don't have to be a grown-up to read. You just have to . . ." Winnie shrugged. "To read."

"Winnie taught herself how to read," Emma announced.

"You did?" Chris looked impressed. "How did you do that?"

Winnie shrugged again. "I just read what was on the pages."

"Wow. That's awesome, Winnie." Natalie, too, was impressed. "Absolutely awesome."

Natalie was about to ask how Winnie knew to make sounds from letters when her phone rang. She glanced at her phone and brightened. "It's Mom. Hello, Mom. I was going to call you in a few minutes."

"We must be on the same wavelength this morning. How come you didn't make it to the bookstore? I thought the girls were looking forward to Grace's story hour."

"They were. My fault. Mom, Chris surprised me and came home this weekend. We thought we might all have dinner together. We haven't all been together since Christmas."

"Hi, Chris . . ."

"Chris, Mom said hi."

"Hi back, Maggie," Chris called from across the room.

"Actually, I was going to call you and see if you all wanted to have dinner here at the house. Linc showed up this morning while Grace was reading, and I thought she'd fall off her chair." Maggie laughed. "It was so cute, Nat. She blushed and stumbled over a few words before she caught herself."

"He must have caught a ride with Chris." Natalie looked across the room to Chris, who was apparently following her part of the conversation. He nodded and gave her a thumbs-up. "Chris just confirmed."

"So nice. Both my girls got a nice surprise this morning. If you don't mind sharing your guy, I hope you'll join us tonight."

"Of course. Looking forward to seeing you and Brett and . . . oh, everyone together."

"Me too, sweetie. Let's make it seven o'clock."

"Perfect. Want us to bring wine?"

"Not necessary. Just bring yourselves. See you then." Maggie disconnected before Natalie could even say goodbye.

"This is perfect. We can announce our engagement and our wedding date at dinner tonight." A beaming Natalie put her phone on the counter. "My mom is going to be so excited. I can't wait to see the look on her face when we tell her."

"It's gonna be epic." He beamed back.

Nat turned to the two little girls and said, "But you can't say anything to anyone, understand? Until Chris and I tell Nana tonight ourselves, you can't say a word about Chris giving me a ring or about us getting married. Promise?"

Daisy and Winnie nodded.

"Pinky promise." Natalie held a hand out to each girl. Winnie grabbed Nat's little finger with her own, but Daisy was slower to act. "Daisy . . . pinky promise."

Natalie knew her chatterbox daughter loved to be the bearer of good news, but this time she was going to have to zip it.

"Okay." Daisy complied somewhat reluctantly.

Chris was still smiling. "This is going to be fun."

~

Chris drove Emma's car to Cottage Street so his mother could sit between the girls in the back seat. Daisy chatted incessantly, Winnie occasionally chiming in with an observation of her own. Natalie was glad to see Emma happy and relaxed with the two children. She'd thought that Emma had been somewhat tense over the past week, but Nat chalked that up to her being so busy with the artists' retreat. Surely the uncertainty of Winnie's situation had been preying on her mind as well, but now perhaps she could relax and not worry as much about having to deal with the girl being sent elsewhere. Right now, everyone seemed to be okay with the way things were playing out, and all things considered, that was probably as good as it was going to get.

Maggie and Brett were in the kitchen, setting out hors d'oeuvres on the island. Linc and Grace were there, Grace helping by setting out champagne glasses. Daisy and Winnie went straight out to the backyard to see the koi pond Maggie had put in the previous week. Natalie kept her left hand turned so that her ring wasn't visible. She wanted to make an announcement before the ring caught anyone's eye.

"Oh, champagne." Natalie grinned as she hugged first her mother and Brett. "So I guess we can celebrate something tonight."

"We can," Brett said.

"Don't start without me," Liddy called from the front hall. "Am I late? I walked from the shop. I thought I'd probably toss back an adult beverage or two tonight, so I left the car at home this morning."

"You're right on time." Maggie took a baking sheet from the oven and placed it on a cooling rack.

"Ooh! Baked brie. My favorite," Natalie said. "Did you use cranberries or roasted onions under that crust?"

"Fig jam," Maggie replied.

"Even better." Natalie opened a box of crackers and arranged them on a plate just as Brett popped open one of the bottles of champagne. She turned and winked at Chris. This was going to be more fun than she'd imagined.

"Natalie, would you please open that jar of olives and put some in this bowl?" Maggie pointed to the jar on the counter. "And, Gracie, find that package of cocktail napkins. They're in one of those drawers near the sink."

Brett quietly filled the glasses with champagne and began to pass them around. Natalie waited until Chris was at her side, his arm around her waist, before opening her mouth to speak.

Someone else spoke up first.

"Everyone," Brett was saying, "I want you all to be the first to know that I've asked Maggie to marry me, and she said yes. So after a forty-something-year wait, Maggie will finally become my bride."

Momentarily stunned, it took Natalie a few seconds to recover. Chris tightened his grip on her waist, and when she looked up at him, she could see the question in his eyes. She shook her head almost imperceptibly, and he nodded in understanding. She couldn't announce her engagement tonight and steal her mother's thunder. Maggie looked gloriously happy, and Natalie would not infringe on that joy. There were squeals and hugs as Maggie showed off the ring Brett had placed on her hand. It wasn't as big or as flashy as the one Art Flynn had given her so long ago, but Natalie knew her mother wouldn't give the size of the stone a second thought: Maggie was finally going to marry her first love. Toasts followed, with everyone taking a turn at expressing their joy and best wishes.

Natalie wore her biggest smile and hugged her mother, then Brett, still trying to hide her left hand. "I'm so happy for you both."

"Thank you, sweetheart. I'm happy for us both, too." Maggie laughed.

"So when's the big day?" Linc asked.

"Brett wanted the Fourth of July," Maggie said. "I tried to talk him into waiting a little longer."

"Till . . . ?" Liddy asked.

"Labor Day weekend," Brett told them. "Sunday of Labor Day weekend."

For the second time in under two minutes, Natalie's jaw dropped. What were the odds her mother and Chris would want the same weekend? Chris was doing his best not to look as horrified as he must feel.

"But I was able to convince her there was no point in putting it off much longer," Brett was saying. "And she was able to convince me she needed a little more time to plan. So we've compromised. It's going to be the last weekend in July."

Natalie thought she would pass out—with relief. She still favored a Christmas wedding—so much to do!—but all the same, she could have kissed Brett. Then she did just that. "Good for you, Brett, and

congratulations for being one of the very few people who could get my
mother to change her mind about . . . well, just about anything, because
the rest of us rarely could."

"Hey, what's everyone doing?" Daisy stood in the doorway, looking
over her celebrating family.

"We're going to have a wedding this summer," Grace told her
happily.

Daisy nodded. "I know. Chris gave Mommy a big sparkly ring."
She went to the island and climbed onto a stool. "Mommy, is this the
kind of olives I like? Winnie, do you like olives?"

The entire group fell silent. Everyone turned to look at Chris and
Natalie, who were both feeling a bit sheepish.

Finally Maggie broke the silence. "Natalie, is there something you
want to tell us?"

Natalie sighed and held up her left hand. Chaos in the form of
cheering, kissing, and hugging followed, everyone wanting to see the
ring and congratulate Chris and Natalie.

"Sweetie, when? And why didn't you tell me immediately?" a clearly
happy Maggie demanded.

"I was going to, but . . ."

"But you didn't want to detract from our announcement."

Natalie nodded.

"No need to worry, my love." Maggie enfolded Natalie in her arms.
After a second or two, she reached out to Chris and brought him into
the fold. "I couldn't be happier. This is the best night ever. The absolute
best."

Chapter Fourteen

"Oh, Preston," Emma called out from her desk at the art center when she saw the tall man walk past the office. She stood and met him in the doorway. "I was just about to come looking for you. You had a phone call earlier. Your son has been trying to reach you."

He took his phone from his pants pocket and his glasses from his shirt. "Guess I forgot to charge the battery. I let it run down and didn't even realize it," he admitted a bit sheepishly.

"Not to worry. I do that all the time. You can use the desk phone," she told him as she stepped out into the large room that served as exhibition space.

"Thank you, Emma. I'll be but a minute."

"Take your time." She walked farther into the space, trying to envision how she'd set up for the local artists' exhibition scheduled for the Fourth of July weekend. She'd scheduled that before she'd gone whole hog into her dream of having an artists' retreat, and now she had both. It had seemed like a good idea at this time last year, when she had nothing else on her mind. No Winnie, no evidence that her husband had been a cheating jerk, no Owen, no wedding on the near horizon, no five artists practically living in her back pocket for the entire summer.

"What was I thinking?" she muttered.

"Sorry?" Luna Moon, who'd been walking through the room, had apparently overheard Emma's grumblings. "Were you speaking to me?"

"Oh, no, Luna. I was talking to myself." Emma laughed, embarrassed to have been caught, but a lifetime of good manners forced her to engage. "How is the work going? Are you finding it easy to work here, or is it distracting to be someplace new? Or doesn't it matter?"

"Oh, it matters. So much. I admit to having been distracted for the first two or three days, but not in a bad way. The town is so pretty, and I've never really been away from home, from my family," she explained. "So new surroundings, new people—everything's fascinating because, well, it's all new. I've always dreamed of living near the sea, so to fall asleep at night listening to the waves lapping at the shore, wake in the morning to the sound of squabbling gulls, the smell of salt water, the morning light just peeking through that front window." Luna rolled her eyes. "Heaven. It's absolute heaven. And I could live in that tiny house forever. Why, I've seen apartments in New York that weren't half that size."

"Well, I'm happy that you're happy." Emma noticed that Preston had emerged from her office. He waved, called a quick thank-you, and proceeded out the door.

"I couldn't be happier. I can't thank you enough for offering this to us. It's been life changing for me.

"I've never had time to work uninterrupted," Luna continued. "These past few weeks, I've been able to try out new techniques and experimented with colors I'd shied away from in the past. Pastels and such. It's probably the most fun I've ever had. I'm going to hate to leave when the program ends."

"Well, there are still weeks between now and then, so you just enjoy the time while you're here."

"Really, words can't express my thanks to you for sponsoring this remarkable experience. I've never felt more like myself."

"You've made my day, Luna. Thank you." Emma turned to go into her office, where she kept her single-serve coffee maker. She could use a good cup of coffee.

"This has been big for all of us, you know. We were talking the other night, and we all agreed this has been the best thing to happen to any of us in a very long time."

Emma paused, the meaning of the woman's words slowly seeping in. She'd hoped that the artists would benefit creatively from the retreat, but Luna made it sound like something more.

"Ah, that surprises you." Luna's mouth widened into an enormous grin. "You really don't know what this has meant to us, do you?"

"Would you like a cup of coffee, Luna?" Emma knew in ten minutes she might regret the invitation, but she was intrigued.

"I'd love to. Thank you."

Five minutes later, mugs of coffee in their hands, Emma and Luna went out to the small patio and sat under the canopy of wisteria.

"We're all from different walks of life, as you know," Luna said. "But we've all experienced some roadblock to achieving our potential as artists. By inviting us here, you've invited us to leave behind those parts of our lives that have stood between us and our art. You know my story—I've been a lifelong caretaker for members of my family. I'm not saying I regret it. Being able to care for my brother throughout his life made me aware of so many things. Mostly how fragile we are as humans, when something as small as a virus or a bacterial infection can bring us down, swiftly or in stages. How the human spirit tries to rise above circumstances that are so dire, so damaging, yet can still inspire with its strength. The specifics aren't important—let me just say that it was an honor to help my brother through his trials right to the end. But it was not without a cost to me. I lost so much time— years—when I could have been learning. I could have been painting. Again, I don't regret what I gave, but I regret what I lost, if that makes sense to you."

"It does." Perfectly. Not too long ago, Emma herself had reflected on what she'd given and what she'd lost. Did she regret her marriage to

Harry? No. Without Harry, there'd have been no Chris. She couldn't have had one without the other, and her son was the best part of her life.

"It seems each of us here have had to make choices that affected our art. You might look at Preston and think he looks like an aging frat boy. He has the look of old money, of a carefree happy-go-lucky guy, doesn't he? You might wonder why he would need to apply for what amounts to a scholarship to spend three months doing nothing but painting. Did his application spell out what his past eight years have been like?"

"No. Though I know his wife passed away after a long illness, I did not ask for specifics nor did I inquire as to anyone's financial status. I didn't intend for that to be an influencing factor."

"For which we all are grateful. Preston left his job as a corporate attorney to be with his wife for the last few years. When they knew there was nothing else to be done for her, he decided to take her to all the places she'd ever wanted to go, to do all the things she'd talked about doing someday, and to do it all while there was still time. So they took trips to Paris, London, Rome, Cairo, Beijing, Tokyo, while she still could travel. They stayed in the best hotels, ate at the best restaurants, saw anything and everything that struck her fancy. As her condition progressed and she was no longer able to travel, he bought a small house on a lake because she loved to watch the sunsets, loved to see the changing of the seasons. When traditional treatments were no longer helpful, he found experimental drugs her insurance didn't cover. The travel and the treatment costs ate away his investments, his retirement funds, until he had very little left. After she passed away, he had to sell their family home, the home where they'd raised their children, but he said he doesn't regret a thing, that he'd do it all over again, spend every last dime to have made her so happy in the last part of her life. Fortunately, he was able to hold on to the lake house, and has been living there while he's been rediscovering his love of painting.

"That's what this summer means to every one of us. It's freed us to leave everything behind and just be artists. Yes, we'll all be returning to our lives when the summer is over, but we'll all go home better than when we arrived."

Emma stared at the coffee in her mug. She'd given no thought to where her artists would be coming from, or what their lives might have been like when she'd first thought about setting up the retreat. She'd simply thought it might be nice to give a few artists some time to paint far from whatever it may have been that was holding them back. She'd never thought beyond that.

"Thank you for telling me, Luna. I had no idea . . ."

"How could you? We all have our stories. Pasquale—you know he's a high school math teacher and that he's divorced. But what you may not know is that his ex-wife has taken their three boys to Colorado for the summer to stay with her parents. It's the first time in years he's had time to himself. Between the alimony and child support for his youngest, and college tuition for the two older boys, Pasquale has to teach extra classes, so he hasn't had any time for himself. He said this is the first summer in years he hasn't taught summer school, and he's loving every minute of it.

"Eva. Well, for most of her life, Eva was a model. She's been in many TV commercials, so if you thought you'd seen her somewhere, it's because you probably have. She's sold everything from diapers when she was a toddler to hand cream and asthma medication. She's still beautiful and elegant, but she's had a run of bad luck, including an agent who cheated her of her royalties and, more recently, a much younger boyfriend who robbed her blind, emptied her bank account, and disappeared. All of which stymied her ability to paint, especially the boyfriend. Sucked the creativity right out of her, she said. She's slowly starting to come alive again."

"I'm not sure you should be telling me all this. I imagine if Preston or Pasquale or Eva wanted me to know their stories, they'd tell me themselves. I've never been much of a gossiper."

"I'm sure they'd tell you if they had a chance. Everyone's been quite open. We've all pretty much bared our souls."

"It sounds as if the five of you have become very close over the past weeks."

"We have. Even Stella, who'd been standoffish, has been joining us at night on the beach, where we've been sharing a bottle of wine or two." She paused. "You know about . . ."

Emma nodded. "Her ex, yes. I'm glad she shared that with you and the rest of your compadres."

Luna smiled at Emma's use of the Spanish word. "You know that, in English, *soul mates, confidants, intimate friends* are all synonyms for *compadre*? That's exactly what we've become, and it's wonderful."

"Well, then, that's a nice bonus, wouldn't you say?"

"I've never had friends like the ones I made here. But it's more than a bonus. It's been a gift. A blessing. I can never thank you enough."

"Just do your best work in the time you have here. Make wonderful art that I can exhibit here at the end of the summer and attract buyers for you."

"That would be amazing."

"It's a goal." Emma's phone rang in the pocket of her skirt. She glanced at the screen, then said to Luna, "I'm sorry. It's my son . . ."

"Take your call. Thanks for the coffee, and the chat."

Emma immediately turned her attention to her phone.

"Chris."

"Hey, Mom. Got a few minutes?"

"Always. What's up?" She watched Luna walk away.

"I thought maybe we could have lunch together today. Just us."

"Of course. When and where?"

"Your choice."

Emma thought for a moment. Between noon and one, all the regular lunch places would be packed with locals as well as people passing through on their way to the Cape. She tried to think of someplace that might be less crowded, where they could talk uninterrupted by old friends or tourists who might recognize him.

"You know, I haven't been to Dusty's in a long time. Let's meet there."

"Seriously? Mom, it's a bar."

"I know, but I heard they have really good roast beef sandwiches, and that's what I'm in the mood for today."

"Their roast beef is the best, and it's my favorite place in town, but are you sure you wouldn't rather go to Mimi's or someplace more upscale?"

"I'm positive. I'll see you there."

Emma ended the call and rubbed the back of her neck. There were classes in progress on the lower level of the center, so she couldn't lock the building, but she could lock her office. Anyone who needed her would have to wait. Chris clearly had something on his mind.

She went back to her office, the empty coffee mugs dangling from her fingers, one on each hand. Laughter from the adult watercolor class drifted up the stairwell, and the sound made her smile. That was what she felt making art should be about at any age, fun and creative and lively. She loved knowing that the art center she'd given so much of her time to was being enjoyed.

She sat at her desk, thinking about her conversation with Luna. Other than Stella, she'd had no idea of the trials her guest artists had endured. She almost wished Luna hadn't told her. Emma felt as if she'd peeked behind too many curtains that morning and seen sad things she wished she hadn't seen. Preston's wife's death, Pasquale's separation from his sons, Eva's betrayal—in a very small way, Emma could identify with each of their troubles. Her husband had died, though in a totally different manner than Preston's wife, but Emma knew what it felt like to feel that other part of you simply disappearing from your life. She, too, spent long periods of time away from her son, as Pasquale was now doing. Of course they stayed close through phone calls and texts, FaceTime and Zoom calls, but it wasn't the same as being in the same room and having time to spend together without the aid of electronic devices. Eva's betrayal by a man she'd loved—well, Emma knew all about that feeling. That empty spot inside that grew with every breath when you discovered that the person you thought you knew was someone else entirely. She could tell Eva that one morning she'll wake up and it won't hurt quite so much when she thought of her ex-lover—that while betrayal can break your heart, it doesn't have to break you, and if Eva ever confided in her, she would tell her exactly that.

Still, there was one huge difference between Emma's circumstances and those of her artists: Harry's death hadn't had a negative financial impact on her life. If anything, with Harry's retirement funds, his vast investments, and his life insurance, she was better off financially than when he was alive; plus, she had a son who had an unfathomable income who couldn't do enough for his mother. She was well aware her life was very different from most others'. Which meant she was going to have to pray her artists created their very best work while they were here, and that she could put together an exhibit that would attract the press and some deep-pocketed buyers by the end of the summer. At that moment, she wanted nothing more than the five artists to leave Wyndham Beach with brilliant portfolios, some good sales, a growing bank account, and contacts with a few galleries who wanted to exhibit their work. Somehow she was going to have to make that happen. She just had to figure out how.

At ten after twelve, Emma locked her office and began her walk to Dusty's. It was only a few blocks away, but her body needed to move.

There wasn't much of a crowd in Dusty's when she pushed open the heavy oak door and stepped inside. It took her eyes a few seconds to adjust to the low-level lighting, but she spotted her son standing at the bar in a lively conversation with the owner.

"Mrs. D," Dusty exclaimed when he saw her. "It's an honor. I haven't seen you in . . . can't even remember when. Someone's funeral, maybe." He reached an arm across the polished bar to take her hand and give it a squeeze.

Emma laughed. "Funerals do bring everyone out of the woodwork around here. Good to see you, Dusty."

Chris opened his arms for a hug, and it seemed to Emma he held on just a tad longer than she'd have expected, even though she'd just seen him the day before.

He'd grabbed a table in the very back corner, far enough from the kitchen to be heard, far enough from the bar to ensure their conversation would be private. Even the two men playing darts opposite them were out of range to hear.

"Are you getting ready to leave for LA again?" Emma sat in the chair her son held out for her and watched as he took the seat next to hers. "Is this why we're having lunch, just the two of us?"

"No. Actually, I've decided to stick around for a while. I called the guys last night and told everyone to take some time off. We've been working around the clock for weeks, so everyone's due a rest, but that's not really the reason I wanted some time here in Wyndham Beach."

"Winnie," Emma said softly.

Chris nodded. "Winnie. And, of course, time to spend with Natalie and plan our wedding."

"When will that be? Have you decided?"

"Actually, we had decided on Labor Day weekend. We figured everyone from the West Coast could take a four-day weekend and spend some time relaxing out here. Eric got married four months ago and hasn't had as much time to spend with his bride, so I figured he'd be looking forward to it. Plus, Linc's here, and he's the one I write my best stuff with, so there's that."

"Oh my gosh, when Maggie announced she and Brett were getting married that weekend . . ."

He nodded, a wry smile on his lips. "Yeah, we were both stunned. Obviously, we'd need to come up with another date. There's no way Natalie would ever want to steal even the tiniest bit of spotlight from her mother. Nor would I. Maggie's entitled to it. She's waited a long time. Thankfully, she changed her mind, and Labor Day is back on the agenda for us. Though Natalie would be happier with a date right before or right after Christmas."

"A Christmas wedding is always beautiful. The church is always magnificent, with all the flowers on the altar."

"We hadn't talked about getting married in the church, Mom."

"Christopher Dean." She leveled him with a gaze. "Your grandfather was pastor at that church for decades. My brother—your uncle Dan—is now pastor. How could you think of getting married anywhere else?"

"Well, when you put it that way, I guess we couldn't." He capitulated easily and good naturedly. "I'll let Natalie know that part's a wrap."

"Just make sure you let Dan know as soon as possible if you change your mind about September and decide on December so he can block off the date for you. Christmas has always been a popular time for weddings in Wyndham Beach."

"Daisy will expect to see Christmas trees on the altar and sparkly lights everywhere. Which, actually, would be beautiful. Hmmm. I'll need to talk to Nat about that."

"It can all be arranged. I think a tree on either side of the altar decorated with white ornaments and tiny white lights would be glorious, but that's up to Natalie and you. The date, the decorations. Whatever the two of you decide." She took his hand. "But you didn't want to talk about your wedding plans today."

"I'm always happy to talk to you about my wedding or anything else you want to talk about, Mom."

"But today, it's Winnie."

Chris nodded slowly. "Yeah, it's Winnie."

"So . . ." She gestured for him to begin.

"I am pretty much resigned to the fact that we're probably never going to figure out who her father is. We've turned over every stone we could think of. Melissa even tracked down the other bands that were stuck in Atlanta that weekend and had them all take DNA tests."

"How in the world did she convince them to do that?"

"She promised them opening acts at one of our concerts." He smiled wryly. "The offer they couldn't refuse."

"But—nothing, right?"

"Right. No matches." He opened his hands on the table in front of him, empty, palms up. "So we can agree, there's almost no possibility of finding Winnie's father?"

"Agreed. Worse than a needle in a haystack."

They sat back in their seats while their waitress, a young woman named Carolyn, handed them menus and offered them water.

"I already know what I want," Emma told her. "I'll have the roast beef and tavern fries and an iced tea. Oh, and horseradish on the side, please."

"Same for me." Chris picked up both menus and handed them back. He turned to Emma and said, "Horseradish, eh? I don't remember you ever eating anything spicier than a salted peanut."

Emma laughed. "This is Mom two-point-oh, son."

"I guess it is." Chris laughed, too.

The sight of his eyes lighting up with humor and the sound of his laughter brought a lump to Emma's throat. She spent too little time in his company, and she was reminded that his laughter had always been easy and true, and she'd missed it.

"So—" Emma gestured for him to get on with it. She wasn't sure which way he was going to go, and the pain in her head whispered to remind her it was lurking right there.

"So we know she's one parent down there. We're not even going to look anymore. Then there's the issue of her mother. Doesn't look good there, either."

Carolyn brought their drinks and placed them on the table. "Your sandwiches will be up in just a few."

Emma smiled her thanks.

"What's the latest from your PI?" Emma said when the waitress had stepped away to chat at the next table.

"He's taken Tish's photo up and down the strip and to bars on the side streets several times, and no one has seen her. A bouncer at one of the clubs said he thought he'd seen her some months ago, right before the big Desert Rose concerts, but not since then. I guess that red hair is memorable."

"That was in November or December of last year."

Chris nodded. "He's staying in touch with the LVPD detective who opened a case relative to the search for bodies in the desert. They have found at least two burial sites that I know of."

"Two!" Emma shivered. It was too terrible to think about what the parents of a missing son or daughter might be going through.

"At this point they're thinking it looks like a serial killer. Without going into detail, the PI said the remains all showed signs of having the same trauma. Of course, they don't want to announce that, but that's how it's shaping up. He said it's going to take months to identify all the victims, and there are some who will probably never be identified. They have Winnie's DNA results to compare, but . . ." He shrugged.

"But we may never know if Tish was one of the victims."

"Correct. We may never know."

"Oh . . ." She didn't finish whatever it was she was going to say, as the waitress served their lunches. Emma stared at her sandwich, her appetite slowly fading.

"What I'm thinking is this." He lowered his voice even more. "We're just going to bite the bullet and say Winnie's mine. If Tish ever shows up—well, we'll deal with her if that happens. But this kid can't sit in limbo. From this day on—Winnie Pine is my daughter, and if she wants to change her name to Winnie Dean, it's okay by me."

"Have you discussed this with Natalie?"

"I have. She's on board. She's spent a lot of time with Winnie this summer—way more than I have—and Winnie's grown on her. And I guess Nat's grown on her, too. There may be issues going forward, but we'll work things out. Winnie and I—well, I have to trust we'll get there, too. Families work things out."

"Have you thought this through?"

He nodded.

"And you're sure? Positive you want to do this?" She watched his face for signs of hesitancy, but found none. "Be sure, Chris, because there'll be no turning back. You can't change your mind once you've told her."

"I've thought it through and talked to Nat until we were both near exhaustion. We've walked it backward and forward. We're sure. And there will be no turning back."

"How are you going to tell her?"

"I'll know the moment when it comes." He picked up his sandwich but didn't raise it to his mouth. "I'm wondering if I have to do something legal. Do I have to adopt her?"

"Your name is on the birth certificate. Why should you have to go through an adoption process if you're already her father of record? You can ask Grace if you're not sure . . ."

"No, no. That's exactly what we thought. So if anyone at any time came back to us to question my rights . . ."

"Her mother named you as the father. The state of Georgia has designated you her father. The father who's raising her and giving her a good and loving home will trump any other claim to her. Even Tish, because there's no question she was a lousy mother."

"Yeah, we were thinking that, too."

"The press will be all over this."

Chris shrugged. "For all of about ten minutes. We'll deal with it."

"And Nat's prepared for that?"

"She is. If Tish's remains are found, and we confirm she's deceased, Nat will adopt Winnie. I've always intended to adopt Daisy, so eventually we'll all be legal. It could take a while before anyone even notices, and then we'll just have to protect Winnie as best we can, and Daisy, too. All of which brings me to the real problem."

Emma raised an eyebrow.

"I don't really know Winnie. You know her better than I do. I'm going to be her father, but I don't know this kid at all. I don't know what she likes except that she likes to read and she likes ice cream. You're with her every day and every night. What does she talk about? What does she like?"

Emma thought for a moment. "Have you talked to Natalie? Winnie spends time every day with her."

He nodded. "Nat said she likes the beach, likes finding shells and sea glass and is always asking what bird is that and what bird is that and why are there so many different kinds of gulls."

"So buy a bird guide and take her bird-watching. There are lots of birds in the woods and on the beaches, and in the marshes, but if you're going to do that, get started before the mosquitoes and the black flies take over."

"Good point. I'll do that. I imagine Liddy has some bird books."

"She has an entire section."

"Okay, good. That's something I can do with her. Anything else you know that she likes to do?"

Emma picked up her sandwich and took a bite, chewed, took another. Chewed it while she thought about conversations she'd had with Winnie. "I think one time she mentioned she liked going fishing with her grandfather when he was alive."

"Fishing. Huh." He began to eat. "I wonder if she meant lake or stream fishing or ocean fishing."

"It wasn't ocean. She said she'd never seen the ocean before she came here. Technically, she still hasn't seen beyond Buzzards Bay yet, just that little bit of it off the beach by the art center."

"Hmm." He chewed thoughtfully, then nodded. "Fishing . . ."

Chapter Fifteen

Natalie and Chris strolled into Walker's Outfitters Since 1975, the big sporting goods store on Route 6, Winnie and Daisy trailing behind them. The shop took up the first floor of a large old house. Some of the walls had been removed to enlarge the sales floor, and classical music played in the background, an unexpected touch.

"Help you folks?" A white-haired man who appeared to be in his late sixties looked up from the rack of waterproof jackets he was arranging under a sale sign.

"We need some fishing gear," Chris told him.

"Rods? Reels? Rigs?" The man hung the remaining jackets. "What kind of fishing you looking to do? Saltwater or fresh?"

"Saltwater."

"Deep-sea or surf?"

"Surf."

"You got a license?"

"Not yet, but I saw your sign in the window. You sell them here, right?"

"I do. What are you hoping to catch?"

"Whatever we can," Chris told him. "I haven't been fishing in a long time, but I remember catching striped bass and flounder off the shore in Wyndham Beach years ago with my grandpa. I thought I'd see if they're still running this time of the year."

"They're running, all right. Guy caught a big bass right off the jetty a week or so ago. Blues are all over the place right now." The man nodded thoughtfully. "You're going to want a fifty-pound test line. Might not need anything that strong but just in case. It's a good option. How's your reel?"

"Good question. I haven't seen it in a while but I think it's still at my mother's. I'm assuming it's still good."

"You check it out, come back if you need to." The man walked behind a counter and looked underneath, then set two boxes of line on the top. "You want monofilament or braided?"

"Mono."

"That's what I thought. You want an extra just in case you hook something that snaps your line." He paused. "I'm assuming you have your rods."

Chris nodded. "But I need a license."

The man went into the back room and came out with some paperwork, which he handed to Chris. "Just fill this out and you'll be in business." He glanced over to where Natalie was holding a sweatshirt up to Winnie, checking for size. "The lady need a license?"

"The lady doesn't fish," Chris told him. "Just me and the little redhead." He turned and addressed Winnie. "Right, Winnie? We're going fishing tomorrow morning."

She grinned and nodded enthusiastically.

"You like to surf-fish?" he asked.

"I never been. But I fished in a lake with my grampa lots of times."

"Now there's an accent I haven't heard around here in a long time. Where are you from, sugar?"

"Georgia."

"You visiting? On vacation?"

Winnie opened her mouth to respond, but Chris replied, "No, we live here."

A look of uncertainty crossed Winnie's face, but she didn't say a word.

"Well, that's nice." He looked over the paper Chris had filled out and pointed to a line and said, "You just need to sign here, and I'll take care of the rest."

"Thanks. Next we all need life jackets," Chris told him.

"Why do we need life jackets?" Daisy asked.

"For when we go out on Linc's new boat," Natalie said.

"What we have left is over there on the right-side wall." The man barely glanced at the paperwork Chris handed him. "This late in the season, there's not much left. I'm still waiting for another big order to come in. Should be here any day now."

"It's only June," Natalie remarked.

"By early April, things are flying off the shelves. Soon as it looks like the cold weather is behind us, everyone wants out on the water. Check back with me next week if you don't see what you're looking for. The order should be in by then."

He helped find four jackets that would suit—though Natalie could have taken a smaller size—and Chris paid for their gear and his license. Since Winnie was under thirteen years of age, she wouldn't require one.

"Anything else while we're here?" Chris asked Natalie.

She thought for a moment. "Maybe a waterproof bag, like a big tote we could pack our food in when we go on the boat. You know, in case it falls in the water somehow."

The salesperson had exactly what she had in mind and added it to the pile.

"Maybe some binoculars," Chris said.

"We just got some in that are very well priced," he told Chris.

Three pairs of binoculars—one adult Nat and Chris could share, and two child size, lest there be a fight—went onto the counter.

"I guess that's it." Chris watched the salesperson total it all up and handed him a credit card.

The man glanced at the card, then at Chris, then at the fishing license.

"You Harry Dean's son?" he asked.

"I am," Chris told him.

"I knew your dad way back. The bank in Wyndham Beach held the mortgage on this building when my father first bought it. Your father was always nice to me when I went into the bank with my dad. Always came out of his office to say hello." He folded and packed their purchases while he talked. "I still bank there. Always had nice people working at that bank—lot of new people these days, though. I only recognize two or three of the tellers now. That woman who used to be your dad's assistant, Carla Dempsey, she's still there. She's nice, too. Always smiling. Always cheerful."

"I remember Carla. She was always so nice to me. Always made it a point to come out of her office when she knew I was there," Chris recalled.

The salesperson handed Chris two bags. "Last I heard, you were a singer or something."

"Or something." Chris smiled and took a bag in each hand.

"You check that reel when you get home, and if you need anything else, stop back."

He assured him they would, then headed out to the parking lot, where they stashed their purchases in the trunk and got into their seats.

"Winnie, are you excited about going out on Linc's boat later this week?" Natalie turned in the front passenger seat to face Winnie, who sat behind Chris, who was driving.

"Yes, ma'am." Winnie answered with her usual politeness, but Natalie sensed the underlying hesitation.

"I think you'll like being out on the water," Natalie assured her. "There's so much to see."

Winnie nodded uncertainly.

"I like boats," Daisy piped up. "One time we went on the boat to Uncle Linc's island and had a picnic with JoJo and Bliss and Aunt Gracie. It was so fun. We went around the island in the boat so we could see the whole thing from the water. And guess what we saw?" Without awaiting a response, she announced, "Dolphins! A whole bunch of them!"

That got nature-loving Winnie's attention. "Dolphins? Real ones?"

"Uh-huh."

"Dolphins," Winnie whispered, clearly awed. Unicorns wouldn't have been spoken of with greater reverence.

But the dolphins and the boat ride to Shelby Island would have to wait. First thing in the morning, Chris told Natalie, he and Winnie were going fishing. Early, he'd said, because dawn and dusk were the two best times to fish. He found his old rod—the one he'd had as a child and had learned to fish on and that Winnie could use—and his grandfather's for him, and brought them along with the old metal box of lures and sinkers onto Emma's patio.

"You know what you're doing, sport?" Natalie watched him tie a hook onto the line he'd bought that day. Next he reached for a small metal object that looked like a teardrop, and he tied that on last.

"It's like riding a bike." He was grinning like a kid, Nat thought, happy to be doing something he hadn't done in a long time. "I'm doing great. As long as my hooks don't fall off, I think we'll be good." He held up the line. "You've heard the expression he swallowed it hook, line, and sinker? Here you go. Hook. Line. Sinker."

"That's a sinker? That metal thing there on the bottom?" Natalie asked.

Chris nodded. "Keeps the lure and the line from floating when you're trying to catch a fish that's closer to the bottom."

"Where's my fishing rod?" Daisy asked.

"Well, we only have one kids' rod, so you and Winnie can take turns," Chris told her.

"What do you do with that?" She pointed to the hook.

"We put the bait onto it, and we throw it into the water and hope a hungry fish comes along and eats it."

Daisy frowned. "What's bait?"

"It's what we put on the hook to attract the fish's attention. Something he would want to eat, like another smaller fish, or maybe a big fat worm."

"Yuck! Worms! I'm never going to fish!" Daisy grabbed Winnie's arm. "Let's go inside and see if there are any Popsicles left."

After the two girls disappeared into the house, an amused Natalie said, "You knew that was going to happen. You knew as soon as you said *worms* it would be all over as far as Daisy's concerned. That's why you didn't pick up a children's pole when we were at the shop."

"She's welcome to come along and look for shells and sit on the beach with you and build sandcastles, but the fishing is for me and Winnie." He looked up at Natalie and said softly, "Winnie and I have things to talk about."

"You're going to tell her tomorrow?"

Chris nodded.

"What are you going to say?" Natalie leaned her elbows on the table next to where he was working.

"I have no idea," he told her. "I'm just going to go with the moment and hope the right words come to me."

The right words did. Eventually.

He'd told Natalie he wanted to leave by dawn, but when she awoke at six the next morning, she could hear him outside in the driveway. She got dressed and went downstairs to see what he was up to.

"What are you doing?" she asked from the stone path that led from Emma's patio to the old Jeep he kept at the house for his use.

"Putting the fishing gear in the car. What's it look like?"

"Looks like a guy who hasn't had coffee yet being cranky."

He laughed in spite of the fact that he was the cranky guy in the driveway. "Sorry. I really wanted to be on the beach by now. Fish get up early." He closed the back hatch and walked toward her.

"Earlier than little girls. I think they're both still asleep." She gave him a kiss when he reached her, and rubbed his back. "It'll be fine. There are plenty of fish out there in the harbor. I bet a few of them will be hanging around, waiting to see what the locals are going to tempt them with for breakfast."

"That reminds me. I have to stop out at Polly's for bait." He rested his chin on the top of her head. "I'm assuming Polly's still there. I think Mom would have let me know if something had happened to her."

"I remember Polly. She was old when we were kids. Always wore a big wide-brimmed hat and a long-sleeved shirt with sleeves rolled to the elbows under her overalls, no matter how hot it was. The overalls were a light-colored denim and always stained with stuff I didn't like thinking about."

"Fish guts." He nodded. "For a few bucks, she'd skin and dress your catch. Split 'em up the middle, take out the bones, cut off the tails and the heads."

"Thanks for putting fish guts in my head. Think I'll be skipping breakfast."

He snapped his fingers. "That's how I'll get the girls to wake up and come downstairs."

"You'll put fish guts in their rooms and the smell will rouse them?"

"No. I'll cook bacon and the smell will rouse them." He looped an arm around her neck and they walked into the house. In the kitchen, he dug a nickel out of his pocket and said, "Heads you make scrambled eggs, tails I make pancakes."

"Okay. But no cheating. Toss that sucker up good so I can see it bounce."

He tossed the coin and it rolled across the floor as far as the refrigerator. They both leaned over to see how it landed.

"Tails." Natalie picked up the nickel and tucked it into the pocket of her shorts. "Guess you better get moving, Dean."

Chris made a face, then laughed and opened the refrigerator door and started pulling out what he'd need for breakfast.

"We could have eggs, Chris," she said. "I don't mind doing them."

"A deal is a deal." He got a large frying pan from a cabinet.

"Well, then, in that case I'll get stuff ready for the beach."

"What stuff?"

"A blanket, some beach towels, snacks for the girls when they get antsy, a couple of bottles of water, Daisy's sand toys so she can build a sandcastle. Oh, and sunscreen. My book." Natalie recited the list from her head.

"How do women do that?" he asked as he got out the flour and a bowl.

"Do what?"

"Just know what everyone needs without even thinking about it much. Like you say, we're going to the beach, and a list of beach things pops up in your head, like little icons?"

"That's pretty much how it happens."

"Really?"

"No." She laughed. "You do things with kids often enough, you just know from experience what you need. And right now, I need the beach bag." She set off for the steps.

Twenty minutes later she was back in the kitchen, both girls dressed and ready for breakfast. Chris set the first stack of pancakes on the table next to a plate of bacon. In what seemed to be the blink of an eye, Natalie had plates and flatware on the table and was slicing strawberries into a bowl. Chris poured syrup into a small pitcher and set that next to the pancakes.

He glanced around the table. "What are we missing?"

"Me. You're missing me." Emma announced as she came into the room.

"Did we wake you?" Natalie asked. "I tried to keep everyone quiet so you could sleep late."

Emma dismissed her concern with a quick wave of her left hand. "I was awake and just being lazy. But I smelled that bacon and decided one piece wasn't going to do me in. But where's the coffee?"

"I knew I forgot something." Chris had started to sit in a chair across from the two girls, but stood.

"Sit and eat, Chris. I'll do the coffee. It's the least I can do after you've made us all breakfast." Emma proceeded to the coffee pot.

Natalie got three mugs from the counter and set them there for Emma to fill when the coffee finished brewing, then helped Daisy with the syrup and put a pile of strawberries on Winnie's plate. She'd noticed that sometimes Winnie was reluctant to serve herself, and Nat knew how much she loved fresh fruit. She added a few more berries to Daisy's plate, lest it appear she was playing favorites, then sat and served herself. Natalie ate quickly, then excused herself to run upstairs.

When she came back down, Chris was loading the breakfast dishes into the dishwasher.

"Oh, honey, leave those," Emma said. "I'll do them."

"Thanks, Mom, but a very wise woman told me once that a cook always cleans up his mess before leaving the kitchen."

"Quoting my mother." Emma grinned. "I like it."

"Actually, I was quoting you. Did Gramma used to say that?"

"Who do you think I learned all my pithy sayings from?" Emma rose, carrying her own plate to the sink.

"I like the word *pithy*." Natalie was stuffing beach towels into the already-overstuffed beach bag. "It should be used more often."

"Pithy," Daisy repeated. "What does it mean?"

"It means the white stuff inside an orange," Winnie said.

The adults in the room all turned and looked at Winnie. When she realized they were staring, she said, "That's what Miz Richardson called it. Pith."

"You're right, Winnie. That's what pith is. But *pithy* means something else, too," Nat told her. "It can mean an orange has lots of pith, or it can mean something is convincing."

Winnie's ponytail bobbed up and down. "Sometimes words mean different things. We learned that, too." She took her plate to the sink, and Chris took it to rinse.

"I know a word that means different things." Not to be left out, Daisy held up two fingers while she, too, handed over her plate. "Two."

"Like, you two run upstairs and brush your teeth, then come right back down," Natalie told them.

"Oh, like go *to* the beach to fish." Winnie led the way to the steps, her voice trailing behind her all the way up to the second floor. "Or, I like that, *too*. I was too hot."

"Someone pays attention in class," Emma noted.

"Well, you did say she skipped a grade," Natalie said.

"We'll have to request her school transcripts from the school she's been going to." Emma's voice was so low, Natalie wasn't sure she hadn't been speaking to herself.

"I guess I should do that"—Chris finished loading the dishwasher—"since Tish isn't around."

"The school might think that's strange, since I imagine Tish or her grandmother had enrolled her. Think they'll just hand over her records just because you asked?" Natalie wondered.

"As Mom reminded me the other day, I'm her father of record, so there shouldn't even be a question."

"What school will she go to?" Emma asked Chris.

He drained the remaining coffee from his cup. "No final decision yet, but it's looking more and more like Wyndham Beach." He opened the dishwasher's door and stuck his empty mug on the top rack. "All I know for sure is that she's not going back to Georgia."

~

Chris stopped at the small shack where the sign over the door consisted of one word: BAIT.

"Wait in the car or come in with me?" he asked as he unfastened his seat belt.

"Wait in the car," Natalie said.

A little more than five minutes later, Chris stepped out of the shack, a small bucket in his hand. When he got in the car, he handed Natalie the bucket. "Mission accomplished. I got some nice fat worms."

"Ewwwww!" Daisy cried, and Chris grinned at Natalie, who was eyeing the bucket with suspicion.

Chris headed toward Cottage Street and the beach. He glanced in the rearview mirror at the girls in the back seat. "Who's ready to catch some fish?"

"I am!" Winnie raised her hand.

Daisy shook her head. "Nope."

Daisy hadn't even wanted to see what was in the bait bucket, but Winnie was totally involved with every aspect of the venture. She helped carry the gear from the car to the beach and helped Chris set up the rods while Natalie and Daisy sat on their blanket, Nat reading, Daisy looking over some shells she found. Natalie slathered sunscreen on everyone.

Chris cast his line into the surf, then asked Winnie if she wanted him to cast her line for her.

"No, thank you," she told him. "I like doin' that part myself."

So she did.

"Nice form, Winnie," Chris told her after her line hit the water. "But maybe a little short. I don't think there are fish that close to the beach. Maybe I could try to get your line out a little farther. Would that be okay?"

Winnie nodded, so he handed her his rod to hold for a moment, then cast her line. They switched rods then, and waited.

"You let me know when you feel something tug or pull on your line, okay? That means there's a fish on your hook."

Winnie nodded silently.

"But you knew that, didn't you?"

She nodded again. "Yes, sir."

"Winnie, you don't have to call me sir."

"I don't know what to call you." Her voice was small, as if it had curled up inside her.

"What would you like to call me?"

She shrugged.

On the blanket, Natalie leaned forward. *Here it comes,* she thought. She leaned a little closer.

"Winnie?"

"I thought I was going to call you *Daddy*," Winnie said.

Chris took a deep breath. "Then that's what you should call me."

Natalie heard him take another deep breath, as if he were trying to decide where to start. She thought maybe he figured the hell with it, just jump in, because he did.

"Winnie, you know that your mother and I weren't together."

She nodded, but her head didn't turn toward him.

"And until you came to Wyndham Beach, I didn't know about you."

"If you knew about me, would you have come for me?"

"If I had known that I had a daughter down there in Georgia, you bet I would have come for you." His line must have gone slack, because he reeled it in.

Good answer. Natalie mentally gave him an A-plus. She could see how difficult the conversation was for both Chris and Winnie even though she couldn't see their faces. Their body language spoke volumes. Winnie stood ramrod straight. Chris was leaning slightly toward her.

"You know that Natalie and I have known each other for a very long time. We love each other very much, and we want to be together and have a family." He paused. "We would like you to be part of our family."

"You do?"

"We both do."

"But when my mama comes back . . ." Winnie's voice trailed off as if somehow she knew the odds were not good that was going to happen.

They were both silent for a long time. Chris checked the bait on his hook and cast it back out into the water.

"I don't think she's coming back," Winnie said. "Do you think she's coming back?"

"I wish I knew for certain, Winnie, but it doesn't look like it."

"Sorta feels that way. She's been gone a long, long, long time. She didn't used to stay away this long."

Just then Daisy jumped up and ran toward the shore. "Winnie! Look what I found! A sand dollar!"

She held it out in front of her and hopped up and down when she reached the water. "Look! You can hold it if you want."

Winnie turned to Daisy and smiled. "That's a sand dollar? I never saw one before. It's not really money, though, right?"

Daisy looked up at Chris. "Isn't it money?"

"Nope," he told her.

"Then why do they call it a sand dollar?" she asked. "Why don't they call it a round sand thing?"

Chris laughed. "I don't know."

"Maybe we can look it up on your mom's computer when we get back to the house," Winnie said, holding tight to her fishing rod.

"Okay." Daisy ran back to show Natalie, who realized that Daisy had gone first to Winnie, and that was a good thing.

"You'll make a very good big sister," Nat heard Chris tell Winnie. "And, you know, when I marry Natalie, Daisy will be your little sister."

"Oh. I didn't know that. I never had a sister."

"Well, you'll have one in a few months. And that would make Natalie your . . ."

"Stepmother," Winnie said. "Will I have to call her *Mama*? Even if I call you *Daddy*?"

"That's something you're going to have to talk to Natalie about, but I know her pretty well, and I'm pretty sure she wouldn't make you call her anything you don't want to call her. You two can decide."

"Okay."

Natalie watched as Chris put a hand on Winnie's shoulder, and she felt all was well in their world. At least at that moment.

"Oh!" Winnie cried. "My fishing rod!"

Chris acted swiftly and stepped into the water to retrieve the rod that was being pulled farther from shore. "Winnie, I think you have a bite!"

Natalie and Daisy ran to the water's edge, where Chris was helping Winnie to reel in her line the way his grandfather had taught him.

"That's how my grampa brought in the fish, too," Winnie was saying. "Pull it in, let it out a little, then pull it in some more."

"That's the tried-and-true technique." He reeled in the line until their catch was in the shallow water. "Winnie, get the net, please."

She grabbed the net off the beach and handed it to Chris, who slid it under the fish.

"Look what you caught, Winnie!" He held the net down so she could see.

"What kind of fish is that?" She peered into the net, her face almost touching the water.

"That's a small blue fish," he told her.

"The fish is blue?" Daisy jumped up and down. "I want to see a blue fish. I have a book about red fishes and blue fishes." She looked at the fish. "Hey, that fish isn't blue."

"Well, it sort of looks blue when it's in the water," Chris explained. To Winnie, he said, "So what do you think? Is it dinner?"

She stared at the fish.

"He's looking at me," she said softly. "I think he's scared."

"He might well be," Chris agreed.

"It would be scary to be swimming along and to see something good to eat but when you bite it, it makes your mouth hurt and then you're in a net." Winnie looked as if she was about to cry.

"We can let it go, if you want." Chris kept the net in the water, but he knelt down next to Winnie on the sand. "Lots of people catch fish for the fun of fishing, but then let the fish go. It's called catch and release. Do you want to do that?"

Winnie stared at the fish. Finally, she said, "Let's let him go."

"I'm sure he's really happy to hear you say that." Chris turned his attention to the fish and to removing the hook with as little damage as possible to its mouth. "If we're real careful, we can do this without hurting him too much. I used a hook that comes out easily and smoothly, so . . ." He worked at the hook for a moment. "There. Winnie, want to hold the net and let him swim out?"

She nodded excitedly and stepped into the water, taking the net's handle in both hands. Lowering the net deeper into the water, she said, "Go, swim home now. Go see your mama and your daddy. And your sisters and your brothers."

As an afterthought, she called after the fish, "And be more careful what you put in your mouth!"

Chris patted her on the back. "Good job, honey."

"Thank you, sir." She gazed up at him with the sunniest smile. "I mean *Daddy*."

Chapter Sixteen

"Chris, are you awake?" Emma walked out to the backyard, where Chris lay in an old hammock he'd found in the garage. He'd hosed it off the day before, then hung it to dry between two trees on the hooks that had been pounded into the trunks years ago. His eyes were closed, but his right leg was on the ground, and he was using it to swing the hammock side to side.

"I am now." He kept his eyes closed.

"Oh, sorry."

"I'm teasing you." He rose up on his elbows, careful not to dump himself on the ground. "I was just decompressing. You know, 'let it go' and all that."

"You need to be careful on that old thing. I'm not sure how old those hooks are in the trees," she told him. "I suppose they could pull out. I'm not even sure when they were put in."

"It seems stable enough, but if I fall on my butt, it'll have been worth it. This is the most relaxed I've been since we were here at Christmas."

"You sure you're not bored? Wyndham Beach isn't the most exciting place. It's certainly not like LA, where there's something happening all the time."

"I haven't been bored one minute since I arrived, Mom. I'm grateful to be in one place with the people I love. I didn't realize how badly

I needed time off to just, well, live for a while. When I'm here, I'm reminded that I have a life outside of music, and as much as I love making music, I love my life here, too."

"Does that mean you might settle here?" She hoped she didn't sound too eager.

"I've been thinking about that. Natalie and I will need to find a home somewhere. Neither of us think LA is the place. I like the Philly area—there are a lot of really nice little towns outside the city. Nat and I have toured most of them over the past few months, but nothing's jumped up and said *home*. So we were thinking about talking to a Realtor here and seeing what's for sale or what might be for sale in the near future. We both love Wyndham Beach, and our families are here, so it makes the most sense. You don't have to look so smug, Mom. You knew eventually I'd find my way home."

"Was I looking smug? I wasn't aware."

Chris laughed. "You need to work on your subtle-ity skills."

"I'm pretty sure *subtle-ity* isn't a word, but of course I'd love to have you and Nat and the girls here all the time. I know it would make Maggie ecstatic as well. Plus, when you're away, you know we'll be looking after them." She hastened to add, "Not that Natalie can't take care of herself and the kids, but sometimes it's nice to have a backup."

"No need for the hard sell, Mom. We're going to look. Know any good Realtors?"

"Of course. I probably know them all, but if I needed a Realtor for any reason, such as maybe to sell this house, I'd call Gretchen Smith at Smith and Armstrong."

"You thinking about selling this house, Mom?" He swung his left leg off the hammock so that both feet were on the ground. "That name rolled right off your tongue, no hesitation."

"I've known her for years. Besides, you know I can't sell this house. It belongs to the Dean trust." She paused. "Would you and Nat want . . ."

Chris shook his head. "Uh-uh. This is nothing personal against you, but most of my memories of growing up here are not good ones. Some are downright painful."

"I understand. I know your father was tough on you, but in fairness to him, what you wanted to do was beyond his sphere of understanding. Men in his family, in his social circle, followed their fathers into whatever business their father was in. He did. His father did as well. He had no reason to believe you wouldn't do the same." She defended Harry at the same time she was mentally asking herself why she felt the need to.

"Until I told him point blank I had no interest in being a banker."

"He believed you'd come around. He never expected you to continue on with your music." That was true. Harry had told Emma many times that Chris's guitar would be stored in the attic as soon as he discovered girls. What Harry hadn't understood was that the guitar would prove to be the gateway to more girls than Chris would ever want.

"But you did."

She nodded. "I believed you had a gift, which clearly you do. And I wanted you to follow your heart in everything, always. I wanted you to be happy." She realized what she'd said, then laughed apologetically. "Not that your father didn't want you to be happy."

"He wanted me to be happy being his Mini-Me. It would only be okay for me to be happy as long as I was doing what he wanted me to do."

Emma couldn't think of a follow-up.

Chris eased himself off the hammock. "I know when he was angry with me, he took it out on you, and I'm pretty sure you must have paid a price for sticking up for me all those years. I've always felt guilty about that, and I never acknowledged that before."

Emma was pretty sure her marriage had been the price for sticking up for her son, but no reason for Chris to know she suspected that

Harry had turned to Carla when he felt his wife and his son had aligned against him.

"You don't have to feel guilty. I did what I thought was right for you. He underestimated how much you loved music. He just didn't understand, Chris."

"Why are you sticking up for him?"

She thought about that for a moment. Why was she sticking up for Harry for all the mean things he'd said and done to their son? Why was she shielding Chris from knowing his father had had an affair? Not just a quick fling, but a love affair that had apparently lasted for years?

"I guess I'm old school, honey. I don't want you to lose respect for him. He was your father."

"That train's long gone, Mom. I haven't felt anything even close to respect for him in years. I hope that doesn't hurt you, but it's the truth. He wasn't always a nice man. Sometimes—lots of times—he was deliberately mean and hurtful."

Emma couldn't argue that point, so she didn't bother.

Chris closed the gap between them and hugged her. "Growing up in this house would have been hell if it hadn't been for you. There is nothing in this world I wouldn't do for you, Mom."

"Hence all the money you've poured into the art center."

"Whatever it takes to make you happy. And I know that supporting other people makes you happy. Like I said, there's nothing I wouldn't do."

She hung on to him, to his words and to his love, for a moment; then she smiled. "So if I asked if you and Natalie would be home tonight with the girls, you'd say . . ."

"I'd say of course. You have plans?"

He took her arm and they walked toward the house.

"Owen called last night. He'll be in Wyndham Beach tonight through tomorrow afternoon. He invited me to dinner." She paused, then added, "At his home."

"Whoa. Dinner at the Harrison mansion?"

"Uh-huh."

"Wow. I don't even know anyone who ever so much as set one foot inside that house." He took his phone from his pocket. "You know how to work the camera on one of these, right? Cause you could take pictures of everything. Whenever he turns his back . . . click." He lowered his voice conspiratorially. "You could probably sell them to your friends, you know? Everyone's always wondered what that place is like inside."

"I've wondered myself. And, yes, I know how to use the camera on my phone, smart-ass. I'm not ancient, you know." She sniffed with faux indignation. "And as much fun as it might be to show pictures of the house around town, I'll pass. My mother would roll over in her grave if I did such a thing."

"Ah, so here's where you are." Natalie came out onto the back porch. "What are you two up to?"

"Mom's got a hot date with Owen Harrison tonight, so we've got both girls."

"We have both girls anyway," Natalie reminded him.

"Yes, but someone's got to be here with them. If we go out, Mom stays in. If Mom's out, we're in," he reminded her.

"So. Owen Harrison again, eh?" Natalie waggled her eyebrows. "And what is it with his popping in and popping out again every few weeks? He seems to be doing a lot of coming and going."

"He's planning on retiring at the end of the year, so he feels obligated to tell all their clients personally that he'll be handing over the business to his younger brother. He wants the transition to be as smooth as possible since he's been the face of the business for many years. So he just stops in when he can squeeze out a few hours here and there between one appointment and the next."

"Is this getting serious?" Natalie asked. "'Cause it sounds like this could be getting serious."

"It's just dinner." Emma's smile teased. "But don't wait up . . ."

~

Emma's own words rang in her ears as she was getting ready for her date. Owen said it would be a casual evening, so she'd decided on a blue linen skirt and a short-sleeved button-down shirt with tiny blue and yellow flowers sprinkled on a white background. Bright-yellow sandals for fun. She touched her ears, which still felt a little naked without the pearls she'd worn for so many years. Emma plucked a pair of diamond studs from their place in her jewelry box. Chris had given them to her for her birthday the year DEAN's album went to number one for the first time. She tried to remember why she hadn't been wearing them. Ah, yes, back then she'd thought that the stones looked too big to be real and were more ostentatious than she was comfortable wearing. She'd never flaunted the fact that she was married to a wealthy man, so, likewise, she'd seen no reason to advertise that her son was a screaming success in the music world. But everyone already knew that, she told herself as she popped the studs into her ears, so why not wear Chris's gift and be happy about them?

"Why not indeed?" She looked into the mirror, turning her head this way, then that, admiring the sparkle.

She stepped back to check her overall appearance. Not too bad for not far from sixty, though fifty had been better. Forty even better than that. But then again, she'd looked pretty much the same all her life.

She decided to change handbags and looked in her closet for a blue leather crossbody bag she hadn't used since the previous summer. She found it and began to transfer what little she'd need for the evening, then stopped. Owen had made a point to mention to her at least twice that he'd be staying in Wyndham Beach overnight. Was he inviting her—maybe expecting her to stay with him tonight? Did she want to?

She didn't know.

This was a new situation for her. Did she assume she was to stay, and if so, was she supposed to pack a bag? What if she got into his car and it became very obvious that he hadn't intended that at all? How embarrassing would that be?

On the other hand, what if he asked her to stay, and she wanted to? She wouldn't have any different clothes with her. She stared at herself in the mirror, feeling frustratingly foolish. This shouldn't be such a big deal, but she'd been alone for more than ten years—ten long, lonely years—and for all that time, she'd never really been interested in anyone, and certainly hadn't spent the night with anyone. It might be nice to have someone to hold on to, especially if that someone was Owen. Then again . . .

Argh! She could go back and forth for the rest of the night, riding the pendulum that was swinging in her brain. She was just going to have to play it by ear.

She put the small blue bag back into the closet and brought out a larger white leather bag. She dumped in her wallet, cell phone, house keys, a few tissues, a pen, the small notebook she was never without. She folded a cardigan sweater and put that into the bag, thinking if she did stay over, she could just put on the cardigan in the morning and button it all the way down, and it wouldn't look exactly the same as what she was wearing now. She took a new toothbrush from a pack of six she'd picked up when she bought a few things for Winnie and tucked one into her bag. Then she paused. Should she pack makeup?

Maybe just mascara, which she wouldn't think of going without, and some blush? Though if she did stay over, she'd probably be blushing for real in the morning, no product necessary.

She felt more than a little silly for being so indecisive, but in fairness to herself, these were unknown waters to her. In the ten years Harry'd been gone, she'd never even contemplated sleeping with another man.

"Emma?" Natalie called from the hallway. "Owen's here."

"Oh, he's right on time, as always." Emma dropped the mascara into her bag and opened the door.

"You look so pretty." Natalie peeked in the doorway. "Love the earrings."

"Thanks. They were a gift from a young man who is near and dear to us both." Emma turned off the overhead light in her room and, pushing aside her inner conflict, went downstairs.

The night would unfold as it was meant to, one way or the other.

~

The Harrison mansion stood by itself in the middle of what would be a full city block, set back amid ancient oak and pine trees, and in summer was hidden from view of the road. The Georgian-style house was huge and impressive and was reached via a curving lane that wound in a precise circle around the front of the house, then off to the left, where it disappeared. Owen parked the big sedan directly in line with the door. He turned off the ignition and got out of the car, walked around the front end, and opened Emma's door.

She got out of the car and looked up at the imposing brick facade. "Your home is lovely."

"I never think of it as my home. It's always been the Harrison house to me. I should say the Jaspers' house. There have been so many of them over the years." Owen took her hand and led her up the steps to the front door, a large oak entrance with clear glass panels on the uppermost sections. He pushed it open and they stepped inside. The house was cool—almost cold—and the long entrance hall was paneled in dark wood. A large crystal chandelier hung from the ceiling, and the walls were lined with framed portraits of faces that looked stern and venerable.

"Ancient relatives," Owen told her as they passed the gallery. "None of whom look like they'd be much fun." He paused in front of a picture of a woman wearing a black dress, a gold pin at her throat, and a black veil over her light hair.

Blonde or gray? Emma couldn't tell.

"Except for her," Owen was saying. "My great-great-grandmother Elora. I'd have loved to have known her. If you look closely, you can see there's a little twinkle in her eye, and just the tiniest bit of a smile on her lips, almost *Mona Lisa*–like." Owen was smiling as he looked up at his ancestor. "She was supposed to be in mourning for—I think it was Jasper two. Maybe Jasper three, I'm not sure. But she was his third wife and much, much younger than he was. Apparently he wore out the other two and put them in the ground. I think she's smiling because she knows he isn't going to get the chance to do that to her—and she and her son—his only son, his other children were girls—had inherited his entire estate."

Owen leaned closer to Emma and whispered in her ear. "The cause of death was never established, but I'm thinking poison."

Emma laughed. "Pure supposition or is there something to support your accusation? Family legend perhaps?"

He shook his head. "Nope. I just like to think she did it. He probably would have deserved it. The family legend is that he was a mean SOB and fell off his horse and broke his neck."

"She must have used a time-released poison," Emma noted.

"Obviously," he said.

"Owen Harrison, stop filling this lovely woman's head with nonsense." A woman who appeared to be close to Emma's age stood at the end of the hall. Her hair was pinned up, and she wore a white apron over a shirtwaist dress of chambray denim. There was something familiar about her, but Emma couldn't place where she'd seen her.

"Just passing on my truth as I know it, Mrs. Fraser." Owen turned to Emma as they walked toward the woman. "Mrs. Fraser is the keeper of the Harrison hearth. She takes care of everything inside these walls, and she's a fantastic cook. I've tried to get her to move to my London house, but she keeps refusing. Something about wanting to stay with her husband."

"My husband is the groundskeeper," Mrs. Fraser told Emma. "He keeps up the outside; I take care of the inside."

"He could come along. Better yet, you can both come with me to Tuscany. He can work the olive grove with me."

"Still determined to grow olives?" she asked him.

"Absolutely."

"You live on the grounds here?" Emma asked.

"We do. We have, for coming up onto forty years now." She put out her hand to Emma.

"Ruth Fraser. It's nice to meet you."

"Emma Dean." Emma shook the woman's hand.

"I'm sure I've seen you around town. In the bookshop and in the general store. Maybe in Ground Me as well."

"Well, I've lived my entire life in Wyndham Beach, and those are my three favorite places in Wyndham Beach, so you probably have seen me around. You do look familiar."

The housekeeper snapped her fingers. "The bookshop. I've seen you there on Saturday mornings. I've taken my grandkids there for the story hour." She turned to Owen. "They have a young woman who dresses up like Mary Poppins and reads to the children."

Emma nodded. "Grace Flynn. She's my friend Maggie's daughter."

"Your friend Maggie who's marrying the chief of police?" Owen leaned against the doorjamb.

"Yes."

"I heard about that," Ruth said. "He used to play professional football but got injured. She's a widow from down south someplace."

"Pennsylvania." Emma nodded. "That would be her."

"Small towns." Owen rolled his eyes, and both women laughed.

Then Emma sniffed the air. "Something smells amazing."

"Ruth promised to make her world-famous roast chicken for us." Owen closed his eyes and inhaled. "Best aroma ever. I hope it's almost ready, because I'm starving."

"It is, and I'd better get back to it. And you're starving because you don't eat regular meals," she said as she went into the kitchen.

"It seems we have a few minutes," Owen said. "Would you like a little tour?"

"I thought you'd never ask." Emma took the hand Owen held out to her.

"This way to the dining room."

They walked into a cavernous room with walls papered in red and gold, and an enormous table flanked by sixteen baronial-worthy chairs, one at each end, seven on each side.

"I've never seen a dining room this big," Emma exclaimed. "It's . . . intimidating."

"I agree. I usually eat in the little morning room off the kitchen. It's cozy and friendlier." He pointed to the portrait hanging over the fireplace. "That's Jasper one. He built the original section of the house, and one of his grandsons expanded it and bought all this grand furniture. He liked to entertain."

"Apparently for a crowd." Emma pictured the dining table with sixteen people seated around it and recalled dinner parties at her own home when Harry was alive. If there were more than twelve on the guest list, she'd set up a buffet. It had been years since she'd entertained more than two people at a time. Recently, it had been only Liddy and Maggie. Now Chris and Natalie, and of course the two girls. The thought of serving sixteen people at once was daunting, and she said so.

"The last time I ate in here was about eight years ago. My brother Ethan brought his wife and children to see the carousel, and they'd brought a few cousins along. Even with that group the room felt empty." He looked around once, then tilted his head in the direction of the front of the house. "Want to move on?"

"Sure. What's in here?" She peeked around the door and looked into another large room, one with several lamps lit on low. The room was furnished with several sofas and chairs in subdued florals, and a massive stone fireplace dominated the outside wall.

"My father always referred to this room as the drawing room. Children were never allowed in," Owen told her. "I have no recollection of ever being in this room as a child. Only since I inherited it and took myself on a tour of all those places I hadn't seen."

Emma couldn't think of a thing to say. How could you expect your children to never enter a room in the house in which they lived? She recalled that as a very young child, he had gone to boarding school, another head-scratcher as far as she was concerned. Why have children if you were going to isolate them from their family?

She was still thinking about that while they wandered from one room to the next. There were two parlors, an office, a den, two sitting rooms, and a library. The house was bigger than she'd suspected, cold and dark even though it had been in the eighties that day, and there were lamps lit in every room.

They wandered to the back of the house and to the small dining room where a table for two had been set. This room, Emma mentally noted, was the only cheery spot she'd seen in the house. The walls were painted a soft yellow, and there was a lovely view of the gardens and the expansive backyard and several outbuildings.

"You're just in time," Ruth told them as she placed a bottle of wine on the table. "I was just about to call you."

"Everything smells amazing," Emma said as Owen held out a chair for her.

"Ruth's roast chicken is one of the few things that can bring me back to Wyndham Beach, present company being one of the others." Owen sat next to her so they both could look out across the grounds.

"Is that a carriage house?" She indicated the building closest to the house.

Owen nodded. "And then there's a maintenance building—we call it the shed—and back near the trees on the other side of the house is the building where the carousel is stored."

"Will the carousel be brought out for the Fourth of July?" she asked.

"Well, five years haven't passed yet since we last brought it out, and the will said . . ."

"The will said no more than five years, not no less than."

Owen laughed. "If you want the carousel brought out, the carousel will be there for the kiddies in town to ride on July Fourth. You can remind me if you think I might forget."

"No, I trust you. The kids loved it last time. The horses are simply magnificent works of art."

"They are. We're lucky to have it, though the circumstances under which it was purchased were sad."

Emma nodded. "Your ancestor who had the carousel created for his terminally ill daughter."

Ruth came in to serve dinner—the roast chicken accompanied by mashed potatoes and sautéed spinach.

"You made mashed potatoes." Owen's eyes lit up.

"Of course. I know they're your favorite." Ruth took a step back to look over the table after she arranged the serving bowls and plates. "Probably not served in some of those fancy restaurants you patronize." She winked at Emma.

"Some do. But none as good as yours," he assured her.

"I know." A smiling Ruth patted him on the back. "Let me know if you need anything else."

"Thanks, Ruth." Owen proceeded to serve Emma before serving himself.

"Oh my gosh, the chicken is amazing," Emma said after she'd tasted it.

"She does something with lemon and garlic and some herbs. It always tastes the same, and no one does it better." He opened the bottle of wine and offered to pour some for Emma.

"Yes, please," Emma said. She took a sip after he filled her glass. "It's delicious."

As was the entire meal. "You didn't exaggerate," she told Owen. "Ruth is an excellent cook."

"She's as good as any chef, anywhere, in my book. The meals she makes are always simple but perfect."

"These days they call meals like this—chicken and mashed potatoes—comfort food." Emma touched her napkin to the corners of her mouth and wished she'd worn something with an elastic waist. She couldn't remember the last time she'd eaten quite as much.

Oh, right. The last time Owen took her to dinner. The lobster shack and their wonderful lobster potpie.

"Would you like your coffee and dessert here, or on the patio?" Ruth stood in the doorway.

"I don't think I could handle dessert," Emma said.

"Maybe you'll change your mind after a walk outside." Owen stood, his hand on the back of her chair, his wineglass in his hand.

"That would certainly help." Emma expressed her thanks to Ruth for preparing the delicious meal, then followed Owen outside through a plant-filled sunroom.

"What a perfect night," he said as they walked through a beautiful garden where peonies were budding out everywhere she looked. "The stars are so bright here. I don't think I ever noticed before."

"How could you live in Wyndham Beach and not notice?" She immediately corrected herself: "Of course you didn't really live in Wyndham Beach for most of your life."

"It's much nicer than I remember. I'm finding I like being here more and more." He looked at her meaningfully. "Specifically, I like being here with you."

He turned her face up to his and kissed her, and any thoughts she'd had of going home if he asked her to stay dissolved. She liked kissing him. She wanted him to kiss her again and again, enough so that she was disappointed when he raised his head and said, "Let's walk down to the pond."

"You have a pond?" She cleared her throat and reached for his hand.

"We do." He took it in his and led her across the lawn. "I think I may have seen your son in town this afternoon. At the coffee shop."

"You very well may have. Ground Me is one of his favorite stops in town. He goes in every day at least once."

"Is he in Wyndham Beach for long?"

"For a while. He isn't quite sure how long, but I expect for at least another week or so. He and Natalie have a wedding to plan, and I suppose they're trying to iron out all the details before he goes back to California." She added casually, "He's been in no hurry since he's trying to bond with Winnie while he's here."

"Winnie?" Owen frowned. "The girl who is claiming to be his daughter?"

"Well, her mother is the one who made that claim. It doesn't matter at this point. They've exhausted their options to figure out who her father really is, and there's a very good chance her mother is deceased. Chris and Natalie have discussed the situation, and they've made the decision to keep her with us, which was a huge relief to me, because I've grown so fond of her."

He sighed. "Emma, you have such a soft heart, but keeping her here is only going to make things harder for you—and for her—when you finally send her back."

"What are you talking about?" Emma pulled up short. "She's not going back. Chris has accepted her as his daughter, and he and Natalie are going to raise her as their own."

"You can't be serious."

"Of course I'm serious."

"Knowing she isn't his daughter, Chris is going to go along with this . . . this game someone is playing with him?"

"There's no game, Owen."

"Oh, please." Even in the dark, Emma could see Owen's eyes roll.

"What exactly do you think is going on?"

"I think your son is being played by someone who will be looking for a big payoff. It's pretty clear he's being set up."

"Set up by whom?"

"Winnie's mother. Her grandmother. Maybe even her mother's siblings. They might all be involved in it."

"Her grandmother has made it very clear she doesn't want anything to do with Tish, and her siblings won't even talk about her." Emma pulled her hand from his. "Winnie's mother is probably dead."

"That's what they want you to think. Trust me, they're going to let her stay with you long enough for her to worm her way into your hearts; then they're going to show up and threaten to take her back. The mother will say she had amnesia or something. They'll name a price, and Chris is going to have to pay up if he wants to keep her. She should have been sent back as soon as she showed up at your door. I can't believe you fell for it."

"And I can't believe what I'm hearing."

"I'm telling you, when they figure the time is right, they're going to go after Chris for a big payoff. And the longer she's with you, the higher the price will be. The only way out of this is to call their bluff. Send her back. Buy her a one-way ticket back to where she came from, but send her back now."

She stared at him, stunned, wondering where fun, kind, sensitive Owen had gone.

When she found her voice, she said, "She's a little girl, Owen. A sweet, funny, smart little girl."

"Of course she is. Otherwise you wouldn't want her."

"You'd really put an eight-year-old child on a bus by herself and send her all the way to Georgia? Alone?"

He nodded, obviously confused by her sudden coolness. "Chris has to protect himself. He has to protect his family."

"She is part of his family," Emma said quietly. "You know what, Owen? I'd like you to take me home. Now."

"Emma, for crying out loud." He reached for her.

"Now." She walked back through the house then right out the front door and stood next to the car for a moment, waiting for him. When he finally appeared in the doorway, he hesitated before coming down the steps.

"I've upset you, and I'm so sorry, Emma. I think we should talk this over."

"There's nothing left to say, except that I'm disappointed, and I'm sad, because I care about you. I thought you were a better man."

He came down off the steps, his arms reaching for her.

"Don't," she said as she backed away. "On second thought, I think I'd like to walk home."

She started down the driveway, turning once to look back at the crestfallen, confused man standing in the light of the front porch.

"Let me know when you remember where you left your heart."

～

Under ordinary circumstances, Emma would be delighted to spend a few relaxed hours on Liddy's deck, drinking her hostess's excellent margaritas, eating delicious snacks, and chatting happily with her two best friends. Tonight she was painfully aware she was faking it—and apparently she wasn't fooling anyone.

"Em, how many years have we been friends?" Maggie asked as she helped herself to Liddy's secret-recipe baked onion dip. "Liddy, you're going to have to cough up this recipe. I want to serve it at my wedding."

"Maybe. But it would have to count as part of my wedding gift to you and Brett," Liddy replied.

"Sorry, Em. Should I repeat the question?" Maggie asked.

"No need. We both know we met in grade school. Even a conservative estimate would bring it to somewhere between fifty-three and fifty-five years. Depending on how old you were when you started kindergarten."

"So almost all our lives, right?" Maggie took a sip of her margarita.

Emma nodded, wondering where Maggie was going with this conversation. It wasn't like her to be oblique when she wanted to say something.

"So I'm wondering—actually, we're wondering, Liddy and I— what's got you so stressed out? Is it the thing with your artist and her abusive ex?"

Liddy put the newly filled pitcher of margaritas on the table between them and took a seat. "Are things not going well with Owen? Or . . ."

"Stop." Emma's hands rose to her face and began to massage her temples. "What makes you think I'm stressed?"

"Oh, please." Liddy rolled her eyes. "We've already established the fact that we've known each other practically all our lives. For the past few weeks, every time I looked at you, it's been obvious you were having a headache. Emma, in all these years, I don't recall you ever having headaches that lasted for days. Something's bothering you, and you're not talking about it."

"I'll be fine when I can finally get some sleep, that's all." Emma hated the defensive note that crept into her voice.

"What's keeping you awake, sweetie?" Maggie asked gently.

"You know you'll feel better if you dump it all right here. It's not like you not to share," Liddy said.

Emma sighed. There was going to be no way around it.

"It just seems like things are piling up. Yes, Maggie, I am worried about Stella, my artist. And yes, Liddy, I am upset about the situation with Owen. Between the three of us, I think I might still be feeling some emotional fallout about Harry's affair. Then there are five artists at the center, and a curated exhibition to prepare for the local artists, and another one at the end of the residency for those artists. And now there's Maggie's wedding, and the wedding of my only child on the horizon, and I just don't know which fire to put out first. Not that I can—I mean, I don't have the power to control everything. Like Stella's situation. And it's looking more and more like Tish might be dead and buried in the Nevada desert somewhere, so there's that. How do you tell a child there's a chance her mother might have been murdered and the police are looking for her grave. And . . ."

"Whoa. Right there." Maggie leaned over and took Emma's hand. "No wonder you're stressed and are having headaches all the time. Em, any one of those things would do it. So let's see what we can do to maybe ease some of that."

Emma shook her head. "Thanks, Mags, but there's nothing either of you can do."

"Au contraire, mon amie," Maggie assured her. "We can help sort this all out. When was the last time any one of us had to go it alone when faced with a seemingly insurmountable problem?"

"Nineteen eighty," Liddy answered without missing a beat. She tilted her drink glass in Maggie's direction. "When you got pregnant in our senior year and had a baby you gave up for adoption. A baby you never told either of us about."

"Okay, other than that," Maggie conceded. "But I had good reasons to keep it to myself."

"None of them valid in our opinion." Liddy pointed to Emma, then herself.

"Still holding that grudge, are you?" Maggie sighed.

"I try not to, but Liddy's right. We could have been there for you, if for no other reason than to hold your hand when you needed one, or given you a shoulder to lean on," Emma said.

"And that's precisely my point, Em. All the things you're going through right now, maybe we can help." Maggie's voice was soothing and confident. "We know you like to control things—there's no shame in that—but sometimes just seeing something through someone else's eyes can help. One thing at a time."

Liddy was nodding. "Let's start with the situation at the art center. I don't mean just the thing with Stella and her ex. I mean dealing with the other artists and the exhibit you want to plan for them. You have an assistant. Why don't you use her more?"

"Marion is part time—and she's also part time with you at the bookstore. There are only so many hours in a day, Liddy. Most of hers are accounted for."

"But she doesn't work for me seven days a week, Em. She works four. Maybe she'd like to pick up some extra hours at the center. You know, her son's wife is having a baby in October. She might like to squirrel away a few bucks to buy a few things for her new grandchild."

Emma was about to protest—it was so hard to think clearly with that drum beating inside her head—but Maggie interrupted whatever it was she would have said.

"Nothing to be lost by asking her. If she says no, well, no harm, no foul. Then you could start looking for another person, someone to work the hours you would have given Marion."

"I admit I'd thought about hiring someone." Emma looked from one friend to the other. "Full time."

"So even you know you need help. Talk to Marion. And if she can't or won't do it, surely there's someone between here and New Bedford who'd be interested." Maggie paused. "Or maybe just hire someone to work on the exhibits. Someone who knows art and who can take care of the details for you. The promotions, for example."

Liddy snapped her fingers. "Keely McGillan."

"Who?" Emma frowned. The name was vaguely familiar but she couldn't place it.

"Eileen McGillan's daughter. I saw Eileen in Ground Me last week, and she mentioned Keely would be home by the end of the week. She majored in art conservation at the University of Delaware, and the job she thought she had lined up fell through, so she's spending a few weeks at the beach down there with some friends before coming home. She'd be perfect."

Emma thought it over. "Well, I suppose I could give Eileen a call and see if her daughter has found something else . . ."

"So let's check that off the list for now. What's next?" Liddy appeared to consult an imaginary list. "Owen."

"Owen. Where to begin with Owen?" Emma felt herself tearing up. "You know, I was all ready to take off with him for New Year's Eve in Italy. I was going to learn to speak Italian, though I've barely looked at the instructional CDs I bought." She paused. "Which in retrospect would probably have been a waste of time."

Liddy and Maggie exchanged a confused glance.

"Truthfully, if I never see him again, it'll be too soon."

Another confused look before Maggie spoke up. "Are we still talking about Owen Harrison?"

Emma nodded, and let the tears fall.

"I thought that was going so well," Liddy said. "Want to tell us about it?"

Emma did. Everything from dinner in the Harrison mansion the previous week to her final parting shot as she walked away.

"I'm stunned." Maggie's eyes were as big as saucers. "What on earth would have made him react like that?"

"Wow, it just goes to show." Liddy shook her head. "He sure had us all fooled. We all thought he was such a great guy."

"He is. He was. I was honestly thinking about staying over that night." Emma rolled her eyes. "I can't believe I was actually thinking about having sex with that man."

"You found out just in time." Liddy patted her hand.

"He showed his true colors, and you did the right thing, Em," Maggie assured her.

"Though the sex might have been really good," Liddy said.

"I'll never know now. I'm just so disillusioned and confused. How can a person be so nice, so good hearted, and be so cold at the same time? It was such a shock I couldn't do anything but leave as quickly as I could."

"Have you heard from him since?"

"I'd left without my purse, so he dropped it off at my house the next morning, but I didn't answer the doorbell, so he left it on the porch. He's called. He's texted. He even sent flowers to the house."

"What did he say?"

"I didn't speak with him, and I deleted his texts without reading them. I can't think of anything he could say that would change what's already been said." Emma reached for her glass as if just remembering she had a drink. "And I sent the flowers to the nursing home over on Jackson Street."

They sat without speaking for a few minutes, the only sound the crunching of crackers.

Finally Maggie said, "There's something odd about Owen's reaction. It just doesn't go with what you've told us about him. It's out of character."

"Tell me about it. I still can't believe he said all those things."

"Jekyll and Hyde," Liddy murmured.

Emma nodded. "Yes, like that."

"There has to be an explanation." Maggie munched a cracker thoughtfully.

The silence returned for several moments.

"I suppose now isn't the time to ask about the Harrison mansion," Liddy said. "Like, what it looks like inside."

Maggie and Emma turned to Liddy, shock on their faces; then the three women began to laugh.

"Sorry. I had to lighten you up some way, honey," Liddy told Emma. "I hate to see you so sad and so down."

"Thank you, my friend. Let's just put Owen aside and talk about something else."

"That's our girl." Maggie poured herself another half glassful from the pitcher. "So what's next?"

"The weddings," Emma said. "Two weddings, one in July, one in whenever."

"You don't have to do a thing for my wedding," Maggie told her. "Just show up and be your own beautiful self."

"Wait, you mean we're not in your wedding?" Liddy looked stricken. "I thought for sure you'd want us to be in your wedding." She turned to Emma. "Em, didn't you think Maggie would ask us to be bridesmaids?"

"Bridesmatrons, maybe, but yes, now that you mention it. I assumed she would."

Liddy and Emma both stared at Maggie, waiting.

"Oh. I guess I just figured . . ." Maggie appeared lost for words. "I mean, my daughters will be . . . well, I guess they could both be maids of honor, so you could both be bridesmaids. Matrons." She laughed. "Attendants. I'm sorry, but I haven't had much time to think about the actual wedding. I've been too busy poring over Natalie's bride's magazines, looking at dresses. Oh my God, have you seen what the modern bride is wearing these days?"

"I've probably seen the same magazines you have. Natalie always seems to have one in her hands." Emma nodded. "Explains why brides might blush. Some of those dresses leave very little to the imagination. Bare in some of the oddest places."

"Want to come with me when I shop for a dress next week?" Maggie asked.

"I'd love to," Emma responded right away.

"Of course," Liddy said. "We have to make sure you buy something that doesn't scandalize the locals."

Maggie laughed. "I promise not to make a spectacle of myself at my wedding." She crossed her heart. "I don't know what I want specifically, just something simple but elegant and gorgeous. Something suitable for an almost sixty-year-old bride to wear for her beach wedding."

"Cottage Street Beach?" Emma asked.

"But of course." Maggie smiled. "It's home base."

"And let us not forget it's where you lost your virginity," Liddy pointed out. "At least you did share that with us."

Maggie laughed and dipped a cracker into the brie. "I had not forgotten."

"So . . . are we in . . . or are we out?" Liddy narrowed her eyes and sent a laser of a glare to Maggie, who laughed again.

"Of course you're in. I'd love to have you in my wedding. I apologize for not thinking that far ahead. I've just been so lost in the idea of actually marrying Brett—after all these years, after me being married to Art for thirty-five years, and Brett being married . . ." She paused to think.

"Three times, but I'm not sure how long he lasted with any of his wives," Emma said. "Three wives, three daughters."

"They all looked like you. The wives," Liddy said. "The way you looked when we were in high school. I always thought it was sad, that he kept trying to marry you over and over again."

"Except of course it wasn't you," Emma added. "But we did feel sorry for him, because we knew."

Liddy nodded. "We definitely knew."

Maggie picked up the pitcher and looked inside. "How much of this stuff have you two been drinking?"

Liddy and Emma ignored her.

"Thanks for listening, guys. I do feel better," Emma told them. "Maybe I'll even skip the Advil before I go to bed tonight. I guess I just have too much on my plate right now."

"Em, there isn't a plate big enough for everything you're trying to deal with," Maggie pointed out. "Anything else we should discuss?"

"Oh, well, Chris's wedding, of course. Whenever that will be. I can't wait to find out when and what their plans are. My big night as mother of the groom."

"The MOG," Maggie said. "That's how all the magazines refer to the mother of the groom. And I'm the MOB. Mother of the bride."

"And I'm the FOB," Liddy said. "Friend of both."

She began to refill everyone's glass.

"No more for me," Maggie began to protest, but Liddy had already topped off her drink. "Oh, well. Just this last one. But, you know, we should have a margarita bar at the wedding."

"I am not playing bartender in my bridesmaid . . . matron . . . dress."

"Good point. And no one makes a margarita like you do, Liddy."

"It's true." She turned to Emma. "So we're good? I mean, you're good?"

"I am. And you're right. It's not good to hold things inside. I held on to mixed-up feelings about Harry for years, even way before I knew about his affair. Things didn't feel the way I thought a marriage should feel. I keep telling myself that I'm beyond caring about his affair, but, frankly, it still hurts."

"Let it go, Em. Now relax. Close your eyes. Picture his face," Liddy instructed. When Emma's eyes were closed, Liddy asked, "Do you see Harry's face?"

Emma nodded.

"I want you to take a black Sharpie—the one with the wide tip?—and draw a fat ugly mustache right there under his nose."

Emma laughed. "Done. Oh, it's not a good look for him. Actually, he looks a little like a porn star."

"Now put a big X right over his face." She paused. "Are you drawing an X, Em?"

"I did."

"Now take that picture, rip it into tiny pieces, and toss it into the harbor. He has no meaning in your life now."

Em tossed her hands up, as if tossing confetti. "There. He's gone."

"Good for you. You know, you keep an eye on the past, it will never be behind you. You'll never move forward. And forward is where it's at. Forward is Maggie's wedding. Forward is Chris and Nat's wedding and maybe some more grandbabies someday in the not-too-distant future. Forward is a future you don't want to miss, whatever it brings. I have a feeling it's going to be a beautiful one. Don't turn your back on it."

Maggie turned to Liddy. "Damn. That was deep. When did you start having such deep thoughts?"

"I was born deep," Liddy said solemnly.

"And yet you've hidden that side of you so well all these years," Maggie said.

"Oh, you two." Emma laughed and picked up her glass. "Here's to forward. Here's to the future."

They all took a sip.

"And here's to the truest, the most loving, the deepest of friends," Emma said.

Liddy stared into her now-empty glass. "Might be time for another tattoo."

Maggie held up her arm and pulled up her sleeve and admired the tattoo on her lower forearm. "How could we top this one?"

Emma studied the matching tattoo on her arm. "Maybe just one wave this time."

Liddy frowned and looked at her own. "Why just one? We already have three."

"Because we are one," Emma said quietly.

"Oooh." Liddy nodded slowly. "Now who's deep?"

Chapter Seventeen

"It's the perfect day to find a wedding dress," Liddy said as Emma got into the back seat of Maggie's car and sat next to Grace.

It would be for me, too, Natalie thought. She'd love to be looking for her gown as well, but she was determined that her mother have her time on center stage. Besides, there were great wedding shops in the Philly area. There was a beautiful shop in Devon—she'd driven past it several times but never had the nerve to go in—and that place in Ardmore where Grace had bought the gown for her wedding twelve years ago. She thought about that for a moment. Had she heard somewhere that it had closed? Maybe not the luckiest place to look. But her day would come when she would step into a fairy tale of a shop and be surrounded by wearable confections, find the dress that would make her feel like a princess. Today was not going to be that day, and she was okay with that.

"Tell us what you've got in mind, Mom," Grace said.

"I'll know it when I see it," Maggie replied.

"Are you thinking white?" Liddy asked.

"Second wedding, two grown kids, grandmother? I guess I have to skip the virginal white."

"Nonsense. These days women of every age wear whatever they damned well please. If you find a dress you love in white, I say go for it."

"Liddy, I know you would. I'm not as much of a risk-taker as you," Maggie reminded her friend.

"It's not so much of a risk anymore, but, Mom, you could do a pale pink," Natalie suggested. "You look gorgeous in pink."

"I have thought about pink. I've been told this shop has an incredible selection, so let's see what we can see."

The selection proved to be more than incredible: it was overwhelming. There were racks of dresses everywhere, and around the perimeter of the shop there were alcoves bearing the names of all the latest wedding designers. They were met at the door by an eager saleswoman who looked over the group of five, then focused on Grace and Natalie, then narrowed down the possibilities to Natalie, who was the only one sporting an engagement ring.

Except of course for Maggie, but as an older woman, she was disregarded in the saleswoman's first pass.

"Stunning ring," she cooed as she reached for Natalie's ring finger. "You're going to make a beautiful bride."

"Well, yes, that would be the hope someday." Natalie took Maggie's arm. "However, on this day, the beautiful bride would be my mother."

The group went past the woman and walked into the shop. They were greeted by a younger saleswoman who was coming out of the back room. She also glanced over the group, then settled on the duo in the forefront. She made a calculated guess and extended her hand to Maggie.

"I'm Hannah," she said. "What can I help you with today?"

"I'm hoping to find my wedding dress," Maggie told her.

"I'll do my best to make that happen for you."

Grace turned and smiled at the first saleswoman, who was being left behind, and stage-whispered, "Later you might ask your colleague for some tips."

"Maggie Flynn," Maggie introduced herself. "My daughters Grace and Natalie. My friends Lydia and Emma."

"Nice to meet you all. Now let's find ourselves a room, and you can tell me what you have in mind." She led them across the room into a small space cordoned off by two curved walls to create a private sitting room. One side was completely mirrored. "So, Maggie." After everyone got comfortable, Hannah sat on the arm of one of the three love seats that crowded the space. "Tell me a little about yourself. How you see yourself on your wedding day."

"Second wedding for me, and I see myself on the beach at sunset exchanging vows with the man I've loved since I was fifteen years old."

Hannah put a hand over her heart. "Sounds like there's a story there!"

Maggie gave her the short version, after which Hannah sighed and said, "I love hearing second-chance stories. It gives me hope that the guy I dated in college will someday walk through the door."

"If he walks through that door"—Liddy pointed in the direction of the store's entrance—"he might have someone else on his arm."

Hannah laughed. "That would be my luck. Now, Maggie, fabric? Style?"

"Nothing too fancy. Something elegant. Romantic. Full length but not full skirted. Not too tight. Not sure of fabric. Nothing trendy."

"And nothing that allows bare skin to show through in awkward places," Liddy added.

"Well, that does help to narrow it down." Laughing, Hannah rose, nodding. "Color preference?"

"I wouldn't mind a pale pink," Maggie said. "Otherwise, cream or ecru maybe?"

"And season? Are you looking forward to the fall or winter? Perhaps next spring?"

"Ah, no," Maggie replied sheepishly. "We're getting married the last weekend in July."

"Next July?" Hannah asked for clarification.

"This July."

"Well, that could be a problem." The saleswoman's eyes widened, but she appeared only momentarily flustered before she said, "But I have a few ideas that we could work with." She went through the opening between the curved walls. "I'll have some refreshments brought in while you wait."

She'd barely left the room before the refreshment cart was wheeled in by a short woman who was cheery and who offered a selection of teas, coffee, and wine. There was a fruit-and-cheese tray and an array of crackers. Another plate held small pastries.

"I say we hit the fruit first, then the scones," Grace said as she looked over the offerings. "Save the little cream puffs for dessert."

"Such a nice idea." Emma gestured toward the cart. She looked at Natalie. "We might have to come back at another time."

"We should." Grace nibbled on a strawberry and elbowed her sister. "Once this one here decides on a date."

Maggie turned to Natalie. "I thought you said Labor Day weekend."

"Chris might have a conflict that weekend. He's trying to work things out."

"A conflict?" Emma frowned. "What kind of conflict?"

"Some fundraiser they'd agreed to do months ago that he'd forgotten about. He's looking into the details. We'll let you know."

A few minutes later, Hannah swept back into the room, several gowns in hangers over her left arm. She hung them separately on hooks that were placed around the room and proceeded to show off each dress in turn. Natalie thought her mother looked slightly disappointed.

"They're all lovely, but . . . ," Maggie said.

"But not you?" Hannah asked.

"But not me. I can't see myself in any of those."

Hannah gathered up the gowns. "Let me see what else I can find for you." She paused in the doorway. "Perhaps if one of your daughters went through the inventory with me, we could find something more suited to your taste?"

"I'll come. I saw a dress recently in a magazine that I think would be stunning on you, Mom." Natalie stood and placed her coffee cup on the cart.

"Do you remember the designer?" Hannah asked.

"It started with a *P*. I'll know it when I see it."

"This way, then."

Natalie followed Hannah to a large room where racks and racks of clear plastic garment bags held wedding dresses in every size and color, from purest white to black. From long gowns to the briefest of minis. Ball gowns to sheaths and everything in between. The saleswoman began to look through the racks.

"So when are you getting married?" Hannah asked.

"Not sure yet. We haven't set the date. We thought the beginning of September, but we might have to change it."

"Have you found your gown yet? Or are you going to wait until the last possible minute like your mom?"

"Believe me, as soon as I have a firm date—and thus, a season—I will be back here in a heartbeat. You have the loveliest gowns."

She stopped to stare at a dress hanging on a hook, no garment bag in sight.

"That would be stunning on you," Hannah told her.

"Thanks." Natalie sighed. "But I can't do that today."

"Do what?"

"Look at gowns. Today's Mom's day."

"And what a good daughter you are to let her have her moment."

"She deserves it."

Hannah unzipped a garment bag. "Was this anything like the dress you saw?"

Natalie stepped closer to get a better look. "Similar but without all that beading on the bodice. My mom doesn't like anything fussy. I think she'd like something really plain but stylish."

"I have an idea." Hannah walked farther down the row. She returned with a garment bag that she hung on a hook. She unzipped it, then pulled a dress of gleaming white satin from its shroud. "She didn't mention white as a color choice, and I'm sure this isn't the dress you have in mind, but there's something about this one. What do you think of this?"

Natalie took one look at the dress, then beamed. "That's so Mom. If she doesn't love that one, I don't know what she'll want. It's perfect for her."

"Let's see what she thinks of it."

They returned to the little private room, Hannah carrying the gown.

"Maggie, come with me to the dressing room. Your daughter believes she's found your dress."

"Oh, it's white. Second-time bride here. And is that satin?" Maggie put her teacup on the tray and stood. "Satin makes you look as broad as a barn."

"Old wives' tale. It's all in the cut," Hannah told her. "And white doesn't mean what it once did. Anyone can wear it. Follow me and let's try this on. At one time we did have it in your size, which would be a blessing because you're not giving me much time to dress you for your big day."

"Still . . . white satin . . ." Maggie's voice trailed behind her as she and the saleswoman found a dressing room.

Grace turned to Natalie. "What's the dress look like?"

"You'll have to wait to see." Natalie felt her smile morph into smugness, but she couldn't help herself. Her mother would be magnificent in that dress—she just knew it.

And she was right.

When Maggie walked into the private dressing room, there'd been stunned silence before a chorus of oohs and aahs and yeses broke out.

The pure white satin perfectly complemented Maggie's blonde hair and her warm skin tone. The style was perfection—a long slim column with a halter neckline that crossed over in the front. The dress was exactly as Maggie had suggested: elegant, classic, slightly fitted but not tight anywhere, and perfectly suited for a romantic wedding on a beach at dusk.

"Mom, you're gorgeous," Grace had exclaimed. "Way to show off those beautiful shoulders of yours."

"What's a word for beyond gorgeous?" Natalie chimed in. "Because that's what you are in that dress. Oh, you're beautiful every day, but wow, that dress, Mom."

"Thank you for suggesting it." Maggie stood up straight and looked into the mirror. "I don't know that I would have thought of something like this. It's perfectly plain, but it's just lovely."

"It's so elegant," Emma said. "It doesn't need any embellishment at all. Its simplicity speaks for itself. Sleek and chic and sophisticated and sexy without trying. Oh, Maggie, you have to buy it."

Liddy began singing "Nights in White Satin," an old Moody Blues song from the sixties. Then laughing, the others who knew the words—including Hannah—chimed in for a few lines.

"So, Mom, are you saying yes to this most perfect dress?" Grace borrowed a line from a popular TV show.

"I am saying absolutely yes." Maggie was staring at her reflection as if not recognizing herself.

"That would be a 'hell yes' from anyone else," Liddy told Hannah.

"Wonderful." Hannah clapped lightly two times. "Inventory says the one we had in your size was sold, but I will try my best to find one for you and have it sent in ASAP. If not, we're going to have to make some alterations to this one. Take it in some here, and definitely shorten it. Do you know what kind of shoes you'll be wearing?"

"On the beach?" Maggie shook her head. "No shoes. Probably pretty sandals for the reception."

"Then we'll definitely need this hemmed."

"Mom, how are you going to wear your hair?" Grace asked.

Maggie half turned toward her. "I haven't thought that far ahead. Maybe just down as it is now but pulled up on one side? I don't know."

"Maybe we could find some sort of pretty thing for you to wear in your hair," Natalie suggested. "While you're changing, we could scout out the hair clips."

"Do that. If you find anything you love, put it aside for me." One last look into the mirror, then Maggie followed Hannah from the room.

While they scanned the display of hair baubles, Grace whispered in Natalie's ear, "You could look while we're here, you know."

"Giving Mom her day."

"She wouldn't care."

"I would. I'll wait until I know for sure when. I can always come back." She smiled. "Okay, so I did take a very quick peek while we were in the back room. I'm pretty sure I'll find something here."

"You definitely will." Hannah came up behind her and handed her a card. "Call me when you're ready to start looking. But do me a favor and don't wait as long as your mother did. It's going to take a village to get that dress in her size."

"I have no doubt if there's one out there, you'll find it."

And Hannah did. She called two days later to let Maggie know she'd found her dress in her size in another shop, and it was already on its way to Hannah. The bride who'd ordered it had changed her mind about it, so it was available. All Maggie had to do was make an appointment for a fitting, which she did for the following week. The five would make the return trip together so that the attendants could select their dresses while the bride's dress was being fitted for alterations. Maggie thought the colors of the sky at dusk would make a lovely palette, but she'd left it up to her daughters and her two friends to choose their dress in any style in any shade of purple or pinky coral. She'd wanted Daisy to be her flower girl, but when Natalie announced that Winnie would from then on be a member of the family, Maggie couldn't bring herself to slight her, so there would be two flower girls. Online, Natalie found the perfect dresses for the two young ones, so she'd ordered those in dreamy chiffon swirls of purple, lilac, coral, and pink.

Everything was smooth sailing for Maggie and Brett's long-overdue wedding. The caterer had been lined up, the florist met with, the tent on order along with tables and chairs to fit under it. The wedding would be on the beach and the reception under a white tent in Emma's spacious backyard. Grace was working on the invitations, which would be hand-delivered in town and emailed to those out-of-towners, and Maggie was still making a decision on favors and whether or not to have a seating chart. She was thinking not, but traditions were hard to break when one has been raised by the book, as Maggie had been.

Natalie tried to ignore the elephant in the room, but at the same time, Chris was getting a little antsy about the fact that they still had no date for their own wedding. DEAN had a commitment to participate in a fundraiser over Labor Day weekend, with live appearances Friday through Monday. If they were going to have a wedding before the band's spring tour, they needed to nail down a day, and fast. They took the girls to the beach one late-June afternoon, and after having walked from Cottage Street as far as Bay Street and back, Chris and Natalie sat at the foot of the lifeguard stand while the girls continued their search for sea treasures.

"I'm sorry that Labor Day weekend fell through. I had no recollection of that weekend-long benefit concert until Melissa reminded me. We'd agreed to do it a year ago, and it must have slipped my mind." Chris sat on the sand with his back against the stand, his arm around Natalie.

"I'm sorry, too, but we'll come up with another date." Natalie rested against his side.

"Still thinking sometime around Christmas?"

"If it's okay with you."

"It's okay with me."

Natalie sat up. "Just like that? No counteroffer?"

"Nope. I think that would be the perfect time."

"Wyndham Beach is glorious at the holidays. Christmas Eve would be lovely, but a lot of our friends wouldn't be able to come because of family obligations. The weekend after Christmas might be better." She pulled her phone out of her bag and tapped on the calendar app. "Christmas Eve is on the weekend, which means . . ."

"New Year's Eve is the following weekend. That might not work for a lot of out-of-towners. Mom was talking about going to Italy with Owen."

"I don't think that's happening now. She and Owen aren't speaking."

"Oh. She hadn't mentioned that. Wonder what happened there. Well, then, at least she'd be there."

"Maybe we should just go with Christmas Eve and whoever can make it, makes it. Or maybe the weekend before—either Friday or Saturday."

"Let's shoot for Saturday. That way we won't be interfering with anyone's Christmas plans with their families."

"Sold. The Saturday before Christmas weekend it is. Let's just hope the weather isn't too wintry by then." She typed a big "!" on the date on her phone. "Next up: Where shall we do the deed?"

"Ahhh, well, my mom is lobbying hard for the church in town where my uncle is pastor. I'm afraid she's quite insistent. She and my dad were married there."

"My parents and my grandparents were married there, too. It's a beautiful church."

"Maggie and your dad were married there?"

She nodded. "And two of my mom's aunts and a bunch of cousins. So yeah. Makes perfect sense." Natalie was already picturing herself walking down that aisle. There would be poinsettias lining the aisle and all around the altar. White ones only, she'd decided. An all-white winter wedding . . .

". . . your mom and Brett aren't."

"What? Sorry. I zoned out. What were you saying about my mom and Brett?"

"I said, I'm surprised your mom and Brett aren't getting married there, but I guess she wanted a different venue this time around."

"That and the fact that she and Brett spent a lot of time on Cottage Street Beach when they were young, so I guess they have memories there."

"Like we do."

"That was the first time you kissed me, and I was a goner."

"I'd waited all summer for that kiss, and it was worth it."

"It was perfect, but then again, you'd had a lot of practice, if I recall correctly. I was crazy jealous the entire summer. You and . . . let's see. There was Anita Jorgensen. Ellie Montgomery. Oh, and Emily Jones. You had a thing going with her for several years, as I recall."

"All mere substitutes for the girl I really wanted. I knew I was too old for you then, and I didn't want you to think I was taking advantage of you. But by the time you were seventeen, the age difference didn't seem as big."

"And here we are, all these years later." She snuggled into his arms. "I think you should write a song about things that are destined and how some things are just meant to be."

"I might be working on something," he said casually.

"Really? Can I see it? Hear it, I mean?"

"When the time is right."

"Is that the name of it? 'When the Time Is Right'?"

Chris laughed. "No, it doesn't have a name yet, but now that I think about it, that might be it." He mulled it over a few times. "When the Time Is Right." He kissed the top of her head. "Yeah. That works. That's it."

"Mommy, look at all the birds!" Daisy called farther down the beach. Overhead, a flock of gulls began to circle.

"Did you give them food?" Natalie called. "Are you feeding them?"

"No. But Winnie dropped a bag of goldfish crackers in the water," Daisy called back. "She didn't mean to."

"Maybe you and Winnie should come back this way. The gulls might be thinking you have something else for them and start pecking at you."

The two girls ran back toward the lifeguard stand. Winnie dropped to her knees and opened her fist to show them something in the palm of her hand.

"See how pretty?" Winnie held up a flat piece of glass that looked luminescent. "I never found white before."

"Good for you, Winnie!" Chris gave her a thumbs-up.

"She always finds the most," Daisy grumbled.

"Daisy, maybe if you took a little more time and didn't try to rush so much, you'd find more, too," Natalie suggested.

Daisy nodded. "Okay. Come on, Winnie. I want to look some more."

"Okay." Winnie tucked the sea glass back into her pocket and made a beeline across the beach.

"Give the gulls a wide berth," Natalie called to her.

Winnie stopped midstride and turned around. "What does that mean, a wide berth?"

"It means give them lots of room."

"Okay." Winnie resumed running to catch up with Daisy.

Natalie turned to Chris. "So you're sure you're ready for this? Starting off marriage with two daughters? And however many more there might be?"

"Sure. I was an only child, remember? I want a big family. I wasn't going to say anything until tonight, but Mom's Realtor friend called while you were at the eye doctor with Winnie. There's a house out on

Channel Drive that's going to be coming up for sale within the next few days. It's empty now, so she said we can see it whenever we want."

"Like tonight?"

"I guess maybe tonight. Want me to call and see?"

"Yes! Yes! Call now!"

Laughing, Chris made the call and was able to report back to Natalie they could walk through the house at six thirty that evening.

"I'll see if your mom is home to watch the girls," Nat told him. "I don't want them to come with us. I want to be able to make an assessment without getting distracted."

Before Natalie could call Emma, Grace called her to see if she and Chris wanted to have dinner with them at the Little House.

"Linc is bringing Brenda's girls with him because his dad and Liddy are going out to dinner and I think he's sleeping over at her place. Duffy is going to be at a sleepover with a friend he met at sports camp. Bliss and JoJo are bringing their sleeping bags, and they're staying over here so I can get them to craft camp in the morning. When I dreamed of getting together with Linc, I never envisioned such madness." Grace laughed. "But they're a package deal now, and he's my Prince Charming." Then she laughed. "Of course, he came riding in in a beat-up old pickup instead of a dashing steed, but hey, modern times, modern methods."

"You deserve a prince, Gracie. I'm so glad you found each other."

"Me too. Life is good. You and Chris are a big part of that good life. So what do you think? You want to come over for dinner?"

"We can do an early dinner or a late one. Chris and I are looking at a house at six thirty."

"Yippee! You're going to stay in Wyndham Beach after all!"

"We both want to. If we can find the right house, we will. So would it be all right if Winnie and Daisy hung out with you all while Chris and I look at this place?"

"Of course. The more the merrier."

"Thanks. We're not telling the girls where we're going. They're going to want to come with us, and I don't want to have to be watching them."

"I understand. Don't worry. I'll find a way to distract them so you two can slip out."

"Thanks, Gracie. You're the best."

"So glad you're finally acknowledging that. See you in a while."

Grace's distraction was s'mores around the firepit on the back patio. Chris and Natalie went out the front door as soon as everyone else went out the back. Chris drove because Natalie was so excited he was afraid she'd forget to watch where she was going.

"Calm down," he'd told her as he fastened his seat belt. "We may not even like the place."

"It's the idea that has me excited. We're moving forward with our life together, and it makes me happy."

"Are you sure you can take all of today's excitement? We have a date. We've agreed on a venue for the ceremony . . ."

"I can take whatever else you've got, bucko."

Chris laughed as he made a left turn. "This is Channel Drive. The house should be . . . oh, there. That's it. The brown-shingled place with the sale sign on the lawn."

Natalie was out of her seat belt before he'd even pulled up the driveway. "Oh, it looks so old New England, with those weathered cedar shakes. Oh, and look at all the hydrangeas along the fence and the front of the house!"

"Is that a good thing or a bad thing?"

"I love the look. But it's what's behind the walls that counts." She jumped out of the car the second it stopped moving. She was halfway to the front door before Chris closed the driver's-side door.

Gretchen Smith stood in the open doorway of the house, and she greeted them warmly. "You're right on time."

Chris introduced himself and Natalie, and they stepped inside the spacious foyer.

"I'm going to let the two of you look around on your own," Gretchen told them. "I have a few calls to make, but don't hesitate to ask if you have any questions."

"We appreciate you fitting us in at the last minute," Chris said.

"My pleasure. But if you think you might want to put in an offer, I'd advise you to not delay. Word has gotten out that it's officially going on the market this week, and there has been a lot of interest." She held up the pad of paper in her hand. "Most of these return calls are about this house."

"We'll keep that in mind," Natalie said. She tugged on Chris's arm. "Let's take a tour."

The house was larger inside than it appeared, and it had recently been partially remodeled. The kitchen was new, though not to Natalie's taste ("Too industrial"), but Chris told her she could redo anything she didn't like. There was a first-floor laundry room, a cozy family room off the kitchen, a dining room as large as Natalie had hoped, an office, a large living room that opened onto a stone patio. A room that could serve as a library. Several fireplaces. Upstairs there were four big bedrooms and the same number of baths, and the attic was a huge unfinished space. The owner's suite was unique in that it had not only two walk-in closets and a large updated bath, but a smaller anteroom as well.

"Nursery? Sitting room?" Natalie wondered aloud.

"Any of the above." Chris poked his head into the small space. "It's whatever we'd want it to be."

"What do you think, Chris?" Natalie asked after they'd completed their tour.

"I really like it a lot, but I'm not overwhelmed. I was hoping to have a place for a studio at home so Linc and I can work right here in Wyndham Beach. I figured I'd sell the place in California, but that's where my studio is. So I have to replace that." He walked around what would be one of the kids' rooms and looked out the window. "I like the view of the sound, though. We can see Shelby Island from here. Linc and I can send messages using lanterns at night. I always wanted to be able to do that as a kid."

Natalie walked up behind him and slid her arms around his waist. "That is a great view. You'd be able to see the island from every room across the back of the house, and I bet the girls would catch on to that whole lantern thing really fast. But if you want room for a studio, that's not here."

"The garage out back's not big enough. And this close to the water, you're not going to leave the cars outside all the time. The salt air will kill the paint." He turned from the window. "There's space on the third floor, but I want my work space separate from my living space; plus we'd have to soundproof the entire attic."

"So I guess that's a no."

"Unless you love it."

"I could love it, but not as much as I'd love to have you working here."

"So let's see what else Gretchen has up her sleeve." He took her hand, and they walked down the steps to the first floor.

They found the Realtor in the kitchen, staring out the back window. "Fabulous view, right?"

"We love the view," Natalie agreed. "And the location is perfect. The space is wonderful, so much room. So much to like. And I keep seeing that library with comfy furniture and endless books on the shelves, and the whole family gathered around reading together on cold nights, a fire in the fireplace."

"Ah, but something tells me you're not loving it." Gretchen looked disappointed.

"This house checks a lot of boxes, but I really need a place where I can work from home. I'm a musician and—"

Gretchen rolled her eyes. "Duh. Like I don't know who you are."

"Okay. So you know what I do. I need a studio at home so I don't have to be flying back and forth across the country all the time. And I don't want the studio in the house. It really needs to be separate."

"Hmm." Gretchen thought for a moment. "Let's walk outside."

"I already considered the garage," Chris told her, "and I can tell it won't work. It's not big enough. Plus we need a place for our cars."

Gretchen beckoned them to the back door. "Humor me."

Chris and Natalie followed her outside. The backyard was wide, and the space between the house and the water deeper than it appeared from inside the house. There was a swimming pool that remained covered and a small pool house and several garden beds that needed some TLC.

"You have a lot of ground here, over two acres, and you have eighteen acres of conserved land beyond that stand of pine trees," Gretchen told them. She pointed off to the left. "At least an acre in that direction between you and the next closest house, and that hedge makes a nice barrier. Because of the topography you can't even see the house next door from here. There's plenty of room for you to build something to your specifications, which probably makes more sense than trying to retrofit your special needs into another space."

Chris walked the entire backyard, from one side to the other.

"This is about as private a property as you're going to find in Wyndham Beach," Gretchen was saying. "And you're not going to find a larger lot in this part of town. I would think privacy would be a concern to you."

Natalie nodded. "People in Wyndham Beach don't bother us, but . . ."

"But once it gets out that Chris Dean lives in town, well, you never know who'll pop up at your door."

"True." Natalie watched Chris walk back toward the house. He paused once to look out at the water beyond the property, at Shelby

Island in the distance, his hands on his hips and a faraway look on his face.

"Nat, it could work. There's plenty of room for a studio over there. I could design it myself, make it exactly what I want it to be, with all the newest, most up-to-date equipment. Maybe even a second floor with room for the other guys to stay over when they're in town. The more I think about it, the more I like it." He turned to Gretchen. "What condition is the pool in?"

They discussed the pool and the roof and the mechanics and the prospect of getting a zoning clearance to build the studio, and by the time they left, Chris and Natalie both had stars in their eyes. They'd taken one more tour of the house, which had been built in the 1920s. They discovered many original charming touches they hadn't noticed the first time around, like beadboard in the bathrooms and arched doorways between the rooms.

"We can make this work, Nat." Chris said when they were back in the car. "What do you think?"

"It needs some work. There are some things I'd like to be different," she said. "But it is a beautiful house."

"We can fix anything you don't like."

She grinned. "Let's go for it. We know we want it, and apparently there's a lot of interest. I don't think Gretchen needed to exaggerate the number of calls she was returning."

"You're right. We should go back in and tell her."

"No time like the present." Natalie jumped out of the car, and they caught Gretchen as she was about to lock up.

"We want to talk numbers," Chris said. "Do you have a few more minutes?"

Gretchen smiled broadly. "I have all the time you need."

Thirty minutes later, they'd agreed on an offer, settlement date, and terms. Gretchen promised to call the homeowner's Realtor and put the offer on the table immediately, and if it was accepted, she'd have the papers drawn up and emailed to them.

"Big day, eh?" he said when they got back into the car. "Picked a date. Agreed on the church. Found a house."

"My head is spinning." Natalie smiled and closed her eyes.

First thing tomorrow she'd call Hannah and make an appointment to try on dresses. She couldn't wait to tell Gracie and her mother all her good news. She was going to be a Christmas bride and marry the love of her life in the same church where her mother had married her father, and she and Chris had found a house right there in Wyndham Beach. She pictured them opening gifts by a huge Christmas tree in the living room, stockings hung on the wooden mantel of that stone fireplace, and the girls playing in the pool on summer afternoons. She and Chris, Daisy, Winnie, and their babies, however many there might be. She wondered if four bedrooms might be enough. Of course, there was all that unused space on the third floor . . .

She pinched herself. Perhaps fairy tales really could come true after all.

Chapter Eighteen

Emma loved walking to the art center in the morning. After two days of rain, a dawn overcast by gray clouds progressed gradually to a brightening sky, so she'd dressed for a warm day: navy Bermuda shorts, a plaid cotton shirt with a Peter Pan collar, and classic white sneakers. She was grateful for the promise of sunshine, and she was grateful for friends who reached out and allowed her to talk out everything that had been preying on her mind. She was starting to think of all those worries as speed bumps she'd maneuvered around. She also recognized there were some things she couldn't change—like Owen's attitude—and some things she'd just have to let play out, like the art exhibits. Some things she could still control to a certain extent, like hiring someone at the art center.

There was so much to be happy about, so many joyous events on the horizon. Not one but two weddings! What could be more wonderful? And Chris and Natalie bought a house less than a mile away. Emma's cup indeed runneth over.

She stopped at Ground Me for a coffee large enough to take her through the morning, then knocked on the front door of Liddy's bookshop. The shop wouldn't open for another half hour, but Liddy saw her and unlocked the door to let her in.

"I wanted to say a quick good morning and to check the progress of Rosalita," Emma said, referring to the tracked shark whose path along the Atlantic coastline Liddy followed on her laptop. The shop's customers were fascinated by the shark's northbound path, and it wasn't unusual to see several people staring at the counter, where the computer screen was always set to what Liddy referred to as Rosalita's Great Adventures. "I see she's already coming close to Buzzards Bay. Is she early this summer?"

Liddy shrugged. "Not sure. I didn't follow her early voyage last year. I didn't pick up on her till later in the summer. But I guess I should tell Tuck to keep the kids out of the water for the next few days. Not that I think she'd come that close to Shelby Island, but Duffy's been spending a lot of time in the water out there lately, so it's good to be aware. Linc made the mistake of telling him how much he'd enjoyed surfing off the island when he was a kid, and once he found Linc's old surfboard in the shed, well, you know how it goes."

"Like uncle, like nephew." Emma took a quick sip of coffee. "Linc's a good role model."

"No argument from me." Liddy picked up a stack of books that had been left on the counter and began to return them to the new-release table at the front of the store. "Anything new?"

"Chris and Natalie have set a date. The Saturday before Christmas weekend at the church across the street."

"Excellent. Your brother's going to officiate?"

"Yes. I was ready to strong-arm the two of them if I'd had to, but he and Natalie readily agreed. But here's the big news: they're buying the old Fleming place out on Channel Drive. They've put in an offer and are already looking for an architect to design a studio for Chris—that's the first order of business—and to make some changes in the house that Natalie wants."

"That is news. Good for you. For everyone, actually."

"Chris is going to call Tuck to line up Shelby and Son to do whatever work is needed inside, and ask him to supervise the building of the studio. Chris wants them to start the day he and Natalie close on the property." Emma was beaming. "I can't wait to get into that house to see it for myself. And, of course, I'm relieved knowing they're going to be right here."

"Everything's falling into place, Em. I couldn't be happier for you. There's been so much going on, so many oars in the water, as my dad used to say. No wonder your head's been spinning."

"It's down to a slow crawl right now, so it's manageable."

The phone on Liddy's counter began to ring.

"Go ahead and answer that. I need to be off anyway. I just wanted to pop in to say good morning and to share all the good news, and to thank you again for helping me get my head in order the other night. You were absolutely right. I need to let some things go completely, loosen the reins on a few others, and take care of the things I can." Emma walked to the door, then realized Liddy had relocked it.

The phone stopped ringing before Liddy reached the counter. She frowned, then told Emma, "You don't need to thank us. It's what we do, right? You were looking so stressed lately, Maggie and I couldn't stand it. But I'm glad you're feeling better."

"Much better. Oh, and I called Eileen McGillan as you suggested, and she put me in touch with her daughter. Keely will be back at the end of the week, and she's ready to start to work at the art center on Monday. She's going to help organize the art show for the locals for the Fourth and then she'll work with me to put together the big showing of the resident artists for the end of the summer. I'm thinking the week leading up to Labor Day would be the perfect time to get as many people in as possible. As far as Stella's situation is concerned, I'm trusting that all will go well for her."

"Brett said she's working out very nicely as a part-time photographer." Liddy unlocked the door, then leaned against the jamb. "He said there have been several auto accidents and one burglary over the past week, and she's taken good shots and gotten them to him that same day. So he's satisfied."

"Let's hope she can work that experience—however limited—into a job somewhere."

"Speaking of jobs—do you know what Natalie's doing about her job? I thought she was supposed to start teaching again in August, but it sounds like she's going to be living here."

"They were talking about cutbacks at the junior college where she's been teaching, so they weren't sending out next year's contracts until the first of July. Natalie said she already told them not to send hers, that she'd decline any offer they might make, so that's working out in her favor. She'll have her hands filled here, with all the work on the house and planning her wedding. Besides, she and Chris decided they want Winnie and Daisy to start school here."

Liddy followed her outside, where she leaned over to deadhead a few spent blooms from the flowers in the long, low planter under the shop's big front window. "It's a beautiful morning, isn't it?"

"Perfect," Emma agreed.

"Stop back on your way home from the art center. Maybe we could run across the street and have a quick cup of coffee." Liddy glanced at the extra-large cup Emma was holding. "Though it looks like you might have a full day's worth of caffeine in your hands."

"Depending on how the day plays out, I might need a booster by then. See you later."

Liddy went back to her deadheading and Emma moved on, crossing the street and walking up Bank Street to Bay. Brett passed her in his cruiser, stopped, and backed up.

"What's up?" she asked.

"Three-car collision at the end of Front Street. Honda, Jeep, and an old VW Bug. Guess which vehicle got the worst of it," he asked through the open window.

"Aw, poor Bug," Emma sympathized, recalling the light-green Bug her brother had when they were in school.

"I'm on my way to pick up Stella to photograph the scene. Since I'm headed your way, want a lift?"

"No, but thanks. I'm enjoying the peaceful morning."

"Let's hope it stays peaceful. See you later." He rolled up the window and took off toward Bay Street. Minutes later, he passed her again. Stella waved from the front seat as they went by.

Twelve minutes later she was unlocking the art center's door and greeting the instructor for the ten-o'clock pottery class. The potter went down the steps to her workroom, and Emma stood in the middle of the large open room, envisioning how the exhibit for the locals showing would be set up. She went into her office and checked the listing of the artists who'd applied to display for the hometown crowd. Some of the works would be brilliant, she knew, but others would be ghastly. She didn't feel she could pick and choose, since the town supported the art center in so many ways, and she didn't feel it was her role to play the critic. Everyone who lived in town could bring a piece to exhibit, and it would be displayed along with a few of Jessie Bryant's.

"What if Walt Hollins wants to hang a nude self-portrait?" Liddy had asked with a straight face. "Whatcha gonna do then?"

Maggie had covered her eyes. "Em, you'd have to turn him down. There could be children there. They could be scarred for life."

Emma had laughed. "The heck with the children. I'd be scarred for life."

"So you admit there has to be a modicum of discretion," Liddy said.

"Someone has to be the arbiter, yes, and yes, that will be me. But short of horrifying subject matter, all are welcome."

Emma checked the list and was relieved to see that Walt Hollins's work was titled *Magnolias in Bloom*. She began making calls to everyone who'd signed up, reminding them that their work had to be delivered to the art center no later than June twenty-eighth. She was between calls when her phone rang.

"Emma, it's Natalie. If you aren't too busy, would you mind if I dropped off Winnie at the center? Daisy has a sore throat and a fever that's rising, and I want to take her to the urgent care clinic out on the highway. It would probably be better for Winnie if I didn't drag her along."

"I wouldn't mind at all. Winnie's never a problem. She'll probably go down to the beach and look for shells. Bring her whenever."

Winnie was in Emma's office twenty minutes later.

"Can I help you do something, Gramma?" she'd asked Emma.

"Unfortunately, not this time. I'm just making some phone calls. Would you like to play on the beach? It's a beautiful day."

"I love the beach." Winnie nodded and was gone the minute Emma handed her a bottle of water.

"Come back when you get hungry, and we'll have lunch together," Emma called to her as she ran out the door.

"I will. Thank you." Winnie's voice trailed behind her.

"What a blessing that child is," Emma murmured. "And what a joy it's going to be watching her grow up. Despite what Owen thinks."

She couldn't deny she missed Owen. She missed his texts and his calls and his company. She missed thinking about what could have been a wonderful future together. But his remarks regarding Winnie made it impossible for her to continue seeing him. Send that child back to Georgia where no one wanted her and where her star was never going to have a chance to shine? Uh-uh. Emma wasn't having any of that. Winnie was theirs, they'd claimed her, and she was staying. If Tish Pine was still alive, which seemed increasingly unlikely, she'd have a fight on her hands for the girl. Then again, some of the remains the LVPD found in the desert could prove to be Tish's. Time would tell.

She pushed both Owen and Tish out of her head and picked up the phone and called the next number on her list.

Emma had almost completed her calls when she heard the outside door open and, seconds later, snap closed. She expected it to be Winnie, ready for lunch, but heavy footsteps echoed through the empty exhibition room and led to Emma's door. Her first thought was that Brett had finished up with the accident and was just stopping in for a moment after he dropped off Stella. But the man who stood in the doorway was not Brett. This man was tall and bald and wore cargo shorts, a sleeveless T-shirt with a button-down shirt open over it, and dark glasses that hid his eyes.

"Can I help you?" she asked.

"Hi, ma'am, sorry to disturb you. I'm on my way to the Cape and stopped in town for lunch, and I overheard someone talking about an art center, so I thought I'd take a look." He glanced over his shoulder. "Doesn't look like there's much going on, though."

"Sorry to disappoint you. We won't have a showing here until the weekend. We won't be setting up for a few more days."

"You get big names to exhibit here?"

"We have had some in the past, but the July exhibit is strictly for local artists."

"You have that many artists in a town small as this that they get their own display?"

Emma smiled and tried to place his accent. "We have a lot of people who like to think they're artists, and we give them an opportunity to show us what they've got. We'll get mostly watercolors, a few pictures of boats out on the bay, flower gardens, and bowls of fruit. But it makes people happy to show off their work, so we're giving them the means to do that."

"Mostly watercolors. Hmm. Well, I'm more interested in photography myself. Anyone exhibit their photos?" He glanced at the nameplate on her desk. "Emma Dean? That's you? You're the director here?"

"Yes."

Emma looked at him thoughtfully. There was something familiar about him—but then again, maybe not. She didn't know too many men that age—he appeared to be around forty—who were totally bald. One of Chris's bandmates had shaved his head a few years ago, but this guy wasn't that guy. This guy gave off strangely weird vibes, though he was friendly enough and polite.

"Photos? We have someone who's taken pictures of every stray cat that's wandered into town, but that's about it." She checked the list that was still in front of her. "Nobody's signed up to exhibit photos."

"Looks like a nice little town, Wyndham Beach." He looked over her head to the window behind her.

"It's a typical small New England town."

"You lived here long?"

"Born and raised," she said.

He nodded, his eyes straying to the window again.

"I saw a flyer in the coffee shop about a Fourth of July parade. You do that every year?"

"It's the same parade you will see in any small town across the country. High school band, local groups marching. Politicians riding in convertibles. Kids' sports teams. You've probably seen the same parade yourself wherever it is you're from."

"Oh yeah. Small Town, USA," he said.

Emma had the feeling he was just making small talk, drawing out the conversation, though she couldn't imagine why he'd want to spend his time inside talking to her when it was a beautiful day outside.

"Like I said, you'll see the same parade in every town on the Cape. You did say you were just passing through?"

He nodded. "That's right. Just passing through."

"I'm sure some of the galleries on the Cape will be having exhibits this summer. Maybe one of those will have something you like."

"I'll keep that in mind." His eyes roamed from the window to Emma and back again, but he made no move toward leaving. "What else do you have going on for a visitor to do?"

"Well, you could rent a boat, if you like sailing or fishing. You can rent equipment and buy a temporary license at a shop out on the highway." She paused. "Not much else, I'm afraid."

"I'm not one to spend much time on the water," he said.

"Well, I hope you find what you're looking for, Mr.—"

"Palmer."

"If there's nothing else I can help you with, Mr. Palmer . . ."

"Actually, now that you mention it, maybe there is." He stepped all the way into her office and stood next to the right side of the desk. "I heard a friend of mine might have been in town not too long ago. She likes to think of herself as an artist, too, so maybe she stopped by. Photographer, though. Not a painter."

He took a photo out of his back pocket, but before Emma looked, she knew whose face it would be. Just as she knew that Palmer was not the name of the man who stood before her.

"Maybe you've seen her?" He extended the photo, and she took it, held it up, and pretended to take a long, careful look, then shook her head and handed it back.

"She's very pretty. I'm sure I'd remember her face, but she doesn't look familiar. Sorry." Emma willed her hands not to shake as she handed back the photo. She needed to call Brett, and she needed him to keep Stella away until George Martin left her office. Unfortunately, he didn't appear to be in a hurry to leave.

Suddenly the outside door slammed and someone was making their way to the office. Martin turned and looked at the open door.

Winnie stopped dead in her tracks when she realized someone was in the office with Emma. She stared at Martin for a moment, then turned and ran out of the building. Emma was glad she'd instructed Winnie not to interrupt if there was someone in her office but wished she'd had time to somehow let her know to go for help.

His face darkened as he glanced over his shoulder. "Who was that kid?" he demanded.

"Just some little girl who likes to play on the beach and collect shells." Emma forced her voice to remain calm.

"Why'd she run like that when she looked at me?"

"She was looking at me, not at you," she told him. "She sneaks in to use the bathroom sometimes, and I've told her several times not to. She probably got scared and ran because she didn't think I'd be here."

Emma slowly reached for her phone, which was on the corner of her desk. She'd managed to slide it toward her and to hit two numbers before he stretched a long arm to snatch it from her hand.

"Nine one . . . let me guess. The next number was going to be another one." He stuck the phone into his pocket. "Now why would you be calling 911, Mrs. Dean?"

He sat in the chair and stared at her for what seemed to be a very long time.

"Why were you going to call 911?" The words hung in the air between them.

"I guess because I know your name isn't Palmer. It's Martin, and I don't believe your stopover in Wyndham Beach was a coincidence."

He nodded. "Then you know why I'm here, and you know who I'm looking for."

Emma nodded slowly.

"Where is she? Where's my wife?"

"I was of the understanding you were divorced. Which means she's no longer your wife."

"We were married in a church of God. What God joined let no man put asunder." He took off his glasses to reveal small, dark eyes. "There's a separation between church and state in this country. A piece of paper from the state of West Virginia cannot override the church. It's right there in the Constitution."

Not what the First Amendment intended, but it didn't seem like the right time for a civics lesson.

"I think you need to take that up with the folks in West Virginia."

"I'll take that up with her. Where is she? I know she's here. I had a feeling she'd run north. It's taken me a couple of weeks, following a lead here and a lead there." His grin held more menace than humor. "Did you know there's a coffee shop down in Fall River that has a newspaper article on their bulletin board about this here artists' retreat?"

"No. I didn't know." *Talk,* Emma told herself. Keep him talking. Maybe Stella can get back to her cabin without him seeing her.

Then what?

"Yep, it was right there where you come in the door. You tell me that wasn't the hand of God leading me here." He nodded. "I know it was. Just like I know you are going to do His will and tell me where she is."

"I have no idea where she's gone or what she's doing." Which was not completely true. With luck, she was still at the intersection of Route 6 and Front Street.

"Then I guess we'll just have to wait for her to show up." He rubbed a hand over his face. "Might be nice to wait for her in that little cabin she's staying in out there."

It hadn't occurred to Emma that he might have figured out where she was staying.

"Those are cute little places. You know, I got out of my car and saw that line of cabins standing there along the dune, and I thought to myself, just the sort of accommodation that newspaper article talked about. So I walked on up, and it took me about twenty seconds to figure out which was hers. Know how?" He chuckled. "She left a note on the door to someone named Luna. Said she'd be back in a bit." He looked at his watch. "It's been more than a bit."

He leveled his gaze at Emma. "It occurred to me that you could live in one of those cabins indefinitely. Is that what she was planning on doing? Staying on here after the summer was over?"

"We never discussed where she'd go once the summer was over." That much was true.

They sat in silence for a few minutes, as he obviously tried to decide what his next move would be.

That will probably include what to do about me. Which probably hinges on what he's going to do to Stella once she gets back.

"I guess the smart thing would be to go wait at her cabin, right? We know she's going back there sooner or later." He motioned to Emma to stand up. "You're going to have to come with me, Mrs. Dean. I can't leave you here alone. We both know what you'll do the second my back is turned."

"And if I refuse?"

"I would have to hurt you, and I would rather not do that. All I want is to get my wife and drive us back home." He took several steps toward her. "You're a married woman, right? You know your place is with your husband, right?"

"My husband's been dead for ten years."

"You could be joining him very soon, depending on how the rest of the day goes."

Emma remained seated, trying to figure out if he was armed with something lethal, a knife or, God forbid, a gun. She hadn't seen any evidence of one, though he had from time to time touched the center of his back with his right hand. Did he have a gun in his waistband, or was that something they did only on TV crime shows? Then again, he probably wouldn't need a weapon since he clearly outweighed her by close to one hundred pounds. Overpowering him wasn't going to be an option.

"My son is coming to pick me up for lunch soon. If I'm not here, he'll know something's not right. He'll call the police."

"I'll deal with him and the police if they show up. I'm not afraid of a few small-town cops or your small-town boy." He gestured to Emma. "Let's go. And if anyone comes out of those other cabins, you keep your mouth shut, got it?"

She nodded and prayed someone would be out on the beach. Surely if she called them by the wrong name, they'd know something was wrong, wouldn't they? She glanced at the parking lot. Eva's car was gone, as was Luna's. They had probably all gone into town for lunch.

She walked to the door, George Martin behind her poking her along with one finger in the center of her back. At least she hoped it was just a finger.

"That is really annoying," she told him.

"Too bad. Keep going." He paused as she opened the door. "Don't even think about running. You're old and slow. I'm younger and faster."

"I wouldn't dream of running." She gritted her teeth at the insult even as she went through the open door, her mind racing wildly.

She knew once she was inside that cabin, her chances of getting away weren't good. Right now he might not be thinking about hurting her, but once Stella returned, it would be a different story. Depending on how badly he hurt Stella—and Emma felt certain he would hurt her because she wouldn't go willingly—he had to realize he was going to have to do something about Emma. She slowed her pace and tried to think. She had no weapon, nothing with which to fight him off.

Why hadn't she taken those tae kwon do classes at the Y when she'd had a chance?

"Keep walking. Go up the side of the dune."

She looked straight ahead and saw nothing but sand.

Sand . . .

They'd just started up the dune when Emma paused. "I hate getting sand in my shoes. I'm taking them off."

"Do it quickly." He stood with his hands on his hips.

Emma leaned over to pull off the first sneaker, surreptitiously filling it with sand before repeating the move with the second shoe.

"Hurry up."

"I'm not moving fast enough for you?" She turned toward him quickly and flung the sand directly into his face.

"Yeow!" His hands flew to his eyes.

Emma ran in the direction of the parking lot, then remembered she'd walked to work that morning. Her car was sitting home in her driveway. Her only other option was to try to make it to Bay Street and hopefully flag down a passing car if she had enough time. George was still bent over, trying to get the sand out of his eyes, but it might be a matter of mere seconds before he cleared them enough to see where she was and where she was going. Barefooted, she stumbled on sharp stones in the driveway, which slowed her pace. She was halfway to the mouth of the drive when a car came flying in and stopped immediately next to Emma. Brett was driving and another officer sat in the passenger seat.

Brett leaned over the console. "You okay?"

She nodded and tried to catch her breath, then pointed toward the dunes just as a second police car appeared.

"He's up there. Martin. Might be armed . . ."

It took Brett mere seconds to reach the building, a little more to take George into custody with the help of his patrol officer.

"Water, please! My eyes are filled with sand! That woman . . ."

Brett nodded to his officer, who handcuffed George, who was still yelling wildly, and put him in the back of the second car.

"I can't see, damn it! I'm gonna sue you. All of you. False arrest. Assault. And that woman—she attacked me. She blinded me!" He was still complaining loudly while the car pulled away.

"How did you know?" Emma's wobbly legs carried her to the center's steps. She sat on the top step and tried to calm herself. Her heart was beating faster than she'd thought possible.

"Winnie. We were still up at the accident scene when I got a call from the desk sergeant that a little girl had come running into the station, calling for me and yelling that the bad man from the picture was at the art center. They put Winnie on the phone, and she told me what was going on." Brett sat down next to her. "That kid ran all the way from here to the police station, you believe that?"

"How did she know who he was? She only saw his face for a few seconds before she ran out."

"She said she saw his picture at Maggie's, that she has a 'picture memory.' She remembered what he looked like."

Emma's emotions caught her between wanting to cry and wanting to laugh. "She told me her teachers said she has a photographic memory. Well, I guess she does. She knew who he was before I did. It took me a while to figure it out. Once I did, I didn't know what to do next."

"Did he hurt you, Em?"

"Only my pride when he said I was too old and too slow to get away from him."

"Guess you showed him."

"Guess I did." Emma looked around. "Where's Stella?"

"I made her stay at the station with Winnie, who by now probably is sitting in my chair and fielding phone calls and getting ready to run for mayor."

"She is quite something, isn't she?" Emma said proudly. "That girl of ours . . ."

"Well, she got the ball rolling, but honestly, Em, I can't believe you threw sand in his face." Brett ran his hand through his hair, waking up his cowlick. "That was some remarkably quick thinking."

"There simply wasn't anything else. You know what they say about necessity being the mother of invention. I had no weapons, and that man is twice my size. I just grabbed onto the first thing I saw."

"It was a great idea—a real gutsy move, but it could have backfired badly if you'd missed his eyes."

"They were my targets. I knew I'd be in worse trouble if I missed, so I aimed really carefully."

"Well, I'm sorry I wasn't here sooner to save the day, but I'm glad you found a way to save it on your own. You're one brave woman, Emma Dean."

"I am, aren't I?" Emma grinned. "I think I'm going to buy myself a Wonder Woman cape. I'm feeling pretty much invincible today."

The officer who'd arrived with Brett walked toward them. "Chief, we're ready to take him back to the station. Unless you object, I'll ride back with Officer Jeffries."

"No objection, Cliff. I'm going to stay with Mrs. Dean for a few."

The officer turned to Emma. "Glad you're okay, Mrs. Dean. Harry would have been proud of you."

He smiled and walked back to the waiting patrol car and its prisoner.

Emma's mouth had dropped open. When she recovered, she all but growled. "Screw Harry. I'm proud of me."

"Don't hold back, Em. Tell us how you really feel." Brett chuckled.

Emma's indignation had reached critical mass. "It's not funny, Brett. I couldn't care less what Harry would think."

"Nor should you. That chapter's done."

"Maggie told you."

Brett nodded. "I hope you don't mind."

She patted him on the knee that was right next to hers. "We've been friends since we were fifteen years old, Brett. I don't mind if you know my secrets. I know you'll keep them."

"Of course I will." He put his hand on hers and gave it a squeeze. "Seems like a long time ago, doesn't it?"

"It was a long time ago."

"Lot of water under that bridge," he said with a nod.

"And yet, here we are." Emma leaned forward to brush sand off the bottom of her foot. "Think you could help me find my sneakers? They're over there somewhere." She pointed toward the dune.

"Ah, actually, they're not. They're in an evidence bag back at the station."

She glanced down at her bare feet. "No car, no shoes. What's a girl to do?"

"She gets a ride home in a police cruiser."

"That should get the neighbors talking."

Brett laughed. "Wait here and I'll drive up."

She watched him walk to his car and sighed. He'd always been a good guy. Back in the day, he'd been a little cocky at times, but when you were the hottest guy in your high school class and a football player who was a shoo-in for all-American, who won a full scholarship to a top school, and who knew the pros were watching, Emma figured a guy could be forgiven for those moments. But he'd left all that behind when he came back to Wyndham Beach, newly graduated from the police academy, and worked his way up through the ranks. He'd devoted his life to the people of his hometown, and they loved him for it as much as they'd loved their golden boy.

He'd been a good friend to her, just as she'd been a friend to him, and she was grateful those ties were still strong. He pulled the cruiser up as close to the steps as he could, and she hobbled over and got in.

Minutes later, as they approached her house, she said, "Thanks for the ride. And thanks for staying with me for a while and helping me settle down. I really needed to decompress."

"I know that was quite an ordeal, Em. You will have to come down to the station to be interviewed about what happened here today, but I'm going to let that go until tomorrow."

"What happens now, to him?"

"He's being charged with enough to put him back inside for a while."

She nodded. "For violating the order Stella filed against him."

"That, sure, but he held you against your will, made threats of bodily harm. I'm assuming you felt you were in danger."

"I did. I know I was."

"That's an assault charge. Kidnapping. Making terroristic threats—and whatever else fits the circumstances. Not to worry. He won't be around for a long time."

He pulled into her driveway. "Now you go on inside, take a shower, and relax while I go get Winnie and bring her home. You want to be composed when she sees you." He grinned the way that had had just about every girl in their high school fall passionately in love with him. "You had a big day today, and you wrestled it to the ground. Emma—one. Bad guy—zero."

~

And that's exactly what she told Liddy and Maggie when they descended on her house later.

"I kicked butt, ladies," she all but crowed.

"That's what Brett said." Maggie placed a tray on the counter. "Appetizers. The caterer dropped off an assortment for a prewedding taste test."

"You should have shared those with Brett," Emma protested when Maggie uncovered the tray.

"Brett couldn't care less about spanakopita or mini goat-cheese-and-fig crepes or these little pastry doodads. He's happy with a couple of oysters and maybe a few little pigs in a blanket. He looked at this tray, shrugged, made a face, and all he said was, 'Okay.' Besides, this could count as my bride's night out." Maggie helped herself to a small round pastry and took a bite. "Yum."

"Mom, I think you mean your bachelorette party." Natalie came in carrying a brown bag, followed by Grace, who carried the same. "In which case you're supposed to gather your posse and take off to some exotic place and party. Maybe have one last fling before you walk down the aisle. You know, like go to Vegas or Miami or someplace like that."

Maggie laughed out loud. "Sweetie, there's nowhere I'd rather be, and my 'posse' is already gathered. No flings necessary."

"Champagne." Grace held up the bag and began to remove the bottles.

"And a bottle of red, a bottle of white." Natalie sang a line from the old Billy Joel song. "For when the champagne runs out."

"We're here to celebrate Super Em." Grace turned to Emma. "Glasses?"

"This calls for the good ones." Emma brought seven flutes to the table. She nodded toward the bottle of champagne and said, "Fire away."

Grace popped the cork, then poured into the glasses for the adults while Emma half filled the other two with ginger ale for Winnie and Daisy. She handed them to the little girls, saying, "These are very special glasses, so be very careful with them, okay?"

Both girls nodded reverently and held the glasses with both hands, their eyes on the flutes and the sparkling bubbles.

"I would like to propose a toast." Maggie waited until everyone had their drink. "First to Winnie, who saved the day with her amazing memory and who ran all the way from the art center to the police station to get help for Emma. Winnie, you are our hero!"

"Yay, Winnie!"

"Winnie, you're a star!"

"Wonder Winnie!"

Winnie giggled shyly, one hand over her mouth, but she was beaming behind the blush.

"Oh, gosh, yes," Emma said. "Honey, you are definitely a hero. Your quick thinking and quick feet saved me. You saved Stella."

"Winnie, how did you know who the man was?" Grace asked.

"Remember that time Chief Brett brought that picture of the man here, and he said to look at it because the man was a bad man, and if anyone saw him, we had to tell Chief Brett right away?" Winnie looked up at Emma over the rim of her glass. "I saw him in your office, and I knew he was the bad man from the picture. I didn't want him to hurt you."

Emma kissed Winnie on the forehead. "I don't know what might have happened if it hadn't been for you."

"That was some smart thinking," Natalie remarked.

Winnie nodded vigorously in agreement. "My teachers all said I was smart."

"Your teachers were right, kiddo." Grace tipped her glass in Winnie's direction.

It didn't take long for Winnie and Daisy to become bored with the adult chatter, and they excused themselves to go outside to play.

"You must have been scared to death today, Emma. I know I would have been," Grace said after the girls left.

"Oh, I was. I don't think I was aware of how shaken up I was after they took Martin away. But Brett stayed with me at the center and kept me talking until I was myself again, and I was able to calm down."

"Anyone would have been rattled. But we're all grateful you're here with us. We all love you, Em," Maggie said.

Emma glanced at the faces of her two closest friends and Maggie's daughters, one of whom was going to be her daughter-in-law. "I love you all, too."

She sniffed for a few moments, then said, "It's been a wild couple of years, hasn't it? Maggie and Brett getting back together. Gracie left her law career behind and discovered skills she didn't know she had, bought herself a house, and fell in love with an amazing young man in the process."

Grace nodded. "I did. And, Liddy, I thank you for making that happen."

"I had nothing to do with you falling for Linc," Liddy said. "You did that on your own."

"No, but you sold me my little house, and I suspect that you tied up Tuck so that Linc would be the one to work with me on the renovations."

"For the record," Liddy said with a straight face, "Tuck likes being tied up."

"Stop!" Emma slapped her hands over her ears. "I don't want to hear it!"

When the laughter stopped, Grace added, "And, Liddy, look at you with your new love. A new outlook on life. Your own thriving business."

"You brought that bookshop back to life and made it a success." Emma raised her glass. "Go, Lids."

"Which gave me the opportunity to live out one of my fantasies and become Mary Poppins once a week." Grace toasted Emma.

"Natalie and Chris finally made it official, and I'm here to tell you the wedding in December is going to be epic." Maggie smiled at her daughter.

"Just a heads-up—Wyndham Beach is going to be overrun with a who's who in the music business. The reception will be one to remember," Natalie promised.

"Where's the reception going to be?" Liddy asked. "Last I heard, you hadn't decided."

"We haven't found a place large enough in town, but we're still looking at options. We want to keep everything here in Wyndham Beach," Nat told her. "But while we're talking about changes in our lives, can we please talk about Winnie?"

"I love to talk about Winnie." Emma smiled. "She's the light of my life these days. I can't thank you all enough for opening your hearts to her. Especially you, Natalie."

"I admit I was aghast and terrified and overcome with insecurity and anxiety at first." She laughed self-consciously, and everyone joined her. "But Winnie grows on you. She's so sweet and she's kind. There is not a mean bone in that girl's body. I don't know where her mother is, but I promise you, if she ever showed up here, she would have the fight of her life on her hands. We will never give her up. This mama bear will do whatever it takes to protect that cub."

Emma looked through the back window, where Winnie was helping Daisy to pick some flowers from the garden. "She's ours, for sure."

"She's going to be so cute in that dress Natalie found for her and Daisy to wear for your wedding, Mom," Grace said. "Chiffon, like ours are, but they're soft shades of a perfect sunset, like watercolors on a canvas."

"We ordered little circles of baby's breath from the florist for them to wear in their hair and baskets of rose petals to toss." Natalie refilled everyone's drink. "Mom, I can't wait for everyone to see you in that dress, and for the wedding and the great party we've planned for after the ceremony."

"And speaking of great parties, are you going to have a July Fourth bash at your house again this year, Mom?" Natalie asked.

Maggie shook her head. "Too much going on. But Grace could invite us all over for a cookout after the parade if she was feeling social."

"Sure." Grace nodded. "Burgers, hot dogs, that sort of thing?"

"We'll pick up some salads from the general store," Natalie said. "Let's just keep it as simple as possible."

"Do you think Owen will have the carousel brought out again this year?" Grace looked at Emma, who shrugged.

"No idea."

"It would be nice," Natalie said. "All the kids loved it."

Emma bit the inside of her lip. If she and Owen were still seeing each other, she knew he'd do it. He'd already said he would. He'd say the word, and the workers would show up and move that gorgeous amusement right out into the park, where the kids would line up for rides and the music would float across the field and into the town. She remembered how she and he had connected two summers ago, and he'd brought the carousel out for the Fourth to please her. It had been a lovely thing to do, a lovely way to begin a new relationship, a most unique way to put a magical spin on their getting-to-know-you dance.

But now she didn't know if he'd feel obligated to hold to that promise.

She'd wanted to take that dance to the next stage, but it didn't appear that was ever going to happen. It was a tough spot to be in at her age—hell, at any age—finding someone you really liked who liked you just as much, and then finding they're not who you thought they were.

As angry and indignant as she'd felt walking away from Owen's home that night, he was still in her head, and she didn't know why.

Unfortunately, there didn't seem to be any way to find out, and she wasn't sure it mattered anymore.

Chapter Nineteen

The night before Maggie's wedding, Emma sat in front of her computer, staring at the screen, immersed in doing something she'd always sworn she would not do: an internet search on Owen Harrison.

There'd been something so out of character in his quick rejection of her reasons why they should keep Winnie, and his insistence that financial gain had to be at the heart of Winnie showing up at Emma's door. His cold assessment had baffled her. She wondered if something in his past had prompted his reaction.

She skimmed all the articles relative to his holdings and his wealth, all the stories of how his company had bought up this or that competitor. She wasn't interested in how much he was worth or how many homes he owned, but she'd lingered over the photographs of his latest acquisition—the villa and the olive grove in Tuscany—with some degree of sadness. She'd daydreamed about walking among those trees hand in hand with Owen, maybe discussing an upcoming harvest. She'd studied the photos of the villa and imagined herself leaning on that second-floor balcony, a glass of wine in her hand, Owen's strong arm around her waist as they shared an unforgettable evening gazing at the dark night sky. The lights of the houses built along the hillside would wink as they were extinguished and their neighbors turned in for the night. Even now she sighed as she pictured it.

Some dreams were so much harder to put away than others, and this one dripped romance. She sighed and read on.

Owen's official biography followed his education from boarding school in the UK to university and thereafter to Oxford as a prelude to him joining his family's business, which he took over at the age of thirty-six. There were photos of him through the years with this British socialite or that Italian countess on his arm, but few appeared more than two or three times. There were vague references to several half siblings resulting from his father's four marriages. Emma found it interesting he'd spoken to her of his fondness only for Ethan, his younger brother. But then several pages into her search, she stumbled on something totally unexpected: decades-old articles about a scandal involving his father's first wife: AMERICAN MAGNATE'S SON KIDNAPPED! MOTHER IMPLICATED IN SCHEME!

She clicked on the article and read it three times to get the full gist of it. The first wife of Owen's father, Jasper VI (known to all as Jay), was British heiress Aster Gordon-Smythe. Jay and Aster had a daughter and two sons together before Jay's affections were won by an American woman named Paulina Stokes, Owen's mother. When Owen was five, his eight-year-old half brother, Simon—Aster's youngest son—disappeared from his bedroom in his mother's home in Derby, England. The ransom demanded had been astronomical for the times, and Owen's father had been hesitant to pay it because, as he said once the smoke had cleared, "Something had smelled off." But he'd paid up and gone along with the demand that he not contact the authorities. Once Simon was safely home in England, Jay quietly employed a private investigator, who discovered that the kidnappers were two young thugs who'd been hired by Aster and her boyfriend and who'd kept Simon in a farmhouse in France until the ransom had been paid. Owen's father had been furious at having been duped and that his affection for his own son had been used to extort money by the woman who should have cared most for Simon: his mother. Jay contacted the police, which resulted in the arrests and convictions of Aster, her lover, and the two men they'd hired to carry out their scheme.

Emma sat back in the chair and mulled it all over. That event had happened fifty years ago, yet it must have made a tremendous impression on five-year-old Owen. On the surface, the kidnapping of his stepbrother and the appearance of Winnie in Emma's life had nothing in common, other than the fact that they both involved children of the same age. But she was beginning to understand why the two situations seemed so similar to Owen. Simon had been kidnapped for a get-rich-quick scheme by his own mother and her boyfriend. In Owen's mind, Winnie's sudden appearance and claim to be the daughter of rock royalty could only be a plan to extort money from Chris by Winnie's mother. Which also explained his insistence that Tish was somewhere waiting for the right time to show up—because in his experience, people weren't above using children to play on your emotions in order to get what they wanted.

Emma remembered that one of the first questions she and many others had when Winnie first showed up was whether she'd been sent by her mother to con money from Chris. But once they realized that Tish hadn't been involved in Winnie's arrival in Wyndham Beach—she'd been missing for months by then—it became apparent that someone did believe Chris was Winnie's father. Granted, there still were questions, like, If Tish believed Chris was Winnie's father, why hadn't she contacted him herself for child support? Why had she allowed so many years to pass without telling him he'd fathered a child? Tish's friend Angel had offered the only possible explanation: Tish really didn't know who the father was, so she named Chris on the birth certificate on a whim, a spur-of-the-moment fulfillment of a wish—but she'd never pushed him because she'd known it wasn't true.

Emma was beginning to see how Owen's opinion had been formed by his past experience. She supposed she could call him, or respond to his next text, but then she'd have to explain how she came by her change of heart. Could she admit she'd searched through his past? As she'd told Liddy once, searching for someone's past seemed underhanded and would make her feel sleazy somehow, like she'd been spying on his life. She knew people did it every day, no big deal, but she thought it was embarrassing. To Emma, it was as rude as insisting that you had a right to know things about someone they didn't want you to know. She wasn't sure she could own up to it.

On the other hand, she really missed him.

~

While Maggie had chosen all the details for her reception, much of the execution had fallen into Emma's lap. The timetable for setting up the tent, the tables, the caterers in the Deans' backyard was very tight. Emma had hoped to have everything except the food delivered the day before, but because they were so late to get onto the vendor's schedule, nothing would be delivered until the morning of the wedding. In the end, it had fallen to Emma—with a little help from Keely—to make sure everything was ready for the guests once the ceremony was over. The guests' tables were set up and the flowers arranged just as Maggie had specified. The dance floor had to be laid down, and the elevated area for the band needed to be set up. But once everything was in place, she left Keely there to watch over things while she ran upstairs to shower and get dressed.

As always, Emma's pixie cut fell right into place—no salon appointment necessary. She rarely wore makeup, but this was a special occasion, so she opted for some blush, eye shadow, mascara, and lipstick. She dressed in the off-the-shoulder dusty purple gown of light chiffon layers—perfect for a very warm late July day—and slipped into pretty gold sandals. Then she opened her jewelry box. The diamond earrings and bracelet that had been gifts from her son? Check.

The huge amethyst ring she'd bought for herself? Double check. She looked in the mirror and declared herself wedding ready.

Liddy was already waiting at the front door when Emma came downstairs.

"Oh! You look gorgeous!" Emma declared as she let her in.

"So do you!" Liddy returned the compliment. "You don't think I look like a big grape?"

"Stop it. You look beautiful. That color is perfect on you."

"Have you ever noticed that when wearing purple with salt-and-pepper hair, the 'salt' takes on a light-purple glow?" Liddy fussed in front of the hall mirror. "Which I guess might be better than blue hair."

"Your hair does not look purple." Emma laughed.

"I'm so happy that Maggie let us pick out our own dresses at the bridal shop." Liddy stopped to adjust the top of her dress in the hall mirror. "Sleeveless is fine for Grace and Natalie with their buff upper arms, but frankly, I have more than my share of arm flap. I wave when I don't intend to."

Emma laughed again. "Technically, these are sleeveless. It's just that deep flounce at the top coming off the shoulders covers up the flub."

"Oh please. You have no flub."

"I have flub. But I keep it under cover as much as I can." She opened the front door. "Come on, Lids. It's time to play hostess at our BFF's wedding."

Maggie knew it would be hot on the beach, so she'd requested cool drinks be served while their guests waited for the ceremony to begin. They'd decided to offer glasses of chilled wine spritzers and bottled water, to be handed out by members of the caterer's staff as people arrived, then flutes of champagne when the officiant announced that Brett could kiss his bride.

The Cottage Street beach had never looked so good. Natalie and Grace had sectioned off an area for the wedding, delineating the space with luminarias. An arch covered with pink roses near the jetty would serve as a focal point for the exchanging of vows. A string quartet began to play as guests trickled onto the beach, and Liddy and Emma played their hostess roles, greeting those they knew and introducing themselves to those few people neither had met before. The atmosphere was light and cheerful, and the breeze from the water kept the mosquitoes at bay.

Twelve minutes before the ceremony was to begin, Brett walked across the beach in a navy-blue jacket, white button-down shirt, and khakis, bare feet, no tie.

"He's still Wyndham Beach's golden boy," Liddy remarked.

Emma nodded. "He hasn't changed a lot over the years. He even still has all his hair."

"And his cowlick," Liddy noted. "Joe has one in the same place."

Brett was accompanied by three young women: his oldest daughter, twenty-four-year-old Chloe (product of his first marriage to Beth, former runner-up to Miss Texas); middle daughter Alexis, who was fifteen (wife number two—surfer girl Holly); and the youngest, nine-year-old Jenna (wife number three, Kayla, who was a dead ringer for Maggie). The three stuck close to their father and to each other, and it was clear they felt uncomfortable being there.

"Psst. Em," Liddy had whispered when the Crawford girls had followed their father to the area where the ceremony would be held. "The one in blue. That's Brett's oldest daughter. I've never seen her before, have you?"

"No," Emma whispered back. "I heard her mother moved back to Texas when she and Brett broke up, and she took the girl with her and remarried. She never made it easy for Brett to see his daughter, so the relationship is strained. She's a beautiful girl, isn't she?"

Liddy nodded. "All three of them are. And they all look so much alike, don't they? You can tell they're all Crawfords."

Emma leaned closer to whisper. "They all look like they wish they were somewhere else."

"Well, I don't know how comfortable I'd have been at my father's fourth wedding," Liddy replied, her voice equally low. "Had he had one."

The area set aside for the wedding was filling quickly. Battery-operated candles in the luminarias had been lit to create an aisle as more and more guests made their way onto the sand where they'd stand to watch the ceremony, which Maggie had promised would be short and sweet.

"Without an aisle," Liddy said, "Joe would have to plow his way through the crowd, dragging Maggie behind him like a dinghy."

"So undignified." Emma glanced at her watch. "Three minutes to showtime. Think Maggie will be on time?"

Liddy nodded in the direction of the small parking lot. "There she is."

They watched Maggie come into view.

"She looks twenty years younger than any sixty-year-old woman I've ever seen," Liddy said. "I could hate her for that if I didn't love her so much."

Emma nodded. "At least twenty years younger."

Liddy left her wineglass on the table the caterer had set up for used glasses, and she and Emma joined Maggie and her daughters and granddaughters at the edge of the beach.

"Maggie, you are positively radiant." Emma kissed her lightly on the cheek.

"You are definitely setting a really high bar for every—oh, let's say mature—bride. The dress, the orchid in your hair is perfect—and those bright-pink toes!" Liddy pointed to Maggie's bare feet after she'd slipped off her sandals.

"I know. I had to dress them up somehow." Maggie looked around. "Is Brett here?"

"Brett's been here for about ten minutes now with all his kids. Well, except for Joe." Emma looked around. "Where is Joe?"

"He just pulled up at the house, and he and his kids are on their way. I can see them from here." Grace waved as Joe and his two children, thirteen-year-old Jamey and eight-year-old Louisa, jogged toward them. "Don't forget, guys—LuLu wants to be called Louisa now. She thinks LuLu makes her sound like a baby, and she will not respond to you if you forget and call her by that baby name."

"Got it. Goodbye, LuLu. Hello, Louisa." Emma nodded.

"And hello, brother Joe." Grace walked into the lot to hug her brother.

"Sister G." He kissed her cheek. "And Sister Nat." He kissed her as well, then looked around. "Has anyone seen Maggie? And who is that gorgeous woman in the white dress?"

"Oh, you." Maggie blushed, but she laughed all the same when he hugged her and gave her a peck on the cheek.

"You look so pretty," Louisa said. "I love your dress."

"Thank you, sweetie." Maggie leaned over and smoothed her granddaughter's hair.

Jamey nodded. "You look pretty, Maggie." He looked around; then his face brightened. "Hey, is that Alexis over there?"

"It is. Why don't you and your sister go join her, and you can meet her sisters. They're your aunts, too."

"We used to have no aunts and no cousins. Now we have . . ." Louisa counted. "Six aunts, I think?"

Joe nodded. "I think you're right. Brett's three daughters and Maggie's two are all my, well, half siblings, so they would be your aunts. We're not doing halves in this family."

"And . . . one cousin? Just Daisy?"

"Right again. Now go on and follow Jamey so we can get started." Joe turned to his mother. "You ready?"

He held out his arm to her.

"I'm ready," she assured him as she looped her arm through his. "How 'bout you?"

"Totally ready to walk my mother down the aisle, then serve as my father's best man." Joe said softly so only she could hear: "What a day, eh?"

"Thank you for being here for me, Joe." Maggie sniffed back a tear.

"Thank you for giving me the honor of escorting you." He touched his forehead to hers.

Grace saw her mother about to tear up. "Mom, don't start. It took me forever to apply your makeup." She took a tissue from the hidden pocket in her dress and blotted her mother's face. "Raccoon eyes on your wedding day are not cool."

"I thought you used waterproof mascara." Maggie held still while Grace took care of business.

"I did. But still . . ." Grace stood back and inspected Maggie's face. "It's fine. Just make sure you save your tears for after the ceremony. You don't want teary tracks through the blush."

Joe signaled the violinists to start playing the processional Maggie'd chosen—Clarke's "Trumpet Voluntary"—and as the music began, Maggie took a few steps forward before Natalie grabbed her by the arm.

"Mom, wait. You go last, remember?"

"Oh. Of course I do." Maggie rolled her eyes. "Stage fright."

"Winnie and Daisy, you know what to do. Just like we practiced. Go all the way up to where you see Tuck. Then you can stand right there with him and wait for the rest of us," Emma reminded the girls.

"Then what will we do?" Winnie asked.

"We'll watch Maggie and Brett get married."

"Oh. Okay."

Winnie and Daisy, dressed in the colors of a summer sunset, scattered rose petals, their faces serious as they went about their task of beautifying the sandy aisle. Next came Emma, then Liddy, both in shades of dusty purple. They were followed by Natalie, then Grace, who wore dresses in shades of sunny coral. Then Maggie, gorgeous in a column of white satin, walked between the makeshift aisle of luminarias on the arm of her handsome son to marry her love.

The vows exchanged were traditional ones, but at the end, Maggie surprised everyone, including Brett, by reciting the poem Robert Browning had written for his wife, Elizabeth: "Grow old along with me! The best is yet to be, the last of life, for which the first was made . . ."

Before she finished the last line—"Trust God: see all, nor be afraid"—the entire assembly of friends and family had tears in their eyes.

But even as everyone assumed Maggie's solo performance marked the end of the vows, Brett had one more surprise for her.

He held both her hands and gazed into her eyes. "I had memorized this thing I saw on the internet that I thought was so perfect and romantic, but now, standing here, looking at your beautiful face, I can't remember all the words. It was something about choices. Something like, in a thousand lifetimes, I would choose you over and over and over, to infinity. I wanted to make that clear, you know? That there will never be a day in my life when I didn't love you with all my heart. When I wouldn't choose you."

He began to say something else, but Maggie silenced him with a kiss that seemed to go on and on, prompting their officiant to say, "Okay, then. I now pronounce you man and wife. And you may now . . . keep kissing the bride."

~

"Oh, Mom." Natalie held a hand over her heart and sighed. "That was just so romantic."

"I know," was all an emotional Maggie could say. She accepted the tissue Natalie handed her and gently blotted her face.

"I hope Chris was taking notes." Natalie looked around for Chris and found him off by himself, his phone to his ear, pacing on the sand. "What's up with that?"

"What's up with what?" Grace asked.

Natalie nodded in Chris's direction. "Look at his face. Something's happened."

"We're going to do photos here on the beach before we head off to Emma's, so don't wander," Maggie was saying. "Oh, here's Brett's sister, Jayne. Girls, have you met Brett's sister?"

They had not, so introductions were made all around.

Grace was about to comment when Joe leaned over and asked, "Who's the dark-haired woman in the back, talking to Linc? Blue shirt, white pants?"

Grace turned and stared. "I have no idea, but she's getting a little too cozy with my guy, so I'm going to go and let her know that that man's dance card is filled for the rest of his natural life. Excuse me."

"Gracie. We need you for pictures," Maggie called after her.

"Be back in a minute." Grace waved without turning around.

"Nat, do you know who that is?" Maggie watched her daughter walk purposely across the sand. "She doesn't look at all familiar."

"I don't know." Natalie, too, watched her sister. "Maybe she's someone's plus-one. Though she does seem to have taken 'casual dress' a little further than most people would think appropriate." She smiled when she saw Chris approaching.

"Nat," he said quietly, taking her hands and leading her a step away from the others.

"What's going on?" Natalie asked. "Who were you talking to?"

"Gannon, the PI. And it's not good news, I'm afraid."

"He's found her? Has he found Tish?" Natalie whispered.

"Chris? What's happened?" Emma moved closer.

"The LVPD has confirmed that some of the remains they found were Tish Pine's." His gaze met Natalie's, then his mother's.

353

"Oh my . . ." Emma's hand flew to her throat. "They're positive?"

Chris nodded. "There was a match to the DNA we sent her. It's definitely Tish."

Natalie's first thought was, *How do we tell Winnie?*

"Should we tell her right away? She's already dealing with so many changes," Chris said.

"If you don't mind me putting in my two cents," Emma said. "There's no easy way nor easy time to find out that your mother is dead, but letting things settle in Winnie's life a bit more might be best for her."

"Maybe it would be better to wait until she's feeling a little more secure with her place in our family. Not that it won't upset or hurt her whenever she finds out, but if she knows for sure she's loved and wanted and she feels secure . . ." Natalie shook her head. "I don't know what's best."

"On the other hand, if she's waiting for her mother to come back, would it be better for her to know now?" Chris couldn't help but wonder.

"This is a really tough call. One I don't think we're qualified to make." Natalie sighed. "I'd like to call Joanne List. She's a child psychologist who's affiliated with Daisy's school in Bryn Mawr. I'd like to see what she recommends."

"Excellent idea," Emma readily agreed.

"I concur. And if she thinks we should arrange for therapy for Winnie, we'll find someone in this area," Chris said. "Whatever she needs."

"Should we contact Tish's family?" Natalie asked.

"I don't know that they'd care." Emma thought for a moment. "But her friend, Angel, would want to know. I can give her a call, and she can tell ArlettaJo if she wants."

"I'm pretty sure the authorities in Las Vegas might be contacting the family," Chris said. "Gannon has their information and shared it with the LVPD."

"What are you three doing with your heads together?" Maggie asked. "I hope you're not planning something crazy. Like have the cake blow up when we begin to cut it."

"Damn, she's onto us." Natalie forced a light tone, reluctant to announce Chris's somber news on this happy day.

When Liddy joined them, Maggie asked, "Liddy, do you know who the woman is who's talking with Grace and Linc?"

"Who? Oh . . . oh!" Liddy's eyes grew wide, and an expression close to panic crossed her face. "That's Brenda, Linc's sister! I better go find Tuck and let him know his wandering daughter has made an appearance. Good Lord, of all days for her to show up out of the blue . . ." Liddy was still muttering when she went through the small crowd in search of Tuck.

"She sure doesn't look like she's spent the last year in rehab," Natalie noted. "She looks like she's been on a cruise. Nice tan, and her hair looks great."

"Does anyone really know where she's been?" Emma wondered.

Natalie shook her head. "No, but I bet Grace finds out."

They watched Grace slip her arm through Linc's and extend a hand to the woman they assumed was his sister. Within minutes, it became clear from the way each woman stood that the conversation between Grace and Brenda was not going well.

"Oh Lord, I bet Grace is giving it to her about leaving her kids all this time." Natalie stared, taking in her sister's stance. Grace was digging in her heels, literally. "And Brenda's probably telling her to mind her own business. Which she should do."

"I think she believes anything that impacts Linc is her business," Emma said, "but this is neither the time nor place for that sort of discussion. Natalie, see if you can break that up before it gets out of hand."

Maggie frowned and called after Natalie. "And tell your sister we're ready to take pictures."

"What's that look for, Maggie?" Brett approached her. "I thought this was the happiest day of your life."

She nodded. "It is."

"Then why do you look like you're about to smack someone?" He leaned closer to ask.

"Because I am." She pointed across the beach to Grace.

Brett stared at the trio for a moment. "Hey, that looks like . . . that's Tuck's daughter."

"So I hear."

"We think Gracie might be giving Brenda a piece of her mind," Emma said.

"Well, I hope Grace gets over it by the time we're ready for the group shots." Brett took Maggie's hand. "Right now, it's time for photos of the bride and groom. That would be us. Put that beautiful smile back on your face, and let's go take some pictures our grandchildren can remember us by."

An hour later, the photo shoot ended, and the wedding party piled into the limousines Brett had ordered to take them to the reception. Everyone was in a party mood, even Grace, who Linc had somehow managed to calm. The long white cars wound slowly through Wyndham Beach to Emma's house on Pitcher Street. The wedding party piled out, one by one, and walked up the driveway. Emma was one of the last to emerge, having been delayed by Winnie's request to fix her ponytail. When she stepped out of the car, she could hear the live band warming up in the backyard and was grateful all her immediate neighbors had been invited to the wedding.

"Can we eat dinner now?" Winnie asked.

"Not for a bit, but there are lots of things to eat before dinner is served, and I'm sure you'll find . . ." Emma stopped midsentence when she noticed a man standing at the foot of her front walk, watching her.

Feeling as if her heart were about to pound itself out of her chest at the sight of him, she took Winnie's hand and walked twenty feet to where he stood.

"Sounds like you have quite the party going on," Owen said softly.

"Maggie and Brett were just married on Cottage Street Beach." She nodded toward the house. "The reception's out back."

"I hope your neighbors like eighties music."

Emma smiled. "Maggie had the forethought to invite them all."

"Ahhh." He nodded. "A good preemptive move." He stood very still, his hands in the pockets of his jacket, looking lonely and more than a little sad. "I guess I chose the wrong time to come to offer my apology."

"There would never be a wrong time."

He looked from Emma to Winnie, then smiled. "I'm going out on a limb here and guess this is your granddaughter. Winnie, is it?"

Winnie nodded. "Yes, sir."

Emma put her hand on Winnie's shoulder. "Winnie, say hello to Mr. Harrison."

"Hello, Mr. Harrison."

Owen bent from his waist and offered Winnie his hand. "I am very happy to meet you, Winnie. Your grandmother has told me wonderful things about you."

"Thank you, sir. I'm happy to meet you, too." Winnie repeated the polite phrase and extended her hand. Owen took it and gave it a gentle squeeze.

"It looks like you may have been in the wedding," he said.

"Yes, sir. 'Cause my daddy is going to marry Maggie's daughter, so we're all gonna be related, and Daisy's gonna be my sister," she explained.

"That sounds like a lot of family."

She nodded solemnly. "Yes, sir, it is. Most family I ever had."

Daisy flew around the side of the house. Seeing Winnie on the sidewalk, she made a beeline, calling, "Winnie! Come see the cake! It has real roses on it!"

Winnie bit her bottom lip and looked expectantly at Emma, who nodded. "Go on back with Daisy and take a look at that cake. It's a beauty. But don't touch it."

Winnie took off without a backward glance. Owen watched her, then turned to Emma.

"About that apology." Owen took a deep breath. "I'm so sorry, Emma. I said things that, looking back, I can't believe I said. I had no right to pass judgment on you and your son or that little girl. She seems every bit as sweet as you said. And it's clear you adore each other."

Emma nodded. "We do."

"I'm very sorry I was such an ass. It wasn't my place to lecture you or tell you how to feel or what to do. I'm embarrassed at how cold I must have sounded, how heartless. Of course you shouldn't have sent Winnie back, and of course you should make room for her in your family. I'm sure Chris has excellent people working for him, so if her mother's still out there, he will find her."

"He already has. The investigator he hired to find Winnie's mother called a while ago. Some of the remains the LVPD uncovered in the desert matched to Winnie's DNA, which Chris sent them. So we know that Winnie's mother won't be coming back."

Owen nodded slowly. "Sorry to hear of any young life cut short, but happy for you that you won't have to worry about her making problems for you."

"I never worried about that, Owen. Winnie belongs here with us. I know Chris would do whatever he had to to keep her here."

"Yes, well, that's good. I'm sorry it took losing your affection to make me understand, to try to see things through your eyes. I'd upset you and I'd hurt you, two things I never wanted to do, because I care about you so much. But the look on your face when you left the house that night—there was such disappointment, such sadness in your eyes. You couldn't get away from me fast enough. I will never forgive myself for making you feel that way."

"Mostly disappointment. I'd thought better of you."

"Again, I'm sorry. I'd do anything to take back those words. But we both know it doesn't work that way."

The music from the band out back drifted across the yard, and they stood in silence for a long moment. She wanted to say more, to let him know she'd come to understand what he may have been thinking, but the words stuck in her throat.

Finally, Owen said, "Well, I'll let you get back to your party. Please give Brett and Maggie my congratulations. I hope they'll have a long and happy life together."

He started to back away, as if to leave.

"Wait. Owen, I owe you an apology, too."

He stopped walking. "What? No, no. There's nothing for you to apologize for."

"There is." She covered her face with her hands. Was she really going to admit this? She took a deep breath. "Owen, I did something that I never thought I'd do."

He looked at her quizzically.

"I'm embarrassed to admit this, but I . . . I googled you." She could feel her face turning red.

"You what?"

"I googled you. I entered your name in a search and . . . and I read about you. About your life. About your family. Things that happened over the years . . ."

"Did you learn anything you hadn't already known?"

She nodded. "I learned about your brother being kidnapped by his mother. That your father paid the ransom."

"And you figured out that that experience probably colored my reaction to your situation?"

Another nod.

"I wasn't conscious of it at the time, but I suppose it was a knee-jerk reaction. Then a week ago, out of the blue, Simon called me. As soon as I heard his voice, it clicked. I've been trying to get in touch with you, but . . ."

"But I've ignored your calls and didn't read your texts. For which I'm very sorry. And I'm sorry I spied on your life."

Owen laughed. "Emma, you don't have to apologize for that. Actually, I googled you before I even met you."

"You did?"

He nodded. "I wanted to know who I was being harassed by. It's really not a big deal."

"Huh." Emma was surprised. Apparently the practice was more common than she'd thought, but then again, she'd never really thought about it at all. "Well, I'm glad you're not angry."

"Actually, I'm flattered," he told her.

"You are?"

Owen walked back toward her. "It means you were thinking about me. Even while you were angry with me, you were thinking about me."

"I was. I really was angry, but I hated not seeing you," Emma admitted.

"I hated not seeing you, too." He took a few steps closer. "Do you think we could pick up where we left off before I blew up what looked like the beginning of a beautiful relationship? Before I acted like such an ass."

"Perhaps we could. And you did."

Owen laughed good naturedly. "So I suppose we're both eating a little crow tonight."

"Crow's not on the menu. Tonight they're serving lobster rolls and lobster potpie."

"From Uncle Steve's?"

Emma nodded. "I suggested it, and Brett went out to talk to them, and they were happy to oblige him."

"The wedding guests are in for a treat." He looked a bit wistful.

"Come join the party," she told him. "You could be my plus-one."

Behind the tent, the band started playing a slow tune, the music drifting on the night. Owen cocked his head to one side, listening, then smiled. "Air Supply."

"What?"

"Air Supply. The band. The song is 'Here I Am.' I know it well." He drew Emma into his arms and swayed with the music, then took several slow steps, taking her along. "When I was at school, one of the seniors down the hall had this album, and he played this song all day, all night, for months. Everyone hated it." He laughed. "But in retrospect, it's a pretty nice tune. And apropos for the moment." He hummed, then sang a few words here and there. Before Emma realized it, they were dancing on the sidewalk in the light of the moon.

"This is a most romantic apology," she said.

"Totally unplanned but hopefully accepted," he murmured in her ear. "Am I forgiven for being such a dunce?"

"You are."

They danced until the band stopped playing.

"Owen. About the Fourth of July," she said. "Thank you for bringing out the carousel."

"I knew it was important to you, so how could I not? I didn't want you to be disappointed."

"Even after I stormed out on you?"

"That was plan B. My ace in the hole," Owen told her. "I thought if the apology didn't work, maybe the carousel would earn me a few points."

Emma put a hand on either side of his face and kissed him.

When she leaned back to look at him, he asked, "So which was it? The apology or the carousel?"

"Toss-up."

"I was all prepared to grovel, if necessary." He nuzzled the side of her face.

"Not necessary."

"You know, I think I'll take you up on that invitation to join you tonight. I'd love to be your plus-one."

"Good. It's going to be a great party."

She took his hand, and they walked up the driveway and under the porte cochere.

"So Maggie and Brett finally got married. Good for them," he said as they strolled along in the direction of the big white tent, where the party was in full swing.

"Oh, that's not the big news," she said. "Chris and Natalie are getting married the week before Christmas. And they bought a house in Wyndham Beach."

"That's wonderful." He paused. "So is our deal still on?"

"What deal?"

"The one where I was to spend Thanksgiving and Christmas with you, and in turn you'd spend New Year's Eve with me."

"Of course you're welcome to come for the holidays." She paused before asking, "New Year's Eve is still on the table?"

"New Year's Eve was never off. If you're still interested, that is."

"Oh yes. I'm definitely interested."

"You know, after the wedding and all the stress from the holidays, you're going to need to relax and unwind. Italy would be just the thing." Without breaking stride, he leaned closer and whispered, "The moonlight over the hills there is something to see."

"Would there be dancing?"

"It could be arranged."

She smiled to herself as the image of the two of them on the balcony of his villa, sipping wine and looking out over a beautiful Italian night, came back into focus.

She gave his hand a squeeze. "I can't think of any place I'd rather be."

ACKNOWLEDGMENTS

Many thanks to Montlake Publishing's fabulous team: rock star editor Maria Gomez, Anh Schluep, Jillian Cline, Ashley Vanicek, Alex Levenberg, Cheryl Weisman, Adrienne Clark, and the art department for those glorious covers! Special thanks to Kyla Pigoni for the surprise and joy of seeing the cover of *An Invincible Summer* on that six-story Amazon billboard in New York City. Thanks also to editor Holly Ingraham for all her hard work on this manuscript—it's a pleasure working with you, and I'm grateful for your insights.

Also a rock star: my agent, Nick Mullendore, Vertical Ink Agency.

What is a book without readers? Many thanks and much love to mine—many of whom have been with me for the past twenty-seven years. To my Facebook family and friends—many thanks for all your support and for loving my characters and taking them to heart. Megathanks to my amazing assistant, Maureen Downey, who keeps me sane. Special shout-out to those who helped name the artists in this book, by volunteering the name of a loved one or a friend, or by making up a name that sounded like fun:

To Robyn Sneed for Eva Sadler, Kathleen LaPlaca Morrone for Pasquale Morrone, Mary Stella for Stella Martin, Shana Box Janner for Preston Hall, Michelle Wilson for Luna Moon, and Irene Peterson for . . . well, Irene Peterson.

Thanks again to Gretchen Smith for being the go-to Realtor in Wyndham Beach!

As always, I have to thank my family for giving me time and understanding when I need it: my husband, Bill; our daughter Kathryn and her husband, Michael, and their fabulous adorable kiddos—Cole, Jack, Robb, and Camryn—and our daughter Rebecca and her husband, David, and their amazing glorious offspring, Charlotte and Gethin. You are my heart, and together, you constitute my world.

ABOUT THE AUTHOR

Photo © 2016 Nicole Leigh

Mariah Stewart is the *New York Times*, *Publishers Weekly*, and *USA Today* bestselling author of several series, including Wyndham Beach, the Chesapeake Diaries, and the Hudson Sisters, as well as stand-alone novels, novellas, and short stories. A native of Hightstown, New Jersey, she lives with her husband and two rambunctious rescue dogs amid the rolling hills of Chester County, Pennsylvania, where she savors country life, tends her gardens, and works on her next novel. She's the proud mama of two fabulous daughters, who—along with her equally fabulous sons-in-law—have gifted her with six adorable (and, yes, fabulous) granddarlings. For more information, visit www.mariahstewart.com.